THE DEVIL'S HARMONY

THE DEVIL'S HARMONY

Sarah Rayne

This first world edition published 2020
in Great Britain and 2021 in the USA by
SEVERN HOUSE PUBLISHERS LTD of
Eardley House, 4 Uxbridge Street, London W8 7SY.
Trade paperback edition first published
in Great Britain and the USA 2021 by
SEVERN HOUSE PUBLISHERS LTD.

British Library Cataloguing in Publication Data
A CIP catalogue record for this title is available from the British Library.

ISBN-13: 978-0-7278-8988-1 (cased)
ISBN-13: 978-1-78029-747-7 (trade paper)
ISBN-13: 978-1-4483-0475-2 (e-book)

All Severn House titles are printed on acid-free paper.

Severn House Publishers support the Forest Stewardship Council™ [FSC™],
the leading international forest certification organisation.
All our titles that are printed on FSC certified paper carry the FSC logo.

Typeset by Palimpsest Book Production Ltd.,
Falkirk, Stirlingshire, Scotland.
Printed and bound in Great Britain by
TJ Books Limited, Padstow, Cornwall.

ONE

'It's a fake,' said Professor Liripine, glaring at the faded scrapbook lying on his desk. Scraps of bubble wrap, untidily removed from the package, lay around his study. He frowned, turned a few pages over, then said, very firmly, 'It can't be anything but a fake.' He sat back and looked challengingly at his companion.

'We can't be sure,' said Dr Purslove, who was examining the scrapbook for himself. 'If it really was found on the site of the Chopin Library—'

'It could have been planted,' said the professor. 'Anyway, no one actually knows exactly where the Chopin Library stood.'

'How did it end up on your desk?' asked Dr Purslove, inspecting the scrapbook. 'It's a long way from Warsaw to your study at Durham University.'

'A former student sent it to me,' said the professor. 'Her name's Nina Randall, and she's doing research in an archives office in Warsaw. Apparently a young graduate from Łódź University found the scrapbook on a building site. He was earning a bit of cash after graduating, and they were demolishing an office block. The bulldozers crunched open part of the old foundations without realizing what they were doing.'

'So this could have been there since . . . well, since the 1940s,' said Dr Purslove. 'You know, most of these documents do look genuine. Some of them have been pasted in – you can see where strands of glue are still on the pages. It's infuriating that almost all of it seems to be in Polish, though. Didn't your student send a translation?'

'I got the impression that she wanted to get the thing off her hands as quickly as she could. She says – wait a minute, where's her letter? Oh, it's here. She explains about the student, then she says:

'"I don't feel that it's something I can look into myself. Partly because of pressure of my own work, but also because I have a feeling that my bosses here wouldn't be very enthusiastic about our department getting involved in investigating this. There's almost a superstition about the Chopin Library, even after so many years. But I can't let this fragile but promising link to the past vanish, so here it is."

'She's only on a very low rung of the career ladder yet,' said Professor Liripine, a bit defensively. 'So she wouldn't want to risk making a wrong judgement. More to the point, she wouldn't want to be seen to make it.'

'In case it really is a fake? Yes, I see that.' Dr Purslove was cautiously turning over the thick card pages. He said, 'There's an untidy look to this that's quite convincing. You could almost imagine that somebody grabbed sheaves of documents and thrust them inside.'

'Yes, but why? To preserve them? None of them looks particularly valuable,' said the professor.

'Then why would anyone bother creating a fake with them? There's no motive, and you're a shocking cynic, Ernest.'

'Whatever I am, I'm in agreement with Nina about keeping this quiet for the moment,' said Professor Liripine.

Dr Purslove said, slowly, 'In case it's a fake, but also . . .'

He broke off and the two men looked at one another. Then the professor said, 'You know perfectly well why we need to keep this under wraps, Theodore.' He turned the pages back and indicated the dim faded oblong of paper near the front.

'To the untutored eye, it simply looks like a handwritten draft for a concert programme cover,' he said. 'A quartet's name at the top, a date, and—'

'And a piece of music to be performed.'

'Yes. But we both know that such a piece of music would never have been performed at a concert, even if—'

'Even if that piece of music had ever been written down,' said Dr Purslove.

'And even if it had actually existed in the first place,' said the professor. 'You do see, don't you, that we can't afford to let it be known we're giving any credence to this?' He was still looking at the programme cover.

'I suppose not,' said Dr Purslove, rather wistfully.

'Of course not,' said the professor, in some exasperation.

'Think about it logically. If we look into this and it does turn out to be a fake, we'd be the laughing stock of both our universities – in fact of half the academic music world. Let's remember all the famous fakes there've been. Piltdown Man. The Cottingley photographs – Conan Doyle was completely taken in by those photographs. And what about William Ireland?'

'We're hardly going to be as gullible as poor old Conan Doyle, with smudgy shots of gauzy fairies at the bottom of the garden,' said Dr Purslove. 'I'll allow you William Ireland, though. Late 1700s, wasn't it?'

'It was. Faked Shakespeare papers, including a full-length play that even got itself on to the stage. It hoodwinked a great many people.'

'Wasn't it virtually booed off the stage on the first night?'

'That's not the point. The point is that reputations have been toppled by good fakes.' The professor looked at Dr Purslove over his glasses, which was a look that was normally moderately successful in quelling unruly undergraduates.

Dr Purslove, who was not going to be quelled by Ernest Liripine's lecture-room tricks, said, 'But we still ought to try getting this authenticated. Only I can't think of anyone we could involve who . . . Oh wait, what about Phineas Fox? We could certainly rely on his discretion.'

The professor considered this, and said, 'That's quite a good idea. But would Phin be interested? It's always been a very vague legend.'

'It's a persistent one, though. Centuries old, I believe,' said Dr Purslove. 'And I think it would fascinate Phin Fox. In fact I suspect him of being a bit of a romantic under that quiet exterior.'

'Being a romantic isn't always a good thing,' said the professor, solemnly. 'Still, we could talk to him. And I should think we could scrape up a bit of a fee to cover his time for a few days. I can probably squeeze something from this quarter's budget towards it, and I could add a bit out of my own pocket as well if necessary.'

'I'd contribute, too.' Theo Purslove thought that although old Liripine had many faults, it had to be said that meanness was not one of them. He said, 'What about the translations, though? Some of it looks like Russian as well as Polish.'

'I think Phin's got a smattering of German, but I shouldn't think he's got any Polish or Russian,' said Professor Liripine. 'But there's that girlfriend he has – Arabella. Isn't she a bit of a linguist?'

'Arabella Tallis,' said Dr Purslove, sitting back in his chair and smiling. 'And you're right about her language skills. We both met her when Phin brought her to that drinks thing for publication of the Liszt book we did[1] – she got stuck in the lift on the way up to the supper room at the hotel, d'you remember? Well, of course you remember. You were one of the people who tried to haul the cable up by hand.'

'They had to call out the fire brigade in the end. But we could see if she might be able to do a bit of translation for us,' said Professor Liripine, thoughtfully. 'This is all starting to sound promising. I'll phone Phineas tomorrow, and try to set up a meeting.'

'Good idea. I might email him, too.'

'I don't expect you'd want to be bothered to come along to a meeting with him, would you?' said the professor, off-handedly, wrapping the scrapbook up in the discarded bubble wrap. 'I know you don't like leaving your ivory tower for very long, and especially not for the rigours of London; in fact you're only in Durham this weekend for the symposium, so—'

'Yes, I would want to be bothered,' said Theodore Purslove, at once. 'In fact, I wouldn't miss it for the world. I don't know where you've got the idea that I don't like London, because I do. And there's no need to make spiky comments about ivory towers, either, because I'm a good deal more in touch with the world than you are, Ernest!'

Phineas Fox only just managed not to sound startled by the phone call from Professor Liripine.

'This is all very unofficial and informal,' the professor said. 'It's simply that we – that's to say Theo Purslove and I – would like to have a bit of a chat with you. Something's come to my

1 See *Music Macabre*

attention that might be worth investigating, and we think it could be very much your field of expertise. I won't say any more about it on the phone – you never know who might be in earshot.'

'Well, no,' said Phin, who had been trying to work on a rather dull commission involving an obscure jazz musician, but who was much more intrigued by this hint of cloaks and daggers.

'Could you manage a meeting reasonably soon?' asked Professor Liripine. 'If so, we could both travel to London and stay over for a night. That's for Purslove's benefit, you understand – he never likes to be away from Cambridge for too long. He's always thinking there's going to be a palace revolution in his absence and that he'll find himself bundled out of a comfortable tenure when he gets back.'

'Would one day next week fit?' said Phin. 'I could book a table at the trattoria near my flat, and we can come back here afterwards to talk.'

'That sounds splendid. I'll let Theodore know. Very grateful to you,' said the professor, and rang off.

Dr Purslove's email arrived that evening, and was in more or less the same vein, if somewhat breezier.

'Looking forward to meeting you again, Phin,' he wrote. 'Old Liripine's getting a bit past jaunting around these days, so just the one night in London will be enough for him. It's a very interesting discovery that we're bringing along.'

Phin, returning to the very uninteresting jazz musician, tried not to waste too much time in speculating as to what the two had unearthed. He also tried not to worry whether he would be able to maintain harmony between them.

But when they met the following week, they seemed pleased to see Phin, and in reasonable amity with one another.

'We'll talk properly when we get back to your flat,' said Professor Liripine, surveying his plate of tagliatelle with pleased anticipation. 'It'll be more private.'

'In a minute he'll say walls have ears, and glance furtively over his shoulder like somebody in a French farce.'

'No, I shan't. Pass the parmesan and don't talk rubbish, Theo.'

The meal progressed smoothly enough, with Dr Purslove wanting to know about Phin's current commission, and offering a few suggestions. The professor disclosed that he had once visited New Orleans where he had taken part in a jam session, which he had greatly enjoyed. 'I was a lot younger then, of course.'

Phin tried, and failed, to visualize this scenario. As they left the restaurant, Dr Purslove expressed concern as to whether the professor would manage to walk as far as Phin's flat.

'It's only a few hundred yards,' said Phin, who had not thought of this.

'Yes, but weren't your feet troubling you, again, Ernest?'

'There's never been anything wrong with my feet. I can outpace you any day, and I could certainly do so after that enormous meal you ate.'

Walking to the flat, they were rather endearingly interested in their surroundings. It was not, they explained, a part of London that either of them knew.

'It's very nice, isn't it?' said Dr Purslove, looking admiringly at some of the houses which were tall and still retained faint traces of former grandeur. 'It's a pity when these lovely old places have to be chopped up into flats, but it looks as if they've been converted very tastefully. Ah, is this the house, Phin?'

'Yes. The flat's on the first floor.'

'No lift?'

'I'm afraid not.'

'Then Ernest might need a bit of help with the stairs,' said Dr Purslove, gleefully.

But they both went very spryly up to Phin's flat, and through to the study, which Phin had tried to tidy up that afternoon.

'I always like seeing where people work,' said Dr Purslove, looking around. 'Beautifully high ceilings and deep windows you've got here, Phin. Shockingly expensive to heat, I expect.'

'Tact was never your strong suit, Purslove,' said the professor, sarcastically.

'I wasn't being tactless, I was diplomatically letting Phin know that we're aware that people have to pay bills and that living in London is ruinous, so we won't be expecting him to do anything without a fee.'

'Pity you didn't say so straight out then.'

Phin went out to the kitchen to make coffee, leaving them

to explore. When he returned to the study with the tray, the professor had ensconced himself in the Victorian leather chair which Arabella had found in an antique shop and had restored for Phin as a present.

'This is very comfortable,' he said, and Phin hoped that the castors did not suddenly propel him across the room, because Arabella had fitted the wrong ones and they were apt to skid the chair forward unexpectedly. 'No piano anywhere though, I notice,' he added. 'You do play, don't you, Phin?'

'Well, a bit, but I'm very out of practice—'

'Of course Phin hasn't got a piano, Ernest,' said Theo Purslove, who was inspecting the contents of the bookshelves. 'For one thing you'd never get a piano up those stairs, and for another you'd have neighbours banging on the walls if you took to belting out concertos at midnight. Phin, did you know that these bookshelves are a bit—'

'Lopsided? Yes, I did.' Phin passed the coffee round, and said, firmly, 'A friend of Arabella's had just started up a DIY business – you remember Arabella, I expect? – and she wanted to help get it going, and I did need more shelves, so . . . No, don't move those books, doctor, because they're all that's keeping the end of the shelves weighted down.'

'Yes, I see that, and . . . Well, yes, I'd enjoy a drop of brandy with the coffee. I daresay Liripine won't refuse, either.'

The brandy poured, Phin sat down at his desk with the idea that it might make him feel at least nominally in charge of the proceedings. Professor Liripine rummaged in a large, somewhat battered briefcase, finally producing a large bundle swathed in bubble wrap, which he handed to Phin.

'We've been calling it a scrapbook,' he said, 'but perhaps portfolio might be a better word. It's a collection of old documents and memos, and concert programmes. A former student sent it to me from Warsaw. It was found in the ruins of what might be where a fairly famous old music centre might have stood.'

'He's looking intrigued already,' said Dr Purslove.

'I am intrigued,' said Phin.

'Wait, I'll find the letter that came with it . . .'

'If,' said Dr Purslove, 'you were at all in tune with the modern age, you'd have everything on an iPad or a tablet instead of that Gladstone bag arrangement you haul everywhere.'

'I don't want to be in tune with the modern age,' said the professor, burrowing into the briefcase. 'And I wasn't the one whose computer images got mixed up in a lecture theatre because of pressing the wrong key when giving a paper on Mozart,' he added, indignantly.

'Pressing the wrong key could happen to anyone. I got everything back after the lunch adjournment.'

'And I don't know how you think a parcel could be stored on a laptop, although – dammit, don't say I've left Nina's letter behind . . . Oh, no, it's here.'

From his seat at the desk, Phin saw that the letter was headed with an address in what was presumably Polish, but that the body of the letter was in English.

'I'll read it out,' said the professor. 'Then you can both hear it together. Theo heard most of it last week, of course, but I daresay most of it's slipped his memory since then . . .

'Dear Professor,' he began reading. 'I hope all is well with your lovely studious world, and also with DUOS . . . Durham University Orchestral Society,' explained the professor, as Phin looked up.

'Yes, of course.'

'She was very involved with it.' He continued reading the letter.

This is a curious thing I'm sending you. I can best describe it as a scrapbook, and it contains a motley collection of fragments and documents – few of them actually complete, I'm afraid. One or two things certainly seem worth investigating, though, and especially the draft of the concert programme. The date is given as 1 Października 1944. (That translates as 1 October 1944.)

The scrapbook was brought to my office by a young graduate from Łódź. He's an intelligent and eager boy, and it seems he found it during redevelopment on the site of where some people think the Chopin Library stood. He was helping with clearing the area after the bulldozers had razed it. (As you know so well, undergraduates and, indeed, graduates, often have to take that kind of casual work to make ends meet.)

I don't feel that it's something I can look into myself. Partly because of pressure of my own work, but also because I have a feeling that my bosses here wouldn't be very enthusiastic about our department getting involved in investigating this. There's almost a superstition about the Chopin Library, even after so many years. But I can't let this fragile but promising link to the past vanish, so here it is.

There is also, of course, the fact that even after your mentoring I don't have a hundredth part of your scholarship or knowledge, especially on World War II's musical associations.

I send my fondest good wishes to you, dear professor. I still have such pleasurable memories of my years at Durham – and in particular that night of the Epiphany Concert! A memorable night indeed – I shouldn't think either of us will ever forget that!

Phin had to quell a strong wish to ask about the night of the Epiphany Concert, but seeing that the professor's face was determinedly expressionless, he asked instead about the Chopin Library.

'I've never heard of it. Should I have?'

'You probably wouldn't,' said the professor. 'It's remarkably difficult to find a reference to it at all. The Nazis destroyed a great deal of Warsaw, of course – in fact, by 1944 the city was practically derelict, the buildings burned or bombed. It was an appalling time.'

'And the Nazis destroyed the Chopin Library?' said Phin.

'It was certainly destroyed,' said the professor, and Phin had a momentary impression of evasion. 'Towards the end of 1944.'

'Are there any records of it? Written stuff? Newspaper cuttings, references in autobiographies? If Nina Randall is based in an archives office, she'd have access to such things.'

'There's nothing,' said Dr Purslove.

Phin frowned, then said, 'What did it look like? Are there photographs, sketches we could see?'

'No. No one's ever been able to find any image of it. It's almost as if it was deliberately wiped from the city's history,' said Dr Purslove.

'A great deal of Warsaw's history was lost, of course,' said the professor.

'Oh, yes.'

Phin went back to the scrapbook, cautiously turning over the thick card pages of the scrapbook. 'Is this the programme you mentioned?' he said, after a moment.

'Yes. It's in Polish and it's handwritten, but it's easy enough to see what it is.'

'A concert.' Phin traced the slanting script with a fingertip. At the top were the words *Kwartet Burzowy*, and under this was a small silhouette of a piano, depicted in considerable detail. There was the date and a time of eight o'clock. The paper was thin and discoloured, and the ink had faded to pale brown. He had an image of someone bent eagerly over this page, deciding what the programme should say, and he was aware of sadness that this was all that was left of a long-ago concert in a vanished Warsaw mansion.

Professor Liripine said, '*Kwartet Burzowy* translates as Tempest Quartet.'

'In Polish, *Burza* means "tempest",' put in Dr Purslove. 'We know that much, at least.'

'But that concert would never have happened,' said Professor Liripine, and when Phin looked up, startled, he said, 'The date, Phin. October 1944.'

'October 1944 . . .' Phin frowned, then, with sudden understanding, 'Of course. By 1944, Warsaw was virtually in ruins. Nobody could have been staging concerts by then.'

'Exactly. More than half of the buildings had been destroyed, and most people had been forced into the camps and the ghettos – the northern part of the city had been turned into a Jewish ghetto,' said Professor Liripine. 'There were still small groups of people hiding out, of course, but living in appalling conditions in ruined houses, determined to avoid the Nazis.'

'Trying to cling to their city,' said Phin, softly. 'Fighting back.' But he was still seeing that image of eager musicians.

He said, 'Couldn't this have been a draft written earlier? For a concert they had intended to hold?'

'No.'

'Why not?'

His two guests exchanged a glance, and Professor Liripine gave a small nod.

'Because of the title of the piece it says would be performed,' Dr Purslove said. 'It reads as *"Temnaya Kadentsiya"* – I think I've got fairly near to the pronunciation. It's Russian. *Kadentsiya* translates as "cadence". And *Temnaya* is "dark". So the translation, near enough, is "Dark Cadence". That's how it's usually referred to in English.'

'When it's referred to at all.'

'Why isn't it referred to?' Phin reminded himself that it was likely that Professor Liripine, wily old boy, had said this deliberately to snare his interest.

'It's death music,' said Dr Purslove.

'But there's nothing unusual about that.'

'Of course not,' said the professor. 'Plenty of very fine pieces have been composed about death and for funerals. Chopin himself wrote a "Funeral March". And there's Handel's "Dead March" from *Saul*.'

'You could even throw in Saint-Saëns's *Danse Macabre*,' suggested Dr Purslove.

'Well, if you were inclined to, I suppose you could, but let's not forget Rachmaninov's *Isle of the Dead*. And Siegfried's "Funeral March" in *Götterdämmerung*.'

'I might have known you'd drag in Wagner. See here—'

Left to it, they would go on like this for hours. Phin said, 'Tell me about the "Dark Cadence". Why are you making it sound so secretive and sinister?'

'Because it is secretive,' said Professor Liripine. 'As for sinister – well, it's not just death music, it's execution music.'

'But again that isn't unusual,' said Phin, determined not to be overshadowed. 'What about Berlioz's "March to the Scaffold"?'

'Phin, the "Dark Cadence" is execution music of a very specific kind. It's supposed to have been heard in many countries, but it's said to only ever be played – only ever heard – when a traitor is being executed.'

'It's sometimes referred to as the "Traitor's Music", in fact,' said Dr Purslove. 'And considering the reference to the "Cadence" on this programme—'

'And the fact that no one knows what happened to the Library itself, and that practically every reference to it seems to have been wiped from Warsaw's history . . . Well,' said the professor, 'you can see there could be a very intriguing story behind all this.'

'Which is why we'd very much like to know if the contents of this scrapbook are genuine,' put in Dr Purslove.

Phin looked at the programme again, then back at the professor and Dr Purslove.

'It's not the mysterious Chopin Library you're interested in, though, is it?' he said. 'You want me to find the "Dark Cadence".'

TWO

'We don't actually believe the "Dark Cadence" exists,' the professor said. 'We'd better make that clear right away. It's just a legend.'

'Oh, of course we don't believe it exists,' said Dr Purslove, at once. 'But we know the legend, and it tells how the music's handed down, probably within families. Father or mother to son or daughter. Perhaps picking it out on a piano or a violin for others to hear and remember. So in a strange way it's been preserved by small groups of people.'

'If it exists,' said the professor, again.

'I meant that. Phin knows I mean that, don't you, Phin? But it'd have been like the old tradition of storytelling,' said Dr Purslove. 'Like our prehistoric ancestors sitting in their caves, spinning tales of what might lie in the darkness beyond their primitive fires.'

'Don't get carried away, Theodore.'

'And the bards,' said Dr Purslove, undeterred. 'Very highly respected in their communities, those bards. Then there were the Irish *shanachie*, who . . . Yes, I did pronounce that correctly, Ernest, there's no need to glower at me. The "Cadence" could have followed all those traditions, Phin.'

'It's said to be a celebration of the death of someone who's betrayed his – or her – country,' said Professor Lirpine. 'People have hated traitors and betrayers all the way back to Judas.'

'And look what happened to him,' murmured Dr Purslove.

Phin said, 'But if the "Dark Cadence" was only ever played at a traitor's execution – does that mean this programme is an advertisement? Sorry, no, of course it isn't. If you were going to put a traitor to death, you wouldn't advertise the fact.'

'Especially if the execution itself was illicit,' said Dr Purslove.

'Illicit?' said Phin, startled.

'If an execution took place, it couldn't have been official,' said Dr Purslove. 'Nobody would have been put to death in a famous old mansion named for Chopin. And as for the "Cadence" itself, as far as anyone has ever known, it was only ever played by one or maybe a couple of musicians skulking outside a prison. In the yard below the condemned cell, or in the shadow of the guillotine, or lurking inside the Tower within touching distance of the block.'

'Stop speaking in purple prose, Theodore.'

Phin looked at the programme again, and was aware of a strong tug, almost amounting to a compulsion. But he said, cautiously, 'There'd be a great many things that couldn't be checked. Starting with the execution itself. If a traitor or a spy really was secretly put to death, which side was he working for? And which side actually executed him?'

'It mightn't necessarily have been a "him",' said Dr Purslove, at once.

'Always one for the ladies, doctor.'

'Plenty of female spies, Ernest. Think of Mata Hari and Odette.'

Before this could develop, Phin said, 'Also, if an execution did take place, how was it done? Traitors were usually hanged or shot.'

The professor said, in a sepulchral voice, 'Traitors suffered a much grislier death in Tudor times.'

'We aren't in Tudor times, Ernest, and if you're really imagining that a beheading – or a hanging, drawing and quartering – was staged inside the Chopin Library—'

'I'm only making an observation. The culprit would be shot,

I expect.' Almost as an aside he said to Phin, 'Difficult to rig up a gallows or a block inside a house.'

'Quite. But all of this would have to be translated,' said Phin. 'I can recognise a few bits of German, but most of it's Polish, isn't it? And that music title is written in Russian, you said.' He thought for a moment, then said, 'I suppose Arabella might be able to help with some of it, and she'd probably know people who could cope with the Polish sections.'

The professor and Dr Purslove exchanged a look, then the professor said, with elaborate casualness, 'We wondered about enlisting Arabella.'

'We don't want to call in outside translators, you see, at least not until we're a bit more sure of this. But if Arabella could spare the time . . . Well, as a matter of fact, we were rather hoping she could.'

'She could do the German far more easily than I could,' said Phin. 'She's got a German godfather, so she grew up with the language.[2] And she's fairly fluent in French, as well. I don't know about Russian and Polish, but I can ask. When are you going back?'

'We thought tomorrow, but we could make it the following day – at least, I could, Ernest probably won't want to stay any longer, of course.'

'Yes, I shall. Especially if Arabella can undertake a bit of translating.'

'Could you manage another meeting tomorrow?' suggested Phin. 'Preferably tomorrow evening, to give Arabella a chance to look at what's needed beforehand?'

They looked at one another, then, in unison said, 'Yes.'

Sharing a taxi to their hotel, Professor Liripine and Dr Purslove thought it had been a very good meeting.

'And it will be nice to see Miss Tallis again,' said Professor Liripine.

Dr Purslove thought, not for the first time, that old Liripine was often surprisingly susceptible, but he merely said he thought the signs were extremely promising for the authenticating of their scrapbook.

2 See *Chord of Evil*

'I still think it could be genuine,' he said, as the taxi stopped at the hotel.

'Only time will tell,' replied the professor. As he got out of the taxi, he remembered he had often noticed how gullible Theo Purslove could be.

'So we're spending the evening with the scholastic double act,' said Arabella Tallis the following morning. She was curled up in the unreliable leather chair, and she had kicked off her shoes which lay near the door. Phin would have to be careful not to trip over them.

'D'you mind?'

'Of course not. I'm intrigued.'

'They fell over themselves to tell me they don't actually believe in the "Dark Cadence",' said Phin. 'But if they can prove that it exists – or existed – their reputations in the music and the academic world would soar.'

'It probably wouldn't do your reputation any harm, either, if you were the one who found the proof. I'm very complimented that they thought I might be able to help, as well.'

'They remembered that stuff you unearthed in Paris last year when I worked on the Liszt project with them,' said Phin. 'They've both got a smattering of German, but it's not much – although I should think they could rattle off most of Schubert's *lieder* with perfect accuracy. But they admitted they wouldn't be equal to translating this. Nor would I. But it wouldn't take you very long, would it? Oh, and they were very definite about a separate fee for you.'

He was unsure how she would react to this; he had no idea whether she might be in need of the work and the relatively modest fee that had been suggested. It was never possible to tell if Arabella's occasional announcements about being ruinously broke or one step from a debtors' gaol were genuine, or were simply Arabella enjoying spinning a dramatic story – which usually included a portrait of herself in a bankruptcy court wearing a hat with a veil to hide her shame. She seemed to ricochet between various commissions, most of which were one-off contracts for PR campaigns, and Phin had the impression that these were fairly well paid. He also had the impression that there might be dry spells between times, however.

Arabella said, 'It is a genuine offer, is it? Not just a put-up thing because you think I need the money? Because—'

'It's not put-up at all,' said Phin, glad he could be truthful. 'Liripine and Purslove suggested it completely unprompted – in fact there was a definite glint in the professor's eye when you were mentioned.'

'Have a heart, Phin; he's seventy if he's a day.'

'I'd bet there's still plenty of life in him. I'm certainly curious about Nina and the night of the Epiphany Concert at Durham.'

'As a matter of fact, I think he's rather a dear under all that frowning,' said Arabella. 'He was very helpful when I got stuck in the lift that night, wasn't he?'

'The entire hotel was helpful, and half the London fire brigade, too,' said Phin, dryly.

'Getting stuck in a lift can happen to anyone,' said Arabella, indignantly. 'In fact I remember once . . .' She grinned and said, 'No, I'll save that story for the long winter evenings.'

Phin repressed a sudden tantalizing image of cosily firelit winter evenings with Arabella, and said, 'What do you think? About the translation? We could work amicably together, couldn't we?'

'I should think so.' She smiled, then returned to scrutinizing the scrapbook. 'Everything's very faded.'

'You'd be faded if you'd been buried under an office block for seventy-odd years and gone through bombs and fires and turmoils.'

'True. It's all fairly legible, though, and I think I could do quite a lot of it with reasonable accuracy. There's certainly some German, which I'd be fine with. There's some Polish, though, and one or two bits do look like Russian. Those would be beyond me, but there are a few fairly reliable websites that do automatic online translations of brief pieces of text – just phrases or short sentences. You've used them, haven't you? I could get on to those, and then cobble everything together, I think. You don't have to register or pay to get an actual person on any of those sites, so it would keep it all under wraps.'

'They'd prefer that,' said Phin.

'All right. How about if we see what we can find this afternoon? Then you could bring the professor and Dr Purslove to my flat this evening and we can share any gleanings. I could cook dinner, and it'd be more private than a restaurant.'

'There isn't much time to cook anything.' Phin had had experience of Arabella's dinner parties, which, if they worked out, could be spectacularly good, extending to four courses and a savoury, but which, if they went wrong, often ended in somebody being dispatched to the nearest fish and chip shop, or a frantic phone call to a pizza delivery parlour. It was a fifty-fifty chance as to the outcome.

'There's plenty of time, because I've got leftovers in the freezer I can defrost,' said Arabella. 'You remember when my cousin Toby brought his new girlfriend to supper? The one he's just whizzed away for a holiday in the Pyrenees—'

'The physiotherapist.'

'We had a great evening and I made beef stroganoff. And I made double – you know Toby's appetite, and there was a lot left. We could have that.'

Phin did remember the beef stroganoff which had turned out extremely well. Relieved, he said, 'That would be very good indeed. And the professor brought a couple of bottles of very nice wine, so we'll open those, as well.'

'Good.' She glanced at Phin's computer, which was switched on. 'D'you want to go on with whatever you were doing earlier, while I take a closer look at the scrapbook.'

'I thought I'd see if I can find anything about the Library online,' said Phin. 'And I want to email the professor's Nina in Warsaw – he's given me her address. I'd like to make contact with the boy who found this if possible, too, and she might forward a message.'

'Good idea.'

As Phin sat down at the desk, Arabella reached for a notebook and pen. For a short time there was only the tapping of the computer's keys and the faint rustle of a page of the scrapbook being turned.

Phin finished his email to Nina Randall, pressed Send, and sat back, glancing across the room. Arabella was absorbed in the scrapbook, making notes at intervals. He thought, as he had done before, that it was invariably a surprise to see how neat and organized her work was, because the rest of her life was anything but.

He turned back to the screen, and typed in a search request for Chopin Library, Warsaw. There were hardly any results, and most simply referred to a once-famous building which had stood in the city until 1944, and which had been named for one of the city's most famous sons.

But one web page gave a little more detail.

> CHOPIN LIBRARY, WARSAW
> Little information is known about this building, which once stood some way out of Warsaw centre, in the quarter of the city known as Ulica Muzyki.

Ulica Muzyki. Phin called up one of the online translation sites Arabella had mentioned earlier. Polish to English . . . Ulica Muzyki translated as the Street of Music, which pleased him. It was almost reminiscent of Old Vienna. He read on.

> The house is believed to have been large, and the name is likely to be a nod to its past and specifically to a series of performances given by the youthful Frédéric Chopin in what was known as the Ivory Salon – named for the painted and decorated ivory panels and ornate wall sconces.
>
> There are said to have been several distinguished directors of music, although sadly, none of their names has survived. However, the final music director seems to have been spoken of as talented and dedicated, although often rebellious.
>
> The Nazis destroyed much of Warsaw during World War II. Libraries, schools, museums, universities and even palaces were burned, or were the subject of controlled explosions carried out by the German forces.
>
> The Chopin Library burned down in the autumn of 1944. Only a few sparse facts about it have survived, and there is no evidence to confirm any of them. Curiously, one detail that has survived is that a famous dessert of the day was created there – the *Mrożony Polonez* – Iced or

perhaps Frozen Polonaise, the name presumably a tribute to Chopin's works.

No photographs of the building seem to have survived, and it is, in fact, interesting that no images of how it looked have ever been traced.

No images. The professor had said the same thing. He had said it was almost as if the place had been deliberately wiped from the city's history. And the text simply said the Library had burned down in 1944. Had the writer of it assumed it went without saying that it had been burned by the Nazis? Or was there more to it?

Phin closed the website thoughtfully. It was almost one o'clock, and he was just wondering about lunch, when Arabella glanced up.

'How are you getting on?' asked Phin.

'All right, I think. Come and look at this.'

Phin went to sit next to her, and looked at the open pages of the scrapbook.

'It seems to me,' said Arabella, 'that there's a kind of progressive deterioration. I don't mean in the actual documents, I mean the assembling of them. I daresay you'll be sceptical, but it's as if whoever put all this together was aware that time was running out and panicking towards the end to get it done. The early material's stuck down relatively neatly – most of it's come unstuck after so long, of course, but you can still see fragments of dried glue, and you can see how things were square with the pages. But the later stuff – here, and again here, can you see? – is loose. Some of the papers are torn, and corners are turned down to keep things in place.'

'Probably not everything did stay in place,' said Phin. 'I should think some of the stuff slid out and maybe even got lost.'

'True enough. But aside from that, I've translated this first document,' she said. 'I could almost believe there's a sequence to these documents, and that this kicks things off. It's a kind of order from some high-up department in the Third Reich. I'd like to check one or two of the terms with a German–English dictionary, but I think I've got it fairly accurately. Listen.'

ATTENTION

On the dates given herein, a detachment of Sprengkommando will commence the procedure for demolishment of the buildings listed, and marked on the map. These buildings are of no cultural or historical interest or interest to the Third Reich.

The entire operation is the command of the Führer and is for the furtherance of plans drawn up by the Third Reich, based on designs created by Hubert Gross, who has visualized for Herr Hitler an entire new city. Warsaw is to become a military transit base.

'It's rather a chilling document,' said Phin, studying it. 'A death sentence for buildings.'

'Yes. But here's the curious part,' said Arabella. 'You said the Library was destroyed in October 1944, didn't you?'

'Purslove and the professor said so. And I've found a website article that says the same thing – not that I automatically trust internet findings, but it does give the same information. Burned in autumn 1944.'

'At the foot of this notice,' said Arabella, 'is the list of the buildings to be destroyed between August and December 1944. I know there could have been other lists, or a page might have been detached, but this looks very comprehensive. Addresses, streets, everything, all clearly marked on a map.' She looked at him. 'There's no reference to the Chopin Library.'

Phin studied the map. 'You're right,' he said, after a moment. 'And it's certainly the right area – the Street of Music is marked.'

'Yes. Ulica Muzyki.' Arabella sat back in the chair. 'I don't believe this Nazi order is in the scrapbook by accident, Phin. It was stuck in quite firmly – you can see the marks of the glue.'

'Yes. And yet,' said Phin, feeling his way along the thought, 'if the Library wasn't part of that demolition, why was this order included? Unless whoever put all this together wanted people to know it wasn't destroyed by the Nazis.'

'But if the Nazis didn't burn it, who did? And why go to the trouble of burning an entire building when so much else in that city was being destroyed? Could there really have been some kind of secret execution in the place?'

'I don't know.' Phin made an impatient gesture. 'Oh – let's put this all aside for an hour and have some lunch.'

'Good idea. I'm starving.'

'We could walk along to the trattoria. Or there's cheese and eggs in the kitchen – oh, and a French loaf. Or we could order something in.'

'Let's have bread and cheese,' said Arabella. 'We can eat and keep looking for clues.'

As Phin cut chunks of cheese and buttered bread in the kitchen, he glanced at Arabella, who was spooning chutney out of a jar. Her hair had tumbled around her shoulders, and there was a smudge of ink on one cheekbone and a biro pushed behind one ear.

He said, thoughtfully, 'It might be a good idea if we don't eat in the study. To make sure we don't get anything on the scrapbook.'

'We could have trays in the sitting room,' said Arabella. 'Or we could lay the table in the bay window – I always like that. It's like a little dining area all by itself, and there's a view over the street.'

'Well, I wasn't exactly thinking of the bay window or even the sitting room—'

'Oh. The bedroom?' Arabella's face lit up.

'It's only an idea,' said Phin. 'But we could carry the plates in there and I could prop the pillows up so that we could eat more comfortably.'

'I've always found your bed very comfortable indeed,' said Arabella, demurely.

The food had been eaten, and the very comfortable pillows returned to their rightful places. Arabella, wearing Phin's dressing gown, had wandered into the kitchen to make coffee. Phin was currently trying to decide whether he could suggest she kept a dressing gown of her own here, but he could not make up his mind whether this sounded like a criticism of her borrowing his, which he rather liked her doing.

'What I find odd,' he said, accepting the coffee, 'is that the

Chopin Library seems to have been quite an important building with an interesting past. That website entry talked about Chopin performing in a marvellous gilt salon. You'd think a place like that would at least have been sketched or painted, or featured in books or articles – that *something* would have survived. But both the professor and Dr Purslove were definite that there were no images of it anywhere. I certainly couldn't find anything online. I'll scour my bookshelves, but even so . . .'

'It's all starting to sound like one of those Egyptian pharaohs who committed some appalling crime or some shattering heresy,' agreed Arabella. 'One of the rulers who had his name chiselled out of the door over the tomb so that the gods wouldn't recognize him when he got to . . . wherever Egyptian gods go to after death.'

'But this is a building,' said Phin. 'Buildings don't commit terrible crimes or shattering heresies.'

'No, but people commit crimes and heresies inside buildings,' said Arabella. 'And then they try to destroy the evidence. But if it was an illicit execution, would people burn a house – and presumably it was a very substantial house indeed – and then try to erase its memory afterwards?' She shivered slightly. 'I can't stop thinking that it must have been something much worse. Something darker.'

'But what?' said Phin. 'What happened inside the Chopin Library that made it an outcast?' He reached for the scrapbook and turned to the programme. 'I wonder how far back this legend of the "Dark Cadence" goes.'

'Why, particularly?'

'I don't know. It's just that I've got a feeling – and it's no more than a feeling – that the reasons behind the Chopin Library's destruction might go much further back than we've been thinking.'

Arabella stared at him. 'Further back than World War II, you mean?'

'Much further back,' said Phin.

THREE

1918

Until the cold, frightening music came, the house had been safe. It was sometimes unfriendly, with the shadowy stairs that went all the way to the top of the house, and the dim rooms that nearly always had the curtains drawn against the daylight, and that must never be entered. But even if the guards came stamping down the stone steps into the scullery, shouting their orders, there were hiding places that could be scurried into.

Being caught in any of those hiding places would mean a bad punishment, but if you were very quiet and if you only ventured out of the scullery when no one was looking, there were corners and unexpected little cellars that people had forgotten about. No one could be told about these places – not Zena, who was the most important person in the scullery, and not even Katya, who was what Zena called a minx, but who was kind and beautiful and made everyone laugh.

The hall was not exactly forbidden, but only the guards could go up and down the stairway. It curved sharply around as it went up so that it was impossible to see what was at the top. But everyone knew about the room up there that was kept locked and bolted, and that always had two of the black-clad sentries, and sometimes three, standing outside. It was a shivery feeling to wonder what might be inside that room, but what was even more shivery was that if you managed to avoid the guards and slip out into the garden, there was a part where you could see that windows at the top of the house had been painted over with white paint. Was that so that nobody could look into that room, or was it so that whatever was inside could not look out?

There was a room that opened off the big hall which was the most beautiful place in the world. There were paintings of people – some of them were tiny paintings, set on a long, polished table. Katya said they were called miniatures. There was one of a girl with grave eyes but a mouth that looked as if it might be ready to smile. She had soft wavy hair with lights in it, like the sheen on chestnuts in autumn.

'She's a bit older than you, but not very much,' Katya said, as they studied the tiny painting. This almost sounded as if Katya knew the girl; it might be possible to ask about this, when Katya was in the right mood.

The room had chairs with beautiful coverings and cushions with golden threads in them, so soft you wanted to stroke them.

'Silk,' said Katya, gravely. 'Very beautiful. And, d'you see, there's a silk cover on the piano stool.'

The piano. It was the most beautiful thing in the room – in the entire house, probably. Propped up over the keys were paper books, open, so that you could see scrolled outlines on them. It was like magic writing – if you knew how to read it, you would be able to chant a spell.

'Those are music scores,' said Katya. 'People learn to read those marks – notes, they're called – so that they can play music.'

'Could I do that?'

'One day you might.'

There were books in the room as well – they were children's books, and they took them down to the scullery. It had to be done quietly because of the guards, but Katya made it into a game, and the guards did not hear them.

Once in the scullery, they spread the books out on the table. They were not new, but there was a sense of them having been read several times. Had the girl in that tiny painting read them? The pages were a bit cobwebby, but they had pictures which showed the people in the stories – there were princesses who had sad lives but who met handsome princes in the end and were happy, and there were wolves and firebirds. Katya knew about them all, and in the evenings, with the guards playing cards in the hall, she read the stories aloud. The marvellous thing was that she seemed able to become each of the story-people in turn, using a different voice for all of them. Even Zena admitted that it livened up the evenings, but then you always did get liveliness from Katya.

But, said Zena, it was to be hoped Katya was not getting mixed up with the rabble who shouted rude things through the railings outside, and who thought they could put the world to rights by screaming and rioting in the streets. Still, the books were very nice indeed, although it was a pity that what looked like half a cup of borscht had been spilled on a corner of one of them, but very likely Alexander Pushkin was a bit over the head of small ears anyway. Also, Zena had the feeling that Pushkin had been part of the nobility, which was certainly not a good thing to be at the present, and most definitely not in this house.

'But all stories are good to tell and to remember,' said Katya. 'And these books can be passed to other children in the future.'

The books had the most beautiful illustrations you could imagine, and in some of them were stories about children who lived in sculleries and kitchens – and who fetched and carried things, sometimes for years and years. But the important thing about those children was that they did not have to do it for ever. They managed to have splendid adventures, or go on exciting journeys, or they helped people to make fortunes or solve mysteries. All kinds of exciting things happened in sculleries, so you never knew what might be ahead. It was good to remember this.

It was especially good to remember it later, when the cold music was being played. It was music that made you think you were walking into a nightmare, and that inside that nightmare would be someone evil and bad, waiting to snatch you up.

There was often other music, though. The crowd sometimes started singing, and the singing reached inside the house. Katya said it was revolutionary songs that were being sung – revolutionary was a new word which could be stored away and the meaning found out later – but Zena said the crowds had been drinking and dancing half the night, never mind engaging in other activities which she would not give name to and especially not in front of an innocent child. Still, very likely the guards would have been out and fired a few shots into the crowd to send them about their business.

But sometimes a man was out there who played music that was so beautiful that it painted marvellous pictures in your mind. Listening to it, you could believe you were gazing across a lake, or walking through a beautiful autumn forest with crunchy golden leaves and sunlight filtering in overhead. You could feel happy or excited or so brave that you could do anything in the world and fight all kinds of enemies.

Katya said it was music to melt your bones, and that you would follow the musician anywhere for the rest of your life, just so you could hear him play his violin. He nearly always came late at night, and it was wonderful to lie in the narrow bed in the little room just off the scullery, and listen to him playing.

* * *

Lucek Socha read the email carefully. It was from someone in London called Phineas Fox, and it had been forwarded by Nina Randall from the archives office here in Warsaw.

It had been sent written in English, and Lucek could probably have just about understood it for himself because he had acquired a small smattering of English at university in Łódź, but Nina had made a translation. It was very nice of her to have gone to so much trouble.

Mr Fox had written:

Dear Lucek,

I've been handed the portfolio/scrapbook you found recently, and which you very thoughtfully took to the archives office and Nina Randall.

Nina sent it on to her old professor at Durham University – he is very knowledgeable about music influences during World War II and she thinks it might be linked to those years. Professor Liripine has asked me to help him verify some of the documents in the scrapbook – a fascinating task, as you'll imagine. With that in mind, I wonder if you would be able to contact me, to let me know a little more about the actual discovery? The professor is fairly sure that you found it in or around the quarter known as the Street of Music.

If you can let me know anything at all about your

discovery, no matter how small or how insignificant it might seem, I would be immensely grateful. For instance, was it actually buried under anything, such as collapsed walls? Could it have been part of some kind of archive department of its own? – perhaps amongst old records from the Library itself?

I'm keen to explore all possibilities, although I'm considerably hampered by not knowing any Polish! However, Nina has kindly said she will be happy to act as interpreter whenever necessary.

I look forward to hearing from you, and thank you again for rescuing this very intriguing piece of the past.

With very best wishes,

Phineas Fox

Nina's email said:

Lucek – I know that Professor Liripine wouldn't have involved anyone who wasn't authentic, so I think Phineas Fox can be trusted. I've looked at his website – it doesn't give many details, and it's more of a calling card than an actual site – but he's apparently a researcher and historian specifically in the music field. He's written several books which were quite highly praised. He also seems to have contributed to a scholarly sounding reference book about musicians exiled by the Nazis in the 1930s and 1940s, so if it really was the ruins of the Chopin Library where you found the scrapbook, this could be very much his glass of vino.

I would like to keep you updated on anything that they uncover, if that's all right?

Hope to see you soon,

Nina

The 'see you soon' part of Nina's note was excellent. Lucek was glad he had taken the scrapbook to her offices, and that he had been directed to her room. He was even more glad that he had managed to wash off most of the dust in the builders' tiny Portakabin, and that he had made an attempt to tidy his hair, which, as usual, was standing up in a toffee-coloured tuft at the front. It did not make him look serious and responsible, which he thought was how he ought to look in an archives office, but it could not be helped.

Nina had been friendly and interested in the scrapbook, and they had got on rather well. So Lucek would reply to her email, and he would reply to Phineas Fox, as well. He thought his English might just about be equal to a reply, but since Nina had offered to act as interpreter, it would be perfectly reasonable to ask for her help. She had said she hoped to see him soon, so he might even offer to buy her lunch. There was a really nice coffee place just along from her offices – one of the nice old fragments of the city that had survived. They did delicious pastries at lunchtime. Or would Nina think he was getting above himself to suggest that? She had seemed to have quite an important position at the archives department, so she might only be wanting to be kind to someone who reminded her of her own student days.

It was, though, quite exciting to have met someone like Nina. Lucek had expected her to be a dumpy academic with pudding-basin hair – certainly not a lady who was only ten; well, all right, perhaps twelve – years older than himself. She had vivid blue eyes and fair hair that caught the light. She had been born and had grown up in England, but she had Polish connections, which she was very proud of, and she spoke really good Polish. She was just about bilingual, really.

Lucek had not expected any of this to happen when he went to work on the building site. It had been casual work, just for a few weeks, just to earn a bit of money, and he probably would not have done it if the builders had not been working in the area that was called the Street of Music. Lucek loved the Street of Music. When he was small Aunt Helena used to take him there and tell him stories about its past.

'It's the old Warsaw,' she said. 'Wealthy people once lived here. Merchants and scholars and writers and even noblemen.'

Lucek loved going there. They usually took rolls and fruit for a picnic lunch, and sat on one of the wooden benches looking across a small garden, and Helena told him how a marvellous mansion had once stood here.

'It was known as the Chopin Library, and famous musicians performed there – including Chopin himself, of course. Can't you almost imagine that all the music that was played over the years must have soaked into the pavements and the stones and into this very square where we are now?'

But sometimes, after these visits, Helena had nightmares. She had two rooms of her own at the top of his parents' house, but Lucek's bedroom was directly below them, so he knew about the nightmares. She would talk – ramblingly and even a bit wildly – about music that contained terror. Sometimes Lucek's mother went up to her. Afterwards, Helena would go over to the little cottage piano she had in her room, and play gentle, quiet music. Lucek was always glad when she did that, because it meant the nightmare had gone. He liked falling asleep to the music, too. He thought Helena played very well.

'We have to make allowances for her,' his mother said to him, once. 'She has no memory of her real family – she was found as a very small child in ruined buildings, somewhere near the Street of Music. It was my grandmother who found her and took her in – your great-grandmother, Lucek. But she never knew who her family were, or what happened to them – I think that's why she keeps going back to that part of the city.'

'To try to find out?'

'Yes. I don't think she ever will, though. And it was a long time ago and dreadful things happened in those years, so perhaps it's better not to know.'

Lucek's parents were interested when he told them about the scrapbook. They were pleased that a fragment of Warsaw's past might have been found, and they were impressed that the scrapbook had been thought of sufficient importance to be sent to an English professor.

Helena was interested in the scrapbook, as well. She found an old map, so Lucek could explain where he had found it.

'I can't tell from this,' said Lucek, helplessly. 'It's all different now. Office blocks and things.'

'Functional, but ugly,' said Helena. 'It's a pity you let go of the scrapbook, though. I'd like to have seen it. There might have been something I would have recognized. A clue – something that would tell me about my family. I don't mean ghosts. In any case, if there ever were any ghosts out there, I should think they fled when the builders arrived.'

Lucek had a sudden cartoon-image of ghosts skipping nimbly through ruins that had been their home, tucking their shrouds about their waists and indignantly telling one another that ruins were one thing, and it was all very well to stay on in the hope that the glittering, music-filled days might one day return, but you could not be expected to haunt grey office blocks with soulless furniture and strange machines. The small image pleased him. He would describe it to Nina Randall; she would enjoy it.

He was starting to feel a bit guilty about taking the scrapbook to Nina's office. Helena often thought she might have come across a clue to her past – she never had, but supposing this time there might have been something? The site had been little more than rubble – there had just been that part where a floor seemed to have caved in, or maybe it was that an old wall had been smashed down, exposing some of the old timbers and sections of stonework. And there the scrapbook had been, lying half in and half out of what looked like a large metal cupboard – maybe an ancient filing cabinet or even a safe. Its door had been hanging off, and Lucek had clambered across the debris to retrieve the scrapbook – which was really more like an artist's portfolio. It had probably been a mad thing to do, but so little of Warsaw's past had survived that it seemed a shame not to rescue something that might contain fragments of its history. It was virtually impossible to find photographs or newspaper cuttings of the old Warsaw now – and especially of the Street of Music. Older people might have such things, but they would be in private photograph albums.

Photograph albums. Lucek considered this for a moment. Were there any photograph albums in this house that might be worth looking at? He had never thought about old photographs before, but finding the scrapbook and meeting Nina had fired his imagination. And old photographs could be interesting – they might be things he could let Nina see. But where would they be stored? In the back of a wardrobe or under a bed? What about the small room near the stairs – it was not much more than an oversized cupboard, used for stashing things that nobody could think what to do with. He ran down the stairs there and then, because there was no point in sitting around thinking about things when you could be doing them.

The half-room, half-cupboard was very cluttered. The walls were lined with shelves which held box files, labelled with things like Utilities, or Guarantees, and Insurance Policies. There were no photograph albums anywhere, although there were some boxes pushed back against the wall that looked promising. Lucek, still fired up with the idea of finding something, dragged a discarded vacuum cleaner out of the way, and moved two large refuse bags containing old clothes, destined for the charity shop. In novels people searching for clues to the past went into attics – they had to fight through swathes of cobwebs and explore ancient trunks big enough to contain bodies, or they opened old desks with secret drawers and concealed compartments. It did not seem to be in keeping with that tradition to have to negotiate around disused vacuum cleaners and bags of old jumpers.

But eventually he managed to drag the boxes out, and to sit on the floor to investigate. They were filled with books, but you never knew what might be between the pages of old books, so he riffled through the pages. But there were no old love letters or mouldering documents with intriguing glimpses of faded handwriting and fragments of sentences about fortunes left to secret mistresses, or plans to topple dynasties. There were certainly no photographs. It seemed that all you got for being romantic and impulsive were indignant spiders scuttling out of their homes, and clouds of dust that made you sneeze. Rather glumly pushing the vacuum cleaner back in its corner, he wondered whether Nina Randall would approve of people who were romantic and impulsive. He had an uneasy suspicion that she was more likely to say, with a tolerant smile, that they were traits you had to expect in young people, and that Lucek would grow out of them. This was such a depressing thought that Lucek kicked a bag of discarded shoes crossly against the wall, and in doing so dislodged a folded piece of faded velvet – somebody's old bedroom curtains, probably – then saw that it had been draped over a battered cardboard box jammed

against the wall. The box might as well be checked – it looked
as if it contained more books, but you never knew.

The box did contain more books, but they were not what
Lucek had expected to see. They were children's books, and
they were very old indeed. The covers were faded and the pages
were yellowed and foxed, but it was still possible to see that
they were beautifully illustrated.

But – and this was the strangest thing of all – they were all
by Russian authors. Pushkin, Aleksei Remizov, and several
others Lucek had not heard of. Even stranger, they were not
translations – he thought they were all in the Russian language.
He flipped through several, then sat back on his heels, frowning,
because as far as he knew, his family had no Russian connections whatsoever. The books looked expensive. The paper was
still satiny, and there were really beautiful illustrations to most
of the stories. He managed to make out some of the publication
dates, and thought that the books were over a hundred years
old. They had lasted well. The box had not, though; it was
practically disintegrating, and the cardboard lid had half fallen
off. Lucek folded it back and in doing so saw that across it was
written in large letters, 'Helena'.

Lucek carried the box up to Helena's rooms and set it down
on the floor.

She was sitting in the chair by the window, reading and
listening to music. The light slanted across the chair, showing
the good bone structure of her face, and giving a gloss to the
smooth, once-dark hair that she wore brushed back from her
forehead. Lucek thought, as he had thought a few times, that
when she was young, she must have been very good looking.
He wondered why she had never married. Perhaps there had
never been any man who had been able to understand, let alone
share, her strangenesses.

Helena stared at the box, then reached down and took several
of the books out. 'Where on earth did you find these? I'd
forgotten all about them.'

'You know what they are?'

'Not exactly. But I remember them turning up,' she said.
'A large parcel – I couldn't have been more than seven or eight

at the time, and nobody had ever sent me a parcel before.' She was turning the pages of the top book. 'They're all in Russian – you realized that?'

'Yes.'

'I didn't know about people speaking different languages in different countries at that age,' she said. 'I thought they might be written in a magic language, but that I might one day understand it – that's something that I do remember. Children believe in magic, of course – at least, they did in those days, I'm not so sure about now.' She turned several more pages. 'The firebird,' she said, softly, her fingertip tracing an illustration on one of the pages. 'I think there are several stories in Russian culture and literature about firebirds.'

Her expression was absorbed, and Lucek thought: she doesn't understand the Russian text, any more than I do. But this is taking her back. But how far and how clearly is it taking her?

Helena said, suddenly, 'There was a note inside the parcel. I can remember your great-grandfather reading it to me. It said something like, "Books stored with me during the war – believe they belonged to Wyngham family of Causwain, and that there is a connection to you. Thought you would like to have them. Very best regards".' She frowned. 'I remember your great-grandfather saying it was a very nice thought by someone – someone who must be a complete stranger,' she said.

'Was there any signature?' asked Lucek, eagerly.

'I don't think so. I forgot about the books over the years, but when your parents moved here I found them again. I was grown up then, so I suddenly saw them in a different light. And that reference to the books having possibly belonged to my family – well, I wondered if they might provide a link to the past – even after so long. There didn't seem to be any way of tracing who had sent them, but there was the name – Wyngham. And Causwain sounded like a place. And so it is. I had to look on several atlases – no internet searches in those days! – but in the end I found it. It's a very small place in England – at least, it was small then. That year I sent a Christmas card and inside it I wrote that I had found the name of Wyngham and Causwain among some old family papers during a move, and it sounded as if there might be a family connection.' She smiled suddenly.

'I assumed I was writing to someone who wouldn't understand Polish, so I wrote in English, very simplistically. Probably the grammar was appalling, because I just lifted the words piecemeal from a Polish–English dictionary.'

'But if there was no address, where did you send the card?' said Lucek.

'I addressed the envelope to Mr or Mrs Wyngham, at Causwain, England. On the map it looked as if Causwain was tiny and I didn't think Wyngham was a very common name. I wasn't very hopeful, and I didn't really expect a reply.' She paused. 'But I did get one,' she said, 'although it didn't tell me anything. It just said it was nice to hear from someone in this country, but that there was no knowledge of any family connection, or of the books. It was signed by a Thaisa Wyngham. I wrote back to ask if there were any older members of her family who might know something, but she replied that her parents were long since dead and there was no other family. After that, somehow we fell into the way of exchanging Christmas cards every year. I didn't ask any more questions – it didn't seem as if she knew anything and there was always the language obstacle. But I liked the small contact each year. And I liked the idea that some long-ago child would have read the books – or been read to from them.'

'And that it might have been a child who came from your own family,' said Lucek, thoughtfully. 'And that whoever sent those books might have known that child.'

'You might occasionally be a bit wild and thoughtless, Lucek – and I don't want to know all the things you probably got up to at university. But I will say you can be very sensitive at times,' said Helena.

'Um, well, thank you,' said Lucek, awkwardly.

FOUR

1918

The scullery was a bit below ground and the two small windows were near the ceiling, almost level with the ground outside. It meant it was nearly always dark in there, and on the day the storm came growling in it was very dark indeed.

Katya loved the storm. 'Lashing rain and crackling lightning, and the skies being torn apart,' she said, a note of what was almost excitement in her voice. 'Imagine if this whole house is swept away.'

'We haven't time today for you to go into one of your play-acting, storytelling fits,' said Zena, crossly, but Katya was right about the storm. It was going to be a bad one, and there was a strangeness on the air – as if the house itself was nervous. Like when you had butterflies in your stomach. Even the guards seemed affected by it; twice during the afternoon they came stamping down the steps, looking around. They peered at the small window catch, and they even tried the handle on the garden door.

'It's locked,' said Zena. 'It nearly always is. The key's on that high shelf over there.'

'You make sure it stays locked,' said one of them. 'You understand?' He glanced around the room, then, in a quieter voice, he said, 'Tonight of all nights make sure that garden door stays locked.'

Tonight of all nights . . . Even after the guards had gone, the words lingered. Nobody dared ask what might be different about tonight, and why doors must be kept locked.

As the afternoon wore on, oil lamps had to be carried up from the storeroom. Zena said nobody should get too close to the lamps, because they had a way of hissing and spitting out little flecks of scorching oil. You might just as well be walking across the devil's own domain, with the lamps' evil imps lying in wait, said Zena.

'The devil lies in wait for us all,' put in Katya, in a voice of doom, and was told to stop being so silly and get on with chopping beetroot, because thunderstorms might well rampage across the skies, and there might be revolutions and riots in the streets, but folk still had to eat.

When, later on, Zena went to forage in the deep larder for something, a curious change came over Katya. She stood very still, as if she might be listening. Then she looked slowly about her, but she did not look towards the little recess behind the range. Hardly anyone ever did, so it was usually a good place to stay out of the way. Katya gave a little half-nod as if she was satisfied that no one was around, then went across to the high shelf where the key to the garden door was kept. She had to drag a stool over to reach the shelf, and then she had to feel along it, moving some of the jars. But she made a small pleased sound, and climbed down. The key was in her hand – it was a big old key, and slightly rusty. Moving quickly, Katya slotted the key into the brass lock of the garden door, turned it, then opened it.

She only opened it a very little way, but at once the rain gusted in. It was silly to imagine that it brought the faint notes of the bad music, but there was a moment when it felt as if the music was out there waiting. Katya stood for a moment, staring into the storm, and even from the hiding place by the range it was possible to see that there was a small frown across her forehead. Was she hearing the music? But after a moment she closed the door and climbed back on to the stool to replace the key on the high shelf. Then she put the stool back beneath the table, and went up the steps that led to the main part of the house.

But she had left the door unlocked – the door that the guards had said tonight of all nights was to be kept locked. It would be better to lock the door again, before the guards found out. There was no knowing why the guards wanted the door to stay locked. It would not be anything to do with the music, of course, but the idea that the music was out there – that Katya might have heard it and even that it might be waiting to get inside – would not go away.

It was easy to drag the stool out again, although it meant standing on tiptoe to reach up for the key, and the stool wobbled a bit. But in the end it was there, and the door was firmly locked. It felt safe when the lock clicked into place, and the key was back on its shelf.

Zena was still muttering around in the larder, and Katya had not come back. She might be in the beautiful room with the tiny paintings. Would it be possible to find her while there was no one around – to steal quietly up the stairs and across the hall? Then they could look at the rest of the books together, and at the piano with the magic symbols that made music.

The storm was still overhead, and the hall was filled with its own strange darkness. There were no oil lamps, and shadows crouched in the corners – they were like hunched-over people keeping their faces turned to the wall so that no one could see what they looked like.

The door into the room with the piano was closed, but Katya was at the foot of the big stairway, looking upwards, as if trying to see all the way to the top. The thunder crashed again, and lightning tore through the hall, sending the shadows scuttling. Katya jumped, and looked round at once. It did not matter about being seen by Katya who would not tell the guards, but she put a finger on her lips, meaning they must both be very quiet. Then she went very quietly up the stairs – all the way to where they twisted around. Might she be going to the locked room with the blind, blank windows? That was quite scary, but going up these stairs was exciting. Once upon a time grand people, wearing beautiful clothes, might have swished down them, smiling and bowing, but it was sad and dingy now, as if nobody could be bothered to dust it or polish the oak banisters any more. In places cigarette ends had been trodden into the oak, burning it slightly. That was the guards, of course.

Just beyond the twisty bit, the stairs widened out, and there was a deep window alcove, with a tall window. The rain ran down the glass making dirty trails, but the window was high enough up to be able to see across the walls that surrounded the house – to see other buildings beyond this one. There was a church with a big tower on one side, but on the tower was what looked like a massive gun. That could not be right.

Churches did not have guns. But there it was, and it was pointing towards these windows.

Then Katya's voice said, softly, 'Are you looking at the gun on the cathedral bell tower? That's what's called a machine gun emplacement. There are several other guns on other buildings quite close by – they're all trained on to this house. But there are guns on the walls of this house, as well, all pointing out.'

'Why?'

'What an inquisitive little creature you are. Don't worry about the guns – they won't hurt you.' *You* was said very strongly. 'But I think you'd better go back downstairs, and . . . No, wait, it'll be better if we go back down together in case you're seen. I can say you're helping me with some of the housework.' She looked towards the head of the stairs, and then said, 'Stay here, but stand in that window recess, and pull the curtain across so if anyone comes they won't see you.'

The window recess was quite a good hiding place, although the thick curtains smelled horrid. That could not be helped, any more than the massive black gun could be helped. The thing to do was not to look out of the window.

The storm seemed to be passing over, but the stairway and the window alcove was filled with rain light, and everything looked blurred and a bit unreal. It even began to feel as if Katya had led the way into an underwater world – one of the worlds where people like the rusalka lived. One of the storybooks told about the rusalka, who lived beneath the seas, and lured people to a watery death with their singing.

Singing. Somewhere in the shadowy corridor at the head of the stairs, someone really was singing. By peering around the edge of the curtains it was possible to see all the way to the top of the stairs – to a long shadowy corridor with doors opening off it. It was impossible to decide if the singing was soothing, like a lullaby, or if it was a bit scary, but it might be possible to creep closer, to see if the words could be made out. But Katya had gone up to one of the doors and was lifting a hand, obviously about to tap on the door. There was a big square of glass in the top half, but it was a frosty kind of glass, so that no one would be able to see through it. There were thin bars crisscrossing the glass, so that even if the glass was broken, whatever was in the room would not be able to get out.

Katya looked back at the window recess and again gave that signal, finger on lips – *be silent*. Then she tapped on the glass. The singing stopped at once, and a shape pressed up against the glass. There was the fuzzy impression of a face. Then there really was someone locked away in there, imprisoned in a windowless room, exactly like all those prisoners and captives in the stories.

In a very low voice, Katya said, 'Can you hear me? Are you all right?'

For a moment there was no response, then whispered words came – they were thready and hoarse, but they were just about loud enough to make out.

'*We think it is to be tonight . . . We are terrified . . . I try not to let them see it, but . . .*' There was a sob, then a hand came up to the glass, as if trying to scrabble through it.

This was dreadful. The words were filled with such terror, and Katya glanced nervously around her. But she said, 'Yes, it is to be tonight. But there's a plan. Dangerous, but it could work. Everything is ready.'

'Thank you – oh, thank you.' The face pressed closer to the glass.

Katya said, 'I promise we're doing everything we can for you. Stay brave.'

Before any more could be said, sharp footsteps sounded from the far end of the corridor. Katya said, 'The guards!' and darted away from the door, down to the window recess. Somehow their hands met and linked, and then the two of them were half running, half falling back down the stairs, still holding on to one another, but tumbling down to the hall, because the guards were coming along the corridor towards the head of the stairs – they were going past the door with the whispering voice, and at any moment they would be on the stair itself . . .

And then, incredibly, it was all right – they were across the hall, and safely back in the scullery, gasping and shivering. After a few moments, though, Katya knelt down. 'Listen carefully,' she said. 'You must forget everything that's just happened – everything you've just seen and heard. None of it involves you – none of it can hurt you.' There was a break in her voice, and then she said, more firmly, 'And tonight you must go to bed, as if this is an ordinary night.'

'But it isn't an ordinary night, is it?'

'No. But we have to behave as if it is.' A pause, then in a softer voice she said, 'Pull the covers over your ears so you don't hear anything. You understand me? Don't listen to anything.'

'I won't.'

But much later, lying in the narrow bed in the tiny room off the scullery, it was impossible not to listen. The guards were stamping around, shouting commands, slamming doors. The crowds were outside as well – there seemed to be far more people than usual, and they were shouting much more loudly than they normally did.

And fear was everywhere, like thick greasy smoke, clogging everything up.

'*It is to be tonight . . . We are terrified . . .*'

The church clock chimed the hours. Ten. Eleven. Soon it would be midnight. It would be very dangerous indeed to slip out of this room and go up into the house, but it might be better to know what was happening than to lie here wondering. And to keep hearing that whisper from beyond the door with the bars . . . *It is to be tonight . . . We are terrified . . .*

In any case, there was so much rushing around and shouting that the guards would not be very likely to notice a small shadow slipping through the rooms. And there were the hiding places – three, even four of them, that could be dived into if necessary. The guards might know about some of them, but they would not know about them all. They would certainly not know about the deep dark secret one. Nobody knew about that.

The idea of becoming a shadow that no one would see was suddenly too tempting to resist. It was very scary to be going up to the hall – as midnight chimed from the cathedral clock, the gas jets in the hall, which someone must have lit earlier, flickered wildly. They sent the shadows prowling and dancing, but that was good, because if the guards appeared it would be easy to become one of those shadows. But no one was around. Just a few steps up the big stairway then, just to peep along the corridor . . . Perhaps the face glimpsed through the glass in the door – the soft, small features, surrounded by the cascade of hair – would be there again.

But halfway up the stairs the guards came marching into the hall below, calling out orders. Would they come up the stairs? Yes, here they came now. There was just time to scramble up the stairs and into the alcove, and pull the curtain across and cower down in the corner. The important thing was to keep absolutely still and absolutely quiet.

The thick old curtains stirred slightly as they went past, then there was the sound of a door being unlocked, then of several other doors being unlocked. There were cries of fear, and a man's voice was raised angrily. Someone began screaming and the man's voice came again, but the guards were still shouting, and it was impossible to follow what was being said. How safe might it be to slip out now and race down the stairs? But there were more guards in the hall as well, and there was the steely clicking that meant they had rifles with them.

The voice of one of the guards suddenly rang out above the cries. He said, 'You ask what we are doing – well, I will tell you. We are moving you out of this house – this place that was called the House of Special Purpose – because it is no longer safe for you.'

'Ipatiev House,' said another guard, scornfully, 'was once a merchant's house, did you know that?'

The man with the angry voice came back at once. 'I did know it,' he said. His voice was different from the guards' voices. Smoother and firmer. As if he was used to telling people what to do, and seeing them do it. 'I also know that this house has a noble background,' he said. 'It was named for the Ipatiev Monastery in Kostroma.' A pause. 'That monastery was the place where the Romanovs came to the throne.'

The Romanovs. With the words – the name – something seemed to stir. Something that was strong and old and powerful; something that called up stories that were hundreds of years old, and that brought images of mighty emperors and golden glittering courts and famous jewels.

'But Ipatiev House is no longer safe for you,' the guard was saying again. 'So you're being moved.'

'Now? At this hour?'

'Yes. Now,' said the guard, and rapped out an order. There was a confused impression of people – it sounded like at least seven or eight of them – being taken towards the stairs, making it necessary to press as far back in the recess as possible and crouch down in the corner. The curtains stirred again, this time allowing a glimpse of the guards half dragging several young women down the stairs. It looked as if there were four of them, or perhaps even five. Behind them were two men and two women, who looked like servants.

In their midst was a figure who was certainly the man who had spoken so sharply, and who had talked about the Romanovs. A woman stood with him, and as they passed under one of the wall sconces, the flickering light fell across the man's face. He had a beard and grey hair that must once have been dark. His eyes were dark as well, and his cheekbones were strongly marked, and it was a face that you would remember for a very long time. But even more memorable was that in his arms the man carried a child – a young boy who was either too terrified, or simply too weak or too ill to walk or even stand. The boy was hiding his face in the man's shoulder, but once he lifted it and looked about him. In all the world there could never have been such fear in anyone's face. Three guards with rifles led the group, and four more, their rifles lifted and pointed at the prisoners, followed.

The man with the child stopped suddenly, and turned to face the guards. He must have said something, but his face was turned away, and his words did not reach the alcove.

But whatever he said infuriated the guards even more. The one leading them said, in a cold, hard voice, 'Very well, since you insist on questioning me, here is the truth. Nikolai Alexandrovich, in view of the fact that your relatives are continuing their attack on Soviet Russia, the Ural Executive Committee has decided to execute you.'

Execute. That meant killing someone for having done a bad thing. A crime. The terror crept closer, like cold fingers creeping around the edges of the dusty curtains.

The man held the boy to him more tightly, as if trying to shut out the dreadful words, and the woman standing next to him seized his arm.

'We knew it was to be tonight,' she said. 'Nicholas, we knew.' It was the voice that had whispered through the barred window earlier. She looked at the four girls, tears streaming down her face. Three of them were clinging to one another, sobbing, and the servants, held by the guards, were trying to get to them. But one of the girls was not sobbing. She was glaring at the guards, as if she would like to leap at them and scratch out their eyes. Her face was small and soft and pale, and her hair cascaded around it, and fell on to her shoulders . . . In the tiny painting in the silken room she had looked as if she were about to break into laughter, but now there was only an angry defiance. Was that simply a mask, though, to hide her fear?

The guards were thrusting their rifles forward, prodding the small group down the stairs. The younger of the women servants tried to push the rifles aside, and shouted something about Bolshevik brutality, and the nearest of the guards instantly hit her across the face and shouted to her to be silent.

The man said, 'So you lied to us when you said we were being moved. You are about to commit murder.'

'It will not be murder. It is execution,' said the guard. 'Lawful and just.' He nodded to the guards who came forward again, their rifles levelled. In the flickering light from the wall sconce the long, spear-like knives fixed to the rifles glinted evilly.

The guard said, 'And now, Comrade Romanov, you and your family will be taken to the death place.'

The woman cried out again. 'No – not all of us. Please not my girls – not my Alexei—'

The guard said, 'Oh, yes, Alexandra Feodorovna. All of you.'

One of the terrible things – one of the things that it would not be possible to forget, not if you lived until you were a hundred years old – was the way the woman reached for the hand of the young boy, and began to sing to him. It was difficult to hear properly, but there was something about not crying, my child, about not weeping in vain, and tears being like living dew.

She sang very softly and very gently, and the boy lifted his head from the shelter of the man's shoulder, to look at her. But he was listening to the singing, and the singing was keeping him safe, because while he listened to it, he was not looking at the guards, and he might not know those guards were going to kill them all.

As they were forced down the stairs, the girl who was in the painting joined in the singing. She knew they were going to be killed, but she still would not let anyone see she was terrified.

FIVE

1918

Even after the guards had forced the prisoners down the stairs, the cries and the sobbing still seemed to echo back up the stairs and into the window alcove.

Earlier, this had felt a bit like an adventure – like the start of something from one of Katya's storybooks – but it was not an adventure at all, it was a nightmare. Might it actually be a nightmare? Might it be possible to wake up? If so, it might even be possible to forget the faces of those young girls and the helpless boy carried in the man's arms. But there was the girl who had sung with her mother to help the boy's fear – even if she was only part of a dream, it would never be possible to forget her.

The curtains made a rattly sound when they were cautiously pulled aside and the old boards of the stairs creaked a bit, but no one seemed to hear. The thing to do was to go very quietly all the way down to the hall – it was still filled with the craftily watching shadows and it would be like going down into a black swirling well. But there did not seem to be any guards around, and there were only seven stairs to go now . . . Five stairs, three . . . Almost there.

As the bottom step was reached, from somewhere deep within the house screaming began – terrible screaming that went on and on, and went deep into your body, and even seemed to cause the shadows to shudder and cower back.

Just when it seemed that the screams could not possibly go

on for any longer, the shots came. Not just a single shot, but guns – rifles – being fired over and over again. It was dreadful. Unbearable. Those people – that man, the boy, those girls – *that* girl – were all being shot by the guards. Their servants were with them, and they were all screaming with terror and pain. There had been the sharp, spear-like knives fastened to the rifles as well – they had been like giant skewers. Were the guards using those, too . . .? There was a lurch of sickness at this last thought – feeling sick could not be paid any attention, though. The screams and the gunshots must somehow be shut out. The only way was to keep thinking none of it was real. That it really was a nightmare, and that eventually you woke up from nightmares.

There was no longer any sense of running across the hall, but somehow it had been done, and the hunched shadows had been got past, and here were the scullery steps. Here was the scullery itself with its familiar shapes of tables and wooden chairs and pans, and the scents of cooking. It was safe, and safest of all was the tiny room with the narrow bed, and the door that could be shut tight against the sounds and the terror.

But after the door had been shut and the sheets pulled up, a different terror began to creep up. Someone was creeping down the stone steps – soft footsteps were coming slowly towards the scullery. Coming to this room? Have the guards realized I saw them take those people away? If they have, they'll shoot me as well! A faint rim of light appeared around the edges of the door – someone was opening it very slowly and carefully, and looking in. Don't move . . . It might be a trick – pretend to be asleep. The rim of light widened and fell across the foot of the bed, then Katya's voice said, very softly, 'Are you asleep?'

Katya! It was Katya who had stolen down here so softly and quietly, and she would make everything all right again. She would make the world safe once more.

'I'm not asleep.' There was no need to tell her – not yet anyway – about going upstairs, and seeing the man and the boy and the girls. 'Um – bad things are happening, aren't they?'

'I'm afraid so. But you're safe down here – they won't hurt you.' She glanced over her shoulder into the scullery. 'And because I know you're safe in here – that there are people in the house who'll look after you – I've come to say goodbye to you. I have to go away. It's all very secret and it has to be very quiet.'

'No. Oh, no!' This was terrible. If Katya went away, the world would splinter and nothing would ever be safe, not ever again. 'Please don't go away.'

'I must. It's breaking my heart, but there's someone . . .' Again the backward glance to the half-open door, and the shadowy scullery. She sat on the edge of the bed – it was very clear she did not have much time, but she sat there anyway, and reached out her hand. 'You heard the screams?'

'Yes. I wanted to—'

'To try to save them? Even if it could just be one of them?'

'It sounds silly. Except when you say it, it doesn't sound silly at all.'

'I am going to save one of them,' she said. 'That's what I'm doing now. And afterwards I'll come back for you, and then there'll be a journey – a really exciting journey it'll be, both of us together, and there'll be marvellous things at the end of it.' Her eyes shone for a moment, and it was suddenly possible to believe her.

There was a quick hard hug, and the familiar scent of Katya's hair and her skin, and then she was out of the room before anything else could be said.

But she did not completely close the door, and a second figure was in the scullery – a figure who was standing very still, with its head turned towards the steps, as if fearful of what might appear. As Katya went across the floor, the light fell across this figure. It was the young servant girl who had shouted that the guards were brutes and had been hit across the face. The bruise showed clearly, even in this light. So it was true what Katya had said – one of those people might be saved after all. This was a good thought

Katya took the girl's hand, and pulled her towards the little garden door. 'Once outside we'll be safe,' she said to her.

'Yes.' It came on a breath of sound, but then, with sudden eagerness, 'Is *he* outside? Is he waiting for us?'

'Oh yes.'

'Are you sure?'

'Yes. He won't let us down.'

For an instant it was as if a light shone in the eyes of both of them, then they were going across the scullery towards the garden door. They were almost there when there were the clattering footsteps of the guards in the hall, and shouts about one of the females having escaped.

'That wretched little servant,' cried a voice. 'The one who shouted curses upstairs earlier. But now she's slipped the net – slithered out of our hands like the Romanov rat-slave she is!'

'We'll find her,' said a second voice, hard and angry. 'She must be in the house – it's sealed. We made sure of that.'

'Drag her down to the cellar – she's as bad as her masters; she can share their fate.'

'That other one'll get a worse end,' said the hard voice. 'That bitch who got her out. That kitchen maid. The crowd's already yelling for her. If we throw her out to them, she won't last long. They'll tear her to pieces. They already know she's a traitor to her own kind – helping those cursed Romanovs. She's been up to her ears in an escape plot, and she's a traitor to the Bolshevik cause.'

'How do you know all that? The crowd have been yelling their heads off all day, but you can't tell what they're shouting most of the time.'

'I do know,' said the hard-voiced guard. 'Listen.'

There was a sudden listening pause, and into the pause . . .

There it was. The thing so much dreaded. The cold, terrible music, filtering into the house.

'You hear it?' said the guard. 'That's the "*Temnaya Kadentsiya*". They call it the "Traitor's Music", and they're playing it for that kitchen maid – Katya, that's her name. And once they get their hands on her . . .'

Katya gave a gasp, and grabbed the girl's hand, pulling her towards the garden door. She was going to take the girl through it with her, and they were going to meet whoever had made their eyes light up with such hope and courage. That was why Katya had unlocked it earlier – ready for this.

But it was not unlocked, because it had been locked again earlier. *I* locked it. I locked it because of what the guards said, and because of keeping out the music. But now it would keep

Katya and the other girl in, because the guards were coming
and there was no time to climb on to the stool for the key . . .
Katya would be thrown to the crowds and they would kill her
while the music was played.

It took two seconds to bound from the bed, and call that the
door was locked. 'But there's a hiding place . . .'

'Where?'

'Here. Quickly . . .'

Of all the hiding places that had been found and kept secret
– of all the places the guards had not known about and that
perhaps no one in the house knew about – this was by far the
best, and it was the one that had never been used. It was as if
it had been necessary to save it for something. For this – yes,
of course for this.

Katya was saying, 'But that's only the larder. That's not a
hiding place – they'll only have to open the door to find us.'

'No – I'll show you. Only you must be quick.'

Once the larder door was shut, it was almost impossible to
see anything, but it was possible to feel a way along – to feel
the marble shelves with the bread crocks and the covered dishes
of leftover food. There was a smell of food and it was dark,
but it was possible to feel the way along.

Katya said, in a fearful whisper, 'Where are we going?'

'All the way to the back. Don't let them hear you.' For the
guards had clattered into the scullery, and they were opening
the little bedroom door – something was said about there being
a pesky child, who must have run into hiding.

'Don't bother about the child – it's those two women we're
after.'

Katya's whisper came again. 'How is this a hiding place?'

'There's a place at the back – a bit like a large cupboard. A
slab that pulls away and a space beyond. You can both go in
there, and I can put the stone back. No one will know.'

'And then you'll go back to face the guards? I won't let you!'

'It's all right, really it is. I'll be in the ordinary larder, and
if they open the door, I'll have been stealing some food – I'll
have some bread or something in my hands. They aren't interested in me anyway – you heard them say so. And once they've
gone away you can get the key and get out.'

There was a moment when it seemed that she would refuse, but then she said, 'Yes. But we have to be quick.'

For a bad moment it seemed that the section of stone that could be pulled away was no longer there – that it had been a dream. But it is there, I know it is. The wall's flat, and you have to run your hands across the surface, but it's here . . . About level with your waist, remember . . .

And suddenly it was there. The two sets of holes, four on each side, positioned so that fingers could be thrust in, and the whole section of the stone pulled back. It did not pull very easily – it had not done so all those weeks ago when it was originally found, but then there was a slow groan of sound, like old, dead bones being forced into life, and the feeling of flakes of dust and dirt showering down, like shrivelled scales falling away from an old snake.

As the stone came away there was the sense that something had breathed out – something that was so cold it would burn your skin if you touched it. Katya and the other girl both shuddered, but they stayed where they were, although there was the sense of the unknown girl glancing nervously back to where the larder door and the scullery were.

The stone was quite heavy, but it could be set on the ground, and there was the square, gaping hole.

'Can we get through that?' said Katya, suddenly sounding doubtful.

'Yes. You'll have to squeeze through, but you'll manage it. And it'll be safe in there.'

'It looks a bit like the opening to a tunnel,' said the other girl, her voice uncertain.

'It isn't a tunnel. It doesn't go anywhere.'

'How do you know? Did you explore?'

'Yes.' There was no need to explain about cautiously climbing through with the oil lamp and seeing that this might one day be a really good hiding place, because one day it might be necessary to hide – properly and completely – from the guards.

'We'll do it,' said Katya. 'You go back and pretend you've been raiding the bread bin, and we'll be safe in here. You can put the section of stone back so it won't be seen, can't you?'

'Yes. And I'll come back as soon as I can, and let you out. But I'll have to wait until the guards have gone and it's safe.'

'I understand that. I trust you.'

They climbed through, first Katya, then the girl.

'Tight squeeze,' said Katya. 'But we're through. It's horrid though – and dreadfully cold and dark.'

'I took some candles and a tinder box from the shelf just inside the larder. Here . . .' And Katya's words about raiding the bread bin had sparked an idea. There was just time to dart back along the larder, to seize from the shelves some pieces of rye bread, and a slab of cheese. What else? The dish of apricots that had been left under a cover. And something to drink. There was a stoppered flagon of milk.

'Take these—'

'A feast,' said Katya, gravely, taking them. 'You're an exceptional child.'

'I'm not.' There was no more time left; the guards were just beyond the larder door, and the stone slab had to be put back. It was difficult to do it in such haste, because it was heavy and it had to be kept absolutely level with the opening in order to slide it back in place. But it was finally scraping back into position, and as it did so, Katya's voice came from the dimness. It was quite close, as if she was pressing against the wall on the other said. She said, 'I love you very much. Please remember it.'

'I will. I love you too. And I'll come back as soon as it's safe.'

There was no way of knowing if she had had heard this, but it was a good feeling to know they were both safe for the time being. Feeling the way back to the scullery, managing to find a chunk of bread and a piece of cheese from beneath a crock, it was important to remember that although they would be cramped and cold, they had the candles which would provide some light, and they had food and milk.

Out in the scullery the guards were prying into cupboards and opening doors. They spun round at once and demanded to know what was happening.

It was surprisingly easy to put on a bewildered voice; to say, 'The shouting woke me up and I was hungry. So I got some bread and cheese from in there.' A vague pointing to the larder.

'I'm allowed to do that.' This came out defiantly, which was good.

The men went into the larder, of course, and moved around suspiciously. But they came out again, shaking their heads.

'A mouse couldn't hide in there.'

'It's not a mouse we're looking for, remember; it's a couple of female rats.'

'Whatever you're calling them, they're not in there. You' – a finger was jabbed angrily – 'you get back to bed in your own room. It's no time for children to be around. And don't come out again. There'll be one of us nearby, watching. I'll stay down here for a while in any case.' As the other man nodded and went back up the stairs, the guard opened the larder door again and went inside. It was all right, though. He came out again with food in his hands and a bottle of something that was probably wine. But he did not go up the stairs. He sat down at the table.

The music was still being played outside – the 'Traitor's Music', the guard had called it. It was trickling through the house, cold and cruel, like shards of ice getting in through the cracks in the bricks and stones, or dripping down from the ceilings.

It would be all right, though. The guard would not stay down here for ever. Presently it would be possible to get Katya and the other girl out, and they would unlock the garden door and escape.

Even like this, in the midst of the fear and with the crowds still shouting and playing the music, it was possible to reach for Katya's words, and feel them like a warm shawl.

'I love you very much,' she had said. Those were good words to hold on to.

SIX

For once, Professor Liripine and Dr Purslove were in agreement about something, which was that the evening ahead at Arabella Tallis's flat promised to be very enjoyable and probably extremely interesting. They were looking forward to hearing if she and Phin had managed to find any clues in the scrapbook's contents.

They dressed carefully before setting off. Dr Purslove had a rather natty bow-tie which he felt gave him a jaunty air, and the professor had had his hair cut at the hotel barber's shop and his beard trimmed into what the assistant told him was a very dashing goatee that made him look ever so scholarly.

They had bought two bottles of wine and some Belgian chocolates to take. Dr Purslove said Prosecco was what people liked at the moment, so they had a bottle of that, and then the professor had noticed some very nice Madeira in the wine shop, and remarked that Madeira had been rather forgotten about, and it would make a nicely unusual aperitif. It was a bit unfortunate that Theodore remembered the fruity old Flanders and Swann song about, 'Have some Madeira, m'dear', even to the extent of trying out a couple of verses in the taxi. The professor hoped he did not start singing the entire song later on – you could never be sure what Theo might descend to after a few glasses. Still, very likely he would not remember all the verses.

Theodore Purslove, remarking that Pimlico had always been considered rather trendily upmarket and it would be interesting to see Arabella's flat, thought that between the Prosecco and the Madeira, Ernest might become quite mellow. They might even find out a bit more about Nina and the night of the Epiphany Concert.

'It looks as if we're here,' said the professor, as the taxi drew up in front of a tall old house with a neat row of labelled bells alongside the front door.

'It does indeed. I see there's one of those old parks in the square,' said Dr Purslove. 'Very nice, too. This looks like the flat.'

'Don't drop the wine,' said Professor Liripine as they clambered out of the taxi.

'I shan't. I'm looking forward to our dinner, aren't you?' said Dr Purslove. 'Phin says Arabella's a very good cook.'

Phin had managed to put in a couple of hours on his current commission for the work on the obscure jazz musician, but the Chopin Library and the "Dark Cadence" were far more alluring than New Orleans and the shape-note hymns of the early nine-teenth century. He finally gave up, and set off for Arabella's flat, where he found her stirring the beef stroganoff, and breaking off at intervals to train a hairdryer on to an amorphous mass in a glass bowl.

'I found this at the bottom of the freezer,' she said. 'It's lemon mousse, so if I can defrost it in time it'll make a beautiful pudding. I can't actually remember when I made it, but it was probably meant to impress somebody, and most likely it was you, so I hope you enjoyed it.'

Phin disclaimed ever having eaten lemon mousse in Arabella's flat.

'I just wish I'd found it sooner and got it thawed out. I daren't try to defrost it in the microwave, because you never know with mousses, do you? Would you mind taking a turn with the hairdryer while I lay the table?'

Phin, warily plying the hairdryer, was grateful that there did not seem to have been any worse catastrophes than a frozen lemon mousse.

The beef stroganoff was delicious, and the professor and Dr Purslove ate with enthusiastic appreciation.

Arabella was wearing a velvet shirt the colour of autumn leaves, with a string of amber beads around her neck. The colours made her eyes look almost golden, and Phin thought that this weekend he would take her out to some very expensive restaurant so that she could wear it again, and the diners could all envy him. It was not that Arabella was beautiful – she was not – and it was not because she was pretty, which she definitely was not. But he knew everyone would still look at her and be envious.

'You were going to have lemon mousse for pudding,' she said. 'And if you'd seen it when it came out of the freezer, you'd have sworn that was what it was. But after the ice was hairdryered away, it turned out to be chicken soup, which is a pity, because if I'd realized in time we could have had it as a starter. But there's plenty of cheese and some fruit, and we'll break open the Madeira to go with it.'

Dr Purslove said he rarely ate pudding, and he suspected

Ernest wasn't supposed to eat it at all. The professor glared at
him, but said, quite mildly, that he was particularly fond of
cheese and fruit to round off a meal. He added that Arabella
was extremely thoughtful to be going to all this trouble.

'And if that's Brie, I'll have just a sliver, please. Oh, and
celery too. Very nice.'

Phin thought there was an unspoken understanding that they
would postpone talking about the scrapbook until they had
finished eating, but he was aware of tension around the table.
It was only when they left the table for the deep sofa and
armchairs grouped around a low table and Arabella had
made a large pot of coffee, that he said, 'If everyone's comfortable, I think this is the moment we start to talk about the
scrapbook.'

It was as if the threads of that tension were suddenly pulled
taut. The two academics exchanged glances, then both looked
at the scrapbook which Arabella had set out in front of them.

'We both think,' said Phin, 'always assuming the documents
are genuine, that they were deliberately chosen. Put into the
scrapbook for a purpose.'

'We even think there's a sequence to them,' said Arabella.
'We don't know if someone was trying to tell a story, or even
send a message, but the whole thing kicks off with a Nazi
command for the destruction of various buildings. It's a horrible
soulless thing.'

'The Nazis did destroy almost the entire city through most
of the 1940s,' said the professor.

'But,' said Phin, 'this order from the German High Command
lists the buildings destined for destruction in the last half of
1944. But the Chopin Library isn't on it. It's almost conspicu-
ously absent, in fact. The order is very detailed – there's even
a map of the area, showing the buildings marked out for
destruction, but the Library isn't one of them.' He was unable
to tell if this came as a surprise to the two men.

'Interesting. Anything else?'

Arabella said, 'Yes, and I only deciphered it about half an
hour before you all arrived. I haven't even had time to tell Phin
about it. Sorry, Phin, but what with the lemon mousse . . . Also,
of course, I might be making much of little, but you could have

been right when you said all this might go back farther than World War II.' She turned the pages of the scrapbook. 'I know you'll have seen this already, professor, but you might not have studied it in any detail, partly because it's so fragile it looks as if it would crumble if you breathed on it – and very, *very* faded – but also because it's in Russian.'

'A music score,' said Phin, leaning forward. 'Very old and faded, but the notes still readable.'

'It's handwritten,' said Arabella. 'As if someone copied it. You can see how the ink's faded to pale brown.'

'I do remember seeing it,' said the professor. 'I only glanced at it, because it wasn't music I recognized, but I remember thinking it looked like the lettering of one of the Eastern European countries – what we used to call the Eastern bloc. I mentioned it to you, didn't I, Theo?'

'It's actually the Russian alphabet, so you did recognize it accurately, professor,' said Arabella. 'I did manage to translate the title, and it seems to be an aria from a Russian opera called *The Demon.*'

Professor Liripine frowned. 'I don't know of it, but Russian stuff is your field of expertise, Theo.'

'*The Demon,*' said Dr Purslove, thoughtfully. 'It's an opera that was composed by – let me think – yes, by Anton Rubinstein. And if my memory serves, he wrote it in the early 1870s – Tchaikovsky's often said to have been influenced by it when he wrote *Eugene Onegin*, in fact. *The Demon* was quite popular in its day, although when Rimsky-Korsakov was invited to a private performance, he didn't think much of it. It wouldn't be at all his kind of thing,' he said to the professor.

'Rimsky-Korsakov was very specific in his likes and dislikes,' agreed the professor.

None of this was said with any sense of displaying or imparting knowledge; it was the offhand familiarity of two people whose daily round is among and within the great composers and musicians of the world. For Phin, it was a reminder of their dedication to their work, and he also found it rather endearing to see the sudden understanding between them.

As Arabella turned the scrapbook's pages, Phin felt again as if it were breathing a strange, sad magic into the room. It was as if trapped memories were blindly trying to find a way out, but were too far back, and too weak, to manage it.

'I've assumed that's the title of the actual opera at the top,' said Arabella. 'And that immediately under it is the name of the aria.'

Theodore Purslove was staring at the music. 'That is the title,' he said. 'And I might not recognize more than a few words of Russian, but I recognize this. The aria is "*Ne plach' ditya moya*". That translates, more or less, as "Don't cry for me, my child", although it's more usually known just as the "Demon's aria". It's beautiful and rather sad, and . . .' He paused, then said, 'And it was an especial favourite of the tsar.' Almost as an aside, he added, 'I mean the last tsar – Nicholas II, who was butchered to death in a cellar in 1918, and his wife and their daughters and son murdered with him.'

With the words, images brushed Phin's mind again, but this time they were familiar and recognizable ones from faded photographs and erratic old movie footage: autocratic and imperious people, the women with elaborately dressed hair and sumptuous gowns, the men in the formal dress uniforms of various regiments, all of them shown against splendid back-grounds of palaces and glittering ballrooms, or wandering in leisurely fashion through beautiful gardens. Also, of course, there were the dozens of books and films and documentaries about their deaths on that long-ago summer night, and the romantic speculations as to whether one of the daughters had escaped.

Dr Purslove was saying, 'The tsarina – Alexandra – is supposed to have often sung that aria to their son – Alexei – to try to calm him when he was ill. The child was haemophilic, as I expect you know, and often seriously unwell and in pain. One source even says she sang it to him as they were all forced down to the cellar to be shot – to try to distract him from what was ahead.' Theo Purslove made a slightly impatient gesture with one hand, as if to brush aside any idea of sentiment. 'I never believed the story, and it's almost certainly one of those romantic tales with no basis—'

'Most likely conjured up by some old servant who escaped

the Revolution and wanted to tell a good story,' nodded the professor. 'Not that I'd want to decry any of the hardships people went through during the Revolution.'

'There's also the possibility that the story could have been started by one of Rubinstein's descendants trying to revive the opera,' said Dr Purslove.

'And then embroidered over the years?'

'Exactly so. Actually, I always thought it rather a mawkish tale.'

'I wouldn't disagree with you on that, Theo.'

This appeared to satisfy them that they were not in the least affected by the small, sad tale, and Phin took the opportunity to say, 'Why would that aria be included here, though? Because if we're accepting that the scrapbook is telling a story, then this particular page points back to . . .'

He stopped, and his eyes met Arabella's.

She said, slowly and deliberately, 'It points back to Imperial Russia in general, and the murders of the last Romanovs in particular.'

Again there was the silence. And again, Phin had the sense of the faded memories reaching out hopefully.

He said, 'Is it relevant to the "Cadence"? We thought the scrapbook was about the Nazis' occupation of Warsaw and the execution of a traitor. I can't see how the Romanovs come into that.'

'I can't see it, either,' said Dr Purslove.

'I think I might be able to throw a glimmer of light on it,' said the professor. 'I don't know if it'll be more than a very faint glimmer, but . . . Where did I put my briefcase? I didn't leave it in the taxi, did I . . . No, here it is. I had an email just as we were setting out, and I didn't have time to read it properly, because we were running late on account of Theo not being ready, as usual—'

'Who's the email from, professor?' asked Phin, before Dr Purslove could say anything.

'Nina Randall. She'd put an attachment to the email,' said the professor, in the careful tones of one who makes a point of regarding the greater part of modern technology and modern communication as intricate and insecure, but is prepared to acknowledge their usefulness. 'I got the hotel reception to print everything out for me while I was waiting, so . . . Does anybody know what I did with my glasses? Oh, thank you.' This was to Arabella, who had found and handed over the glasses.

'I heard from Nina as well,' said Phin, as the professor donned his spectacles and burrowed in his briefcase. 'She was going to see if there was anything in their archives office or any of the old newspaper records about the Library, wasn't she? She didn't sound very hopeful of finding anything, though, because—'

'Because the Chopin Library became an outcast,' said Arabella, softly. 'It's hardly referred to anywhere. No photographs or images of it seem to have survived. It's almost as if people wanted to expunge it from the records – even from their own memories and the memories of their descendants. Sorry if that sounds melodramatic.'

'It does, a bit, but you're right,' said the professor, looking up from his briefcase, and regarding Arabella over the top of his spectacles. 'Nina said almost exactly the same thing.'

'Ernest, I think we'd all like to know exactly what Nina Randall did say, so will you find the email and read it, please.'

'I have found it,' said the professor.

Nina had written:

> Hello professor,
> You do hand me some fascinating tasks, and they frequently take surprising twists. I've never forgotten that time you set up that weekend study group focusing on Elgar, and I came back to Durham to help out. Eight of us decamped to the Malvern Hills – that was when we discovered the cobwebby antique shop with the ancient ciné footage of Dame Clara Butt, dressed as a mermaid, performing some of the songs from Sir Edward's *Sea Pictures*. In retrospect I'm not sure if my attempt that night to recreate her performance down to the actual costume worked as well as it might have done. But it was certainly a research project that led us down some unforeseen paths.

Without looking up from the page, the professor said, 'That was a particularly interesting study project.'

'Yes, I'm sure it must have been.' Phin did not dare meet
Arabella's eye.

The professor turned to the second page.

> But as to the Chopin Library, as I told you, I thought it
> would be looked at askance if I started to delve into its
> history from here, but I did take a stealthy look in a few
> old files. I came up against a remarkable number of blank
> walls, though, and I think I might have abandoned the
> search altogether if it hadn't been for the charming young
> man, Lucek Socha, who found the scrapbook in the first
> place. He's taken this whole project to his heart and he's
> determined to get at the truth of it.
>
> So, I hope you might find the attached useful. It's
> certainly primary research material, which – as you once
> taught me – is always good to have.
>
> It was in a file relating to one of the original fire services,
> of all things – somebody, at some time, seems to have
> compiled a kind of memorial to the firefighters of the city,
> and the file found its way to our archives offices. The
> original is in Polish, of course, but I've made a translation
> for you. There's a curious part at the end, which didn't
> mean much to me. I thought this was about the Library,
> but I'm wondering if there's another aspect you haven't
> mentioned.
>
> I haven't done anything about verifying this – again, I
> don't want to draw attention to the delvings. But it looked
> like a genuine first-hand account from a man who saw the
> Chopin Library burn, and it reads as if he wrote it shortly
> before Warsaw was liberated.

Professor Liripine paused to readjust his spectacles and drink
some of his coffee, then he reached for what was clearly Nina
Randall's translation.

As soon as he began reading it, Phin felt as if those struggling ghosts had crept even closer. They want to be heard, he
thought. They want it known what happened inside the Chopin
Library that night – that's why the scrapbook was made.

SEVEN

'It is being rumoured around the Street of Music that an enquiry may be made into aspects of the work of the Verbrennungskommando (Burning Detachment), and the Sprengkommando (Demolition Unit), during the occupation of Warsaw,' began the document. 'None of us expects to be questioned, but memories fade with the months, so I am setting down my recollection of an event that happened near to my restaurant – the night when a building which holds a special place in my heart was burned.

'The Chopin Library always meant a great deal to me, and I am not ashamed to say this. My father was head chef there in the years of its greatness, and in my own time I knew some of the modern musicians, as well – among them the remarkable young man who was the Library's director of music, Yan Orzek, whose tempestuous ways and attraction for the ladies were as famous as his musical talent.

'I should explain that I am a chef by profession and also by inclination, and that my restaurant is near to the Street of Music. It is known as Anatol's, this being my name and that of my father and grandfather, also.'

The professor glanced up. 'Yan Orzek,' he said. 'And Anatol. I think those are the first names we've actually found, aren't they?'

'I'm making a note of them,' said Phin, who had already reached for his pen.

'In the bad years, we were dirt under the boots of the oppressors, and it was a great struggle to keep my restaurant open. But there were loyal friends who came to dine, and to enjoy the music which we managed to provide, even though it was only a single pianist and the piano itself a jangling old instrument, sadly in need of tuning.

'There were people gathered in my restaurant on the night I write about. A good supper was being served – it was still sometimes possible to get food if one knew where to go. It was known that I opened my doors for an hour or two on most evenings, and no objection was made.'

As the professor paused, Arabella said, softly, 'How dreadful that he had to justify a perfectly normal thing like running a restaurant. Sorry – go on, professor.'

'I was determined to remain in the city for as long as I could,' Anatol had written. 'Even though there was constant danger, and even though it was terrible to see ravaged streets and scarred wastelands where buildings had been burned or destroyed from the relentless bombing.

'On the night of which I write, there were perhaps ten or a dozen people dining. Everyone had enjoyed the food and there had been a flagon or two of good wine as well, although how that was acquired I shall not explain . . .

'When the reports of a fire nearby came, most of us ran out to see what was happening. At first it was thought, of course, that it was another of the planned demolitions, although there was usually a notice sent to the buildings, telling them what was to happen. That was something people feared to receive, for if residents did not leave, often they were taken to one of the ghettos – terrible places surrounded by high walls and barbed wire.

'But there had been no such notice for any of the buildings in the Street of Music – we knew this, for many of my customers lived nearby.

'I ran towards the Library with the others, going as fast as I could manage. (I have enjoyed my own cooking over the years, but this adds to the girth and results in the buying of larger-sized trouserings.)

'The square was crowded when we got there – the oppressors had come running, of course, but it was at once clear that their commander was shocked by the fire. He marched angrily around the square, vanishing and then reappearing from out of the billowing smoke like an avenging god, demanding to know what had happened, and shouting that this was a waste of resources and men – the Library had not been marked for demolition; it was of no significance, culturally or historically, and its contents were of no value to the Third Reich, so it should be left to burn to ashes. Hearing that, I wanted to run across and punch the man's face to a pulp, but I was restrained by several of my customers.

'It was while we were trying to quench the fire, in defiance of the order, that through the smoke and the flames and the confusion, I heard the music.

'The Chopin Library has been a place of music for more than a hundred years – I could remember how it had always been impossible to cross that square without hearing it in some form coming from within the mansion. It was named for a great and famous composer, and I had often heard it said that the very stones and the pavements of the Street of Music were soaked in wonderful and memorable music, not only from Chopin himself, but from other men in whom the lamp of genius burned.

'But no music should have been heard from within a building burning to its own death.

'I stood there, not speaking and not moving. Because I knew that music. No one who had ever heard it would forget it. It requires no ability to play an instrument, or understand a music score; it is music that burns into your very soul and stays there for ever.

'And there is a belief that to exorcize a devil – a demon – it must first be named. So I shall name this demon, and perhaps that will draw its teeth.'

'Demon,' said Phin. 'He actually uses the word.'

'Yes, but there's no reason to connect Anatol with the contents of the scrapbook and the "Demon's aria",' said Dr Purslove.

'There's reason to connect him with the Chopin Library,' said Phin. 'Sorry, I'm theorizing ahead of the data, aren't I?'

'You are a bit, but it's understandable,' said Professor Liripine.

As he reached for the next page, Arabella said, 'I rather like the sound of Anatol. I like that he was angry and defiant, and that he refused to be cowed by the Nazis.'

'I do, too,' said Dr Purslove. 'Get on with reading, Ernest, and stop milking it.'

'An elderly gentleman – frail, but learned and wise – lived near to my restaurant, and often I visited him. He had an old piano and sometimes he would play for me. Religious music, mainly – Bach and Handel and Fauré.

'But one night – and it was shortly before he died – he played strange and chilling music that I did not know.

'"Its name is the *'Temnaya Kadentsiya'*," he said, when I asked. "More usually known as the 'Traitor's Music'. I first heard it many years ago, and I have never forgotten it."

'"When? Where did you hear it?" I asked.

'He paused, then said, "It was in a place called Katerinburg. Outside a house called Ipatiev House. It was played there on the night the tsar and his family were butchered to death."'

Dr Purslove drew in a sharp breath, then, as the professor looked up, he waved impatiently to him to go on.

'He had been a learned and devout man of the Church, and I trusted what he told me about the music – that it is played to mark the execution of someone who has committed the sin of betraying friends or comrades to an enemy. Its legend tells that it has been handed down within families and small, close communities – perhaps over several centuries. No one ever dares write it down for fear of being subjected to terrible questioning as to how and why and when the knowledge of it had been acquired.

'He played it for me a second time, and then a third, and I thought he was seeing ghosts, or perhaps even Death itself. But looking back, I believe he was seeing a long-ago night when he had stood outside a house in which brutal murders had been done.

'And on the night my beloved Chopin Library burned, someone played the "*Temnaya Kadentsiya*", the music that I have since come to know is recognized in many countries as the "Dark Cadence".

'But I wish to set down that I do not know who played it. Also that I do not know for whom it was played.'

For what felt like a long time, no one spoke.

Then Phin said, slowly, 'That's an extraordinary story.'

'Yes. And,' said Professor Liripine, 'how far do we accept it?'

'It sounds like another strand in the legend,' said Phin. 'It fits with what we already know.'

'Also,' put in Dr Purslove, 'this might be the proof that there really was an execution in the Library on that last night.'

'A traitor burned to death? It's an extraordinary method,' said the professor. 'The Nazis would have shot a spy – or hanged him. This doesn't sound as if they even knew it was being done.'

'Could somebody have played the "Cadence" that night without knowing its meaning?' asked Phin, rather hesitantly.

'No,' said Arabella, at once. 'Sorry to disagree with you, but that was a ravaged city – occupied by the Germans. There'd have been Nazis and SS yomping all over the place. Nobody was likely to say, "Has anyone got a violin conveniently to hand, because I think I'll just bash out a bit of a tune while we watch this place burn." And if you so much as *mention* Nero and Rome—'

'Let's remember that Anatol's report of the "Cadence" is hearsay, anyway,' said Professor Liripine. 'He was told about it by an elderly priest who claimed to have heard it on the night the tsar and his family were murdered: 1918.'

'Which takes us back to the Romanov connection,' murmured Dr Purslove.

'Why did Anatol's frail priest play it to him at all?' demanded the professor suddenly.

'An old man, his mind back in the past?' said Phin. 'Do you believe Anatol's account, professor?'

'Against all logic, I think I do.'

Phin said, 'I think I do, as well. Doctor, I'm not particularly well up on the Russian Revolution, but weren't the deaths of the tsar and his family regarded as a straightforward execution by the Bolsheviks?'

'Yes. I don't think there was ever any rumour of traitorous involvement,' said Dr Purslove.

'So no reason for the "Cadence" to be played at their deaths?'

'None I've heard of. There were a few murmurs about escape plots, but there usually are after that kind of event. There was the Anastasia legend, of course, but that was disproved in – oh, somewhere in the 1990s. People liked the idea, but I don't think it was ever given much credence.'

Arabella said, 'Professor, was there anything else in Nina

Randall's email? Was it just a cover note with the translation?'

'Mentioning how you all cavorted around the Malvern Hills re-enacting Elgar's *Sea Pictures*,' said Dr Purslove, slyly. 'What Arabella is saying – very politely – is did you read the entire email, Ernest.'

'Of course I read it.' The professor reached for the email again. 'Oh,' he said, 'there is a bit more, well, it's almost half a page, actually, and I don't believe I did read it – that'll be because Theodore was running late.' He scanned the printed sheet, then suddenly looked pleased. 'How astonishing.'

'What? Ernest, *what?*'

'Nina says Lucek Socha – the boy who found the scrapbook – has an aunt or great-aunt whose family are thought to have lived in or around the Street of Music.'

> I think 'aunt' is a kind of courtesy title, because her own family vanished at the end of the Second World War. The aunt – her name is Helena Baran – was found wandering in the ruins, and she has vague memories of some childhood tragedy or loss. She was only a very small child at the time, and all she can remember is being extremely frightened. Lucek says she still has nightmares about it. I have a feeling that there might be something in his family's history that stretches back to the war years, and possibly even the Library itself, if that isn't a coincidence too far.

'What a sad thing, though,' said Arabella.

'A great many families were wiped out in those years,' said Dr Purslove. 'Apart from being carted off to ghettos and concentration camps, there were bombing raids towards the end.'

'But,' said Phin, 'the records suggest that the Street of Music was never targeted by the Nazis in any way. It was on the outskirts of the city. Anatol mentions that – he says the commanders were startled and angry at the fire.'

'And he'd have said if there had been any bombs that night,' nodded Arabella.

'I wonder if the ruins where the aunt was found could have been the ruins of the Chopin Library,' said Phin. He was remembering that when he first saw the scrapbook, he had had a mind-picture of four musicians who had called themselves the *Burza* Quartet, eagerly planning a concert for an October night in 1944. Now, he had another image – that of a tiny girl, bewildered and frightened, scrabbling through rubble. He was just trying to calculate whether he could afford time away from the jazz book to travel to Warsaw to meet Helena Baran – and whether, given the ease of modern communications it would be worth it anyway – when the professor said, 'Apparently a plan is being put together for Helena and Lucek to come to England so that she can see the scrapbook. Nina says Lucek was going to email you, Phin.'

Phin reached for his phone, and flipped it into life. He said, 'Yes – there is an email from him. It looks as if he sent it this evening.'

Lucek wrote:

> Dear Phineas Fox,
> It was very good to hear from you again.
>
> After a lot of family discussion, we are trying to make a plan for myself and my Aunt Helena to come to England. My aunt has lived with my parents since before I was born, and she has a few fragmented memories of her childhood, which seem to link to the Street of Music.
>
> There is a slight acquaintance with a lady my aunt has never met, but whose family might have known her family. This is a lady called Miss Thaisa Wyngham, who lives in a small place called Causwain, so we hope to visit her.
>
> Neither of us has been to England so we are very excited at this journey. I have a little English, and I think we could manage the journey.
>
> Would it be possible to meet you, also? I would very much like to talk about the scrapbook and my aunt would like to see it and talk about her memories of the 'lost' Warsaw. Perhaps those would be of some help in your research.
>
> With kind regards,
> Lucek

That small girl must be well into her seventies now, of course, but Phin would be able to talk to her, to see her reactions to the scrapbook. To see if it shone a light on to her lost memories . . . He reminded himself not to get carried away, and said, temperately, 'Could we set up a meeting for us all? Where's Causwain, do we know?'

'Welsh Marches,' said Dr Purslove. 'Marchia Walliae. One of those places where England crosses over into Wales, and nobody's ever quite sure where the boundary is. How does he spell Causwain – oh, yes, I see. I believe there are ruins of a Caus Castle somewhere in Shropshire – one of those old Norman strongholds that's crumbled away with the centuries.'

'As most of us do,' observed the professor, dryly, then, in an elaborately casual voice, said, 'Nina's added a note that she thinks she might be able to come over with them. She has some holiday leave due, and she can act as interpreter if it's needed. Helena Baran doesn't speak English, and I shouldn't think this Thaisa Wyngham speaks Polish.'

'I wonder if we could all meet up in Causwain,' said Phin. 'Could you both manage that? If there's a reasonable pub or B & B we could book in and use it as a base.'

'That sounds a very good idea,' said Dr Purslove, pleased. 'We could work around our commitments, couldn't we, Ernest? Make it a weekend, perhaps.'

'I might manage something. Purely to compare research, of course. Always supposing Nina really can get away. And that I can fit it into my schedule.'

Phin caught Arabella's eye and looked hastily away.

After Phin had seen the professor and Dr Purslove into a taxi, he helped Arabella collect the plates.

'One of the nice things about you,' said Arabella, as he came into the kitchen and reached for a tea towel, 'is that you help with the washing-up.'

'I have other talents,' said Phin, but he sounded preoccupied.

After a moment, Arabella said, 'Will those two go to Causwain?'

'Undoubtedly. As they got into the taxi they were discussing meeting up halfway – Shrewsbury was mentioned – and arguing about train times. I don't think either of them would miss this for the world. And the professor certainly won't find it a hardship to meet Nina Randall again.'

'Far from it. The night of the Epiphany Concert, wasn't it? And now an Elgar weekend. What wouldn't you give to know the story of those?'

'I'm trying to maintain a gentlemanly lack of curiosity' said Phin. 'And the professor is certainly maintaining a gentlemanly discretion.'

Arabella looked at him. 'Phin, my love, I have the feeling that you'd quite like to head home now,' she said. 'To chase up some of the ideas this evening's sparked.'

'Leaving you to a virtuous and solitary bed?'

'I have a good book to read,' said Arabella. 'Or I might try to get at a bit more of the scrapbook for an hour or so. You can let me know later or tomorrow if you turn up anything interesting.'

'One of the nice things about you,' said Phin, kissing her, 'is that you understand that sometimes an idea is too fragile to even put into words. Bless you. Don't ever change, will you?' He reached for his jacket, kissed her again, and went out to flag down a taxi.

It was only just after ten o'clock when Phin reached his own flat. He made himself a mug of coffee, switched on the computer, and called up Chopin's *Ballades* from the playlist. This is your world I'm trying to reach, Frédéric, he thought, as the soft notes began. So you might as well accompany me on the journey.

Anatol's account had intrigued him, but one part had intrigued him very particularly, and that was Anatol's reference to a priest – the 'wise old man' who had talked to him about the night the Romanovs were killed – hearing the music as the killings happened.

Phin thought that in the chaos and confusion that must have been raging that night, in practical terms the "Cadence" could only have been played by a single musician – at a stretch, by a couple. How close had this wise, frail old priest been to the house? Outside? Had there been a street outside? Had there been grounds? Or could he have actually been in the house itself? Either way, it seemed to suggest that his church had been close by.

He typed in a search request for Ipatiev House, scrolled through the hundreds of sites devoted to the execution of the tsar – in fact of earlier tsars, too – and finally found one that focused on Ipatiev House itself.

> The tsar and his family were kept in Ipatiev House for the last few months of their lives. The house was built in the 1880s, and owned by several merchants before the Romanovs were imprisoned there.

There followed a description of the cellar in which the killings had taken place – how, at the tsar's request, chairs were brought for the tsarina, Alexandra, and the young Alexei, and how, with so many people crammed into a small cellar, the slaughter had been messy and inefficient. Phin frowned, pushed away the harrowing images these words conjured up, and read on. There must be a church nearby . . .

There was. He read the section eagerly.

> Ipatiev House was situated opposite the Cathedral of the Ascension, and the cathedral was, for a time, part of rumours that there had been a plot to rescue the imprisoned tsar and his family, organized by a mysterious brotherhood, which some sources identify as the 'Brotherhood of St John of Tobolsk'.
>
> As is known, the attempt failed, but one source tells how a priest at the Cathedral of the Ascension was part of the plot. By February 1918 the Russian Church was becoming fragmented; the Bolshevik-controlled govern- ment had enacted the Decree on Separation of Church from State, and School from Church, and there were violent clashes between Bolshevik officials and the Russian Orthodox Church.
>
> The priest, one Father Gregory, is said to have vanished on the night of the Romanov slaughter. The truth of this story has never been verified and his body was never found,

but locals claimed to have heard shots from within the cathedral that night, and screams. Some time later, an unmarked grave was located in the cathedral gardens, bearing only a small cross, which had the appearance of having been hastily nailed into a cruciform.

However, reliable sources say that 28 bishops and 1,200 priests were executed in those troubled years, so it is just as likely that Father Gregory lost his life in that way.

Or, thought Phin, that he escaped to Poland and lived in the Street of Music. Were you Anatol's frail old man, Father Gregory? Did you play the "Cadence" to him shortly before you died? I think I'm chasing phantoms and running after will o' the wisps, and I don't think it will be possible to find out any more about you.

But whoever you were, you knew about the music.

EIGHT

When Nina had said she thought she might be able to accompany Lucek and Helena to England, Lucek was so delighted he was quite unable to speak for a moment. Fortunately, Nina did not seem to notice. She said, 'I do go over at least once a year to see my family, so I could time that to coincide with your trip. But if you and your aunt would prefer to go on your own – if it's private thing for you to do – please say, and I'll entirely understand.'

'I'd love you to come with us,' said Lucek, before he could help it.

'Would you? Oh, good. I'd like to find out more about the scrapbook, and it would be nice to see the professor again.'

Lucek reminded himself that Professor Liripine had been Nina's tutor at Durham University, and that she would regard him almost as a father-figure.

'I could come with you to meet this Miss Wyngham,' Nina was saying. 'Sort of hand you and your aunt over to her and make sure you were all OK with enough English and so on. Although your English is actually better than you think, Lucek.'

She had a way of pronouncing his name that made electrical thrills of pleasure run all over Lucek's skin. They were in the little coffee place near her office – they had been here a few times now, and the staff had got to know them. It was almost like when couples just embarking on a romance had 'our song' and 'our restaurant'. Lucek wondered whether he and Nina might one day look back fondly at this little coffee house and think of it like that. Perhaps the people who worked here felt indulgent towards them, telling one another there was a blossoming romance taking place at the corner table.

He contemplated this possibility happily, then thought that the truth was that they were more likely to be admiring Nina, and wondering what on earth somebody like that was doing with such a scruffy boy. Or even – horror of horrors! – telling one another it was probably her nephew or a work experience boy at her office she was being kind to.

'And we can book a hire car at the airport, and . . . What? Oh, sorry, I didn't realize you didn't drive.'

Lucek, fearful of seeming immature or indolent, explained that he had simply never got round to it. 'What with being away and everything. And there wasn't really any need for a car at university.'

'That's not a problem,' said Nina. 'I can do the driving. I like driving, anyway.'

'It seems a pity to put it on you. I'm sorry.'

'Don't be,' she said, and somehow she had put her hand on the table between them, and somehow Lucek had reached out to take it. In a soft voice, she said, 'I think this is going to be a really exciting trip, Lucek.'

Lucek hoped it was going to be exciting, as well, and in ways that had nothing to do with scrapbooks and professors. But most likely Nina was simply being friendly. He reminded himself that there must be ten years between them – well, all right, twelve or thirteen if you were going to be finicky. But there must be a great many very successful relationships in which the lady was a bit older than the man. He tried to think of some and failed, but there were bound to be a lot.

As the trip approached, the question of clothes, which Lucek did not normally think about very much, suddenly loomed rather worryingly. He wanted to look right for Nina on this trip. Well, for Thaisa Wyngham and for Professor Liripine and Phineas Fox as well, of course.

Eventually, he yielded to the persuasions of his father to go along to a decent tailor's to buy a suit, or at the very least a jacket and some smart trousers. Lucek could not actually afford any of these things, but in the shop his father handed over his own card, and Lucek ended up with a very nice dark brown jacket which his father said would look good almost anywhere. He then said they might as well do things properly, and added a cream shirt and trousers that toned.

Faced with this magnificence, and also with the possibility that he might not sleep in his own bedroom absolutely every night, Lucek later made a discreet expedition of his own to buy new pyjamas and underthings. It was almost certainly pointless, because almost certainly he would never dare make any kind of approach to Nina, but he bought the pyjamas anyway.

Helena was already sorting out her own clothes for the trip, waving aside the protests of Lucek's mother, who said they were not going on safari for six months and anything she found she needed could certainly be bought in England, and of Lucek's father who said Helena would have to pay a massive excess-baggage charge on the plane.

Helena said she did not care. 'If I'm going to meet my past,' she said to Lucek, later on, 'and if I'm going to find out even the smallest scrap of information about what happened the night the terror came, then I'm going to look my best for it.'

'"Night"?' said Lucek, and Helena looked surprised.

'Did I say night?'

'Yes. You said, "the night the terror came".'

'I did, didn't I?' A tiny frown creased her brow, then she said, 'It *was* night. I've never seen that before, but I can see it now. It was dark, and there were night scents – they're different from daytime scents, always. And people were behaving oddly, as if they were expecting something to happen. Perhaps they knew the terror was going to come that night.'

Lucek never knew how to respond when Helena became

intense like this. He hoped she was not going to be intense during their time in England, and he hoped the unknown Thaisa Wyngham would be able to cope with his aunt.

Thaisa Wyngham had no idea if she would be able to cope with the visit of this unknown Helena Baran and her young nephew. She had never been able to decide whether she had done the right thing all those years ago, when she had replied to the rather stilted Christmas card from an unknown woman in Poland.

Now, reading an actual letter from Helena Baran – a typed sheet of A4 with a signature at the foot – something akin to panic swept over her, and she wished that she had followed her instinct, and thrown that first card away.

For most people that long-ago Christmas card would simply have been an unexpected and rather friendly contact from someone who thought there might be a family connection. The trouble was that Thaisa's family was not like most people's. Throughout her entire childhood there had been rules, restrictions, constant reminders of how she must behave.

'None of us must ever do anything that might draw attention to us,' her mother used to say, while her father, a quiet man whom Thaisa never felt she really knew and who was constantly immersed in his music studies, said that Thaisa must follow exactly the same routine every day. That was the safe way to live. It had not occurred then to Thaisa at the time that 'safe' was an odd word for him to use, although it had occurred to her since.

It was certainly occurring to her now. She had to be safe – she had to keep the past locked away. It did not matter what it took to do that. She had been brought up in that belief, and she would keep to it now.

She should have ignored that first Christmas card from Helena Baran, of course, but she had thought that if the woman was wanting to make contact with any English branches of her family, she might start a wider search for anyone called Wyngham. What might that stir up?

In the end, she wrote a note in a conventional card, saying she did not know of any other family, and that her parents had both been dead for many years. Posting the card, she thought with relief that it would be the end of the matter. But it was not. The following Christmas another card arrived, with a similar note – this time apologising for Helena's lack of English, and hoping her good wishes could be understood.

From there, somehow the custom of exchanging cards became established. Thaisa went along with it, because it meant she knew what Helena Baran was doing – if the woman started to investigate the Wyngham name any further, Thaisa would have warning. After a time, when she saw the familiar writing and the Polish stamp each December, she was reassured. She knew Helena was still in Poland. As the years went along it began to seem unlikely that Helena – no longer so very young – would ever come to England.

Until now.

The letter started with 'My dear Thaisa', which in itself felt strange, because no one had called her Thaisa for years. She was Miss Wyngham to everyone. Her piano pupils and people in the church group – she played the piano for the local choir rehearsals – all called her Miss Wyngham. It was the same with the library volunteer group, where she worked for one morning each week. She thought that if any of the people in those places thought about her at all, they probably regarded her as quite old-fashioned. Bit of a dull life, they probably said to one another – never had a man in her life, so far as anyone knew. Approaching sixty most like – late fifties, certainly. And rather a solitary existence, living alone in that house inherited from her parents. Still, people lived as they wanted.

The gist of Helena Baran's letter – which she explained had been translated into English for her by a friend – was that she was finally coming to England. She sounded excited and pleased about it, and she said she certainly wanted to meet Thaisa – she was trying to trace her family, she said; some new information had recently come to light. She would be in the country for at least two weeks and probably three, so she could fit in with whatever dates would be convenient for a visit of long or short duration.

New information. Thaisa felt the panic surge upwards at once. What new information? Whatever it was, Helena could not be allowed to get anywhere near Thaisa's past. Ever since she could remember, her parents had instilled into her that nothing must ever be done that might draw attention to the family itself, and above all to the past.

No matter what it took to stop people, it must never be allowed.

It had been shortly after Thaisa's seventh birthday when her mother had called her into the big double bedroom and said she wanted to talk to her.

It had been a dull afternoon, and the bedroom was gloomy and a bit dingy, because her parents would not have workmen in the house unless it was absolutely necessary. People at school talked about their fathers – and quite often their mothers – decorating rooms in their houses, and said it was quite fun, because you could help with sloshing paint around, and you had to have picnic meals or even takeaways while it was all going on. Thaisa had never had a takeaway in her life, and she certainly could not imagine her father coping with rolls of wallpaper or paint and stepladders.

She felt awkward being in the bedroom. Her mother closed the door which made her feel even more awkward, because it was as if embarrassing secrets were about to be told. But she listened obediently to her mother explaining about the rules they must all follow. It was because of the war, said mother. It often seemed to Thaisa that the whole house and her parents' entire lives centred around the war, even though, as far as she could make out, the war had happened absolutely ages ago. Nobody else's parents talked about it, although Thaisa's parents were older than most of her schoolfriends' parents, which might mean they remembered it more clearly.

'You took us by surprise when we were middle-aged,' her mother had once said to her, which was as near as she had ever got to saying anything in the least bit private. Father never said anything private; in fact he hardly ever said very much at all. He was interested in Thaisa's piano lessons, though, and occasionally he talked to her about a piece of music or a composer, comparing one with another. Sometimes called her into his music room to listen to something on the Third Programme, but that was pretty much all. It was always a bit of an event to go into the music room. Thaisa always felt that if there were secrets from her parents' past, that was where they would be.

But today, with rain pattering against the windows and the dripping of water from the broken gutters, mother talked about the past in a different way. She said that in his young days Thaisa's father had been an important man in their own country, and when the war came he had become involved in secret work. This was the first that Thaisa had heard about Father doing anything so exciting and mysterious as secret work, and she would have liked to ask questions. But Mother was talking in a near-whisper, as if she was worried that people might be listening, and there was an odd look in her eyes that made Thaisa feel a bit scared, so she did not dare say anything.

Mother said the work Thaisa's father had done meant there were people who had hated him. Lies had been made up about him – terrible stories which she would not repeat, because if she did, Thaisa would never be able to get them out of her mind. Thaisa was later to wonder whether it would have been better to know what the terrible stories actually were, or whether it was worse being left to imagine them.

But on one point Mother was clear. The people who had hated Father had decided to kill him. Even though it had all happened in another country, and even though it was a long time since the war had ended, those people could still be watching and waiting, hatching more plots against him. At this point, Mother got up to look out of the window, peering down into the garden, which made Thaisa feel even more frightened.

For some of those men – and women too – the war had never properly ended, said Mother. And those people had made vows – they had sworn solemn oaths. She knew it sounded like something from a book or something on the television, but Thaisa must believe that it was true. Even though her parents had managed to reach England and make a new life for themselves, if Father's real identity ever came out, their lives could still be in danger. Her eyes darted from side to side when she said this; almost, thought Thaisa nervously, as if she suspected the plotters might be hiding in the wardrobe.

It was all very scary and worrying, but Mother promised that if the rules were followed, Thaisa would be perfectly safe, and she and Thaisa's father would be safe, too.

One of the rules was that Thaisa could not accept invitations to other children's houses – to birthday or Christmas parties. 'Not to be thought of,' said Mother when the subject first came up, and Father looked up from his book to nod agreement. If you accepted an invitation, he said, politeness required that you must later return the hospitality, and that was impossible. He was very sorry – they both were – but they could not allow anyone to become close to them, which meant they could not let anyone come to the house.

No one ever did come to the house. Occasionally there did have to be workmen to fix a leaking tap or mend a fuse, because Father had no idea how such things worked and he would get into a panic if called on for help and have what Mother called one of his heart spasms, for which he had a series of pills. And Mother certainly could not mend taps or fuses; she could not even change a light bulb. But she always stayed in the room with any workmen who came, and watched as they worked, as if to make sure they did not sneak out while her back was turned and search the house. Father always shut himself into his music room, and did not reappear until the workmen had gone.

Thaisa went to and from school, which was a short bus ride through the little town, and just beyond it. On two afternoons she stayed late for piano lessons, which her parents thought she should have and that she would like. She found she did like the lessons, and her parents were pleased when she reached Grade V and then VI. Every Saturday she and Mother went shopping for the week's groceries, and on Sunday they went to church – always to Evensong because it was a choral service. Other than that, nothing much happened.

She worked hard at school, especially at history, which she liked. The history teacher was an enthusiast about her subject, and tried to imbue her pupils with her own interest, often taking them a little outside of what Thaisa later guessed was the curriculum.

When they got to the twentieth century and World War II, Thaisa paid very close attention, in case she might find a clue to her parents' past. There might even be some mention of 'unnamed heroes'.

There was nothing, of course. The textbooks were standard school issue, simply providing facts and dates, and giving lists of treaties and pacts, which most of Thaisa's class yawned over. But the enthusiastic teacher showed them images of the Nuremberg Rallies, with Hitler whipping people into a frenzy, and old newsreels of Mr Chamberlain waving a piece of paper on the steps of a plane and saying 'Peace in our time', and hunted out scratchy wireless broadcasts of Winston Churchill telling people they would fight on the beaches. There were photographs, as well – grainy images of bombed cities like Warsaw, which the history teacher said had been a beautiful city and which had lost most of its wonderful buildings and a great deal of its cultural history.

But nowhere was there anything about unnamed heroes, or any reference to 'brave men and women who worked in secrecy and danger and were never recognized'.

After a good deal of thought, Thaisa wrote a careful reply to Helena Baran's letter regarding the visit. She explained that she had a great many commitments, but that she hoped Helena would enjoy being in England. This sounded politely friendly, but ought to set Helena at a distance. She did not give any email address, although she had a laptop and an email account, which was sometimes useful for her piano pupils and the choir rehearsals. Other than that, she rarely used it, and to give it to Helena would have felt like opening a door for the woman to get into her life. She would stay with the old-fashioned method of a written letter and a stamp on the envelope. She posted the letter and thought that should be the end of it.

But Helena wrote again, giving the exact dates she would be in England, and asking if there was somewhere in Causwain or the immediate vicinity where she could stay. She would very much like to come to Thaisa's house to hear about her family and see what the connection between them might be.

This was dreadful. Thaisa's parents had virtually lived the lives of recluses, and Thaisa had never known any other way of living. She did not think she wanted to know any other way.

But it became clear that Helena was not going to be put off, and it was also clear that she was going to come to Causwain, and she would expect to come to Thaisa's house. Looked at from one point of view, it was a perfectly reasonable expectation. In the end, Thaisa wrote to say that she believed the White Hart in the little town offered bed and breakfast. She added once again that she did not know anything about the families of either of her parents.

Her mother had told her that there would come a time when Thaisa would be on her own. She and Thaisa's father would not always be there.

'And when you're on your own, you'll be vulnerable,' she said. 'People might try to come into your life. It might be a long way in the future, and they might appear in a way you won't expect. So you must always be on guard, and you must be prepared to do whatever is needed to keep them away – whatever is needed to keep the past sealed up.'

Whatever is needed . . .

It was at that point that a small, sly voice began to whisper inside her head. *Do whatever is needed to keep the past sealed*, it said. *It's what they did – your parents – both of them . . . Because they were both murderers . . . It's your legacy – a taint . . .*

And then, even more shockingly and insistently, the whispering memory that she had never been able to banish . . .

And you didn't escape it, Thaisa, did you . . .? Remember . . .? Remember that day in your father's study . . .

NINE

The summer leading up to Thaisa's eighteenth birthday had seemed, to begin with, to be like any other summer. It had even seemed as if it might be a better summer than previous ones. Thaisa's music teacher had introduced her to another pupil – a young man who was two years older. His name was Alan, and the teacher said they were her

very best pupils, and she thought they might join forces for a forthcoming music festival in Ludlow. They might do a duet, she said.

Thaisa's parents, warily approached, eventually gave guarded
permission. Thaisa suspected they had tried to think of reasons
to refuse, but had decided a refusal might look strange and
cause comment. And it was to do with music, which would
have swayed her father. She pretended to Alan and the teacher
that her parents would come to the festival, although she knew
they would not.

The three of them discussed what should be performed. It
was a free choice, so it would be nice if they could hit on
something a bit unusual – something that would make their
performance stand out for the judges. Thaisa offered to look
through her father's music scores to see if there was something
that would be different from all the other entrants' choices. He
had dozens of scores, she said; there might be something among
them that no one else would think of.

It was a pity that when she got home her father was having
what her mother called one of his off days. A few heart twinges,
she said. Nothing to worry about; he had taken his pills and he
was lying down.

Thaisa would have liked to talk to her father about the duet
and ask for suggestions, particularly since music was one of
the very few subjects on which they could communicate. Still,
she had always pretty much had the run of his books and the
stack of music scores, and he would not mind if she looked at
a few pieces. She would do that and talk to him about it all
tomorrow when he felt better.

The music room was at the back of the house. It overlooked
the gardens, and it was always a bit dark, even in summer,
because large shrubs grew immediately outside the windows.
Thaisa had often thought her father had deliberately let the
shrubs grow up like that because they made it feel as if the rest
of the world was safely shut out.

The music scores were all quite old. Thaisa always thought
they had come from those distant, mysterious years, and sometimes, handling them, it felt as if she was brushing her fingertips
against those years.

Her father kept everything in alphabetical order and he was

a bit finicky about that arrangement, so Thaisa would have to be careful to put them back in their right places.

There was a lot of Chopin and some Debussy, and there was a fair amount of Mozart. Mozart had composed some lively stuff, and it would be technically challenging and effective. The trouble was that other contestants would think the same thing. It did not look as if she was going to find anything, and there were certainly no duets so far. She wondered briefly whether they could do a two-instrument piece, with herself at the piano and Alan on the violin. He had learned the violin as well as the piano, and he was quite good. She would ask if the festival rules allowed that.

There was, though, a deep old box under the desk – an oak chest with some carving around the edges and a hinged lid. It had always been so much part of the room that Thaisa had scarcely ever noticed it. But it might be worth checking what it contained, so she pulled it out. It was a bit dusty and the lid resisted, as if it had been closed for so long that it had almost sealed itself up. But the lid finally came up, its hinges groaning, showering what was probably the accreted dust of years out on to the carpet. Thaisa would have to sweep that up or smuggle in the vacuum cleaner.

As she folded the lid all the way back there was the sense that something breathed out into her face – something that was old and shrivelled and tainted. It was only the smell of old paper and dust, of course, but for a moment it had almost felt as if she had forced open an old tomb.

But when she began to sift the sparse contents, it looked as if there was still nothing that would be any good. There were certainly some old scores, all of them curling at the edges, and most of them spotted with mildew. There was the cover of an old concert programme, which had a really lovely sketch of a piano at the top. It was a tiny sketch, but it was quite detailed, and Thaisa examined it with interest. It did not actually tell her anything, though, and the programme was printed in a language she did not recognize. At first she thought it was German, then she thought the lettering was wrong for that. As far as she could tell, it was a programme for a concert in a place called the Biblioteka Chopina. *Biblioteka* would be something to do with books, wouldn't it? A bookshop or maybe a library? Chopin Library, perhaps? Thaisa rather liked the sound of that. She wondered if she might ask her father about it – had he been to the concert, or had he known someone who had performed in it? Might he even have performed in it himself? The trouble was there was no way of knowing how he would react. Best say nothing.

She replaced the programme cover, and she was about to close the lid when she saw the small leather box at the very bottom. It had been pushed into a corner, and it was very dark leather, and almost invisible against the old wooden sides. Thaisa hesitated, because it might contain something private. Probably it was nothing much at all, and certainly she ought not to pry any more, but there was still that feeling that this room was so much a part of the past, and her mother's words on that long-ago afternoon had stayed with her.

'*Your father was involved in secret work,*' Mother had said.

Secret work. Might this box hold a clue to that secret work? But if her parents had wanted her to know any more they would surely have told her by now – she was nearly eighteen, she was grown up.

Her mother had said something else on that long-ago afternoon, and that, too, had stayed strongly with Thaisa.

'*There were people who hated your father so much that they decided to kill him,*' she had said. If that was true, wouldn't it be better to know as much as possible?

Thaisa reached down and lifted out the small box.

It was like the boxes you saw in jewellers' windows, but the leather was so old and rubbed that if there had ever been a jeweller's name on it, it had long since vanished.

This was starting to feel like the worst kind of intrusion, but having got this far, Thaisa had to go on. Inside the box was a pad of faded velvet. It might once have been dark purple, but now it was the colour of dust. Lying on it was a small silver ring. Something her father had given her mother in the past? But it was not a conventional ring in any sense at all, and it was a bit large and thick to be a lady's ring. It was clearly a man's ring, and at first Thaisa thought it was one of the really old signet rings – the kind that had crests engraved on them so that gentlemen could press them into melted wax and seal letters and documents with their family emblem.

But this carving was certainly not a crest – it was a skull's head, unmistakable and macabre, and as Thaisa stared at it, a coldness began to trickle across her mind. Fragments of those eagerly attended history lessons came trickling in. The history teacher, constantly keen to snare her pupils' interest, had talked to them about the personalities of the wars of the twentieth century – of the Second World War in particular, wanting to bring to life the major players in those dark years. She had told them about the brave commanders and the famous men who had fought for their countries – not just England but the Allied countries who had fought alongside.

But she had also talked to them about a man who had been the head of the SS – a ruthless Nazi who had been the overall controller of the concentration camps. He had had a curious and unexpected side to his character, she said, in that he had been deeply interested in occultism and pagan mythology – to the extent that he had tailored several of the myths to chime with Nazi ways and rules.

One of the myths he had adopted was the story of Thor – the god from the old Norse mythology – who had possessed a pure silver ring, over which people took oaths. From there had come the strange, sinister concept of creating a silver ring for the Nazis – a ring that would be a high and exclusive honour.

The man had been Reichsführer Heinrich Himmler, and the rings had been known as the Death's Head rings. They had become woven into Himmler's legend and into the legend of high-ranking Nazi officers.

Sitting on the floor of her father's shadowy music room, staring down at the circlet of silver with the carved skull's head, Thaisa knew that she was looking at one of Heinrich Himmler's infamous Death's Head rings.

After what felt like a very long time, she snapped the box shut and thrust it back to its dark corner of the oak chest, piling the music back on top of it.

She sped up to her bedroom. At the deepest level of her mind she knew she was right, but she needed to make absolutely sure. It was possible that she was remembering those history lessons completely wrongly. In her bedroom was a set of encyclopaedias, a gift from her parents on her sixteenth birthday. 'To help with your studies', her father had said. Thaisa pulled out the 'G to I' volume, and riffled through the pages to see if there was an entry for Heinrich Himmler. There was, of course. Most of it was about his war record; how he had risen within the Nazi Party and the SS, and how he had been deeply involved in what was called 'Germanization', which had included the destruction of so much of Poland.

But near the end was a small section about Himmler's interest in myth and mysticism, and about the creation of what the book called the *Totenkopfring*.

'The concept and runic form of the ring was undoubtedly adopted by Himmler from pagan German mythology,' said the book. 'Each one comprised a band or a wreath of oak, embossed with a skull's head, and with several symbolic runes. The runes were considered by Himmler to be symbols from his country's past. The wreath of oak leaves, in particular, was and is a traditional German leaf.'

The book went on to describe how the recipients of the rings had been made to swear that they would never sell the ring or allow it to fall into the hands of anyone not entitled to wear it. On the death of the recipient – or his demotion or dismissal from the SS – the ring must be returned.

'Probably not all the rings were returned, of course,' said the entry. 'But those that were were kept in Himmler's Castle at Wewelsburg, which was blast-sealed to prevent the Allies finding them. To this day they have never been found. It is not known exactly which officers were awarded the *Totenkopfring*.'

Alongside this section was a very clear photograph. Thaisa studied it for several moments, then she took the book back down to the music room. She would compare the book's image with the ring she had found, and there would be differences, and she would know that what she had found was nothing to do with the Nazis or the legendary *Totenkopfring*.

She had to force herself to open the oak chest again and reach down for the leather box, but she did it, and then she placed the silver ring on the open encyclopaedia, next to the photograph. And there it was. As clear as a curse. Detail for detail, the ring she had found was exactly the same as the one in the illustration. The wide death grin, the empty eye sockets . . . Macabre and terrible.

Thaisa sat back on her heels, staring at the ring and the open book. Perhaps her father had acquired the ring or inherited it and kept it as a curio, and forgotten about it.

Stupid, said her mind. You know it's not that. You know it's all to do with his past – the past they never talk about; the past they fled from and have spent their lives trying to keep secret.

She was dimly aware of the distant noises within the house – the clatter of crockery from the kitchen where her mother would be preparing the evening meal; the faint sound of the radio, because she would be listening to the evening news.

Then came another sound. It was the door of the music room opening. Her father stood there, looking at the Death's Head ring.

He did not speak, but his eyes went from Thaisa to the tiny box with its damning silver circlet. The expression on his face frightened her so much that she shrank back, pressing against the wall, wanting to run out of the room, knowing her legs would not support her.

After a moment he walked forward, his steps slow and uncertain – like a faltering old man, thought Thaisa, horrified. But he's not an old man – or is he? He put out a hand as if to pick up the Death's Head ring, then snatched his hand back, as if something had burned it.

Almost to himself, he said, 'The *Totenkopfring*,' and eerily and terribly Thaisa heard the foreign pronunciation. He sat down on the music stool, moving slowly, leaning back against the piano, one hand pressed to the left side of his chest. A spasm of pain twisted his face, briefly, then the door of the music room opened, and Thaisa's mother stood there. For a moment it seemed that she did not understand what was happening, then she, too, saw the box and what it held.

The same shock flared in her eyes, but she stayed where she was, silhouetted in the doorway. Then Thaisa's father said in a strained voice, 'I told you to get rid of it. I *trusted* you . . . But there were always too many secrets to be sure of losing them all, weren't there? And you were always such a liar – always such a fucking deceitful bitch.'

It was like a blow across the eyes to hear him use those words. Thaisa cowered back in her corner, one fist crammed into her mouth so that she would not make any sound.

'You're in pain,' said her mother to him.

'Bit of a spasm. The shock . . . Seeing that . . . You gave me your word. But you always lied – I should have remembered how you always lied . . .'

'We both lied,' said Thaisa's mother. 'And we both did other things. We had no choice.' Her voice sounded strange, as if it was the voice of someone else. In this unfamiliar voice, she said, 'But it was a bad way for them to die . . .' And then, her voice sharpening back to its normal tones, she said, 'D'you want your pills?'

'Spray,' he said. 'Desk.'

He directed the spray beneath his tongue. Once. A second time. Then he leaned back against the piano again, his eyes half closed, one hand still pressed to the left side of his chest. A trace of colour seemed to come back into his face, but then, incredibly, he twisted around on the piano stool, and his fingers groped for the keys. And then the music started.

It was an extraordinary moment. Thaisa knew with absolute certainty that this was not music she had ever heard, but even with the first notes she thought it was the coldest, cruellest music ever written. There was a kind of prowling, cat-after-mouse pattern, and then sudden greedy triumph, as if something was saying, *Now I've got you!*

'You remember it?' The words were strained, difficult.

'Yes. Oh, God, yes. Stop playing it – *please stop* . . .'

He lifted his hand from the keys, and turned to look at her directly. 'We're the only ones left who know the truth.'

'Yes.'

The moment seemed to stretch out and out, until something must surely snap. Then her father gave a rasping cough and fell forward, crashing on to the keys, sending the strings inside the piano jangling and jarring. His hand clawed at the left side of his chest again.

He said, 'Help me . . .'

Thaisa's mother was already half running into the hall, to the phone. Her father was lying across the keyboard of the piano, one hand still against his chest, but the other reaching out as if trying to grasp something that was not there. His eyes were wide and staring, and a dreadful cold grey look was creeping over his face, as if he might be turning to stone.

Thaisa heard her mother saying, in a panic-stricken voice, 'Ambulance – quickly, please. My husband – a heart attack, I'm sure. As fast as you can, or it will be too late . . .'

But even as she heard her mother say this, Thaisa knew it was already too late. She knew her mother must know it, as well.

TEN

Everyone at the hospital was very kind. A massive heart attack, the doctors said, using medical terms which Thaisa did not understand and which she did not remember afterwards. They explained about the history of angina, which they said had impaired Mr Wyngham's heart quite severely. They were so very sorry, but he had been dead when the paramedics got to the house.

The funeral was four days later. It was attended by Thaisa and her mother, two neighbours with whom they had exchanged the occasional 'good morning' over the years, and unexpectedly by Thaisa's music teacher and Alan.

After the service, Alan and the music teacher came up to express their sympathy, and Alan asked if he could call to see them – perhaps next week.

'No,' said Thaisa's mother at once. 'We don't want visitors – not now, and not in the future.' As if in afterthought she said, 'Thank you, though,' and then almost pulled Thaisa into the waiting funeral car, and they drove off.

Back in the house, she said, 'No one is to come here, remember?'

Thaisa pretended not to care. She went upstairs to take off her coat, and sat in the window chair, watching the shadows creeping across the garden. Her father had once said he liked to speculate what music should be played for night gardens such as theirs.

'*Clair de Lune*?' Thaisa had said, tentatively, fearful of saying the wrong thing and spoiling this rare moment between them.

'Much too soft,' he said. 'When the garden looks like ours does at twilight, darker music's needed. Perhaps Schoenberg's *Verklärte Nacht*, with the doomed lovers walking through the cold night forest. Or, no – how about this?' He began to play the opening notes of the famous Bach fugue that started most horror films with a crashing sequence of chords. Then he laughed, and for a moment, incredibly, he was no longer the withdrawn man who seldom spoke; there was amusement in his eyes, and Thaisa had suddenly seen that he must have been good-looking as a young man.

When, at last, she went nervously downstairs, everywhere was in darkness, and the music room door was closed. Was her mother in there? Thaisa opened the door warily and reached for the light switch. Yes, she was here. She was slumped in a chair, and there was a half-empty glass of water at her side, the pack of pills her father had taken for his heart problems next to it. The pack was empty. A note was propped on the music stand. There was no name on it and no signature, but there did not need to be.

> My death will be seen as suicide, but it is murder. You murdered me, Thaisa, just as you murdered your father – as surely as if you stuck a knife into both our hearts. You pried and snooped and you found the Nazi ring. He could not bear the sight of it – he could not bear knowing all the menace and the threats of the past had woken. I can't bear it, either.
>
> It was that past – those black memories – that bound us together, and now he has gone there is nothing. I can't face being the only one left who knows the truth.
>
> Finding the ring will mean you will have guessed something of our past. And so never forget what you are,

Thaisa. Never forget the legacy we have given you. You
are the daughter of murderers. We killed – we caused
bad deaths . . .

But now you have caused two deaths, because you are
responsible for the death of both your parents.

Thaisa, shaking almost uncontrollably, tried to feel for a pulse
in her mother's wrist. She was not entirely sure if she would
actually recognize whether there was one, but it was what you
were supposed to do. There did not seem to be anything, though.
But supposing there was a thread of life – that she could still
be revived? To tell people what she had written? To accuse
Thaisa of having caused her father's death?

It was only then that Thaisa saw that in her other hand, her
mother was clutching the Nazi Death's Head ring. Evidence,
thought Thaisa. The note and the ring together . . . Would people
believe that I was responsible for all this?

Shuddering violently, she uncurled the cold fingers from
the ring and dropped it in her pocket. She burned the terrible
note, but she left the empty pack of pills and the glass of water
for them to find, because it would be the normal – the innocent
– thing to do.

Only then did she feel safe to call the paramedics.

There had to be an inquest, but the verdict was 'accidental
death'. A mind unbalanced by grief after the death of a beloved
husband, said the coroner. Mrs Wyngham had taken pills that
she thought would help her, and in her distress and confusion
had taken a second and possibly a third dose of them. No blame
could be attached to Miss Wyngham, to whom he extended his
heartfelt sympathy and condolences.

Thaisa suspected that the coroner might have directed the
verdict out of sympathy for a young girl who had lost both her
parents within a week of one another. She was massively
relieved, though, that it had not been a verdict of suicide, which
might have opened up questions and investigations.

The next day she buried the Nazi ring in the garden, doing
so openly, during the afternoon. If any of the neighbours were
looking out, they would just see her planting a new shrub at

the edge of the lawn, and think perhaps she was doing so as a memorial to her parents. She dug as deep as she could and dropped in the ring, still in its box, covering it with earth. But that night she had nightmares about it clawing its way to the surface, the grinning skull peering over the edge of the ground, looking for her so that it could tell people that here was a female whose parents had been murderers, and who had, herself, been responsible for both their deaths. In the dream, the music her father had played when he was dying was calling to the *Totenkopfring*, showing it the way through the dark garden and into the house where Thaisa was sleeping. She woke gasping and drenched in sweat, and she got up and went all round the house, making sure all the doors and windows were locked.

But as the days, and then the weeks, went along, she began to think she would be all right. She would have to keep people at a safe distance, because nobody must find out the truth about her parents' deaths.

You murdered me, Thaisa, just as you murdered your father – as surely as if you had stuck a knife into both our hearts . . .

No one must ever find out about her parents' pasts, and she must never let anyone suspect that her mother had died after writing that terrible accusation. But Thaisa had been brought up to keep the world at bay, and she could go on doing it.

On a financial level, she thought she would be just about all right, as well. There was the house, and there was a little money. Each of her parents had had an insurance policy, although her mother's would not have paid out for suicide. Thaisa experienced a lurch of fresh panic on reading that. Supposing anyone ever found out about the note that she had burned before calling the paramedics?

A man at the bank explained about using the money to buy an annuity which would bring a small income. It would not be a fortune, but if she was careful, it might be enough to live on – although there would not be enough for things like a car or holidays. Thaisa did not say it had never occurred to her that she might have a car, or that she had never had a holiday in her life.

But of course Miss Wyngham would be thinking of work – a career, he said, comfortingly. He believed she had recently left school. Thaisa did not say, either, that the thought of embarking on a career – on work of any kind – terrified her, because it would bring her into close contact with too many people. When he suggested she might sell the house and buy a smaller one, to release what he called equity, she did not say she could never leave the house because of what was buried in the garden.

Neighbours called, doing so a bit warily, but offering sympathy, and wanting to know if they could help in any way. Thaisa, totally unused to giving or receiving even the simplest hospitality, invited them in and made tea or coffee for them. It felt strange to be doing things that most people regarded as everyday, but not to have done so might cause comment. The neighbours were kind and prepared to be friendly, but they could not be allowed to get any closer. '*Always too many secrets,*' her father had said as he was dying. And her mother had written, *You are the daughter of murderers.*

Thaisa's music teacher called at the house to ask if she might like to help with coaching one or two very young pupils who were just starting piano lessons. It would be very informal, of course, because these days you had to have so many qualifications to teach in any official sense. But it might be something that could be arranged on a friendly, unofficial basis. Thaisa could supervise their practice sessions, for instance – perhaps help them prepare for exams. The parents would probably pay a small sum for the sessions. Thaisa thought she could do that; it would fill up some of her days, and the practice sessions would be at her old school, which would be comfortably familiar. She supposed Alan had been driven away by her mother's words on the day of her father's funeral, and when, the following spring, she caught sight of him in the town, hand in hand with a girl, she knew she was right.

Surprisingly, the small, casual arrangement for helping young music pupils worked, and built up over the years of its own accord. A request that Thaisa accompany the church choir for their rehearsals was made as well, and then someone in the choir asked her if she could spare a little time to help at the local library, as a volunteer. These were all things she could do quietly and without attracting any attention. There was a tiny income from the music pupils and the choir rehearsals.

None of the activities made for a particularly exciting life, but it was at least a life of a sort. She liked working within music. And as long as she was always watchful, and never did anything to cause comment . . . As long as nobody found out that she was the daughter of murderers . . . Of a man who had been awarded the Nazi Death's Head ring. Or that she had brought about the deaths of both her parents. *As surely as if she had stuck a knife into their hearts* . . . And that she had covered up her mother's suicide.

If it had not been for the Death's Head ring, Thaisa might have been able to retain that romantic image of her father as a spy. But the Nazi ring could only mean he had been in service to the Nazi regime. He must have killed – if not with his own hands, then he would certainly have given orders to others to do so, condemning victims to be shot or sent to the gas chambers. Her mother had killed, too – she had said so in her note. *You are the daughter of murderers.* 'Murderers' plural. *We killed*, she had written. *We caused bad deaths* . . .

Sometimes Thaisa wondered how they had felt when they killed. How did it feel to take life knowingly and deliberately? After you had done it, were you racked with guilt, or were you horrified and remorseful? Or frightened of being found out?

And how far did you have to be pushed before you made a decision to kill someone in order to preserve your own safety?

After Helena Baran wrote to say she was coming to England to look for her family, Thaisa thought about these things for a very long time.

1918

It was important to find a way of not listening to the cold, evil music that was still being played beyond the house. The black-clad guard had called it the 'Traitor's Music', saying it proudly and sneeringly, but clearly liking to show off his knowledge.

It was impossible to know who was playing it, but certainly it would not be Katya's violinist, who would never play such music. But whoever was playing it, it would not be shut out, no matter how hard you pressed your hands over your ears or burrowed under the pillow. The memory of the screams would not be shut out, either. They had gone on for what had seemed to be a very long time before they had finally stopped. But the silence that had followed had been almost worse, because it could only mean the guards had shot those people – that they were all dead.

Even when the screams stopped, a tiny thread of them remained – as if, instead of hearing them, you were feeling them. A long time in the future, would people who came to this house feel those screams? Will I keep feeling them in my mind? And the soft singing of the woman with high cheekbones who had tried to calm the boy – will I still hear that sometimes, and will I keep seeing the face of that girl with autumn leaf hair, the girl who had refused to let the guards see how terrified she was at the end?

But think instead about other things. Think about how soon you can get Katya and the girl who was with her out of their dark hiding place. Think of how to do what Katya had tried to do earlier – unlock the garden door and get outside. The other girl had asked, eagerly, 'Is *he* outside? Is he waiting for us?'

And Katya had smiled, and said, 'Oh, yes,' as if the unknown *he* could make everything right. It *would* be all right.

The guard was sitting at the table that Zena used for chopping vegetables, and he was cramming food greedily and messily into his mouth. It was only a question of waiting for him to go back up to the main part of the house, though. People were still up there – there were the sounds of them going across the hall, slamming doors, shouting orders.

The guard finished his food, then went across to the chair in the far corner that Zena always used. He did not seem to have noticed that the door of this room was slightly open, allowing a narrow view of the scullery. He had thrown himself down in the chair, leaning his head back. Zena was not going to like it if the man's greasy, slicked-back hair left marks on her cushion.

Katya and the other girl would be dreadfully cold and cramped, but the hiding place was a good one. They must not be found, because the guards had called Katya a traitor – that was because she had helped the servant girl to get away before she could be shot with the others. And they had said that if the crowd outside got their hands on Katya, they would tear her to pieces. A betrayal of her own people, they had called it. Betrayal was not a very familiar word, so it had not been easy to entirely understand everything, but it had been clear that Katya would be killed if the crowd got hold of her – and probably the girl who was with her, as well.

The guard was still in Zena's chair, and incredibly he had fallen asleep. People had been killed in this house tonight – there had been screaming and pleading for life and shouting, and yet he was able to fall asleep as if nothing important had happened. His eyes were closed, his mouth had dropped open, and faint snores came from him. He was horrible and he was ugly and hateful, but he had a rifle, and it would not take much for him to wake.

Could Katya and the other girl be got out without him waking up? The crowds were still outside, but they would not know who Katya was. And she had said that *he* would be waiting. Curiously, there was a sudden surge of reassurance in remembering that.

It could be done. They would all have to be quiet and slow and careful, but Katya would know that, without having to be told.

Which first, though? Unlocking the garden door? Yes, because once that was done, even if the guard woke up and caught them stealing out, they might be able to run to the door and get through it before he could do anything.

Even turning back the blanket on the bed and sliding down on to the floor had to be done inch by inch. It was important to watch the sleeping guard, and be ready to dart back to the bed if he woke. But he was not stirring, and bare feet made no sound on a floor. The stool was set under the shelf with hardly a sound, although climbing on to it was perilous, because one misstep, one wobble of the rickety legs . . . But it did not wobble, and it was easy to reach the key from its place.

Unlocking the door was the riskiest part yet, because the lock would click and it might creak. But the key slid in smoothly enough, and if only it would turn as silently . . .

It turned, but it did so with a scrape of sound that was like gunshot in the quiet scullery. There was a grunt from behind, and then the guard was lumbering up out of the chair, coming forward, the rifle lifted . . .

There was a moment of sheer blinding panic – what do I do! – and then the knowledge that there was only one thing to do. The guard shouted, 'Stay there! If not, I'll fire!'

If he fired, no one would ever know about the two girls shut in the dark old tunnel – there would be no one alive to tell them. There was only one thing to do, and that was to pull the garden door open, and run as fast as possible into the darkness beyond.

ELEVEN

1918

The darkness beyond the garden door was frightening, and beyond the high walls were the sounds of the crowd – some of them were clearly drunk, and bottles were being smashed somewhere close by.

Confusion and panic came rushing in. I don't know what to do – except that I must keep running and not let the guard catch me. Was he coming through the gardens? Yes, there was the sound of his voice shouting angrily. Only I don't know where I can run to, because there are high walls, and I don't know how to get out . . . But there was nothing for it but to keep running, even if it was only running round and round the house itself, and to hope there would be somewhere to hide.

Then arms came out of the shadows, and there was the sense of being pulled almost roughly into a patch of dense blackness against the nearest bit of the wall. A voice said, very softly, 'Don't scream. You're safe. I've got you. Crouch down under this overhanging part of the wall, and you won't be seen.'

'Who . . .?' The single word came out in a gasp, but the question did not need asking, because at some level had already come the knowledge of who this was. Katya's violinist – the one she had said made music to melt your bones, and the one she would follow for the rest of her life if it meant she could keep hearing his playing. And he would know what to do and how to do it, and in the end they would all be safe. Like the stories where you went through dangers but at the end you lived happily ever after.

Keeping his voice very soft, the man said, 'Katya? Where is she?'

There was a note of such urgency in his voice, that it was good to be able to say, 'She's all right. She's inside the house – there's another lady with her. I managed to get them into a hiding place and nobody will find them. Only they can't get out of the hiding place on their own – it only opens from this side – and I can't get them out yet, because—'

'Because the Bolshevik guards are still everywhere,' he said. 'I understand.' Almost to himself, he said, 'But I do thank all the gods that she's alive.'

'Yes, but if the guards get her, they're going to give her to the people out there – the people shouting beyond those walls. And if they get her—'

'She'll be executed as the Romanovs were,' he said at once. 'Only for her, it will be an even worse death, because they believe she's betrayed her own kind. She helped the Romanovs – at least, she helped one of their servants to get away.'

'You know all that?'

'I know all that.'

The grounds were still mostly in shadow, but the windows of the house were still blazing with light, and glow-worm lights from oil lamps were moving around the gardens.

'Are the guards searching the grounds? Are they looking for me because I got out? But I'm not very important.'

'You're important to Katya,' he said, at once. 'And you're important to me. But if the guards think you know where Katya is, they might try to find you. We'll fool them and get away, though, never fear.'

Never fear . . . The thought formed that, with this one, you would never fear anything.

'What they're doing at the moment, though, is dealing with the . . .' A hesitation, then he said, 'There are things they have to deal with because of what happened earlier.'

'They executed those people, didn't they? The Romanovs?'

'Yes. You shouldn't have to know about things like that at your age. You shouldn't have to have seen what I think you did see. Don't look too closely at the memory of it, though. If you do that, you'll be able to forget.'

He paused, tilting his head, as if listening. 'I think the guards are over on the other side of the house now. So if ever there was a moment for us to get out, this is that moment.'

'What about Katya?'

'We'll come back for her very soon, I promise. It'll all quieten down in a few hours. Can you crawl along this part of the wall – keep on all fours and you won't be seen. There's plenty of shrubbery to hide us.'

'Where are we going?'

'I've managed to make a kind of tunnel just under a corner of the wall,' he said. 'I did it earlier when everyone's attention was on what was happening inside the house. We'll go through the gap. It's narrow, but it's how I got in, so you'll manage it. I've covered it with branches, but it won't stay covered long, so we'll have to be very quick and very quiet. Here it is – d'you see it?'

'You promise we'll come back for Katya?'

'I promise.' Incredibly there was the sound of a smile in his voice. 'I would never leave Katya,' said the musician, softly. 'But we need to lie low for a little while until it's safe to come back. You go through the wall first, and when you're through, stay there while I follow. Never mind all the people out there – they'll think we're part of them.'

It was easy to squeeze through the narrow opening, but once through it was very scary indeed to be standing on the other side – to see the crowds surging around and hear them shouting. And the music. The music was still going on.

The musician had squeezed through the gap, and now he was here it was not very frightening at all. His hand came out, warm and strong and reassuring.

But he said, 'Can you hear the music?'

'Yes. The "Traitor's Music".'

There was a small start of surprise. 'You know about that?'

'I heard one of the guards say about it.'

'It is the "Traitor's Music". They're playing it for Katya – for both those girls. It's for them to die to. It's sometimes called the "Dark Cadence", and it's very old and very vicious.'

Somehow, like this, in this dark place with fear and memories swirling everywhere, it did not seem strange to hear music described as vicious.

'Where did it come from?'

The dark eyes glanced down. 'No one knows,' he said. 'It's very old, but no one's ever written it down. But it's always been known as the "Traitor's Music", and these people out here believe Katya is a traitor because she tried to save the last Romanov.'

'Yes.' A pause, and then, speaking, hesitantly, 'I don't even know your name.' It was not very polite to ask such a question of a grown-up, but the musician smiled at once, so clearly it had been all right.

He said, 'I've been known by several names, but to Katya – and to you – I am Vadim.'

Vadim.

Vadim had spoken truly when he said the crowds would think they were part of them. As they walked along, no one gave them a second look. Vadim even joined in with them as they went, shouting a few things, and waving an arm. He looked down, and said, very softly, 'I told you we'd seem to be part of them. I can shout rebellious cries as well as any one. And they don't know who or what I'm rebelling against. Here we are now.'

'The church?' This was a surprise, but the rearing outline was familiar from seeing it through the windows of the house – although it was strange to be seeing it like this, and to be so close to it. Like having stepped into a dream where things did not look quite as you expected.

'In fact it's a cathedral – the Cathedral of the Ascension.'

'Will we be safe here?'

'Yes. Churches are places of sanctuary. And the clergy themselves . . . Well, the Bolshevik government is very strongly resented by a great part of the clergy.' The smile came. 'That's too much for you to take in or even understand, isn't it? It doesn't matter. It means, though, that most of them are on our side – including Father Gregory. Despite that massive gun placement in the tower which they put there without his consent – even without his knowledge, I think – despite that, he'll help us.'

The dreamlike quality increased as they went through a wide door into the shadowy cathedral. There were glimpses of soaring archways and stone pillars, and of ikons and beautiful, elaborately carved screens.

Father Gregory was thin-faced and older than expected, but he had the same air of reassurance as Vadim. Tumbling at last into an exhausted sleep in a small room at the top of a winding flight of stairs, there was a sense of safety. As long as Katya could be got out, everything would be all right. But Vadim would manage it.

The last conscious thought was that a faint light was starting to streak the sky outside, which must mean it was almost morning. That, too, brought a sense of safety. Whatever might happen – whatever tragedies and terrors might stalk the world, each day still dawned with new light and new promises.

And Vadim was here.

The exhausted sleep must have lasted for a long time, because suddenly there was bright sunshine pouring into the room, and Vadim was coming in, carrying a tray. On it was a dish of cooked eggs, a twist of warm bread with butter – real butter! – melting in it, and a mug of milk.

'Late breakfast,' he said. 'Very luxurious to have it brought to you in bed, isn't it? I thought you deserved it, though. While you eat it, I'll go back to the house to get Katya. I daren't leave her there any longer, and it looks quiet over there.'

'I'll come with you.'

'No. You'll stay here. It'll be safer for just one of us, and I can get through the hole in the wall again. But you'll have to tell me exactly where the hiding place is.'

He listened closely, asking one or two questions about the scullery and the larder and the stone slab, and then about the people who worked there.

'If I meet any of them, I'll say I'm a travelling tinker,' he said. 'A mender of pots and pans. I can be anything I want, you know. A man of a thousand disguises.'

'Will they believe you?'

'At worst, they'll think I'm just taking advantage of the upheaval to get a bit of business. Impudent, they'll say. Trading on tragedy. But no one will be particularly suspicious, because there's no longer anything to be suspicious about. Listen to me. Last night – what happened last night – was the whole reason for Ipatiev House being turned into a prison. That reason no longer exists, because—'

'Because they all died. Murdered.'

'Yes. You shouldn't even know the word at your age,' Vadim said, angrily. 'But there was a plan to get the tsar and his family away. It failed – except for Katya's part in it. She got that servant away from the killers.' A shadow touched his eyes, and then he said, 'Perhaps ours was only one of several plans. But I only know about the one I was part of.' He gave a slight shrug. 'In time to come, those plans, those people, will probably be lost or overlooked by history,' he said. 'Or the stories about them will be regarded as lies. But perhaps fragments of the truth will survive. Do you understand all of this? I keep forgetting how young you are—'

'I understand it all.'

'You're an exceptional child,' Vadim said. 'But that's to be expected.' Before he could be asked what he meant, he went on. 'There won't be the patrols any longer, and the guards won't be expecting trouble. They're still there, those guards. I went up into the tower earlier and I could see them in the grounds. But they won't be on the lookout for plotters or people trying to get in to stage a rescue any longer – after last night there's no one who needs rescuing. And I'm one man – I haven't a gun or any kind of weapon, and if I can get into the scullery, even if the guards see me they'll think I'm part of the household.'

He had gone before he could be asked any questions, and the food could be enjoyed. But the day stretched out, and it began to seem a very long time since he had left.

Once, Father Gregory said, 'Vadim's being longer than I expected. I hope nothing's wrong.'

It was towards the end of the afternoon when at last they heard the sound of footsteps coming through the main door.

Vadim at last? But if so, there was only one set of footsteps, and there should be three. Katya and the other girl should be with him. And the steps were wrong – they were slow and dragging, as if their owner could hardly stand . . .

Together they ran across the stone floors, and down to the main door. Despite his look of fragility, Father Gregory was quick and agile, but he stopped abruptly, and let out a cry of anguish. 'Vadim – oh, dear God, no!'

Vadim was there, but he had fallen forward on to the stone floor just inside the church – it was as if he had been determined to get into the place he had called a sanctuary. His face was white and there was blood on his chest and over his hands, and when they knelt down and tried to speak to him, he did not seem to hear. Father Gregory tried several times, asking what had happened, and asking about Katya, but Vadim's eyes were unfocused and blurred with pain.

'Father, can we get someone – a doctor? A surgeon?'

Father Gregory glanced towards the door. 'It would take a long time, and even if we could find a doctor, there's no knowing who can be trusted. But we'll get him into a bed and do our best.'

In the event, there was very little they could do.

'Gunshot wound,' said Father Gregory, presently. 'Those guards must have caught him – they must have guessed he was part of one of the plots . . . Only God can know how he managed to get back here to us with that bullet in him. It should be removed, of course, but we haven't the knowledge – we could make things worse.'

Between them they bound up the gaping wound just below Vadim's left shoulder, and as the light outside began to drain, Father Gregory produced a tiny flagon of some thick dark liquid. 'For the pain,' he said, briefly. 'It might help a little.'

And the liquid, spooned in tiny drops between Vadim's lips, seemed to revive him a bit.

'He's trying to speak, isn't he?'

'Yes. Take his hand, can you.'

Vadim was struggling to speak, but his voice was weak, and the words were like fragments of cobwebs. Even so, it was possible to understand him.

'In my pocket – jacket pocket . . . Take it and destroy it.'

He was moving restlessly, as if trying to escape the pain from the bullet wound, and his breathing was becoming shallow and harsh.

'Do what he's asking,' said Gregory.

The jacket had been flung over a chair. It was blood-soaked, but that did not matter. Inside the pocket was something wrapped in thin, smooth cloth. Silk? Whatever it was, it was so thin that it might shred and fall apart. But unfolded, it showed a single sheet of music score – recognizable as music because of the piano in Ipatiev House. There were the same scrolly marks that would tell you how to make music. Katya had explained about that. Katya . . .

The music paper was so thin that it might be nearly transparent if held up to the light, and the marks were dim and faded. There was a sense of extreme age, and the feeling that someone, a very long time ago, had sat down at a desk and written the music symbols down very carefully, dipping a pen into an inkstand, doing so with doors locked, and by candlelight because no one must know . . .

Vadim's voice came again. 'Destroy it,' he said. 'You must destroy it.'

'It's the "Traitor's Music", isn't it?'

'Yes. The "*Temnaya Kadentsiya*".'

'The "Dark Cadence",' said Father Gregory, softly. 'Heard in many countries. In England on gallows and scaffolds. In France it was heard in the grim shadow of what the French call Madame La Guillotine.'

'They played it for Katya,' said Vadim. 'But it must be destroyed – promise to destroy it.' His hand came out, cold but still firm. 'Promise you'll destroy it.'

The church had never seemed entirely silent, but it was suddenly very silent indeed, as if the stones and the ikons were listening for the answer. And there was only one answer that could be given.

'Yes. I promise I'll destroy it.'

Vadim gave a half-smile and a half-nod, as if satisfied. 'Exceptional child,' he said. 'How could you be otherwise, though?' His eyes were misting over, but his next words were perfectly clear. 'How could you be other than exceptional with Katya for your mother?'

Katya. My mother. The remarkable thing was that the words did not come as any surprise. The only feeling was of delight and then of fear, because they still did not know what had happened to Katya – if she had been found; if she was all right. But Vadim was dying, and it was impossible to ask him the question.

Somehow, though, it was possible to lean closer, and to say, 'If Katya is my mother, who is my father?'

Vadim's hand tightened briefly, the fingers cold but still firm. 'Do you need to ask?' he said, in that frail, cobweb voice.

'Oh, I'm glad. I'm so glad.' The tears that had been kept back fell then, hot and scalding; they fell on to the clasped hands, and Vadim felt them and for a brief second the smile showed in his eyes. His lips moved, and although his words were no more than a faint stir of sound, they were clear. 'I'm glad, too,' he said, and then his head fell back.

Even at the moment of making the promise, there had been the knowledge that it was a promise that could not be kept. It's the only thing I'll ever have of Vadim – my father – and I can't destroy it and I won't destroy it. And somewhere inside the desperate sadness was a deep pleasure at having known him and known what and who he was. But now there was Katya. Could Vadim have got her away somewhere?

Father Gregory was saying, 'You understand we have to go away from Katerinburg? Immediately, I mean.'

'Where to?' This was something new to face.

'Some of my fellow priests have managed to get to Poland. It's a long journey – difficult and perhaps dangerous – but I think we could do it together. Will you come with me? Will you trust me?'

'Yes.' Vadim had trusted Father Gregory, so it was sure to be all right. 'Why do you have to go away?'

'It's difficult to explain – you're so young – but there've already been violent clashes between the Bolsheviks and the clergy . . . We're trying to stay out of the conflict, but we're caught in the crossfire. The Bolsheviks are already calling some priests counter-revolutionaries.' A shadow seemed to pass over his eyes. He said, 'Last night's executions won't be the only ones, I'm afraid.'

They put things in two carpet bags that Father Gregory took from a deep cupboard. A few clothes – 'They won't fit you very well, but the cloak will be warm.' Food that could be wrapped and that would last, and a kind of leather drawstring bag into which the remains of the milk was poured.

Inside the cloak was a deep pocket. Into this went the music score in its wrapping of silk.

'All ready,' said Father Gregory at last. 'We'll wait for first light, and then we'll set off. Until then try to sleep. I'll do what needs to be done for Vadim.' A hand came out. 'Don't think too much about it. But he'll be treated with gentleness and committed to God's mercy, that I promise.'

'Thank you. And Katya?'

A shadow passed over Gregory's face. 'I don't know,' he said. 'If we can get to her we will, but you mustn't count on it. But tomorrow we'll be walking away from this place and going towards a new life. There's only a few hours left for us in Katerinburg.'

Only a few hours left in Katerinburg . . . Then I only have a few hours to find out what happened to my mother . . .

And then . . .? And then, somewhere at the end of a long journey, would be another life, a life beyond Katerinburg and on the other side of the terror and the tragedy of Ipatiev House. The child who had listened with helpless fear to the 'Dark Cadence' being played for Katya could vanish for ever.

TWELVE

Lucek had enjoyed the journey to England. He thought people had looked admiringly at Nina. She had on a plain linen jacket that made her eyes look very blue, and a small cotton hat which she pulled over her bright hair when it rained as they went across the tarmac to the plane. Lucek thought she looked very nice indeed.

Helena, on the other hand, had put on a velvet trimmed jacket, with a cape flung negligently over her shoulders. She was wearing high heels, and she looked as if she had stepped out of one of the old newsreels you saw about rich people in the last century boarding ocean liners or luxurious railway carriages with monogrammed seats.

'She looks terrific, doesn't she?' said Nina, happily. 'I bet people think she's exiled foreign royalty or an international jewel smuggler or something.'

She smiled, and went to help Helena up the steps of the plane, because the high heels made them a bit perilous, and Lucek saw that of course it was perfectly all right and even quite fun for Helena to be so extravagantly dressed, and perhaps make people wonder who and what she could be. He was suddenly proud of her.

He and Nina sat next to one another on the plane, and talked about the scrapbook. Nina had done some research of her own, although she had had to do it a bit furtively, because there seemed to be a kind of superstition about the Chopin Library – if you wanted to be fanciful you might almost wonder if there had once been a conspiracy to keep it out of the record books, she said. One day she would like to find out the reason for that. But she had managed to find a very interesting report mentioning it.

'It was apparently written by somebody who actually saw the Library burn down. I emailed a translation to the professor, and I've brought a copy with me. You can see it later.'

It was really nice to talk like this with Nina, and it was extremely nice to be sitting so close to her that several times their thighs touched. This was not something that Lucek would have engineered, even if it had occurred to him, which it had not. In fact, a couple of times it was necessary to concentrate on not having any kind of physical reaction that might be noticed and that might put Nina off, and that would certainly shock Helena.

After they landed, Nina telephoned her professor to let him know they had arrived. Lucek pretended to be rearranging their luggage so as to give her a little privacy. He thought that he probably would not have been able to follow much of a one-sided conversation in English, but he did hear her laugh softly, and say something about Elgar, who Lucek knew was a famous English composer, and then about the Malvern Hills. This would refer to her studies, of course.

Afterwards she said she was greatly looking forward to meeting Professor Liripine again – he would be at the White Hart, and a colleague was coming with him – someone from Cambridge University.

'The professor says he's very learned, and extremely interested in the scrapbook,' she said.

Lucek was quite nervous about meeting this distinguished gentleman and the equally distinguished-sounding colleague. He was also slightly worried about meeting Phineas Fox, who might ask all kinds of searching questions about the finding of the scrapbook, none of which Lucek thought he would be able to answer. He did not say this to Nina, of course.

Helena did not seem in the least nervous or intimated, either by the journey or by the forthcoming meeting. She said it would be interesting to hear what this professor that Nina thought so highly of had found out.

'We're booked into a place called the White Hart,' Nina said. 'It's quite near to Miss Wyngham's house – about a ten-minute drive, she said. She's booked three separate rooms for us,' said Nina, meeting Lucek's eyes, guilelessly.

'Oh, good.'

'And we've got a drive of about three to four hours, but we can have little stops along the way. I've worked it all out and timed it.'

Lucek thought it was good to be with someone who was so efficient. He managed to squash a sudden worry as to whether Nina would be equally efficient in a more romantic setting. It was to be hoped she did not map things out, or even – this was a dreadful thought – time anything.

But he enjoyed the drive to Causwain. At first the roads were busy and crowded, but gradually the traffic thinned out, and there were lovely wide roads with glimpses of mountains in the distance. The White Hart, when they reached it, was low-roofed and white-washed and there were oak beams across the ceilings, and flowery curtains and wallpaper.

Helena liked it very much.

'This is how foreign visitors expect England to be,' she said.

'It's a lovely old place, isn't it?' said Nina, looking about her, clearly pleased.

'I have a feeling that I'm getting closer to finding out about my past,' said Helena.

When they went downstairs, there was a phone message from Phineas Fox. Lucek could only follow parts of the rapid exchange between Nina and the hotel receptionist, but he gathered that there had been something about a lost key, and that it was likely to be late afternoon before the professor's party arrived.

Nina suggested that they might as well have lunch, and the receptionist explained that they did not do anything formal at midday, but their bar lunches were always very popular.

As they studied the menu, which was chalked on a black-board, Nina pointed to a pork dish that she said sounded like one they had at their own restaurant in Warsaw. They might try that – it would remind them of home.

Lucek was so pleased to hear her call their little café 'their own' restaurant, that he began to feel much more confident about meeting Professor Liripine.

He ordered the pork dish, but declined the garlic bread, because there was no knowing what the night might bring.

Phin had got up early in order to put in a couple of hours' work before collecting Arabella to drive out to the far side of Shrewsbury, where they would pick up Professor Liripine and Dr Purslove.

Arabella had worked out the journey to the White Hart, explaining that they only needed to get off the motorway for a short distance in order to scoop up the professor and Dr Liripine, whose respective trains would arrive at a particular station within fifteen minutes of one another. Phin hoped this optimism would be justified.

For the moment he had set aside Father Gregory and the Cathedral of the Ascension, and he was concentrating on the Chopin Library itself. He had abandoned the online search, and he was working his way through his own books, a great many of which contained obscure references which would not have found their way into the digital world, and most of which had been published at least a century earlier anyway. It was time-consuming, and it would probably not yield any information, but Phin wanted to make sure he had trawled all possible sources.

By ten o'clock he had scoured several turgid descriptions of theatres and opera houses and concert halls, and had ploughed doggedly through a number of architectural tomes on old European buildings, any one of which might have included a mention of the Library. One of these was a hefty volume bearing the title *Paean to the Vanished Temples of Music*, which initially looked promising, but which turned out to be a kind of textual dirge for old religious houses. It was unbelievably dull, and Phin could not imagine why he had acquired it in the first place. He could not imagine how it had even come to be published.

He was just thinking he had better return some of the books to their shelves – it was remarkable how books could scatter themselves over the floor when you were looking for something – and in any case he would soon have to drive out to collect Arabella.

He had replaced most of the books, and he was reaching for his jacket and car keys when the phone rang. A vaguely familiar voice announced itself as being a neighbour of Arabella's.

'Marjorie Gilfillan – I live in the flat facing Arabella's. I expect you remember we met that night when Arabella got the fire alarm stuck on the "on" position, and we had to get the fire service out to disconnect it.'

'I do remember that night.'

'She's asked me to phone you,' said Marjorie Gilfillan, and Phin, with vivid memories of other calls made to him on Arabella's behalf, said, warily, 'Is anything wrong?'

'Not to say wrong, but Arabella wondered if you could delay collecting her. Perhaps by about an hour.'

'What's happened?'

'One of those small, stupid things that might happen to anyone . . .' She paused, and Phin thought they were sharing the thought

that small, stupid things happened to Arabella far more frequently
than to anyone else.

'It's her door-key,' said Marjorie Gilfillan. 'She took some
rubbish out to the bin – there's a kind of communal chute at
the back of the building for tipping the rubbish down into the
communal dustbin in the basement. I should say waste-disposal
container, I expect, but whatever you call it, it's a monstrous
great thing and the men have to use a kind of grab mechanism
to empty it.'

Worrying images were already forming in Phin's mind. He
said, 'Yes?'

'Arabella wanted to be ready for when you collected her –
parking is so difficult here, isn't it? – so she locked the flat and
trundled her case into the main hall. But,' said Marjorie Gilfillan,
'she brought out the rubbish at the same time, so it could be
put down the chute on the way. Very sensible, of course, because
you don't go off for a couple of days and leave rubbish to
moulder in your kitchen, do you?'

'No.' Phin already had a fair idea of what was coming.

'And she had the rubbish bag in one hand and the key ring
looped over a finger, and when she flipped open the chute—'

'The keys slid off her finger and went down the chute along
with the rubbish,' said Phin, resignedly.

'Yes, and although she says being locked out isn't too much
of a problem, because at worst you can always get a locksmith,
she refuses to leave a set of keys among the rotting cabbage
leaves and the remains of number five's Chinese takeaway,
because you never know who might pick them up.'

Phin could hear Arabella's voice coming through this very
clearly. He said, 'Had I better come over anyway?'

'Arabella said you'd offer, but she said not to. For one thing,
you'd never get a parking space within a mile of the flat. She'll
ring as soon as she's rescued the keys and got back into the
flat and cleaned up. She's having to sift through all the rubbish,
you see. Potato peelings and so on.'

'Yes, I do see. All right. Would you tell her I'll contact the
people we're meant to be collecting. Thanks. Good luck with
the potato peelings and cabbage leaves.'

He picked up the *Paean* which he had left open on his desk, and he was about to close it when an entry in the index caught his eye. 'Lost Music Accolades – *A memory of trophies abandoned and extinct.*'

The chapter would not be very likely to contain any mention of the Chopin Library, but helpful snippets could crop up in the most unexpected of places. Phin turned to the appropriate page, and almost at once the Library's name leapt up off the page. He blinked, then sat down at his desk to read the entry.

It was quite short, and its main focus was on the presentation of a music award – the Żelazowa Award.

'Considerable interest was expressed in this Polish music award,' said the text. 'Sadly, there was only ever the one recipient, since the award seems to have vanished without trace – obviously because of the ravages inflicted on Poland as World War II advanced.

'However, the award is intriguing, in that it appears to have been sent anonymously to the Academy of Music at Łódź, with the stipulation that it be presented to the most gifted final-year student. There was speculation as to identity of the donor, but as far as the author can ascertain, that donor was never discovered. It was, though, named for Żelazowa Wola, the tiny village in Gmina Sochaczew, which was the birthplace of Chopin – one of Warsaw's most famous sons. It has not been possible to establish whether there is any actual link between the award and Warsaw's Chopin Library – particularly since the Library itself was destroyed more than ten years ago – but it is an interesting possibility.'

Phin thought, ten years, and turned to the opening pages to check the book's publication date: 1957. Which fitted with what he knew so far. It also meant, though, that it would probably be difficult, if not impossible, to trace any sources the book's author might have used – they were likely to be very widespread. Textual evidence was probably no longer in existence, and people interviewed were most likely dead.

'The announcement of the winner and the presentation was made at the Chopin Library,' went on the book, 'which does suggest a connection. The recipient was a Miss Tanwen Malek, who had just finished her studies at Łódź. Your author found a brief report of the actual event in a publication of the day – the *Kultura Ludowa (The People's Culture).*'

If it had not been for Anatol's account of the Library's fate which Nina Randall had found, Phin thought he would by now be starting to wonder if the Chopin Library had ever existed – if it could have been what people today called a unicorn story. Fabulous and beautiful, but almost certainly mythical. But he had believed Anatol's report and, if this book's author could be trusted, here was an article that had been written by someone who had actually attended an event in the Library. He was aware of a slight feeling of unreality and even a faint eeriness, because this seemed to be virtually primary source material – something straight from the horse's mouth. Phin reminded himself that horses' mouths could sometimes be the mouths of unicorns in disguise, that Anatol's story had still to be verified, and began to read.

A brief accreditation was given to the translator of the *Culture*'s article, then came the article itself.

A relatively illustrious company assembled at the Chopin Library in the Street of Music, last Friday evening, to hear the announcement of the first ever recipient of the mysterious Żelazowa Award.

Various suggestions have been made as to the identity of the award's donor – a few have been credible, while others have been startling. This magazine will do its utmost to uncover the truth, and will report all discoveries to its readers.

The ceremony took place in the famous Ivory Salon, where both Chopin and Paderewski are said to have performed. After suitable speeches, the announcement was made that Miss Tanwen Malek, a graduate of Łódź University, was to be given the award.

On being presented with the trophy, Miss Malek expressed her delight and was careful to also express her extreme surprise. However, she then treated the assembled company to what we were told was an impromptu perform-ance of the third movement (the rondo) of Mozart's Violin Concerto No. 5 – often referred to as 'The Turkish'.

This magazine does, of course, join in congratulating Miss Malek on her award, and would not dream of understating her ability. It does, though, take leave to question whether the performance of the concerto was indeed impromptu in the strictest sense of the word. To your humble correspondent it appeared to have been rehearsed, giving rise to the suspicion that Miss Malek knew all along that her name would be announced as the winner.

It was observed that the Library's director of music, Yan Orzek, was later seen talking to Miss Malek with what more than one lady has been known to describe as the "darkling look of the maestro".

Phin had no idea how far to trust any of this – and certainly not that description of a musical director given to darkling looks, and apparently well regarded by ladies. It was perfectly possible that something of the original meaning had been lost or misunderstood in translation, of course, or that the translator had been of a romantic turn of mind, but even so . . .

Yan Orzek had been mentioned in Anatol's account of the fire. He reached for it, to find what Anatol had said about him. Here it was. 'Tempestuous and attractive to the ladies.'

He turned to the next page, hoping there might be more, and was greeted by a black-and-white photograph of Tanwen Malek. The caption merely said, 'Miss Tanwen Malek, the only ever recipient of the anonymous Żelazowa Award.'

The photograph was a head and shoulders shot, and it had not reproduced particularly well, but it was easy to see that Tanwen had had a cluster of soft dark curls. She was smiling at the camera, but Phin thought it was rather a smug smile, almost verging on a simper. He thought that, however talented she might have been, he would not have liked her very much.

Malek was a name that might hail from several countries, but Phin could not remember ever encountering a Tanwen. The article ended by saying that Miss Malek had been invited to join the group of musicians who performed at the Chopin Library, and would make her debut at a concert there later in the year. It would, stated the article firmly, be a wonderful event.

Phin marked the page and closed the book thoughtfully. He was just putting it in his case, because Arabella and the others would certainly be interested in it, when the phone rang. This time it was Arabella, saying buoyantly that she had found her keys, although it had taken absolutely ages, and there had seemed to be a positive ocean of rotting vegetation and decaying fish-heads – had Phin realized people still actually bought entire fish and gutted and beheaded them? – not to mention soggy newspapers and foil trays with the remains of people's takeaways. But she had had a swift shower and dunked the keys in disinfectant just in case.

'So if you could dash over now, we can head west and pick up the prof and Dr Purslove from their respective trains,' she said. 'And after grubbing around in chicken carcasses and the remains of somebody's macaroni cheese, not to mention potted shrimps that had gone bad, I'm looking forward to the drive.'

Phin said, 'With that precious pair on board, it's likely to be a bumpy journey. But did I tell you the White Hart had a double room with a four-poster?'

'I hope you booked it,' said Arabella.

THIRTEEN

After a great deal of agonizing, Thaisa had invited Helena Baran and her young nephew, and Nina Randall to Sunday lunch. Nina had accepted the invitation with pleasure, and then had explained that some other people were coming to the White Hart. The Warsaw scrapbook had caused quite a lot of interest, she said, and there was a professor of music and a researcher who were going to be with them. They would certainly hope to meet Thaisa.

The mention of a professor of music and a researcher almost threw Thaisa off balance altogether, but she managed to listen to Nina Randall saying cheerfully that of course they would not all expect to come to lunch.

'But if Helena and Lucek and I could come, and then the others turn up later – mid-afternoon, say – that would be really good. Could you manage that?'

What was there to say, other than that they would all be welcome?

'Lunch will only be very simple,' said Thaisa. 'I'm not used to entertaining.'

'A sandwich and a cup of coffee will be more than acceptable,' said Nina Randall, at once. 'The visit is primarily about Miss Baran meeting you, so please don't go to a lot of trouble.'

After the call, waves of panic swept through Thaisa. It was the nightmare from the past – the thing her parents had always feared and tried to avoid. People investigating the past – delving and prying and turning up goodness-knew-what facts. And this was not just a few inquisitive people, it was a group of professionals, with a professor of music who would know about music history and musicians – who might know of musicians who had been in Poland – in Warsaw in the 1930s and 1940s. Not for the first time, Thaisa wished she knew exactly what her father had done during those years, and how well known he had been. Supposing there were documents – photographs, concert programmes – in this scrapbook that had apparently been found in Warsaw. Supposing it held evidence of old crimes?

There were always too many secrets to be sure of losing them all, he had said, as he was dying. And, *We both lied*, her mother had said. *And we both did other things . . . But it was a bad way for them to die . . .*

In the investigating of the past – of Helena Baran's past; of the Warsaw scrapbook's origins and provenance – what questions might be asked about the deaths of Thaisa's parents?

Even though Thaisa had never entertained anybody to a meal in her life, she knew you could not offer just sandwiches and coffee to complete strangers who came to lunch. In the end, she thought she would cook a casserole the day before; she found a recipe that looked fairly straightforward, and it said the dish could be left to cool, and heated up before serving; in fact casseroles were often better if you did that. It recommended serving it with a potato dish that Thaisa had never heard of and that looked complicated. But you often saw people on TV eating food with wedges of French bread, so she would buy some crusty loaves and arrange them in a wicker basket.

She wondered about wine. You saw people on television offering wine to guests who came to eat. It would be a normal thing to do – it might even be thought odd not to do it. After thought, she went into the little wine section of the supermarket, and asked a helpful assistant what he would recommend to drink with a chicken dish.

'Some quite special guests, and I want to get it right,' she said. 'But I'm not really a wine drinker myself.'

The young man said he would suggest a Sauvignon Blanc. And Prosecco was popular these days. Also, of course, there was Chablis, which was a bit more expensive, but they currently had quite a good offer.

The prices shocked Thaisa, but she bought a bottle of each and hoped three bottles would be enough, although she had no idea if they would. She added a bottle of sherry, so that she could offer that as well before the meal. Her mother had often had a glass of sherry before Sunday lunch, and there were still the sherry glasses in the sideboard which she had insisted on using, saying they might have sunk low, but she hoped she had not sunk so low as to have to drink her sherry out of a beaker.

By this time, Thaisa had decided it was not particularly Helena Baran and the nephew who were frightening her so much. She would be polite to them, of course – she would say to Helena that it was very nice, very interesting to be meeting after all the years of Christmas cards, but she did not see any way of establishing a link. She could say, with truth, that she did not know anything about the parcel of books apparently sent to Helena – that if they had been sent from her parents or someone linked to them, it would have been before Thaisa herself had even been born. As for any documents or photographs of her parents linked to their pasts, she could say with truth there was nothing – and that neither of them had talked about their early lives, so that she knew nothing at all.

Except, said her mind, for the fact that your father had been given a high Nazi award. And except for the fact that your mother accused you of murdering him, and that when he was on the brink of death, she had said that about people dying a bad death.

It was, of course, the professor of music and the researcher who were worrying her. Nina Randall had said the researcher's name was Phineas Fox, and Thaisa, who seldom used the internet, suddenly thought she would try to find out a bit more about him. It was an unusual name – there were not likely to be many people called Phineas who were researchers.

There was, in fact, only one, and there was a small website. It was clearly the right person, because he was described as a music researcher and historian, and there was an agent's name, email and phone number for enquiries. But although there were few details about Mr Fox himself, there was a list of books he had published, and among them was quite a scholarly sounding one on German and Jewish musicians prior to World War II. World War II. It all kept coming back to that.

Thaisa closed the website and switched off the laptop, but her mind was churning with fear. This Phineas Fox was the one who would pose the most danger. He knew about World War II – he knew about the musicians who had lived then.

Lucek had changed his mind several times about what to wear for the meeting with Nina's professor and the others at the White Hart. This was not at all like him. Usually he just pulled on whatever was nearest in his wardrobe, or, more often, lying at the foot of his bed. In the end, he put on the new brown jacket with a cream shirt which he decided to leave open at the neck. He thought it was casual but smart, and he was pleased when, having tapped on Nina's door, she said, 'Wow, don't you look great.'

Helena had not gone for casual, at all. She had on a dark red jacket with what Lucek thought was some sort of brocade embroidery all over it, together with several strings of black beads that caught the light.

He managed not to blink, but Helena picked up his reaction, of course, and said, sweepingly, 'Lucek, there's no need to look so startled. If I'm going to be meeting ghosts from the past, I'd like the ghosts to think that at least I'm reasonably stylish.'

Lucek was somewhat relieved to hear the familiar, ironic note in her voice, although he hoped she had not gone over the top with the outfit. But then Nina – dear, tactful, warm-hearted Nina – said, 'I think you're brilliantly stylish, Helena. In fact I'm going back to get my silk wrap so that you don't outshine me.'

At this, Lucek immediately wondered if he should go back to his own room to put on a tie, but Helena was already sweeping towards the stairs, so he followed. Nina caught them up, wearing a vivid blue wrap that made her eyes look like mischievous sapphires, and as they reached the turn in the staircase, she winked at him, which went a small way to alleviate the dreadful stage-fright he was now experiencing.

They went into the bar, and a man rose from a corner table and came towards them.

'Nina,' he said, and put out his hands.

And Nina said, 'Professor,' and took the outstretched hands in hers.

'You don't look a day older,' he said.

'Nor do you.'

They stood looking at one another, their hands still clasped. Lucek had the impression that something passed between them, but whether it was simply the affection of old friends, or whether it was nostalgia for something that might once have existed between them – or even gentle regret for something that might have existed, but had not – he could not tell.

Ernest Liripine was one of those people whose age was impossible to estimate. Lucek did not actually want to assess it, and in any case he would probably have got it wrong. But the thought went through his mind that the professor could be anything from fifty-five to seventy-five. He was wearing a rather untidy jacket and trousers, with a check waistcoat. He took Helena's hand and smiled at her, and then said to Lucek that he was extremely pleased to be meeting them both, and he hoped they had had a smooth journey.

Nina translated this for Helena, who smiled and nodded. Lucek, however, had thought out what he would say, practising to get the English pronunciation as accurate as he could, and he said, very carefully, that the meeting was a great pleasure, that he was loving England, and that he and his aunt were happy to be here.

This appeared to go down well, and the professor's colleague, who was Dr Theodore Purslove, shook their hands, and said good evening and welcome in Polish, which seemed to annoy the professor, who said something about it being typical of Theo to score a point by learning a few Polish words, parrot-fashion. Dr Purslove had wiry grey hair and he was wearing a plain dark suit, but with it he had put a very colourful bow-tie, and he seemed enthusiastic about life in general, which Lucek liked. He found it rather endearing that Dr Purslove had an English–Polish dictionary, from which he exchanged a few phrases with Helena.

He began to relax, and when Phineas Fox and his girlfriend, who was called Arabella Tallis, came in, he relaxed even more. He liked Mr Fox at once, and he was rather relieved to see that he was wearing a dark grey corduroy jacket over a pale grey shirt, but without a tie, so it looked as if Lucek had got that right. He was not startlingly good-looking, but Lucek had the feeling that most ladies would find him extremely attractive, possibly because of his voice which was nice, but also because he had such unusual eyes – they were a very clear grey, and fringed with black lashes. Lucek saw Nina look at Mr Fox with a very alert interest; not that this was anything to worry about.

At first Arabella was not at all the kind of girlfriend he would have expected Phineas Fox to have – he thought she was very nearly ordinary. She was wearing a rather peculiar patchwork-velvet top, and amber beads, and she had apparently pinned her hair on the top of her head, but had not done so very securely, because some of it had tumbled down. And then she smiled at him, and said she was more grateful than she could possibly describe that he had found the scrapbook because it was just about the most fascinating thing she had ever worked on. By the time Lucek managed to reply that he was looking forward to hearing about the scrapbook, he had completely changed his mind about Arabella being ordinary. He thought it might be the smile, and then he thought it might be the way she seemed so delighted with everything and everyone, and he saw that Phineas and Arabella were actually extremely well suited to one another.

He managed to have quite a good conversation with Arabella and Mr Fox, who said he liked to be called Phin, and he began to think he was not acquitting himself so badly. Dr Purslove was resorting to his phrase book to translate the menu for Helena – there seemed to be some amusement between them over that – and the professor and Nina were engrossed in what looked like quite an intense discussion. They would be reminiscing about her days as his student, of course.

Lucek was not sure how it came about that they all ended up in what the White Hart called a coffee room after their meal, but Phineas Fox seemed to have come to some arrangement with the White Hart that they would use it as a semi-private sitting room for the evening. Lucek regarded Phin admiringly, and wondered whether he would ever possess that kind of confidence. It was polite and understated and Lucek would probably never manage it if he lived to be twice Mr Fox's age.

Arabella had brought the scrapbook down with her. 'I've become completely neurotic about leaving it on its own and it being pilfered,' she said, confidingly.

Lucek asked what a 'pilfer' was, and it was explained that it was English slang for stealing.

'*Old* English slang,' murmured the professor. 'Nina, do you remember that walrus-faced visiting lecturer at Durham reading a paper on street musicians in Victorian London?'

'Dr Glaum,' said Nina, nodding. 'I do remember him. I also remember you standing up halfway through and accusing him of lifting his entire lecture from Henry Mayhew. The two of you nearly came to fisticuffs.'

Dr Purslove instantly demanded to know more about this, and Lucek was about to ask what a fisticuff was, when Phin Fox said, 'I think I'll ask them to bring another pot of coffee in, and we can let your aunt look through the scrapbook.'

Phin thought there was a strong sense of closeness between Nina and the professor, although he would not have taken any bets on whether it was physical, mental, or even spiritual. He liked Nina, and he liked Lucek Socha as well. When he commented on how good Lucek's English was, Lucek was delighted.

'I've been practising,' he confided. 'We can talk of the scrapbook better if I can follow you, and I can tell it to Helena, without troubling Nina each time.'

Helena. All the way to Causwain, Phin had been thinking of her as that forlorn abandoned child, lost in the ruins of a dying city. The reality was that she was rather a striking-looking lady in her seventies, with the high cheekbones that Phin thought might be characteristic of Ukraine – even of Russia – rather than Poland. But, shaking her hand and managing to exchange greetings, the image of that long-ago child was still with him. He thought: Helena, you might be one of the few people still alive who once actually saw the Chopin Library. Those ruins where you were found might have been what was left of the Library, and somewhere in your lost memories, you might have some scrap of knowledge that would unlock the mystery of that place.

Partly with the help of Lucek and Nina, he tried to tell Helena that he hoped it would not be an upsetting experience for her to see the scrapbook.

'She says it might be rewarding,' said Nina, having relayed this. 'There may be memories, but they may be good ones.'

Phin looked at Helena, and hoped Nina was right.

Then Arabella folded back the bubble-wrap, and began slowly to turn the pages, and Helena and Lucek leaned forward eagerly. Nina occasionally murmured something, and once or twice Lucek pointed to a page or a scrap of a document. But each time, Helena shook her head, as if saying, No, this did not mean anything – nor this . . . Phin began to be aware of disappointment, although he was not sure if it was disappointment for Helena or for himself. But she had been so very small when she had been found, that surely she would not really remember anything.

And then Nina turned to the page with the concert programme, and the reaction Phin had been waiting for was there.

Helena did not quite recoil, but she almost did. But then she looked more closely at the programme, and very tentatively touched the paper's surface, tracing the words at the top – *Kwartet Burzowy* – Tempest Quartet, and then the words beneath it – '*Temnaya Kadentsiya*'. Phin felt the sudden tension around the table. She's recognized something, he thought. But what? Is it the Tempest name or is it the '*Temnaya Kadentsiya*'?

Helena said something to Lucek, who turned to the others. 'There is something – um – that she knows on this page.'

'Recognizes?'

'Yes, recognizes.'

Phin said, 'The name of the quartet? Or . . .' He hesitated, then said, 'Or is it the title of the music?'

'It's the piano,' said Lucek. 'The drawing of the piano.'

'The piano?' Phin thought none of them had expected this.

Lucek indicated on the page. 'The music stand on the piano,' he said. 'Very clear – very carefully drawn. She says it's a firebird.'

Dr Purslove leaned closer to see. 'I believe it is,' he said. 'How extraordinary. D'you know, I hadn't realized that until now.'

'Helena thinks she remembers the piano from when she was very small,' said Lucek. 'She says she can remember listening to someone playing it.' Helena said something else, and Lucek nodded, then said, 'She thinks it was that memory that encouraged her to learn to play later on. My great-grandparents arranged for lessons for her, I think. She's actually very good,' said Lucek, anxiously.

'It'd certainly be distinctive enough for a child to remember. And I shouldn't think you'd find many music stands like that,' said Dr Purslove. 'Ernest?'

'No. Possibly even custom-made?'

'The firebird,' said Dr Purslove, thoughtfully. 'It's one of the famous Russian symbols, immortalized in all those classic fairy stories.'

'It makes for another link,' said Phin, thoughtfully. 'And the piano – and the pianist – must have been important for her to remember it and recognize that sketch. Lucek, what exactly is the link between your aunt and this Thaisa Wyngham?'

'A very little link,' said Lucek. 'There was a parcel of books sent to Helena when she was small. It was never known where it was from, but it mentioned a Wyngham family in Causwain, and that there might be a connection to Helena. Later, Helena managed to find Miss Wyngham – Causwain is a small place, so not difficult. Christmas cards have been exchanged for many years.'

'That's interesting,' said Phin. 'What were the books?'

'Children's books – very old ones, but very beautiful,' he said. 'Illustrations and smooth, expensive paper.'

Children's books . . . Or the books of just one child? Phin saw again the small lost girl in the ruins of a city.

Lucek said, 'The books were all in the Russian language.'

There was another of the silences, but then Dr Purslove said, softly, 'Russia again.'

He leaned back, and Phin saw that he suddenly looked tired, and he remembered that neither Dr Purslove nor the professor were young men any longer, and that Helena Baran must be well into her seventies. He said, 'This is all very thought-provoking, isn't it? But we've all had quite long journeys – what does anyone think about calling it a day, and returning to the fray tomorrow?'

'I'm in favour of that,' said Dr Purslove. 'Nina, you and Miss Baran and Lucek are going to Miss Wyngham's for lunch, aren't you?'

'Yes, and we're taking the scrapbook to show her. The idea is that the rest of you come along later – mid-afternoon, if that's all right – and we can have a kind of general discussion about any discoveries. Thaisa Wyngham sounded a bit daunted at the prospect of so many people at once, so that should dilute it a bit.'

'In that case, the rest of us can have lunch here,' said Dr Purslove. 'And then Ernest can have his post-prandial snooze.'

'I do not have post-prandial snoozes. In fact, I shall most likely go for a brisk walk and look round Causwain.'

'Then I'd better come with you, because you're bound to get lost,' said Dr Purslove.

'I've got a better sense of direction than you have.'

Arabella reached for the scrapbook and its wrappings. 'And where did I put my glasses? I thought they were here, but . . . You all go on up, and I'll follow when I've found them.'

'I'm certainly ready for bed,' said Nina, and Phin thought she sent a quick glance at Lucek and that Lucek blushed slightly. Ingenuous young man infatuated with a slightly older woman? Why not, thought Phin. It might even work.

FOURTEEN

Lucek was afraid he had blushed when Nina made that remark about being ready for bed, but no one seemed to have noticed, or, if they had, they had been too polite to say anything.

Once in his room, he washed, undressed, and got into bed. It was a very nice room, and the bed was comfortable.

It had been strange to see the scrapbook again, and it was even stranger that Helena had recognized the sketched piano with the firebird music stand. The Russian books had several really lovely illustrations of firebirds.

He was glad he had given the scrapbook to Nina, and that she had passed it to Professor Liripine and Phin Fox, but it had been odd to see it covered in modern bubble-wrap and to know that there were going to be analytical discussions about its contents. To him, it was a fragment of the past, shrouded in dust from the rubble beneath which it had been buried for so many years. He found himself hoping the ghosts were not minding being dragged into the present. This was an absurd idea, of course. Nina would certainly think so.

Nina.

Her room was at the end of the corridor, so he would hear her go past his door; not that he was going to lie awake listening. Or perhaps he would lie awake for just a little, to make sure she had got safely to her room. Or in case she tapped on his door to talk about the evening. She might do that.

Supposing she did not come back to her own room, though? The memory of how she and the professor had laughed, and said, 'Do you remember . . .?', several times during the evening came to him. The professor's bedroom was at the other end of the corridor – instead of turning left at the head of the stairs for Lucek and Helena's and Nina's rooms, he would turn right. What if Nina had turned right with him?

No, he was being ridiculous. The professor was much too old

to be having assignations in hotel bedrooms. There must be a good twenty-five years between him and Nina. Probably more. Say the professor was seventy and Nina was thirty-five. That would mean thirty-five years' gap. On the other hand, the professor might not be much over sixty, which would narrow the gap considerably. And he had a nice smile when he forgot to project that frowning image – Lucek had noticed that several times.

It was eleven o'clock. That was not very late. Lucek would leave his light on, so that if – no, *when* – Nina came along to her room, she would see the light, and know he was still awake. In case she did that, he got up to make sure his hair was fairly tidy. He got back into bed, and arranged the pillows to look inviting. Then he got out again to brush his teeth for a second time, in case he had not brushed them sufficiently thoroughly the first time.

It was absurd to be nervous. It was not as if he had not had several girlfriends. It was not as if he was entirely inexperienced, for heaven's sake. Still, with somebody like Nina, who had probably had quite a lot of lovers, he would want to – well, to put up a good performance. Then he began to worry whether, if it came to it, he would be so nervous he would not be able to put up any kind of performance at all.

In the White Hart's coffee room, Nina made to follow the professor and Dr Purslove, then hesitated.

'You're looking a bit wistfully at the scrapbook,' said Arabella, who was still searching for her glasses.

'It's just that while I was looking at the scrapbook with Helena . . . Well, near the back, it looked as if letters had been stuck in. And old letters often have all kinds of useful information.'

'Indeed they do,' said Phin.

'I'd really like to take a swing at them,' said Nina. 'But if you'd rather leave it until the morning . . .'

'I only said that because I thought people might genuinely be zonked,' said Phin. 'We've all had quite long journeys, and Dr Purslove and the professor aren't young men any longer.'

Nina laughed. 'Phin, I've never known Professor Liripine be zonked by anything.'

'I'd like to know what's in any letters,' said Arabella. 'I've even found my glasses. Where exactly—? Oh, yes, I see. Three or four of them.'

'Yes. The top edges are very tattered and it's impossible to see any dates. This first one is addressed to the Chopin Library Trust, though.'

'A Trust?' said Phin. 'That's something we didn't know about. But the Library would have to have been funded by something, of course.'

'Or someone,' put in Arabella. 'Nina, if you're going to try to get a translation, can I type some notes on to the tablet at the same time? I can transfer it to my laptop and Phin's later.'

'Yes, of course.'

'Good.' Arabella delved into her bag for the tablet. 'OK, fire away.'

Dear Sir,

Firstly, I must thank you for the excellent lunch you gave me yesterday. It seems it is still possible to obtain good food and wine in Warsaw. I do not come to the city very often, as you know, but our meeting was both pleasurable and useful.

I am very glad that you see my request in such a favourable light. The young lady is a gifted musician, and will, I feel, make a worthy addition to the group of permanent musicians at the Chopin Library. Having been awarded the prestigious Żelazowa Award, she is likely to bestow considerable kudos on the Library.

Once her appointment is confirmed by Mr Yan Orzek, I will be happy to make the payment into the Trust funds – the amount to be as discussed.

I am, my dear sir, yours very faithfully

'Yes?' said Phin, as Nina broke off. 'Very faithfully who?'

'No signature,' said Nina, staring at the page. 'That's annoying. It's just a squiggled initial, splodged by damp. It could be G, but I wouldn't put money on it.'

'Whatever it is, I don't like the sound of G,' said Arabella.

'I'll bet he had an ulterior motive for getting that girl appointed to the Library.'

'Next is what looks like the chairman's reply,' said Nina.

> Sir,
>
> I am pleased to tell you that this afternoon I have a meeting with the Chopin Library's director of music, when I will confirm that the Trust directs him to appoint the lady whom we have agreed to refer to merely as your protégée. (One never knows into whose hands messages and correspondence might fall, and in these times it is necessary to be vigilant.)
>
> However, I must remind you of Mr Orzek's annoying way of resisting what he calls 'outside interference'. Even so, I believe that if the matter is represented to him in a calm and sensible way, and if it is made clear that the appointment of our young lady means that a substantial sum will be credited to the Chopin Library Trust, he will be amenable.

'That's signed, "Chairman, Chopin Library",' said Nina. 'This next one is from Yan Orzek himself, and it doesn't look nearly so formal.'

> Sir,
>
> I refuse utterly and categorically to include Tanwen Malek in the Chopin Library's permanent group of musicians. She may well have been awarded the Żelazowa Award, but I don't care if she's been given fifty awards, because I don't approve of awards, and half of them are rigged beforehand anyway.
>
> Since you were present on the evening when the award was made, you will recall that Miss Malek played for the company a Mozart rondo. She certainly possesses considerable technical skill, but even setting aside the ill-mannered behaviour in her playing it without an invitation, her performance was flamboyant, showy, and unprofessional. She waved her bow as if directing traffic or even (God help us all) as if she were conducting an entire

orchestra of her own, throwing back her head during the bouncing *jetés*, and making wholly unnecessary use of the springing *sautillé* stroke. In addition – and this is perhaps the worst sin of all – she included several flourishes and trills that Mozart did not intend, or, indeed, compose.

I am perfectly well served with my present musicians. I also have Bruno Sicora as a second-in-command. He may well deserve the label I believe you once applied to him as frivolous, and his moral behaviour may indeed be sometimes flexible, but he is an excellent pianist, a useful second violinist, and a trustworthy assistant. He certainly has the Library's best interests firmly at heart.

I do not care a jot if somebody is even prepared to bestow as much as 50,000 złoty on the Trust, I do not want Tanwen Malek.

Yan Orzek

'Strong stuff,' said Arabella, as Nina turned the page. 'And didn't our Anatol refer to Yan Orzek?'

'Yes. He said something about his tempestuous ways being attractive to the ladies.' Phin was studying the letter. 'In places that last letter looks as if the pen dug into the page,' he said. 'Thick black ink and several blots. What comes next, Nina? It looks a bit like minutes of a meeting.'

'I think it is,' said Nina. 'It doesn't seem to be complete, but it's headed "Meeting of Chopin Library Trust Board". It lists the people who were present, but . . . Damn, no names, though. Just people's positions within the Trust. Oh, except for Yan Orzek. He was present. And his assistant – Bruno Sicora. All right, Arabella?'

'Yes. Keep going.'

Minutes of Meeting of the Committee of the Chopin Library Trust.

Those present: Chairman of Trust Committee. Treasurer. Secretary. Accountant.

Also present: Mr Yan Orzek, Director of Music. Mr Bruno Sicora, Assistant Director.

Proposal made by the chairman that Miss Tanwen

Malek be appointed to the permanent musical staff of the Chopin Library.

Seconded by the secretary.

Proposal objected to by Mr Orzek, but objection not seconded or supported.

Mr Sicora's suggestion that Miss Malek would be a decorative addition to the group was regarded as superfluous.

The treasurer distributed the newest figures for the Chopin Library, and asked that it be minuted that there is a dwindling bank balance. He also asked that it be recorded that the appointment of Miss Malek would release a large sum of money from the donor of the Żelazowa Award – the identity of which person was unknown.

Mr Orzek left the meeting at this point.

In his absence, the proposal to invite Miss Malek to become one of the permanent musicians at the Chopin Library was carried.

The secretary agreed to obtain estimates for the repair of the door, which had become detached from one hinge due to Mr Orzek's abrupt departure.

Nina sat back, and Phin said, 'We knew about Yan Orzek, but I know about Tanwen Malek as well. While Arabella was grubbing around in the refuse this morning, I was reading an entry in a very dull book about lost – I mean defunct – music awards.'

'That does sound dull,' said Arabella.

'It was, apart from one brief section. If you can stay for another five minutes, I'll show you – I brought the book down with me.' Phin reached into his briefcase for *Vanished Temples of Music*, and turned to the page on Lost Music Accolades.

Arabella and Nina leaned over to read it, and a brief silence fell. Then Arabella said, 'I think the whole thing sounds like a put-up job to get Tanwen into the Library.'

'I do, too,' said Phin. 'A newly created award from an anonymous donor – a good-looking young female being shoe-horned into the Library as resident violinist—'

'And being referred to as "G's protégée",' put in Arabella.

Nina was studying the photograph of Tanwen Malek. 'What do you think of her, Phin?'

'I wouldn't trust her from here to that window,' said Phin, promptly.

'I wouldn't, either. Are we thinking that "G" was the anonymous donor of the award?' asked Arabella.

'I wouldn't go that far yet, but I wouldn't dismiss the idea.'

Nina got up, and stretched her arms and shoulders. 'Whatever we think or don't think,' she said, 'if you don't mind, I really will say goodnight now, and go to bed.'

'Good night, Nina. Thanks again.'

As Nina went out, Phin said, softly, 'I wonder which bed she's going to.'

Arabella grinned. 'Don't you know?'

'Oh, yes. I was wondering if you did.'

'Of course I know.'

Lucek had decided to forget his wild idea that Nina might come to his room. He was just reaching up to switch off the light when there was a tap on his door.

'I wasn't sure whether to knock or not,' said Nina, pausing in the doorway after Lucek had called to come in. 'But I saw your light under the door, so I thought you must be still awake, and I thought you might like to hear about what we were doing.'

Lucek managed not to say, Well, as long as whatever it was, you weren't doing it in Professor Liripine's room. He sat up in bed, and said he would like to hear it all very much.

'I didn't realize you were all still downstairs.'

'Only Phin and Arabella and me,' she said, at once. 'Purslove and the prof went up to bed almost straight after you.'

'Oh, I see.' Lucek managed not to sound too pleased.

Nina closed the door and came over to the bed. 'You look very cosy in there,' she said.

'Do I look a bit solitary, though?' Lucek could hardly believe he had managed to make such a suave response, but it sounded rather good. Cool, in fact.

'You do, rather.'

'You could alter that by joining me in bed.'

Nina smiled. 'I was beginning to think you'd never ask,' she said.

'Phin,' said Arabella, when they reached their own bedroom, 'does Helena's recognition of that piano contribute anything?'

'I don't know. She might just have seen something like it at any time, and be – well, projecting the image of it on to her lost childhood. Does that make sense?'

'Yes. I suppose it was the sketch she reacted to,' said Arabella, slowly.

'What else?'

'Might she have recognized the title of the music? The "Cadence"?'

'And wanted to throw us off the scent? It's seems a bit unlikely,' said Phin. 'And what would be the point? In any case, on the night the Library burned, and someone played the "Cadence", she couldn't have been more than three years old – say four at the most.'

'You're looking thoughtful, though.'

'If I am, it's because I'm thinking about Tanwen Malek,' said Phin. 'G certainly got her into the Library, didn't he?'

'Assuming G was a "he", of course.'

'It sounded like it. I wonder if he was an oily old seducer – what they used to call a sugar daddy – or a manipulator? Was it a case of, "Come to bed with me, my dear, and you'll find yourself resident violinist at the famous Chopin Library"? Or was he something more sinister? This was the 1940s, and Warsaw was an occupied city, let's not forget. I think G sounds ruthless under all that bonhomie and lavish lunching and promises of money. Speaking of "come to bed", that four-poster looks extremely tempting, doesn't it?'

'You read my very thoughts,' said Arabella. But as Phin slid beneath the duvet and reached for her, she said, thoughtfully, 'If G was a manipulator, I wonder if Tanwen knew.'

'You mean did she go in there knowingly, or was she an innocent puppet – a dupe?'

'Also,' said Arabella, 'I wonder how Yan Orzek reacted when he found out that Tanwen had been forced on to him.'

FIFTEEN

Warsaw, late 1930s

Until the award ceremony, Tanwen had never met or seen Yan Orzek, but during her last term at the Academy, several of the girls had talked about him – saying that he was generally considered irresistible. He had what people called compelling eyes – a bit like you might imagine Svengali, if Svengali had been younger and better looking.

Accordingly, Tanwen took considerable trouble over her appearance for the Żelazowa Award announcement at the Chopin Library. She wore black, very understated, but with a neckline that dipped with just the right amount of promise, and pinned her hair into a scholarly chignon. After the award was announced and presented, she played a Mozart rondo by way of expressing gratitude – and perhaps, just a bit to demonstrate how extremely good a violinist she was, too. It was a perfectly acceptable thing to do, certainly not warranting Yan cornering her at her very first rehearsal and telling her that she had behaved unprofessionally, that he had agreed to her appointment against his better judgement, and that he would not put up with such behaviour again.

Tanwen, with downcast eyes and trembling lips, had said she was deeply sorry. It was just that the whole occasion had been overwhelming – the famous Ivory Salon, the lights and all the people. Everything had gone to her head. She contrived to sound humble, even though she was boiling with rage, because how *dared* he speak to her like that! Now that she had met him, he was not so very wonderful or so attractive, anyway. She would allow that he had dark, compelling eyes, but as for the rest . . . Well, his hair looked as if it needed cutting, and although some people might find high cheekbones attractive, to Tanwen's mind they simply pushed his eyes up at the corners. Still, he might be useful to her career, just as the Chopin Library might be useful.

Father had been very keen for her to join the musicians at the Library. He'd said it would be her first step on the road to a glittering career on concert hall platforms – the career he had prophesied for her since she was six years old and strumming experimentally on the family piano. Sweetly pretty she had looked, and he and her mother had taken dozens of photographs. Most of them were framed and on display in their house; the rest they brought out to show proudly to visitors.

Tanwen had gone along with Father's suggestions about the Library. The wretched war that had come boiling out of nowhere, engulfing them all before she had realized what was happening, was causing all kinds of problems. She felt as if it was cheating her out of all the things she should be having. When you were approaching your twentieth birthday, your life should be filled with parties and nice clothes and lovers, not with bombs and curfews and people being dragged from their homes and sent to horrible labour camps. It was all extremely tiresome, and the Chopin Library might serve as a reasonable stopgap until it was all over.

She had been quite surprised when it transpired that Father knew one or two people connected with the Library, just as she had been surprised at him knowing about the arrangements for the Żelazowa Award. Once or twice she had even wondered if he knew who had donated it, because there had been rather a knowing smile when she had been nominated. But, of course, he had met and worked with a great many people during his professional life. He was more or less retired now, and living some way out of Warsaw, but he was still in touch with former colleagues and associates.

From the first rehearsal, it was clear to her that Yan Orzek was held in very high regard by everyone at the Library, from the musicians all the way down to the kitchen staff who prepared and served the Ivory Salon's suppers. Bruno Sicora, who was the pianist and also the assistant director of music, told Tanwen that if Yan included a piano performance of his own at a concert, huge sums of money were paid for seats, and places were booked for weeks ahead so that people could see him and hear him play. He was a maestro, said Bruno, without the least trace of envy.

Studying Yan, Tanwen began to see him in a slightly different light, and when Bruno called him a maestro, she wondered if he would also be a maestro in the bedroom. She had gone to bed with several young men at the Academy, partly because it was a good idea to practise – practice meant you became skilled, whether it was playing the violin or engaging in bedroom activities. It had not made her a cheap tart, it had simply been that it was a good idea to acquire any skills that might be useful. Also, she had been curious to know what the bed thing was like, and whether it was as good as people said. Mostly, it had not been; it had been messy and undignified and even a bit boring. She had tried it with a couple of older men, who ought to know a bit more about such things – and also, who might be of use to her career in the future. They had been a bit better, although not much, and they had vanished politely from her life after a couple of sessions.

But with Yan it might be very different indeed. She might even forgive him for the way he had spoken to her about that first night when she had been given the Żelazowa Award.

It was annoying to find that nobody at the Chopin Library seemed very impressed by the Żelazowa Award. Alicja, who was currently the Library's resident cellist, even said, in a die-away voice, that she had never heard of it.

'But I suppose it's something they award in provincial schools, is it?'

Tanwen knew quite well that this remark came from pure jealousy, because it was obvious that Alicja was in love with Yan. She gazed at him with open adoration – once or twice Tanwen even wondered about suggesting that if Alicja did something about her stringy hair and the complexion which did not look as if it had ever known the touch of a powder puff, she might have a better chance.

Bruno Sicora asked if the award had taken the form of a silver cup or a bowl, because if so, he and Tanwen might fill it with wine some evening and share the drinking of it. Tanwen had no intention of drinking wine from silver cups with mere assistant directors; it was perfectly clear what Bruno's intentions were, and she was not going to jump into bed with somebody she had just met, which really would be the behaviour of a cheap tart.

Yan Orzek was angry that he had been forced into taking Tanwen into the Library. He had always chosen his own musicians, but in the end the Trust's chairman had huffed a bit and talked about dwindling bank balances, and she had been appointed despite Yan's objections.

'The truth is,' said the chairman, 'that the Chopin Library, distinguished and historic as it is, won't run on nothing. Even,' he said, meaningfully, 'with a musical director as gifted and as knowledgeable as yourself.'

The message was clear. Appoint this girl, and someone is prepared to deposit a substantial amount of money in the Library's coffers. But continue to refuse, and you'll find there are other, equally gifted and knowledgeable musicians who will be more amenable and who could take your place.

And so there had been a somewhat pretentious award ceremony, at which Tanwen had behaved like a precocious six-year-old showing off in front of the grown-ups. When Yan had made it clear at her first rehearsal that he was not prepared to put up with such behaviour, she had stared at him with shock and then with fury, clenching her small fists. The fury was quickly suppressed, but for a disconcerting moment, Yan had caught himself wondering how she would look if her eyes were not glowing with angry defiance, but with an entirely different emotion – and how she would look if her hair were unpinned and tumbling around her bare shoulders.

Such thoughts – such feelings – had to be suppressed. And it was not very surprising if some unknown person was prepared to help Tanwen's career in return for certain favours. If Tanwen was indeed bestowing those favours on some unknown Library benefactor, or even on the entire Trust board, it was no concern of Yan's. He would acknowledge that she was a skilled violinist, and he would admit that she would be an asset.

But preparing for the concert at which she would make her debut, he wondered, as he had done more frequently of late, how much longer the Chopin Library could survive. He would fight for it, but he was afraid there could not be many more concerts. Nobody actually came out and said that the Nazis were tightening their grip on the city – most people would be too worried that such comments could be overheard and reported – but it was what everyone thought.

But this concert, at least, would go ahead, and the chef came puffing up from the kitchens to discuss the supper that would be served. He said they could not be expected to provide the kind of food that had been possible a year or two ago, but they would do their best. They would, of course, serve the *Mrożony Polonez* – Anatol was shocked to his boots to think of a Chopin Library concert without it. He became loquacious on the subject, describing how his father, who had been chef here thirty years ago, had always led the procession up the steps from the old ice room, deep in the bowels of the building – they would forgive the use of the word *bowels* in this context, Anatol hoped – and how the procession was always accompanied by two violinists playing one of Chopin's own polonaises. He paused, overcome by the emotion of the memory, then went on to describe how servants would carry wax candles in gilt holders. 'Lighting the *Mrożony Polonez*, they used to call it.'

'I wish I could have seen it,' said Yan.

'It's a very great pity, Mr Orzek, that that original stairway became unsafe and they had to block it off,' said Anatol. 'It was done during the last tsar's visit – before he was assassinated, of course.'

'Of course.' From the corner of his eye, Yan saw Bruno grin, but they all liked Anatol, and they enjoyed his stories about the Library's past and its traditions.

'These days,' said Anatol, 'we have to use the scullery steps which are narrow and deep, and no kind of background for a ceremonial procession, at all. Also, they are difficult for persons of larger girth to ascend.'

After Anatol had gone, Bruno observed that it was a pity they could no longer have the full ceremonial procession and the Lighting of the Iced Polonaise.

'I didn't know there was an ice room here, though,' he said. 'Did you, maestro?'

'What? No, but logically there'd have to have been one in the place's heyday. And all houses of this size had ice rooms or ice pits.' Yan sounded preoccupied. They were in the big rehearsal room, and he was at the piano, a Debussy score propped up in front of him. Alicja was in the other corner, drooping over her cello.

'I might explore sometime,' said Bruno. 'A closed-off stairway going down to an old ice room sounds nicely spooky. You could come with me, Tanwen. We'll hold hands and hunt for ghosts.'

Without looking up, Yan said, 'More likely you'll find nothing but cobwebs and spiders. I wouldn't worry about ghosts, Tanwen. I never do.'

Bruno said, 'Your trouble, maestro, is that you have no romance in your soul.'

'So I've been told,' said Yan, returning to Debussy.

Yan hoped that Tanwen was not taking Bruno's teasing for anything other than the mischievous flirting it undoubtedly was. Whatever else she might be, she was still quite young and probably not very worldly, and Yan had a responsibility towards his musicians. He wondered whether he ought to speak to Bruno, but he would find it difficult and embarrassing. Bruno would not be in the least embarrassed, of course, in fact he would consider it amusing.

Bruno had rooms in the same house as Yan, on the floor immediately above, which could be convenient and friendly, although sometimes awkward. There were times when it was impossible not to hear female giggles and shrieks of delight, or groans of an unmistakable rhythm and character. It was occasionally quite difficult to face Bruno in the rehearsal room on the mornings after those nights.

Once, Yan had said, carefully, 'Bruno, I never pry, as you know, but these days you do need to be careful about who—'

'Whose bed I get into and who I let into my own bed?' said Bruno. 'Are you wondering if I'm unwittingly passing information to the Nazis? Because if so—'

'No, of course not.' Yan hesitated, then said, 'You go to some of the meetings, though, don't you? The secret ones?'

'Yes,' said Bruno, in a low voice. 'And so, I think, do you.'

*   *   *

As the night of the concert drew nearer, the city began to feel more and more uneasy. People in the streets began to have a hunted look; they did not exactly hide in their homes, but they kept off the streets as much as possible, and they tried to avoid the patrols that regularly marched through the city.

Anyone with even the smallest vein of Jewish ancestry now went in genuine fear, because by this time it was known that Hitler was hell-bent on purging Poland – and probably as much of Europe as he could get at – of anyone with Jewish blood. There were a number of theories as to the reason for this, one of which was that the Führer had caught a venereal disease from a Jewish prostitute in the Great War and this was his revenge. Nobody dared say this very loudly, of course, and not many people actually believed it, although Yan thought most people would like to.

He knew that soon he would have to talk to his musicians about the Library's future and their own futures. This was a daunting prospect. How would they react? Alicja would be sympathetic, but in the wrong way. She would fix her large, burned-out-lamp eyes on him, and say this was another of life's tragedies, and that her family had known many of them. Then she would vow to shut herself away and compose music that would express anguish and sorrow. Alicja was always composing music expressing anguish and sorrow.

'When the Muse visits me, I cannot ignore her,' she said, with a sad, brave smile.

Yan always accepted Alicja's compositions when she presented them to him, and they were always terrible.

'A nocturne,' she might say. 'A haunted piece, born of sad dreams. Or perhaps it might be an étude. You shall decide.' Several times, after Tanwen's arrival, she said, 'I've brought a piece that I composed with you in mind, maestro. We could rehearse it together – just the two of us, I mean. Anyone else would be an intrusion.' She sent a disparaging look towards Tanwen.

Tanwen . . .

But so far she was accepting Yan's direction without demur, and it was hardly her fault that when she sat by a window during rehearsals, the afternoon sunshine fell across her hair, making it look as if a glowing sunset shone through it.

SIXTEEN

Warsaw, late 1930s

Bruno said that they would all rattle around like four peas in a pod at the concert.

'Personally, I prefer the bigger events,' he said. 'Thirty-piece orchestra and footmen in liveries and wigs and all the rest of it.'

'I don't suppose there'll be much of an audience, anyway,' said Alicja, mournfully, and added, 'the Germans are everywhere. Their boots are like huge steel claws scraping on the cobblestones. I lie awake listening for the sounds of their marching in the street outside my window.'

'Personally,' said Bruno, 'if I hear anything untoward in the street outside my window, I pull the sheets over my head. And,' he said, with a wink at Tanwen, 'over the head of anyone who might be in bed with me at the time.'

Tanwen said firmly that she had never heard the marching boots, and Bruno added that if you let the Third Reich squash you to the extent that you stopped trying to entertain people with your music, you might as well give up once and for all. For himself, he would fight to his last breath, said Bruno, and for a disquieting moment something seemed to blaze from his eyes, so that it was no longer the familiar flippant, careless Bruno – the man who liked to sit down at a piano and pour out music of all kinds and slide mischievously into modern swing or jazz. It was someone very different indeed.

Father had written to say he could not get to Warsaw for the concert. He found travelling tiring these days, and, of course, travelling of all kinds was becoming difficult. But he would telephone Tanwen the morning after at her lodgings, and they would have one of their talks. Father loved to know about her days and about her new life at the Library. He said it made him feel that he was sharing it with her, and she must be indulgent of an old man's foolishness. He would look forward to hearing who had been at the concert, and which rooms had been used.

They had to wear traditional black for the concert, of course. Evening or semi-evening frocks for Tanwen and Alicja, and white tie and tails for the men. It was becoming impossible to buy new clothes, but Tanwen scoured the second-hand clothes shops – the good ones, where aristocratic ladies sent their clothes after they had only worn them a couple of times, but were too mean to actually give them away – and found a really beautiful silk cocktail frock in black silk jacquard. It fitted perfectly, the skirt swished alluringly around her ankles, and there were black shoes with glacé bows to match. The shoes pinched a bit, but Tanwen could put up with pinched toes for a couple of hours.

It was annoying to find that Alicja had been right about the audience being small, but they were very appreciative and Yan looked marvellous in his sharp, formal evening dress. Tanwen thought the very air sizzled with his energy.

After the audience had gone, the rooms were cleared and swept, and the gilt chairs carried back to their store cupboard by the two girls who helped Anatol. The leftover food was diligently gathered up – by some strange and secret method it would be taken to Anatol's cousin who kept sheep on the slopes beyond the Kampinos Forest. Presently some racks of lamb and loin chops would make their appearance in various larders by way of payment. It was what was being done nowadays. If the Germans knew about it – and probably they did because they knew most things that went on – nobody seemed overly concerned.

What was left of the *Mrożony Polonez* would not go to the Kampinos pigs, of course. In any case, it would have melted to nothing by the morning. It was carefully scraped into a large bowl and carried away. Alicja said, mournfully, that she supposed it would be refrozen so that it could be served up in the future to a different audience, and added that most things in life were rehashed and re-served in a different form, but essentially they remained the same and you lived a life of leftovers.

Tanwen wondered if this was meant as a philosophical

observation or whether it was just Alicja's usual pessimism, but she was only half listening, because her mind was too alive with her own plans.

Yan was glad they had gone ahead with tonight's concert. Walking through the empty rooms, he felt, as he always did, how different the Library seemed immediately after a performance. Often, when he was on his own here, he would imagine the Library's glorious days, when glittering and famous people flocked here – when Paderewski and Chopin himself performed and the Russian tsars came to hear them. Surely, if ever there were to be a time when the ghosts of those great composers ventured out, this would be it. He thought they would be polite and unobtrusive, tiptoeing back to see if their music was still being played, shying away from the light, because they had never known electric light – only candlelight, or lamplight.

Lamplight. Something stirred at the edges of his mind, and with it came the feeling that this was a night when other ghosts might stir, and that they would not be the shades of inquisitive composers or musicians. He frowned, and went into the Ivory Salon. This, too, was in shadow, but through the tall windows he saw that storm clouds were scudding across the night sky, and that rain was lashing against the glass. There had been a storm when those other ghosts had walked . . .

Don't look at the memory, said his mind. Do what you always do when those ghosts try to push their way into the present – turn to music, and pretend, as you always pretend, that the music might one day take you back. And that if by some fantastical chance it does, you'll be able to change what happened.

He crossed to the dais, but once seated at the piano, he hesitated. Normally on nights like this he reached for Mozart, because nothing drove away ghosts like Mozart at his insouciant best. But tonight, different music was taking hold of him, and it was music that had been sung on a long-ago night, the words only heard in fragments, but the whole learned and understood years afterwards. *The Demon* by Anton Rubinstein, beautiful and sinister and melancholy, with, at its heart, the Demon's impassioned farewell.

Don't cry . . . your tear will drop on my hand

And tomorrow I'll be left without you . . .

Only the storm light illuminated the Ivory Salon, but for this, of all music, Yan did not need light. His fingers found the piano keys, and the soft sad harmony stole into the room, mingling with the storm.

He was still lost in the music and the memories, when on the edges of his mind he became aware of soft footsteps. With the footsteps came singing – soft and sweet, the words those of the aria he was playing . . . The words that had been written when this music was composed nearly seventy years earlier.

'. . . *I'll fill all the pages with my rhymes for you*
And if I meet you in a crowd
I'll never let you out from my life again.
I'll steal you from all the people and you will be only mine
for ever . . .'

It ought not to have been strange to hear someone singing inside this building. The Chopin Library was a place of music – it was alight and alive with music for most of its day – and the 'Demon's aria', although seldom performed these days, was quite well known in the music world.

But the light, feminine singing was sending a tidal wave of memory tumbling through Yan's mind, and his hands were shaking so badly that he could no longer play. He stopped, and went out to the hall. The storm was still growling overhead, and several times lightning flickered, so that the hall and the stairway came sharply into brilliance.

The stairway.

She was at the head of the stairs, and for a moment Yan was not sure if she was real, because it was like seeing an outline traced on transparent paper. The lightning crackled again, showing up the rioting hair like a copper curtain, and he saw that she was no paper cut-out – she was real and alive.

She was still singing the 'Demon's aria', and she was smiling, and coming down the stairs towards him, as if she was very sure of her welcome. Everything blurred and Yan had the sensation of something wrenching his mind from the present, and sending it spinning into the past.

You can't forget me, and you can't shut me away, Yan . . .
I've always been with you . . .

Always with him . . . That girl with autumn-leaf hair falling around her shoulders, who had sung this aria as she descended a stairway, doing so in order that the people with her would not be afraid, and doing so to hide her own fear . . .

The past surged forward and he was again in an old house with menace thickening in its shadows, and he was watching a girl walk down a stairway. The girl he had been powerless to help, even though he had known, and she had known, that she and her entire family were walking to their brutal deaths.

Tanwen had been annoyed when the storm came grumbling in, because her new frock might be spoiled, and also the rain would cause her hair to come loose, and it would stand out around her face like a mist, which was very unfashionable and not the look she wanted to present to Yan Orzek.

She had waited in the square outside the Library, finding a corner that gave her a view of the main doors, and watching everyone coming out. Bruno and Alicja were together, Bruno talking and waving his hands as he described something. Then came Anatol, with the two waitresses. They carried large bags, which probably meant they had liberated some of tonight's food. Tanwen did not care if they had ransacked the entire kitchen, providing they left her way clear to get to Yan.

It looked as if everyone had gone and as if it would be safe to go back inside. She had it all planned. When she found Yan – or when he came to see who was there – she would tell him that she had got halfway to her lodgings when she realized that she had left her bag in the musicians' room. Her latch-key and her purse and everything was inside it, she would say, and she had run all the way back, praying he would not have locked everywhere up and left. She would be apologetic and breathless.

Then, of course, it would be natural to walk with him through the silent, shadowy old building, making it easy to brush against him. She was aware of a shiver of delight at how it would feel if he took her hand. Earlier, she had looked into the smaller reception rooms that were kept for entertaining guests and for Trust meetings. Two of them had deep sofas with plump soft cushions. *Very* suitable. And the Ivory Salon itself had deep chaise longues set against the walls, once reserved for really eminent guests. Tanwen smiled even more at the thought of that. This was going to be a memorable night.

She turned up her coat collar, and sped across the square, skipping across the puddles, going towards the side door which Yan generally used. There was a heart-stopping moment when she thought it was locked, and that after all she had missed him, but the handle turned, and she was inside.

At first she thought he was not here, after all. The door of the Ivory Salon was closed, and the reception rooms at the back of the building were in darkness. But he might be upstairs in the rehearsal room, so Tanwen crossed the hall and went up the stairs. This was all starting to feel slightly creepy, but she walked along the landing, glancing down over the gilt railings into the big hall below. It was then that she heard the music coming from the Ivory Salon.

At first she did not recognize it, and then, quite suddenly, she did. There had been a fossilized old professor at the Academy who had had a passion for Russian composers. His lectures had been unbelievably boring, but Tanwen had gone to them all and made notes, because you never knew when things might come in useful. A couple of those lectures came in useful now, because she was able to identify this music. It was from an opera by Anton Rubinstein called *The Demon*, and this was the Demon's own aria. It was called 'Don't cry for me, my child', and it was the demon's farewell to the doomed heroine. Tanwen supposed it was all very dramatic and that it made for good theatre, but to her mind a few fireworks from Mozart or Tchaikovsky were far more effective. Some lively swing or ragtime that you could dance to was even better.

It sounded as if the pianist – and of course it was Yan – was wrapped in his own world as he played. What if Tanwen were to enter that world, by way of the music? She was fairly sure she could remember most of the words of the aria. She began to descend the stair, singing as she did so. Father had always said she had the sweetest, purest voice he had ever heard. It was as well he could not see her using that sweet, pure voice in these circumstances.

The music stopped, as abruptly as if someone had slammed

a lid down on it. The door of the salon opened, and Yan stood there, framed against the storm light.

Tanwen went on singing, sliding into a later verse because she could not remember the second one, but managing to blur the words without losing the melody.

She went towards him, her hands outstretched, but he seemed frozen to the spot and almost bewildered. She still had the story of the forgotten bag ready to produce, but it was looking as if it would not be necessary, so, because there were times when it was a good idea to take the initiative, she went up to him, wound her arms around his neck, and pressed against him. His body responded at once – there was no mistaking it.

In a soft voice, deliberately giving him the title that clothed him in such authority, Tanwen said, 'Maestro – isn't it about time you stopped fighting with me? And that we went to bed?'

How they reached the Ivory Salon, Tanwen was never, afterwards, sure, but somehow they were there, and he was clinging to her as if he would never let her go. And then there was the feel of the silk covers of one of the couches, and the cushions had fallen around them, and he was kissing her so fiercely she thought she might faint. Tanwen, who had certainly not expected quite this level of reaction, found her own senses leaping to respond, and she pulled him against her, taking his hands and sliding them beneath the folds of her evening frock. He gasped, and said something in a language she did not recognize, but she did not care what language he was using, because it was as if an explosion was happening between them, and she would not bear it if he drew away from her.

Through the soaring waves of passion, she had a distant memory of having intended this to be a light, one- or two-night affair – of how she could then boast that she had enslaved the maestro. But there was nothing light about this – in fact it felt as if it might be Tanwen herself who was being enslaved, and if he did not make love to her properly, this very moment, she might faint from sheer longing.

There was a moment when he drew back, as if suddenly unsure whether he dared go on, but Tanwen reached down to enclose him with her hand, and he cried out. Somehow their clothes were discarded – she thought there was even the sound of the silk of her dress tearing slightly, which could not have mattered less by this time.

When at last he entered her, the room blurred and almost seemed to recede, and she understood with dazzling clarity that all those fumblings and bouncings with other men had been as nothing. This was real – it was what the poets wrote about and the music-makers sung about and it was what the painters tried to depict on their canvases . . .

There was no longer any sense of their being two separate beings, nor was there any sense of time. When finally he cried out and gave a helpless thrust and Tanwen felt the passion drain from him, it might have been ten minutes or ten hours or ten years since they had fallen, entwined, on the sofa.

His head fell against her bare shoulder, his hair like silk on her skin. She managed to turn her head to look down at him, and saw the faint sheen of sweat on his eyelids, and she tightened her hold on him and wanted to stay like this for ever.

He turned his head on the satin cushions and looked at her, and faint unease brushed her skin, because his eyes were dark and unreadable, and there was something wrong – something different about him.

Then he said, 'I've reached you. I've saved you. I knew one day I would.' He touched her hair, and said, softly, 'Sunset shining through autumn leaves. It's how I always thought of you. Katya tried to help you – did you ever know that? But she couldn't do it.' He tried to sit up, looking about him, and with increasing concern Tanwen saw he was not recognizing his surroundings.

Who was he talking about? What was all this about sunset hair and somebody called Katya trying to save someone? Tanwen pulled him back so that he was facing her again.

'Yan,' she said, speaking as calmly as she could, 'Yan, who is Katya?'

He stared at her, and she saw he did not recognize her, either.

'Yan – it's me – Tanwen. We're in the Ivory Salon – in the Chopin Library.'

He looked round again, and his eyes seemed to clear a little.

'Yes,' he said, still in the same faraway voice. 'We're in the Chopin Library. I see that.'

The distant look was fading from his eyes, but he still seemed to be a long way from her.

Tanwen tried again. 'Yan – you said Katya tried to save someone. Who is Katya?'

He turned to look at her, and for a terrible moment a picture seemed to light up, as if the lightning had flickered across it. It printed itself on Tanwen's mind, and it was the picture of a young woman crouching in a deep, dark place, sobbing and shivering . . . There was a candle flame, casting wild shadows on dripping stone walls . . . And Yan's face, lit from below by the candle's light, staring down at the young woman . . .

A sick horror was starting to sweep over Tanwen, but she gripped his hands. 'Tell me. Yan, tell me about Katya.'

Yan said, 'Katya . . .' And then, 'I murdered her.'

SEVENTEEN

1918

Father Gregory had said, as he and Yan sat together in the shadowy church overlooking Ipatiev House, that there were only a few hours left for them in Katerinburg.

Yan had not dared ask where the two of them would go after all this, in case they were simply going to walk and walk until they reached somewhere safe, or until one of them dropped from exhaustion. Instead, he obediently put together things for the journey in a kind of carpetbag, and tried not to count how many hours Katya and the other girl had been in the cold darkness.

Gregory would not let him help with Vadim's body, and Yan was guiltily grateful. He did not know how he would have borne to look again at the cold dead thing that had once been Vadim. He would never be able to forget him, though, and he knew that, despite his promise, he would keep the music – the

'*Temnaya Kadentsiya*' – that Vadim had given him in those last moments. It was like a talisman, a tiny memory of the father he should have known for longer. But Father Gregory could be trusted to do everything that should be done for Vadim's body. Yan knew he could trust him, in the same way he had known he could trust Vadim himself.

And in the same way he had known he could trust Katya.

Katya.

He was frantic to get to her, but when he climbed to the top of the bell tower and looked down over the walls of Ipatiev House, the guards were still around. He would never get past them, and even if he did, he would never get Katya past them without being seen. But he could not leave her . . .

'The guards won't be there much longer,' said Father Gregory. 'There's no reason for them to keep patrolling the grounds – Ipatiev House is no longer a prison.' Almost to himself, he said, 'The Bolsheviks' goal has been achieved.'

Yan understood that he meant the Romanovs had all been executed. All of them, including his copper-haired girl who had sung so bravely as they were dragged to their deaths. You would have been brave to the last, he said silently to her memory. And I will never forget you.

'Once we see the guards have stopped marching around,' said Father Gregory, 'we'll go back in the house.'

'How? We can't just walk up to the door and ask to be let in.'

'We'll use the tunnel Vadim made under the corner of the wall. It should still be there.'

'He scooped it out of the earth,' said Yan. 'And he covered it with branches and leaves to hide where the ground was disturbed.'

'Then, please God, it's still covered,' said Gregory. 'Stay at the top of the bell tower, and when you see the guards have gone, come and tell me.'

A thin light was streaking the sky when finally the guards stopped their ceaseless patrolling. Yan watched for a little longer to be sure, then sped down the stairs to where Gregory was kneeling before the altar. He waited for Gregory to look up, then said, quietly, that he thought it was safe to get into the house now. He tried not to sound too urgent about it, because of this being a church, but it was something they had to do quickly.

Father Gregory understood at once. He made a kind of semi-bow to the altar, as if politely ending a conversation, then took Yan's hand to lead him out of the church. As they reached the door, he paused. 'We'll need a light of some kind, Yan. It would be very dark in that place?'

'Yes, but there'll be candles just inside.'

'Take my tinder box in case you need it,' said Gregory, going quickly into a small room near the church's main doors. 'And for the love of all the angels, don't drop it, for it'll clang like the sounding of the Last Trump. And now,' he said, as they went outside, 'we must walk across the street openly and without seeming furtive, because that would attract attention. You are one of my pupils and we are taking an early morning walk after our devotions, and we are a little curious about Ipatiev House. All that is natural.'

Yan had been worried that he would not be able to find the tunnel that Vadim had made – or that it would have been discovered and filled in by the guards – but as they walked around the high walls he saw it.

'Just there.' He dared not point in case anyone was watching. 'You stay here, Father, while I go in.'

'Of course you aren't going in there on your own—'

Yan said, very politely, 'Father, two of us might be noticed. But I've lived here, and Zena and the others might not know that I ran away. They'd think it was normal to see me.' He could not believe he was talking like this to a priest, but he knew he was right. The moment lengthened, then he said, 'Also, Father . . .' He broke off and glanced down at the narrow indented section of ground.

'Also,' said Father Gregory, smiling, 'you're doubtful as to whether I could squeeze under there and be sufficiently agile to sprint through the gardens. You're right. I might be more of a danger than a help. But if you aren't back here within an hour, I'll find a way to come in and get you.' A hand came out and rested lightly on Yan's head for a moment. 'God be with you,' he said. 'Your father called you an exceptional child, and he was right. I'll be waiting here when you come out, and I'll be praying it will be with your mother.'

My mother. Katya.

Yan did not trust himself to speak, so he just nodded, and dropped flat on the ground to squeeze through the narrow space.

The dawn light was starting to touch the trees and the stones of Ipatiev House, but there was still a strange, other-world quality everywhere.

There did not seem to be anyone about, but as Yan went through the gardens, he stayed in the shelter of the trees. It was very quiet. There was the occasional chirrup of birdsong, but that was all. He came out of the trees, and saw the garden door ahead. He could be there within a minute if he ran. But would the door be locked? He had left it unlocked when he fled into the night with the guards giving chase, but would anyone have locked it since? Yan was trusting that there had been so much turmoil within the house, it would not have occurred to anyone to see if a small back door was locked. If it was locked, he would see if he could break a window and climb through, because he was not going to have got this far to turn back.

He took a deep breath and began to run forward. His feet made hardly any sound, but with every step he expected to hear shouts and to see guards spring out and seize him. But nothing moved, and he reached the door, and, his heart pounding in his chest, grasped the handle. Please let it turn, *please* . . .

It was all right. The handle turned and the door opened when he pushed it, and he was inside the familiar scullery with its scents of food and the shapes of the tables and chairs – there was Zena's chair, where the guard had sat last night – and there was the door to his own little room, still partly open, as he had left it. No one was here, but soon people would be coming downstairs – at any moment someone might come in.

He crossed the room and opened the larder door, and the blackness reared up almost as if it was a solid wall. He had been prepared for that, though, and he left the door slightly open behind him so that he could see to get a candle. Here they were, exactly where they always were; a box of thick tallow candles. He thrust two in his pocket and, trying not to let his hands shake, he managed to strike a light from the tinderbox to fire a third. The small flame came up from the candle, and Yan wrapped a bit of rag around it so it would not scorch his fingers. In his mind he was calling to Katya that he was almost with her, that she would be soon out and they would get away. Just another few minutes . . .

Again, he tried to work out how long the two of them had been in there, but time had become blurred. Had it been last night? No, it had been the night before last, because he and Father Gregory had sat with Vadim for most of yesterday. That was a long time. But they had had light and food and the flagon of milk.

As he made a cautious way through the stone larder, the shadows made by the candle flame leapt and danced on the walls. They were quite small shadows, because the candle flame was small, and Yan tried not to think they formed them-selves into prowling shapes, like creeping goblins. There were goblins in some of the stories in the book Katya had found. They would read those stories together again – he would believe that they would.

The back of the larder with the stone wall and the hidden panel seemed much farther than he had remembered, but he went determinedly on, moving slowly so as not to dislodge anything from the shelves, or trip over the bags of flour and rye on the ground and make a noise that would bring people running. There was the sound of water dripping from some-where; it formed a kind of rhythm – a light, creeping pattern, as if the shadows really were goblins, coming after him on their bony goblin feet. He turned sharply, holding up the candle. Had something dodged back out of sight? No, there was nothing except the lumpen sacks sagging against the walls, and the rows of jars and flagons on the shelves.

And here, at last, was the stone wall – the wall that looked like the blank end of the larder itself, but was not. All he had to do was feel across the surface for the fingerholes, and pull the stone out. And please, oh please, let them both be all right.

He tilted the candle carefully so that some melted tallow ran on to the ground, set the candle in this, and turned to the stone slab. His heart was hammering in his chest, and he realized he was whispering a prayer. Then he felt the chiselled holes, and he was pulling on the stone. It did not resist this time; it scraped against the sides, then came free. A breath of cold sour dankness came at Yan, and he set the stone on the ground. But as he did so, the light from the candle fell across it, and to his horror he saw that there were long scratch marks on the inside of the stone. As if fingernails had scrabbled frantically at the surface – fingernails belonging to someone trying to dislodge the stone from inside to get out.

For a terrible moment Yan could not move. He was too terrified to lift the candle to look inside the yawning blackness, but he was even more afraid to run away.

Somehow he managed to pick up the candle, and, still shaking violently, he thrust it through the gaping hole. Please let there be some movement – some sound – something to say they're still alive.

There was no sound and no movement. The candle flame flickered wildly again, making fantastical shapes on the enclosed space, as if some monstrous insect was darting back and forth. And there was a wild, joy-filled moment when he thought they were not in there, and with that moment came a rush of gratitude, because they must have managed to dislodge the stone from inside, after all. They had been able to push it through, and they had climbed out, replacing the stone so no one would know anything. But even as these hopes were forming, he knew they could not have got out. The stone could only be moved from the outside, and Yan was positive that no one knew it was there. Even if anyone had, there was no reason why they would come in here to remove it.

He moved the candle again, and a cold dread closed around his heart. He heard his voice murmuring, 'No – oh, no . . .'

They were there. They were huddled together in a kind of scooped-out oblong in the floor, Katya's arms wound around the girl from behind, both of them facing the same way. The girl's face was turned upwards, towards the panel. Watching for it to move, thought Yan, sick with the horror of it. Waiting to see a light show around the edges, waiting to be rescued, because their own attempts to get out had failed. Even though they clawed at the stone they couldn't dislodge it . . . I was so much longer than they expected – were they hungry, thirsty? But I left them with food and milk.

There was a dreadful whiteness to their faces, and their eyes were open and staring. But the worst thing of all – the terrible nightmare thing that would stay with Yan if he lived to be a hundred – was that they both looked old. *Old.* Withered and shrunken and dried out, as if something had sucked all the moisture from them. As he stood there, unable to move, he began to be aware of something he had not seen earlier. The candlelight was showing up a glassy whiteness in sections of the walls. It was within the floor, as well, and straw was strewn across it. Yan frowned, at first not understanding. And then, with a rush, he realized that the whiteness within the walls was ice. *Ice.* It must have been chiselled from the ground in winter, and brought in here to form an ice room. This would be where the people who had once lived here had stored their rich food and their wine to keep it cool and fresh.

He had shut his beloved Katya – his mother – and her good friend who had tried to rescue the Romanovs, inside an ice room. They had had light and food and drink, but it had not helped them, because they had died by freezing to death.

'You did nothing wrong,' said Father Gregory, as Yan huddled in a corner of the church, sobbing and shivering. 'You were brave beyond the bravery of almost any child I can think of – of most grown men, in fact. You tried to help them, and you had no evil intent. If they had been caught, the Bolsheviks would have executed them anyway. Yan, you must believe this wasn't your fault. No one would ever blame you. Katya – your mother – she would never blame you.'

Yan said, 'But if I had gone back sooner—'

'You couldn't. The guards were everywhere. They would have stopped you – perhaps killed you as a tsarist spy, young as you are.'

Don't forget that they killed the tsar's children . . .

'But if I had found somewhere else to hide them—'

'There was nowhere else.' Gregory was holding Yan's hands in his, and Yan felt a faint, far-off warm comfort. 'It would have been a gentle death,' he said, although his voice wavered as he said this, and Yan had no idea whether to believe him, or even if Gregory believed it himself. 'A gentle death,' he said, more firmly. 'They would have slipped into a deep sleep – and then a deeper one. And from that into death itself.'

It was impossible to say: But they clawed at the inside of the stone first to try to get out. To say, They *knew* what was going to happen. Instead, Yan sat up and managed to wipe his tears with the handkerchief Father Gregory handed him.

'They were huddled together, Father Gregory. Katya was behind the other girl . . .' Tears welled up again as he remembered he had never known the girl's name, and this was bad, because people should have their names remembered after they were dead. He said, 'Katya's arms were wound around her shoulders, but – but her head had fallen forward on to the girl's . . .'

As he broke off, Father Gregory said a strange thing. Very softly, he said, '"Two souls frozen in one hole, so close that one's head served as the other's hood."'

Yan stared at him. 'Yes,' he said. 'Yes, that's exactly what it looked like. As if she – the girl – was almost *wearing* Katya as a cloak with a hood. How did you know?'

'I didn't. The words are by Dante.' Then, as Yan looked at him, not understanding, he said, 'Dante Alighieri. He was an Italian poet, and he depicted heaven, hell and purgatory in a very long poem. In one section, he describes hell, and those are the words he uses to portray the fate that's reserved in hell for—'

'For what? Who?'

'For traitors.'

Traitors. That word again. And two nights ago, the guard had said of Katya that she was a traitor to her own kind, and a traitor to the Bolshevik cause. He had said the crowd beyond the walls of Ipatiev House were playing the 'Traitor's Music' for her. Vadim, giving the music itself to Yan, had called it the 'Dark Cadence', and had said it was vicious and old, and that Yan must destroy it. But I won't, thought Yan, fiercely. It's all I have of those two. I won't destroy the music because it's a memory. If I keep the music always, it will mean I keep the memory of my parents.

*   *   *

They were ready to set off on their journey almost at once. They dared not stay any longer, Father Gregory said. They would try to get to Poland; it was a long journey, but there would be places to stop and rest on the way – churches, religious houses. And once in Poland, there would be people – people within the Church – who would certainly give sanctuary and help.

Sanctuary. It was a good word. A word to hold on to, a word to take on their journey, together with the small memories.

Memories . . . There was another memory he had brought out of the house this morning.

He had felt as if he was walking through a nightmare when he came back into the scullery. Without thinking he made for the garden door, and then stopped, and darted back to the stone steps that led up to the hall. No one was about. This was incredibly dangerous, but it would not take long.

The door to what he had always thought of as the Silk Room was slightly open, and, glancing about him, he stepped through it. Incredibly, the room looked exactly as it always had done. Yan could not believe it did not bear some imprint of what had happened in this house, but the drapes hung in the same soft folds at the windows and the chairs were all in their places. The piano stood open, the silk-covered stool drawn up to it, as if someone might walk in and sit down and play. One day I'll know how to do that . . . I'll be able to read the strange marks on the paper that are music. And on the desk, the pale brocade curtains behind it, were the miniatures.

She smiled from the ivory surface and it was an untroubled smile, with no shadow cast by what was lying in wait for her. Her hair had been allowed to flow loose for the painting, and it rippled on to her shoulders. Autumn leaves and polished copper, and sunset shining through trees. Beautiful. The miniature was so small he could put it in his pocket, and no one would ever know – probably no one would even notice it had gone. He looked round the room. In the far corner, in a glass-fronted cupboard, were rows of books, most of the titles visible in the soft morning light. The memory of Katya smuggling those books into the scullery, one at a time, and reading the stories, came strongly to him. How difficult would it be to take those, too? How heavy would it be to carry them? But I'd be taking something of you with me, he said to Katya in his mind, and with this thought he went over to open the cupboard. Impossible to take all the books, of course, but there were just six that Katya had read from, and they were not especially large . . . He seized one of the silk drapes lying across the back of a chair, and folded the books inside it, knotting the corners.

You'll both be with me now, he thought. Katya, when I open these books, I'll hear your voice reading to me, laughing, pretending to be the different people in the stories.

In his pocket was the miniature. You'll always be with me too, he said to the painted image. I'll always have that memory of you singing as you walked to your death and the deaths of your parents and your sisters and your brother.

EIGHTEEN

Warsaw, late 1930s

Yan had no memory of leaving the Chopin Library after Tanwen had run out into the night, or of going through the streets. He only knew that he found himself in his own rooms near the Street of Music, and that he had opened the box containing the miniature taken from Ipatiev House all those years ago. His emotions were in turmoil. I thought you had come back to me, he said, holding the miniature between his hands, and looking at the painted features. I thought I had been able to go back and that this time I could save you.

The memory of the girl had never left him – just as the memories of Katya and Vadim had never left him, but he had known who Katya and Vadim were. He had never known which of the tsar's four daughters his girl had been. Olga, Tatiana, Maria? Or Anastasia? It was tempting to allot to her Anastasia's identity, of course – the stories told that Anastasia had been the mischievous one of the four, the one most likely to cause disruption. If Yan could believe his girl had been Anastasia, it would mean he could call up the vague rumours and stories that she had escaped the Bolsheviks and was living in safe, secret exile somewhere. He did not really think those stories were more than romantic legends, though.

Growing up, managing, with Father Gregory's help and encouragement, to study music, there had been good times – friendships with like-minded people with whom he could share music and conversation and companionship. There had certainly been nights when he had not slept in a solitary bed, as well. The trouble was that the emotions of those nights – even the most intense of them – never lasted. He sometimes thought it was because none of the young women with whom he spent extremely pleasant nights, could ever match up to his sunset-haired girl.

Once he had asked Father Gregory whether he would stay in Poland. Gregory only said, 'I go where God's work takes me. But we won't lose one another, Yan.'

Yan was determined they would not, and they had not done so. Gregory had rooms in the city – Yan was always welcome there. He hoped that one day he might find a way of repaying Father Gregory for all he had done. They seldom mentioned Katerinburg and Ipatiev House, and after a time Yan found it easier to keep the memories banked down.

And then Tanwen Malek came to the Chopin Library, and those fleeting resemblances to Yan's lost Romanov girl – the way the sun lit her hair to copper; the way she had been able to sing the 'Demon's aria' – had resulted in that astonishing, explosive love-making. It had been as if something had spun him back to that night inside Ipatiev House, and from out of that spinning confusion had come the damning admission. It had been dredged up from the deepest level of his mind, but Yan knew it had always been there. Guilt. I killed Katya.

He had seldom looked at the thought, and he had certainly never voiced the fear. But tonight he had done so. Tonight he had told Tanwen that he had committed murder.

Once outside the Chopin Library, Tanwen had run through the dark streets, not noticing that it was still raining, not seeing the darkened streets or the tall buildings with their shuttered windows. All she saw was that image that had seemed to come from Yan's mind and print itself on to her own mind. The girl helpless in the cold darkness, trapped and terrified. And Yan looking down at her, his face lit from below by the light of a single flickering candle.

Katya . . . I murdered her . . .

It was only when she reached her lodging house that she realized she was soaked to the skin from the pelting rain. She pulled off all her things, thrusting the black evening frock into the back of the wardrobe. She would never want to wear it again, because it would always hold the memory of how Yan had unfastened it, and how he had peeled it back from her skin, his eyes dark with passion and longing . . .

She wrapped herself in her dressing gown and sat down on the bed, shivering violently. Tonight she had allowed a murderer to make love to her – no, she would be honest, she had seduced a murderer, and the fact that she had not known what he was did not seem to matter.

After a while she managed to boil a kettle for a cup of tea and filled a hot-water bottle. She had a bed-sitting room and a minuscule kitchen at the very top of the house. Father had heard about the lodging house from somebody, and he said there were rooms she could have there which sounded very suitable. At the time, Tanwen had supposed the rooms would be all right until she could find something better – not realizing that it was as difficult to find rooms in Warsaw as it was to buy new clothes. There was also the point that Father was paying the rent here, which perhaps he would refuse to do for somewhere he had not found for her. This was a large consideration.

She was about to get into bed when she saw that a note had been pushed under her door. It was from the landlady, saying that the Exchange had telephoned to say the person-to-person call booked for Miss Malek would be connected tomorrow morning at eleven o'clock, rather than the ten o'clock time originally requested. The landlady added a note at the bottom to say she would ask Miss Malek to kindly be downstairs in the hall to take the call, because she could not be running up and down the stairs all the time like an errand boy. Her writing looked like her – it was thin and spare.

Tanwen wondered if she would have stopped shivering in time to take Father's phone call. Then she tried to think if there was a rehearsal scheduled for tomorrow, and was deeply thankful to remember there was not. She had no idea how she was going to face Yan – she had no idea if she even wanted to face him. This feeling, along with having remembered that there was no rehearsal tomorrow, made her feel desperately lonely. Always before a rehearsal had been the fun of planning what she would wear, and how she could attract Yan's attention.

She would never do any of that again.

By morning she was still shivering, and her stomach was churning with misery. Perhaps getting drenched on the way from the Library might have caused her to get influenza or something, which would at least mean she could send a perfectly genuine message to the Library that she was unwell, and could not attend any forthcoming rehearsals for a while.

She got dressed, putting on two thick sweaters, and at five minutes to eleven went down to the draughty hall and sat on a hard, uncomfortable chair by the coat-stand to wait for the call. Somehow she would have to put on a bright and happy front for her father, and tell him about the concert, which seemed to have happened a very long time ago. Perhaps the call would not come in, though; the telephone service was increasingly erratic.

But the call did come, and there was Father's voice, wanting to know all about the concert – how Tanwen's performance had been received, how many people had been in the audience. Had she met any of them afterwards, and were they important people who might be of use to her career?

Tanwen reeled off a few names, managing to give the impression that she had talked at considerable length with them all. Local dignitaries, she told Father, airily. They had all been very friendly and nice, she said, and of course there had been supper, with the ritual of Lighting the *Mrożony Polonez*. She told him how Anatol had made a splendid entrance, beaming with delight, and how it was a very old tradition, and there was supposed to be an old boarded-up staircase going below the mansion. The ceremony had originally made use of that old staircase, said Tanwen, but nobody used it now, of course.

Father was very interested in this. He wanted to know whether Tanwen had ever heard where the staircase might have been, but she did not.

'Bruno – Bruno Sicora, that is – said we should all look for it sometime, but I don't know if he meant it.'

Father asked if it had been a late evening, and hoped she had not had to walk home on her own. Tanwen heard her mother's voice call out something at this, and Father chuckled, then said, 'We're really wanting to ask if anyone saw you home. Anyone special, that is.'

Tanwen tried not to wince at the sudden sly coyness in Father's voice, because no matter what either of them said, he would not really want her to have had the intimacy of being walked home in the dark. And if he had the smallest suspicion of what had happened last night, he would come steaming in and threaten to flog Yan. He would use outdated terms like seducer and libertine, and it would all be too embarrassing for words. He belonged to the nineteenth century, and it was a constant source of surprise to Tanwen that he had allowed her to go off to the Academy to study music, never mind coming to live in Warsaw on her own.

In answer to his questions, she managed to say that several of them had left the Library together.

'And your director? Mr Orzek? Was he with you?'

It came as a shock to hear Father refer to Yan almost as if he knew him. Tanwen said, 'He stayed behind.' This was true, at any rate.

'In that big old mansion? On his own?' Father sounded surprised. 'Does he often do that?'

'I think so,' said Tanwen. 'He works very late. He doesn't seem to mind being there by himself.'

As she rang off, she thought it was a bit odd that Father had been interested in Yan. But of course he was interested in everything about Tanwen's life in Warsaw.

Yan's note, the following day, said:

Dear Tanwen,
I was so sorry to hear from your landlady (who called at the Library earlier) that you're unwell – possibly with an

attack of influenza – and that it seems to have started on the night of our concert. Perhaps that isn't very surprising – it was a strange, unexpected evening.

If you would like to talk to me about that night, please will you let me know. Also, if there are any aspects about your work and your future with the Library that you feel we need to discuss – or that might benefit from explanations of any kind – again, don't hesitate to get in touch.

I send you my very best wishes, and hope you will quickly recover.

Yan

It was a note anyone could have read, but Tanwen knew Yan wanted her to read beyond what he had actually written. She knew he wanted to give her some kind of explanation for those words. *Katya . . . I murdered her . . .* Was there an explanation, though? And would she be able to believe whatever he told her, anyway? Thinking about it made her head ache and made her feel sick, and for the moment it was easier to lie on her bed and just be ill.

Father telephoned several times, concerned and wanting to be reassured that she was all right. Influenza could be extremely nasty, he said. He would try to visit her, although travel was becoming so very difficult. Her mother was nervous at the very thought of it – she only really felt safe in their small village these days. But if there was anything Tanwen needed, she must tell him, and they would find a way of getting it to her.

'There's nothing,' said Tanwen, managing to sit on the uncomfortable hall chair for the duration of the call, and wishing he would hang up. 'I'm getting better, honestly I am. And Irina – the landlady here – is being very kind.'

This was true, if surprising. Irina had brought up trays of food and bowls of broth. She sometimes stayed to talk, and once or twice she brought a newspaper, so that Tanwen could know what was happening in the world.

Tanwen did not care what was happening in the world. She did not want to know about the hateful war, which was not only killing people by the thousand, but was likely to spoil her whole life. Whatever happened with Yan and the Chopin Library, the world was changing, and it might change so much that she would never reach those concert halls that Father had always insisted were her due.

She tried not to read stories about all the people who were taken away to labour camps, and the mass executions that went on if the Gestapo unearthed what they believed to be nests of rebels and dissidents.

Irina said that the way things were going, Tanwen was better remaining inside the house for a time. Rumours were even circulating that parts of Warsaw were going to be demolished – blown up or burned – before much longer. People would be sent notices telling them that their homes or offices or shops were scheduled for burning and that they must leave. Probably it was all only speculation and even a new form of propaganda, said Irina, but she was going to pray she never received such a notice, and that she never heard the tramp of marching feet in the street outside, or the midnight knock on the door.

Tanwen nodded, remembering what Alicja had said about the soldiers' boots sounding like huge steel claws, and their marching seeming to be some huge monster prowling the streets, scratching at doors for victims. She told Irina she would also pray that the soldiers did not come to this house or to this street.

But a short time afterwards she found herself praying for something very different.

In the Ivory Salon with Yan, Tanwen had been in the grip of such intense passions that she had not given a thought to consequences. She thought neither of them had. Even if the thought of what was sometimes called nature's cheat – that hasty scramble to uncouple at the last moment – had occurred to them, she did not think they could have achieved it. They had both been too far lost in their emotions.

But now it seemed that nature was having her revenge.

Tanwen was at first disbelieving that such a thing could have happened on one single encounter; she tried to think she had miscalculated dates, or that she was simply upset by the whole thing. And the situation in Warsaw was enough to send anybody's monthly rhythms off balance, on its own account anyway.

But a tiny part of her knew the truth, and panic began to take

over. Several times, she tried to think she would have to tell
Yan and that perhaps he would marry her, but she knew she
could not do it. How could she marry a murderer? And equally,
how could she bear to watch a child grow up knowing what its
father was?

There were things you could try to get yourself out of this
particular predicament, of course. Scaldingly hot baths. Gin.
But the bathroom in the lodging house was a very basic one,
and the hot water was unreliable, to the point of being non-
existent for much of the time. You had to boil kettles and sit
in the enamel tub in the kitchen. And gin, gulped shudderingly
down in large quantities, only made Tanwen even more sick.
She tried to be quiet about that in case her landlady heard and
asked awkward questions, but the most ladylike person could
not be sick in complete silence, and of course Irina heard. She
came up to the room after the fourth bout, giving a perfunctory
knock on the door, and coming into the bedroom where Tanwen
was huddled miserably over a basin, retching and gasping.

'You've fallen, haven't you?' said Irina, accusingly. 'You've
been with some man, and now you've got to face the shame.'

It was not something that could be hidden for ever, so Tanwen
nodded, helplessly.

'Won't he marry you? Or is he married already?'

'He isn't married. But there are things about him – I can't
marry him.' Tanwen could not go on, but thankfully Irina did
not push for more.

She sat down in a corner of the room, frowning, as if trying
to solve a problem. Tanwen supposed there would be a tirade
of disapproval, and probably a request to leave the lodging
house there and then. What would happen to her in that
situation?

Then astonishingly, Irina said, 'I'll help you.'

Tanwen had stopped being sick, and she managed to sit up,
and stare at Irina.

'I can't help you to get rid of it, and I wouldn't even if I
could,' went on Irina. 'Is that understood?'

'Yes.'

'We could let it be thought you've gone back to your family,'
she said.

'I can't possibly do that—'

'No, I know you can't. But you wouldn't actually go. You'd stay here – although you'd have to remain virtually in hiding until after the birth. But it could be done. And then afterwards . . . I suppose it will have to be adoption.'

Something deep in Tanwen flinched at the thought of giving away Yan's son or daughter, but she could not see what else to do, so she said, 'There must be good families who've lost a child to the war. People who'd be grateful to adopt a baby.'

'I might be able to help with that, as well.'

'I could pay you,' said Tanwen, at once. Father made her a small allowance, so even if she left the Library she would have money. She might even ask for a bit more – Father could always be twisted round her little finger, everyone had always said so. But one thing had to be made very clear, so she said to Irina, 'My father must never know about any of this. Will you promise me you won't let him find out?'

'You have my word that he'll never know.'

'Supposing he comes here before the birth, though? He doesn't often come to Warsaw – and it's so difficult now – but he's done so in the past. He might do so again.'

In a voice Tanwen had never heard anyone use ever, Irina said, 'Georg Malek will never come to this house.' She paused, then said, 'And if he does, I will certainly kill him.'

NINETEEN

Lucek woke in the White Hart's comfortable bed to the sound of taps running in the small bathroom. He had no idea how he would manage to greet the others when they met up in the dining room for breakfast. Would he be able to say 'Good morning' in a completely ordinary tone? Would he blush furiously if anyone asked, in complete innocence, if he had spent a comfortable night? He was just wondering whether it might be easier to miss breakfast altogether, even though he was actually very hungry, when Nina came out of

the bathroom, wrapped in a towel, her hair pinned on top of
her head. She looked marvellous. Even with strands of damp
hair clinging to her neck, she looked so wonderful that Lucek
forgot about breakfast and stopped worrying about how he
would answer questions.

'The water's beautifully hot,' she said, sitting on the edge of
the bed. 'But I'm sorry if I disturbed you.'

Lucek considered whether he could say that she had caused
him to be very disturbed indeed several times during the night,
but he could not think how to put this without it sounding a bit
wince-making. So he said that if she had finished, he would
have his own shower, and then he supposed it would be time
to go down to breakfast.

'It's not quite eight o'clock yet,' said Nina. 'And the dining
room notice says they serve breakfast until nine.'

She looked at him, mischief in her eyes, and Lucek said,
'That means we don't need to go downstairs for at least half
an hour.'

'Well, it does. But you were going to have a shower . . .'

'I'll allow ten minutes for that later,' said Lucek, pulling her
back into bed.

The professor and Dr Purslove had gone together into the White
Hart's dining room for breakfast. Scrambled eggs and bacon
were set out on hot plates on an old-fashioned sideboard,
together with mushrooms and grilled tomatoes. The toast was
freshly made, and the pot of coffee brought to them was piping
hot. It was extremely pleasant to be enjoying this very good
breakfast and to speculate on the meeting with Thaisa Wyngham
later on. That was going to be very interesting. The professor
had made notes of points to discuss, but Dr Purslove was inclined
to go for spontaneity and see where the conversation went.

Helping himself to toast, he looked round the dining room,
then said, 'There's Phin and Arabella coming in. I don't see
Lucek or Nina yet. I suppose they'll be down fairly soon, though.'

'I shouldn't think they will,' said Professor Liripine. 'Not
yet, anyway.'

'Pass the marmalade, will you. Why won't they be down
yet?'

'Theodore,' said the professor, 'you can be unbelievably naïve at times.'

Dr Purslove stared at him. 'You don't mean to say that Nina and that boy—'

'Almost certainly.'

'Well, I'm . . . But there must be at least twelve, if not fifteen years between them.'

'When did twelve or fifteen years between two people matter?' demanded the professor, pouring himself a second cup of coffee.

'Well, it doesn't, it's just that I didn't think . . . He's a very nice boy, of course,' said Dr Purslove.

'He is. And,' said Professor Liripine, 'I daresay Nina will have taught him a thing or two since last night.'

Dr Purslove was unable to decide if Ernest had smiled reminiscently when he said this.

On Sunday Thaisa got up very early, and from ten o'clock onwards alternated between the kitchen to make sure the food was all right, the dining room to check nothing had been forgotten for the table, and the window to watch for a car.

She had spent most of Saturday cooking the chicken casserole, consulting the recipe every step of the way, and tasting it at anxious intervals. She had bought a corkscrew and practised using it on a cheap bottle of fruit juice, and she thought she would manage the wine all right. The house was cleaned to within an inch of its life, and she had put specially bought scented soap and fresh hand towels in the little cloakroom by the front door.

But all through these preparations the fear was ramping up, because in the hours ahead the past might be broken open, and the secrets might come spilling out. And Thaisa had no idea what these secrets might be. She knew about the Nazi connection and, on their own admission, her parents had been murderers, but what else might there be? She had never been able to entirely forget her mother's words. *It was a bad way for them to die . . .*

But whatever it was, it can't matter after so long, thought Thaisa, frantically. Whatever those things were, they happened before I was born. No one would care now.

You'd care, though . . . And you'd care if people knew that you brought about your parents' deaths – and that you covered up your mother's suicide . . . That you lied about her death, and took the insurance payment when the policy specifically said it wouldn't pay out on suicide . . .

But I didn't mean any of it, thought Thaisa, in panic. I couldn't help finding the Nazi ring that day. And I didn't know about the insurance policy clause – I was barely eighteen, for pity's sake, and I didn't understand half of what was happening!

I won't listen to any of this, she thought. This isn't some gothic Victorian drama or one of those ghost stories where dead relatives whisper at people out of the shadows. This is nothing but guilt for having covered up her suicide – and a kind of hangover from all those years of having it drummed into me that the past had to stay hidden. *At all costs . . .* And even if my mother committed a dozen murders, and even if my father ordered the deaths of thousands, and no matter how bad those deaths were, it's nothing to do with me. I *can't* do anything about what's happening now and I won't do anything, because it doesn't matter!

But even as this last thought formed, the sly voice inside her head was saying, *Doesn't it matter . . .? Are you sure about that? And couldn't you do something if you had to? Because there's always something that can be done . . .*

Miss Baran and her nephew, together with Nina Randall, arrived shortly after midday, and Nina made the introductions half in English for Thaisa's benefit, and half in what was presumably Polish for Helena's. Thaisa liked Nina, who had a lovely warm smile. The nephew – Lucek – had tow-coloured hair and an air of looking forward to whatever might be ahead, which was rather attractive.

But the minute the sunlight from the narrow hall window fell across Helena, Thaisa knew there was a link. Helena knew, as well. They took one another's hands in a rather awkward handshake, and something passed between them. As if a connection had been made – like electricity sparking between two points.

Then Helena said, in careful English, 'We meet at last. How very good that is.'

It was obvious she had prepared these words, but Thaisa had managed to find a greeting in the Polish phrase book, and she was able to say in return, 'I am glad to meet you.'

Helena was looking at her with rather disconcerting intensity. She said something, and Nina said, 'She's saying that although you have never met, she feels as if she knows you. The word she used translates as "recognition", but I don't think she meant it literally.'

Thaisa knew it was recognition at a deeper level that Helena had meant. She could see it in the other woman's expression, and she could feel it within her own mind as well. She had no idea what to make of it, or how to deal with it, though.

Helena was a little older than she had been expecting, but she was very smart and Thaisa thought her clothes were expensive. Her hair was grey, but it was thick and glossy and clearly well cut. Thaisa began to feel dowdy. She had put on a green two-piece – a skirt and matching jumper with a collar, and a necklace of green amber which had been a seventeenth birthday present from her parents. But next to Helena she felt like a frump, and next to Nina Randall, who was wearing casual cotton trousers with a loose open-weave linen jacket, she felt old-fashioned.

They had brought flowers, which was disconcerting. Nobody had ever given Thaisa flowers before, and she was not sure whether it was correct to put them in water at once, or leave them in the wrapping. But somehow Nina was saying she would take them through to the kitchen – just here was it? – no, she could find her own way perfectly well, and that would let Miss Wyngham and Helena get to know one another for a few moments.

'Lucek will translate,' she said. 'His English is very good.' She smiled at Lucek, and Thaisa thought he blushed slightly.

It was difficult to know quite how to talk to Helena, but Lucek was helpful, explaining about the scrapbook which he had found in some ruins in Warsaw, and which they thought might contain references to his aunt's family.

'She has hardly any memory of her early childhood,' he said.

'But Phineas Fox and the professor are bringing the scrapbook later for you to see, in case you recognize anything.'

'The professor thinks there might be a connection to the old Chopin Library,' said Nina, coming back. 'It was quite a famous centre of music before the war, and all this is very much his field of study.'

'And Helena has always believed it was in that part of Warsaw that she was found,' put in Lucek.

'So we're hoping that the two of you' – Nina smiled at Helena – 'can look through all the documents and see if anything sparks any memories. Helena's seen some of it already, and there was an old sketch – a curious, rather unusual old piano – that she thinks she recognizes.'

Thaisa, horrified at all this, and appalled at the mention of a famous house of music, said it would be interesting to see the documents.

'I really don't think I'll be able to help, though. I told you, didn't I, that I don't know anything about my parents' early lives. They never talked about . . . about their past or about any relatives.'

'But they were from Poland?'

'Yes,' said Thaisa, not seeing how else to answer this.

'And someone sent those books to Helena all those years ago, with your name included on the box,' said Nina. 'So we're hopeful something might emerge.'

By this time it was almost a quarter to one, so Thaisa felt she could take them into the dining room for lunch, which might make it easier to change the subject.

The meal seemed to go well. Nina helped to serve the casserole, and Helena passed round the bread. Lucek very politely picked up the corkscrew and offered to open one of the bottles of wine which Thaisa had put ready.

'Ladies can find this difficult,' he said, and Thaisa smiled and thanked him, and thought how well-mannered he was.

She had bought a fairly upmarket apple tart for a dessert – the upside-down kind called Tarte Tatin – and she warmed it, slid it on to a china plate and served it with cream.

'Beautiful,' said Lucek, beaming. 'Please, yes, I would like a little second helping.'

Thaisa began to relax. If Helena Baran had virtually no memory of her childhood, there might not be anything to worry about. But then she remembered that in about an hour she would be facing two – no, three – men who were musically knowledgeable, and that one of them had written a book about musicians of the World War II era. They would bring with them old documents unearthed from the ruins of Warsaw's music quarter. She remembered that Helena had already apparently recognized a sketch among those documents. But there still need not be any links to her parents – there must have been dozens of musicians in Warsaw in those years, and for all she knew, her father might simply have been a teacher or even a talented amateur. But he was also a Nazi, said her mind, slyly, let's not forget about that. The apprehension spiralled into fear all over again.

Lucek thought things seemed to be going quite smoothly so far. Thaisa Wyngham had clearly been nervous, but she had cooked a delicious lunch, although Lucek had not realized that people actually sipped sherry out of dainty glasses before a meal. He thought Helena rather appreciated this small formality. And Thaisa had seemed to relax by the time they sat down to eat. Nina had helped with the serving, and Lucek had thought it would be all right to offer to open the wine which was on the table, because Thaisa had seemed as if she did not quite know how to handle that.

He was, though, still a bit worried about meeting Professor Liripine later on. He had not seen the professor since last night, but he could not possibly know that Lucek and Nina had spent the night together, and even if by some weird alchemy he guessed, it would not matter. Lucek did not really believe there had ever been anything between Nina and Ernest Liripine, but he was still worried.

But when the professor and the others arrived, they did so on the crest of some story about Arabella having opened the curtains in the White Hart's bedroom, and the curtains having fallen off their moorings and engulfed her.

'And that's why we're a bit late, because I couldn't get free of the wretched things, and Phin was no help; in fact he was practically hysterical with laughter, because he said it was like when children dress up in a sheet and pretend to be a ghost, only I was a Sanderson print ghost. Brown and orange floral pattern.'

Phin said, 'The only regret I have is that I couldn't get to my phone in time to video it.'

They were all laughing at the tale, and Arabella was enlarging on the details about the curtains having to be put back up and a search for a stepladder, and somehow Thaisa and Nina, and even Helena, became swept up in it, and were laughing as well.

During this, Professor Liripine suddenly turned to Lucek, and said, 'You're coping with this English expedition extremely well, I think.'

'Um, well, yes.'

The professor looked at him for a moment, and Lucek absolutely knew he was blushing, and hated himself for not being able to control it.

But Professor Liripine only said, casually, 'I have the impression that you're finding England – and perhaps also Nina's company – very agreeable. If so, I'm very glad.'

They looked at one another, and Lucek suddenly saw that it was all right. He said, 'Yes, I am finding those things extremely agreeable. Thank you, professor,' and Professor Liripine nodded, and turned to Thaisa to say what an interesting house this was, and he was intrigued to hear from Nina that Miss Wyngham actually had a music room.

'Hardly anyone has such a thing nowadays,' he said.

'Hardly anyone has a large enough house nowadays,' put in Dr Purslove. 'It's only desiccated music professors with comfortable tenures at universities who have such luxuries.'

'It was my father's room,' said Thaisa, and then suddenly looked frightened, as if she might have given something away. 'I've kept all his books and most of his music, just as he left them.'

'It'd be a link to him for you,' nodded the professor. 'I can understand that. And you teach music yourself, don't you? I'm sure Nina said you did.'

'Only quite young children and only sort of supervising their practice.' Thaisa said this quickly as if, Lucek thought, she did not want to sound pretentious.

'It's the young ones who need the most careful tuition,' said the professor, seriously. 'Theo, you'd agree with that?'

'Yes, certainly. Get them to about Grade V and you've probably got them hooked. You have to weave in a bit of the modern stuff, too, of course. Hip-hop and rap.'

'Well, as to that—'

Nina said, 'Don't listen to the professor being dismissive of the modern stuff, Thaisa. He wrote a terrific paper a few years ago about influences on modern music lyrics – tracing it all the way back to several astonishing sources. It was hailed with huge acclaim and all the scholarly journals lapped it up – several mainstream pop-music-culture magazines, as well.'

'It was only a few jottings,' said the professor, clearly aiming for a dismissive note, but looking pleased.

Arabella said, 'Thaisa, the truth is that these two would love to see your music room and find out what kind of music you play and teach.'

Lucek thought there was a moment when Thaisa seemed to be thrown off balance, but the professor was saying, 'It's true that it's interesting to see where people work. I mean people who work and study music.'

'And who teach it,' put in Dr Purslove.

Thaisa said, 'It's just across the hall.'

TWENTY

As they went across the hall and into the music room, Thaisa was fighting against a new tide of mounting fear. She had been more or less all right with Helena and with Lucek and Nina, and she had even found that Professor Liripine and Dr Purslove were unexpectedly easy to talk to. She liked Phineas Fox and Arabella, as well, although she was rather nervous of Mr Fox, because she was nearly always nervous with young and attractive men.

The request to see the music room was perfectly reasonable, though, and once in the familiar room, she found she could talk

almost naturally when they asked about her pupils – talking
about the first, tentative five-finger exercises and how she found
for them simplified pieces to try, then played recordings of those
same pieces by some of the great pianists and orchestras.

'That's a good method of teaching,' said the professor.

'It gives the artless little grubs something to aspire to,' nodded
Dr Purslove. 'Phin, were you given things to aspire to?'

'Not as far as I remember. Which is probably why I'm a very
indifferent pianist,' said Phin.

The professor was looking along the rows of CDs.

'I see you've got almost all of William Boyce's work,' he
said. 'He's a particular favourite of mine.'

Thaisa was pleased. 'I play some of his music for the church
groups,' she said. 'I think his work is very elegant.'

'So do I. In fact, I've wondered about doing a paper on him.
There's a very good group in Durham who might be interested
. . . The books are quite an eclectic collection. Several on
Russian composers.'

'Those were my father's. He had a liking for the Russians.
Performers and composers.'

'I can see that. Stravinsky, Borodin, Glinka. Rimsky-Korsakov
and Tchaikovsky of course . . . Oh, this is interesting.'

'What have you found?' demanded Dr Purslove. 'Miss
Wyngham, don't let him start plundering your bookshelves,
because he has no conscience if he sees something he wants to
add to his collection.'

The professor said, 'It's a study of Anton Rubinstein. It's
quite well-worn, too. It's not often you find a mention of
Rubinstein these days.'

Thaisa, sensing that some tension had come into the room,
but unable to see any reason for it, said, 'I think my father had
one or two scores of Rubinstein's work.'

She thought Phineas Fox started to say something, then
stopped. Instead, Dr Purslove said, 'Is any of your father's music
still here? Russian music is very much my field of study, and
it's always interesting to see other people's working scores – to
see any notes or directions in the margins.'

Thaisa had scoured this room and everything in it, and there
was nothing anywhere that might cause comment. She had burned

the old concert programme cover that had seemed to point back to the war years and a place that might have been known as the Chopin Library, so she felt safe to point to the oak chest pushed against the wall. 'All his music's in there,' she said, and, as Phin pulled the chest into the centre of the room and pushed up the lid, she reached, almost automatically, for the switch of the wall light over the piano. It cast a soft glow over the piano and over the open chest.

The three men lifted the music scores out, studying them, then placing them to one side of the oak box. Their expressions were absorbed, and they were careful with the old, brittle paper. This is an everyday thing for them, thought Thaisa, and she began to relax slightly. She was about to ask if they would like a cup of tea, when Dr Purslove suddenly said, 'My God, look at that. Ernest . . . Phin—'

'What is it?'

Dr Purslove said, 'This. D'you see? Would you have expected to find a second copy?'

'It's the aria from Rubinstein's *Demon*,' said Phin.

'Yes. "*Ne plach' ditya moya*".'

The professor said, 'The Romanovs again. But it's not so unusual to find it, surely? Except that . . .'

He paused, frowning, and Phin said, 'Except that this one is handwritten, as well. And I think—'

'That it's by the same hand?' said the professor, looking up.

'I'm not sure. Hold on, I'll get the scrapbook.'

As Phin went out, Thaisa thought: there's something wrong. It's only an old score, though – handwritten, but that's not so remarkable, surely. But the fear she had been struggling to hold in check was flooding through her. She had missed something. She had left a clue, and they were about to pick it up. But what was it? *What?*

Phin came back with the scrapbook, Helena, Nina, Lucek and Arabella following him. There were not enough chairs, but Arabella curled up on a padded stool, and Lucek perched on the windowsill on the side of the French doors, with Nina next to him.

Dr Purslove said, 'Thaisa, you said this music was your father's?'

'Yes. It's all been in there since he died. That's a good thirty-five years ago.'

Phin had opened the scrapbook, and was holding the music score next to one of the pages. The professor and Dr Purslove leaned over, and a curious silence seemed to come down. Then Phin said, slowly, 'It would need an expert to be sure, but I think the writing on both is the same.'

'Even down to the ink,' said Professor Liripine, nodding.

'Yes, but . . .' Dr Purslove frowned.

'Something else, doctor?'

'I'm not sure.' Dr Purslove was looking more closely at the two music scores.

Phin looked at him and then at the score. Then he said, 'Thaisa, would you object if one of us tried this out on your piano? Pure curiosity, nothing more.'

What was there to say to that, except that of course she would not object.

'Thank you.' Phin lifted the stack of music on the floor to one side, and said, 'Doctor, do you want to do the honours? This is your field, after all.'

'Ernest's the better sight-reader,' said Dr Purslove, and Thaisa saw Professor Liripine make a half-gesture of refusal. They don't want to play it, she thought. None of them wants to. But why? I don't understand what this is about, but I think it could be the thing I was always afraid might happen – no, the thing I always *knew* would happen . . . My parents were so watchful, but even they don't seem to have known about this music . . .

Then the professor gave a small shrug, and sat down at the piano, propping the music on the stand.

He looked at it for a moment, then began to play.

As the first notes came into the room, Phin, who was nearest the piano, saw the professor frown, and Dr Purslove made an abrupt gesture that might have been surprise.

The professor hesitated, played several more bars, then stopped. He looked more closely at the score, and played more of it. Then he turned to face the room, but before he, or anyone else, could speak, there was an abrupt movement from the corner. Helena Baran was pressing back into the recess by the hearth, almost as if she wanted to hide inside the bricks. Her hands were covering her ears, as if she was trying to shut out something so dreadful she could not bear to hear it.

Arabella went forward at once. 'Miss Baran – Helena – what is it? Nina, Lucek – ask her what's wrong.'

But Lucek was already at Helena's side, trying to take her hands, flinching when she pushed him away.

Dr Purslove said, 'It's the music. She's recognized it, hasn't she?'

'Yes,' said Phin, his eyes on Helena. He looked back at Dr Purslove. 'That wasn't Rubinstein's aria, was it? It wasn't the Demon's lament?'

'No,' said Dr Purslove. 'You didn't think it was, did you?'

'I wasn't sure,' said Phin. 'Professor?'

'I wasn't sure, either.'

'Are we thinking the same thing?' said Dr Purslove. 'Phin – Ernest?'

'I should think so. I suspect,' said Phin, 'that what you've just played, professor, was the "Dark Cadence".'

'Yes. Dear God.'

Lucek had taken Helena's hands, and he was speaking to her in a voice that shook slightly. Then he said, 'She's saying it's the – um – *koszmar*—'

'Nightmare,' supplied Nina.

'Thank you, nightmare. Helena has always had bad nightmares and in them is music that is part of it. She says it's the music you've just played. You called it – what did you call it, Professor Liripine?'

'The "Dark Cadence".'

'Helena only ever called it the terror. I think I've got the word right.' He looked at them, his young face creased with anxiety. 'She is a normal and intelligent lady,' he said, earnestly. 'A pianist of great skill, also. Not – um – disturbed or flawed in her mind. Am I saying that right?' he said to Nina.

'I think so.'

'But there were childhood tragedies – my parents never knew what they were. No one knew. Helena came here because of the scrapbook – to meet Miss Wyngham because of it. To see if she could find the truth about her past – the family that was lost.'

Phin saw again his inner image of the small frightened child in the devastation of Warsaw's once-beautiful city. Pity closed around him, and he said, gently, 'Lucek – tell her we understand – that we're sorry.'

Nina said, 'Should we call a doctor? Or . . . Thaisa, how far is the nearest A & E department?'

'No, she will be all right in a little time,' said Lucek, looking, Phin thought, rather horrified at the prospect of hospitals and doctors. 'It will be like the nightmares – soon over.'

'Perhaps better to take her into the other room,' said the professor. 'Away from the sight of the piano and the atmosphere of music altogether— I don't mean that to sound discourteous,' he said to Thaisa. 'And I'm sorry if we seem to be taking over the house.'

'It isn't discourteous. Shall I make a cup of tea?' said Thaisa, rather helplessly.

'The great British remedy,' said Phin, managing a smile to reassure her, because she was looking white and rather frightened.

'Can we help you?' This was Arabella.

'No, I can manage, thanks. You all go into the sitting room – I'll bring everything in.'

Nina and Arabella took Helena across the room; Nina was talking to her, and Helena was listening and nodding, and already seeming calmer. But as Nina opened the door, Helena turned back to stare into the room. She's looking at the music again, thought Phin. And then – or is she? Is there something else in here? But when he looked round the room, he could not see anything out of the ordinary.

Dr Purslove was still studying the score, but as the door closed, he glanced up from it, and said, 'Ernest, there's no need to look as if you've just chanted the Black Mass by mistake. If Phin's right, we could have uncovered definite evidence that the "Cadence" did exist. We could even have the score of some music that legend said no one ever dared write down. Think what fireworks that's going to make in the music world.'

'We can't prove anything, though. If it is the "Cadence", it's in disguise.' The professor made a gesture expressive of exasperation. 'I'm sounding as if I'm talking out of a Victorian melodrama,' he said. 'Disguises and sinister legends and forged papers.'

'The "Cadence" is pretty melodramatic, though,' said Dr Purslove.

'But why would it be disguised as Rubinstein's *Demon*?' demanded Professor Liripine. 'And where have two separate copies come from? One in the scrapbook and the other somehow in this stack of old scores?'

'If the scrapbook really did come out of the Chopin Library, the one in it could have been to let people know there was a traitor,' said Phin. 'It could be a clue.'

'Pity whoever put it there didn't make it clearer, then,' said the professor. He scowled at the music, then said, 'Is Helena all right? And Thaisa? Because to have seven strangers descend on you, and then for one of them to succumb to hysterics—'

'She seemed all right, but I'll go and find her,' said Phin. 'She went to make some tea.'

When Phineas Fox came into the kitchen to ask if she was all right, Thaisa was slightly startled. But she said it was all a bit unexpected and she was concerned for Helena, but she was perfectly all right.

She was not in the least all right, of course. Her mind was tumbling with fear and confusion, although she thought no one had noticed. She set out the cups, trying to hear what was happening. It sounded as if they had all gone into the sitting room, so after a moment she went across the hall and into the music room. Someone had switched off the light over the piano, and the room was in semi-darkness. Through the open curtains, the old shrubs and bushes were dark crouching shapes.

It was more than thirty years since she had heard the music the professor had just played, but she had never forgotten it, just as she had never forgotten the sight of her father struggling to play it before he died. And whenever it had been that her parents had first heard it, she knew now that neither of them had forgotten it, either.

She pushed the memories away and carried the tray with the tea into the sitting room. It appeared that Nina had produced paracetamol for Helena, who was sitting quietly in a chair by the fire. Helena accepted the tea with a gesture of thanks, and Thaisa went back to the kitchen to refill the kettle in case more tea was wanted. She could hear everyone talking in the sitting room, but their voices seemed a long way off. It was like a bee buzzing against a windowpane from outside. Everything felt unreal, as if an old, old dream was trying to wake. But was it her own dream or was it someone else's? And mightn't it be a nightmare rather than a dream? The music was still going on in her mind – it was distant and even hesitant, as if it was tiptoeing around her. But when she went back into the hall, she realized with a prickle of horror that the music was not in her mind – it was real. Someone was in the music room, playing it. It was rather stumbling and uncertain, but the strange cold harmony was unmistakable.

There was no reason to feel afraid, though. It would be the professor playing it again, or Dr Purslove, or even Phin Fox. It was absurd to think that if she went into that room she would see her father seated at the piano, his face haggard with pain and with some deep dark memory of his own . . .

To dispel this idea, Thaisa took a deep breath and opened the door. The music stopped at once and the figure seated at the piano turned. It was not her father, of course, but nor was it the professor or Phineas Fox. It was Helena. They stared at one another, and Thaisa thought: we can't understand each other's language, but there's an understanding between us at some deeper level. And I know that she's playing the music because she thinks it might take her back to her lost memories. That's what she's here for. She remembered all over again that Helena had apparently been in Warsaw during those savage war years – she could only have been four at the very most, but four-year-olds could be astonishingly observant and perceptive. Something had already been said about the scrapbook – about Helena having recognized something in it to do with a piano. And now she had recognized this music. I can't let her remember anything else, thought Thaisa.

Do whatever it takes . . .

She started forward, although she had no idea what she was going to do, and then stopped. Propped up on the piano was a small, framed photograph. Helena stood up and reached for it, turning to look at Thaisa. In her other hand was the music score.

The photograph and the music. Somehow they had fused, and caused Helena to remember what had happened to her all those years ago.

The photo had been on the mantelpiece in this room for a great many years, and clearly Helena had picked it up and set it on the piano before she began to play.

But it was impossible that she would have seen it before today. And that being so, why had it had such an effect on her? Who did she believe it to be?

TWENTY-ONE

Warsaw, early 1940s

Inevitably, the day came when the Trust issued Yan with a definite directive to close the Chopin Library. Any musicians or staff who might still be in the city were to be politely dismissed, and the building made as secure as possible. If any kind of check could be kept on the Library – if anyone trustworthy was still in the area and could perhaps go in sometimes – that would be greatly appreciated, but it was acknowledged that it might be impossible.

Yan had no choice but to comply. Going about the necessary and deeply depressing tasks, he wondered what the future held for this place – whether the Ivory Salon would ever be lit to glowing life and filled with music again. He wondered, as well, if Warsaw itself would ever be the same. It was tearing at his heart to see the once-beautiful city being ruthlessly partitioned by the Nazis, and to hear about the creation of ghettos for anyone with Jewish connections. People did not exactly hide in their homes – Yan hoped it would never come to that point – but they certainly kept off the streets as much as possible. It was starting to seem as if no one was truly safe any longer. People who could leave – and who had families or friends to go to – left. Those who remained locked their doors every night, shuttering their windows and turning the gas jets low so as not to attract attention.

But there were some who remained. One of these was Anatol, who had been the Library's chef. He had found tiny dining rooms near to the Street of Music, and had actually been able to open a small restaurant.

'I refuse to leave my city,' he told Yan. 'For where would I go? I will stay here, and I will preserve my family's tradition of providing good food. Always providing there is food for me to cook,' he added, pragmatically.

Of Tanwen there was no trace. Yan had called at her lodgings, but the thin, dark-haired woman who owned the house said that Miss Malek had left. She was sorry that she did not have any address, but if she were to get in touch, a message could be sent to Mr Orzek. Yan gave her the address of his rooms, then, as an afterthought, said he and a couple of the remaining musicians frequently ate at Anatol's restaurant, and that he could usually be found there. This seemed to interest her, and she looked at him carefully for a moment. Probably it was only curiosity about people who were attempting to scrape out a life in the city though.

His memory of the night with Tanwen in the Ivory Salon was still confused. At times her face blurred into the features of his lost Romanov. Several times, in his own rooms, he unwrapped the miniature stolen from Ipatiev House all those years ago, and sat for a long time studying the gaze of the girl whose name he had never known. The painted features were as clear as they had ever been, and the memory was as clear, too.

Bruno, and rather unexpectedly, Alicja, had both remained in the city.

'Only because I haven't anywhere else to go' said Bruno, cheerfully, and Alicja observed, sadly, that you did not abandon a place in its death throes. 'Warsaw is doomed – it will become a lost, dead world,' she said. 'But I shall compose a requiem to it.'

'It's not dead yet,' said Yan, angrily.

Other things were dead, though. Links with his own past were being snapped cruelly off. And among them was one link that Yan had desperately hoped would never break.

*   *   *

He had just finished a solitary supper at Anatol's, when Anatol came over to his table, his face sombre. 'Yan, there is someone you must come with me to see.'

'Now? Who is it?' Yan instantly thought: Tanwen? And was aware again of the familiar clash of emotion and confusion.

But as they went together through several of the side streets, skirting the Library's own square, he recognized the area.

'I know where you're taking me,' he said to Anatol.

'Yes. You come here often, I know. I, also.'

The room was at the very top of the house, and there were views across the city. How many times had Yan sat in this room, looking out of that window as night stole over the city, seeing the silhouettes of the buildings dark against the sky? Talking, reminiscing, speculating. Playing music . . .

The evening light filtered into the room, and from the bed, a soft voice said, 'Yan. My dear, exceptional boy.'

Yan said, 'Father Gregory.'

He went forward, and as he took the thin hand with the skin that was now almost transparent, Father Gregory said, 'I'm dying.'

The thing Yan did not believe he would ever understand was that there was no sadness in Gregory and no fear. His life was ending, and he would be grateful to hold on to the hands of his two dear friends, Yan and Anatol, until those other Hands took over from them. But there was no fear.

Yan said he would bring a doctor, but Gregory tapped the left side of his chest and shook his head.

'I'm beyond doctors.' His hand, lying loosely in Yan's, tightened, and he said, 'But there is something . . . The music . . . Yan, you must put my mind at rest – please give me your word that you destroyed it?'

The dark eyes, still filled with intelligence and such compassion, were fixed very directly on Yan. The moment stretched out, then Yan said, 'Yes, Father. I destroyed it.'

'Ah.' Gregory seemed to relax against the pillows. 'An old man's obsession,' he said, as if apologizing. 'But it's been in my mind so much these last days . . .' He looked at Anatol, who was sitting near the window, listening. 'Anatol knows how much,' he said.

'We have talked of the music,' said Anatol. 'I understand about it – or as much as anyone can understand about it. I know it's recognized as the "Traitor's Music", and as such should never be written down, because if it were to be found—'

'Especially in these times,' said Father Gregory. 'If the oppressors were to find it—'

'Would it be of any interest to them, though?' said Yan. 'What use could they make of it?'

'They will make use of anything they think they can turn against us,' said Anatol. 'Music that is written down – music with a sinister history – is a tangible thing for them to seize on. They would find a way of making it into a weapon against us. But if the music is only in the mind, in the memory, then they cannot reach it.'

Yan's eyes went to the small, rather battered piano in the corner. He and Father Gregory had seen it in the corner of a dim old shop near to the Street of Music. Even dull and unpolished as it had been then, it had attracted their attention. Yan knew that was largely because of its music stand. It was the most unusual and the most beautiful music stand he had ever seen on a piano. It was carved into the shape of a bird – a smooth and lovely bird, positioned as if it had alighted for a brief moment to clasp the music, and as if, once that music had been played, it would take flight again.

Gregory, staring at it, had said, very softly, 'It's a firebird. The creature that survived when the world was destroyed by fire and flood, but that revived and lived again.'

Yan said, 'Allegories in all places.'

Gregory smiled, but only said, 'In some cultures the firebird is recognized as the phoenix – even as a representation of divine power. The Jews teach that the phoenix was the only creature in the Garden of Eden not to taste the forbidden fruit. For that, it was rewarded with immortality.'

Yan's mind had gone back to his childhood – to Katya telling him of the firebird legend, but he only said, 'Stravinsky's music for *The Firebird* ballet is very beautiful.'

He had known that no matter its cost, he must get the instrument for Gregory, and he had done so that same day, brushing aside the Father's protests, not caring if the purchase completely drained his small bank balance. Gregory had polished the scarred wood until the firebird music stand glowed and looked almost golden, and Yan had found a piano tuner who had said the instrument had a beautiful mellow tone, that it was a sin and a scandal that it had been left to rot somewhere, and Yan had done a splendid thing in rescuing it.

Now, looking at the piano, Yan understood that Father Gregory must have played the 'Dark Cadence' for Anatol on it. An old man's memory of the past, or a shrewd man wanting to preserve a strange music legend? It did not matter. What mattered was that, facing death, he had wanted Yan's assurance that the tangible evidence of the legend – the score given by Vadim all those years ago – no longer existed. Yan was glad he had been able to meet Gregory's look straight, and tell him the music score no longer existed.

He and Anatol sat quietly by the bed as darkness stole over the city. Once, Anatol went down to the tiny kitchen to warm some milk, to which he added a spoonful of brandy.

'Shall I meet my God slightly inebriated?' said Gregory, the gentle, ironic smile showing briefly.

'God wouldn't mind,' said Anatol.

Beyond the windows the darkness hung over the city, but at last a faint, hopeful dawn began to streak the sky. At first there were only slender threads of light, but, as Yan watched, the threads became swirls and streaks, rose and gold. It was then that Father Gregory gave a small sigh, and took his hand away from Yan's clasp. With a gesture that Yan would never forget, Gregory's hand seemed to reach up.

In echo of Yan's earlier thoughts, Anatol said very softly, 'He's reaching up for the other Hands that are taking him.' And then, as Gregory's hand fell back on the coverlet, Anatol said, 'It's over, Yan. He's gone.'

Walking back to his rooms, Yan thought, and now the last link has gone. Now there's no one who knows what happened in Ipatiev House all those years ago.

And then a tiny disturbing voice in his mind said: but there is. There's Tanwen. She knows. That night, when past and present seemed to fuse, when you were no longer sure where you were, you talked about Katya. You said, 'I murdered her.'

How much had that meant to Tanwen? It was impossible to know. As well as calling at the lodging house, Yan had written to her, but she had not answered, and no one seemed to know where she was. And surely, in the midst of such turmoil in Poland and in the world beyond Poland, Tanwen would not remember those words with any real attention.

Despite the turmoil and the fear and devastation, there were tiny threads of hope in Warsaw. Very quietly, people were seeking ways to fight the Nazi oppression, and many of them had stayed on, determinedly clinging to a semblance of normality. Some shops were still trading, although supplies were erratic, but a number of small cafés and coffee shops were open for an hour or two in the evenings. Anatol's little restaurant was one of these. It opened several times a week, and there was a regular clientele. The electricity supply frequently failed, so that candles had to be lit, but Anatol insisted this did not matter.

'Except,' he once said, indignantly, 'if you are in the middle of preparing kielbasa. I cannot served you with half-cooked sausage, my friends, so tonight there will be only bread and cheese, but there is also pickled cucumber and some of my own pickled cabbage with apples.'

In fact the food was nearly always excellent. Yan suspected a great deal of it came from Anatol's cousin, who had a small-holding near the Kampinos Forest, although it was anybody's guess how it was smuggled into the city. There was almost always wine available, although the wine's provenance was even more dubious. But at least twice, from the window of his own rooms, Yan had seen Anatol's portly figure together with one of his helpers, furtively carrying large crates through the streets at one and two o'clock in the morning. He guessed that Anatol was discreetly liberating it from the Chopin Library, a crate at a time, but he would not have dreamed of telling Anatol he knew this, and he was glad that Anatol's customers could enjoy the wine.

Between them, Yan and Bruno had managed to wrestle the

firebird piano down the stairs from Father Gregory's rooms and install it in the restaurant. Often one of them would play for the customers – anything from Mozart to Chopin to modern pieces. Several times Bruno gave them an evening of jazz and ragtime, and on other nights there were songs from the repertoire of the American crooner, Sinatra, and music from the light operas of the English composers, Gilbert and Sullivan. Hardly anyone knew any of the English words of these, but nobody cared, because the music was wonderful and it made for a happy, lively night, and if the Germans wanted to come stomping in and break things up, by ten o'clock of an evening most people had drunk so much of Anatol's contraband wine that they were prepared to take on the entire Third Reich.

By contrast, Yan played the much-loved folk songs of the country. '*Płynie Wisła*' – 'The River Flows' and '*Hej Sokoły*' – 'Hey Falcon', which had been sung by soldiers for decades.

Anatol was delighted; he said singing had always been a strong part of Polish life, and some of the old ballads had accompanied the most dramatic moments of the country's history.

When one night Yan played '*Nie Daj Sie*' – 'Don't Give Up/ Don't Let Go', the women in the restaurant sobbed openly, and Anatol climbed on to a table, and delivered a speech saying they would not give up and they would never let go, they would resist the sweeping evil of the Nazis while there was breath in their bodies. He drank two more glasses of wine, mopped his eyes unashamedly, and repeated the sentiment, while one of the helpers went to look out of the door to make sure no one was outside, because you could not trust the Nazis not to come marching down the street and carry you off for sedition or incitement when all you were doing was singing.

But often, walking back to his rooms, Yan felt as if the world had become distorted – as if it had been dislodged from its axis. Or was it more as if the Earth's rotation had altered and its people had not altered their pace to match it? Once, he tried to explain these feelings to Bruno, but Bruno said he did not give a tinker's toss if the world was off its axis or slowing down or racing ahead, or whether it was performing somersaults across the universe. Whatever it was doing, it wasn't likely to make any difference. Better to concentrate on not sinking into the Slough of Despond and not letting the Nazis crush them once and for all.

'You don't seem to fall into the Slough of Despond very often,' remarked Yan.

'You'd be surprised,' said Bruno, suddenly serious. 'I have a dark side. But then who doesn't?'

It was early evening, and shadows were spreading thickly across the ground, turned to a mosaic of crimson and gold by the sinking sun, so that it was like walking across one of the Persian carpets out of the old legends.

'It's a beautiful city,' said Yan, in sudden anger. 'And it's *our* city. Yet here we are tiptoeing through the streets, constantly looking over our shoulder. There's a line of poetry from somewhere – I don't know the author's name, and I'm not sure if I ever did, but I think it was an English poet. One of the eighteenth-century Romantics. Something about a man tiptoeing down a lonesome road in fear and dread . . . "*And having once turned round walks on, And turns no more his head; Because he knows, a frightful fiend doth close behind him tread . . .*" That's us, my friend.'

'Well personally, maestro, I'm inclined to think we're more like characters in one of those French farces,' said Bruno. 'Trying not to be caught in the wrong bedroom. Not that I'd necessarily object to that, because at least you'd have the promise of a lively night ahead of you.'

But he frowned, and Yan felt, as he sometimes did, Bruno's mood change. I have a dark side, Bruno had said. What might that dark side hold? After a moment, Bruno said, 'All we can do in these times is trust to God's mercy – or the devil's, if the Prince of Darkness is likely to be more kindly disposed to us – that the Nazis don't find out what's happening in quiet corners of Warsaw.' They looked at one another. 'We both know what I mean, don't we?' he said.

'Oh, yes. And don't you think that those things – those quiet activities, are gaining strength?' said Yan. 'You can almost feel it happening. Like a storm that gathers strength as it gets closer.'

'A storm,' said Bruno. And then, very softly, 'Or a Tempest.'

He did not say any more, but he did not need to. Yan knew

that Bruno was referring to the embryo organization first conceived in southeastern Poland, started by the Polish Home Army, and intended to culminate in an uprising in Central Poland that would drive out the Nazis.

The Resistance movement that had been given the name of *Burza*. Tempest.

It had been Anatol, and – rather astonishingly – the thin dark woman, Irina, from Tanwen's old lodging house, who drew Yan and Bruno into the Tempest movement.

Irina was often in Anatol's restaurant, and somehow – Yan was not sure how – she had got into the way of coming to sit for a while with himself and Bruno – also Alicja on the nights she was there.

Alicja thought Irina might be one of Anatol's casual waitresses – there were several who came and went – but Bruno said it was more than that.

'I think she's here to pick scraps of useful gossip,' he said.

'You mean she's a Nazi spy?' This did not sound as far-fetched or dramatic as once it would have done.

'I think we ought to keep the possibility in mind. She's an odd, secretive woman.'

'Of course she is secretive,' said Anatol, when this was put to him. 'She had a sister who was married to a Jewish man – a respectable, hard-working bookseller. A very nice family. But the Nazis burned his shop and took his entire family to one of the camps.' A plump shrug. 'I do not know which one, and I don't think Irina knows. But for that reason alone she would never work for the Germans. Against them – oh, yes, she would definitely work against them.' He glanced to where Irina was sitting. 'You may be approached by her,' he said, very softly, under cover of the piano that was being played in a corner by one of the customers.

'To help in her – um – work?'

'Yes.'

Anatol was right. The approach came two nights later.

'Radio transmissions,' she said, seated at the table with Yan and Bruno, her thin face intent, her dark eyes glowing, but her expression as bland as if she were discussing with them which dish to choose from the menu.

'Radio?'

'It could be a way of sending messages without being seen or heard. And I believe, Bruno, that you have knowledge of such things.'

'A very little,' said Bruno.

'But enough. The equipment can be got, but there's the question of where it can be set up.'

Anatol, who was hovering with a wine flagon, sat down. 'If I could set it up here, I would do it,' he said. 'I would throw my entire restaurant open for such a purpose, but it is quite small, and the oppressors can walk in and out at their will.'

'A warehouse or offices would be best,' said Irina. 'There are plenty of empty buildings. But it must be somewhere that wouldn't be noticed very much. A place where we could come and go without comment.'

Yan and Bruno looked at one another, and Yan knew the same thought was in their minds. But Bruno did not speak, and at last, Yan said slowly, 'There might be somewhere.'

TWENTY-TWO

Warsaw, early 1940s

'I never found the old staircase,' said Anatol, as they went cautiously inside the Chopin Library much later that same night, and crossed the big empty hall towards the kitchen area. 'There was never time to search for it. But my father talked of it.'

They found oil lamps in a storeroom, and went down the steps to the kitchens by the flickering light of them. Their footsteps echoed in the emptiness, and it felt strange to know that overhead were the high-ceilinged, ornate rooms where once silken-clad ladies and gentlemen had gathered; where royalty of all races and creeds had come to hear music played by the finest musicians of the day. Were you ever here? said Yan in his mind to his Romanov girl. Might you and your sisters have been brought here as children – as a treat, for a special event, or simply to attend a concert? But he had no idea if that doomed family had ever travelled to Poland, let alone to Warsaw. Pointless speculation. Concentrate on trying to find this boarded-up stair.

But as Anatol cautiously investigated an old larder, Yan felt his mind loop back over the years to that other larder with its stone slab that could be pulled away to open up another ice room. The stone that could not be moved from within . . . Don't think about it, said his mind, angrily. Think instead about what's happening now, and that this might be something that will help the Resistance movement. Tempest. *Burza.*

'It can only be somewhere in here, that boarded-up stair,' said Anatol, as he and Bruno tapped on walls and sections of planks.

Bruno said, 'I think there's something here – listen.' He rapped on a section of timber a second time.

It gave a dull echo, and Yan said, 'A hollow space behind?'

'Let's find out.' Bruno was already plundering the drawers for suitable implements. 'Hammer and chisel,' he said. 'Anatol, why did you have a hammer and chisel in these kitchens?'

'There were sometimes small jobs to be done – maintenance – shelves to be fixed . . .'

But Bruno was already hammering against the wood, and sliding the blade of the chisel between the planks when they loosened.

'Carefully,' said Anatol. 'For if this is what we're looking for, we'll have to replace those boards when we come and go.'

Between them they worked free a large oblong of timber, roughly six feet high and eight feet wide. As it came away, a breath of cold, sour air gusted out.

Bruno reached for one of the oil lamps and thrust it inside.

And there it was. A wide staircase, partly stone, partly timber, but the timbers rotting and sagging. Thick cobwebs like veils hung down from the vaulted roof above, and strange cold echoes drifted across the dimness. But unquestionably, this was the ancient, famous stairway, up which sumptuous banquets had once been carried for glittering and often royal audiences.

'Wall sconces,' said Anatol softly, pointing to the walls. 'They were for the best wax candles – for light so that the musicians could play the Iced Polonaise all the way up here and through the rooms to the Ivory Salon.'

'Do we investigate?' said Yan, peering at the stair rather doubtfully.

'Maestro, you astonish me,' said Bruno. 'Of course we investigate. This is romance and history at its best. Also,' he said, on a more practical note, 'it could be a place we can use as a secret headquarters for the radio transmissions.'

'You should not get carried away yet, Mr Sicora,' said Anatol. 'First we have to see what is down there. Also, we must be careful not to fall through the rotting parts of the steps.'

Descending the old stairway was a strange experience. The echoes whispered all round them, and it was necessary to constantly push aside the thick cobwebs. Several times Anatol tried to burn them out of the way with the oil lamp, but the air was so damp that the oil flare was struggling to remain alight at all.

'And it's so bloody *cold*,' said Bruno, turning up his coat collar, and shivering so that the glow of the lamp he carried shivered with him on the walls. 'I don't believe I'll ever be able to get warm again after this. I'm cold right through to my bones.'

For Yan, the old nightmare was still trying to break into the present, and when Bruno said this about it being cold, he thought it must be how those two had felt as they died – his beloved Katya, and the girl who had been with her. Bone-cold, so that you would never believe there could be warmth anywhere in the world ever again. And there had not been, not for those two.

The stairs finally opened out on to a large area, which had the same stone floor as the scullery overhead. There were deep shelves, waist-high, along one wall.

'The original sculleries,' said Anatol, pointing to an ancient sink and the remains of what looked like a massive iron range.

'We could bring chairs down here,' said Bruno, shining the lamp around. 'And if we really can get a radio transmitter, it could go on one of those stone shelves.'

'Wouldn't the roof block out the signal? And all the rooms overhead?'

'I don't know. Yes, they might. We'd only find out by trying. But even so, as a . . . a centre for information, it would work,' said Bruno. 'We could post lookouts in the square or even in the main hall upstairs, and have a warning system in place.'

Yan said, 'And even if the Nazis came into the building, I don't believe it would occur to them that there might be this place down here. We'd replace those sections of wall planks every time.'

'I think you're right. Well?' said Bruno, looking at them, a light of excitement glowing in his eyes. 'What about it? Are we going to try?'

And this time the images that were crowding Yan's mind were quite different. They superimposed themselves over those older, disturbing images, and they were pictures of himself and Bruno – perhaps Anatol and Irina too, and maybe even Alicja – working stealthily in this place. Sending out secret messages. Coded radio signals for the Resistance if it could be managed, but in any case somehow spreading information that might help their fight and that might add to the growing momentum of the organization. And doing it all under the very noses of the oppressors. It was impossible not to be fired by the audacity and the dangerous glamour of the idea, and by the eventual aim it might achieve. It was also impossible not to be fearfully aware of the certain outcome if they were caught.

He said, 'Yes. Oh, yes, we're going to try this.'

It was Bruno who came up with the idea of using the opening notes of Sibelius's incidental music for Shakespeare's *The Tempest* over the transmitter.

'Short and recognizable and appropriate,' he had said. 'Whichever of us is here can play the notes each time – we can keep one of the violins down there for that. And whoever's listening will pick up and know it's a signal that a message or some information is imminent.'

'Whoever's listening might include the Nazis one night,' Yan said.

'Yes, but we'll have to risk that.'

Others joined their small group – all vouched for by Anatol and often by Irina. Alicja was among them, prophesying sadly that the Chopin Library's days were probably numbered. 'It will end in being one of Warsaw's most tragic losses, you'll all see.'

'Oh, the old place has weathered worse,' said Bruno, cheerfully.

'I shall ensure its memory lives on, though,' said Alicja, ignoring this. 'I shall compose a symphonic poem, telling its story, and my pen will be dipped in tears and the notes written with my heart's blood. People who hear it will be moved to tears.'

'I wouldn't be at all surprised,' said Bruno, with unmistakable sarcasm. But afterwards, he said to Yan that Alicja might be impossibly gloomy, but she was very committed to what they were doing. 'And she's entirely trustworthy.'

'I know.'

With them was a man who, when the world was normal, had owned a small printing business. He suggested creating what would appear to be advertisements for concerts, but which could contain hidden messages.

'But the Nazis will know we can't stage concerts any longer,' objected Yan.

'Yes, but if they found them, we'd say they were ones ordered ages ago,' said the printer. 'Old advertisements or programme covers for concerts you had in your schedule. I'll even print a fake schedule, for heaven's sake!' he said.

'That's quite a good idea about fake programme covers,' said Bruno. 'We could use them to keep our people informed – and to tell them about our meetings. In a strange way it might be safer than word of mouth, because you never know who might be listening in.'

'It's a pity we aren't strong enough yet for anything other than meetings,' said Irina, who was present. 'But we will be.' Her eyes glowed and she suddenly looked unexpectedly attractive. 'Before too long we might be able to get hold of arms and supplies – break into the German munition stores. We need to counter the threat from the Soviets, and when the Polish Home Army gathers its strength—'

'We'll start with the meetings,' said Yan, before Irina could become too carried away. 'I like the idea of the fake advertisements. We could incorporate symbols to let people know where meetings are to be held. A different one for each venue. A heart when we're meeting in that abandoned warehouse near Holy Cross Church in the Krakowskie Przedmieście.'

'Where Chopin's heart is supposed to be sealed inside a pillar,' nodded the printer.

'And when there's a meeting here in the Library, we'll make it an open book,' said Bruno, eagerly.

'And,' said Yan, 'on the nights we use Anatol's cellar we'll have a small sketch of Father Gregory's firebird piano. It'll look like part of a poster for a concert, but it's very distinctive, that piano, and if we draw it clearly enough, people who know will recognize it.'

Anatol said, 'Father Gregory would have liked to think of himself as playing a part in this.'

Tanwen had to constantly remind herself that there was nothing to feel ashamed of in having left Warsaw. Irina had said it was the only thing to be done – Tanwen must go while it was still possible to leave, and the baby could be left with her.

The baby. Born in painful, struggling secrecy in the bedroom at the top of Irina's house, with only Irina to help her. The months leading up to that night had been unutterably tedious. Irina had books, but there were only so many books you could read, and sewing and knitting were boring in the extreme. Tanwen had her violin, but there was not much satisfaction in playing when you did not have an admiring audience.

Once or twice she even made a few half-hearted attempts at housework. Cleaning and polishing were, of course, the ultimate in tedium, but Tanwen had been brought up in a house where such things were important, and Irina's own rooms were shockingly untidy, with old papers strewn around and spilling out of half-open drawers. Sorting everything out would at least give her something to do.

But Irina would not hear of it. She had better things to think about than filing letters and receipts and seed catalogues, she said, closing a drawer with an angry forbidding snap. So Tanwen did not bother.

When the birth began, Tanwen thought she was going to die. She clung to Irina and sobbed and gasped, and begged her to do something to end it. But then, incredibly, at the end of the pain was a tiny scrap of humanity, who, even from the first, had a disconcerting way of looking at the world with her father's dark eyes. And Yan's daughter had his instinctive response to music as well. Early on, when she cried, Tanwen tried playing one of Brahms' lullabies on her violin. The effect was magical. The baby was at once calmed and entranced. None of that could be allowed to get under Tanwen's skin, though, and the child must never find out that every time her mother looked at her she was pulled back to a night that should never have happened. A night when barriers had come down, and this baby's father had confessed to committing a murder.

When it was time to leave the child, Irina said Tanwen would have to steel herself to do so.

'You can't take her with you,' she had said. 'And I have a friend – a restaurant owner near the Street of Music – who has a cousin in the Kampinos Forest. Some help is wanted there, so that's where I'll be going. Helena will come with me.'

The Kampinos Forest sounded safe and rural and rather peaceful. Tanwen was glad to think of the small, helpless Helena being safe.

The journey out of Warsaw to her parents' home was long and tiring, and also quite dangerous. Twice SS men boarded the train, demanding to see everyone's papers. They glared suspiciously at Tanwen for what felt like a very long time. She glared back, because her papers were all in order, and there was no reason why they would haul her away to some sinister destination. Even so, it was a relief when the officers left the train, and it rumbled on its way again. She had not been especially frightened; in fact she looked forward to telling her parents all about it. Her mother would listen, round-eyed with astonishment at such dreadful things, and Father would say she was a brave girl and he would like to punch those men who had intimidated her.

Father.

Irina's words that day had stayed with Tanwen; they had gnawed at her mind. 'Georg Malek will never come to this house,' she had said. 'He knows that if he does, I will certainly kill him.'

What could Tanwen's father possibly have done to warrant such hatred – because there had undoubtedly been hatred in Irina's voice and in her face. Father could be a bit of an old fusspot, of course, and he was shockingly old-fashioned and irritatingly prim and prudish, but that hardly warranted somebody wanting to kill him.

When at last she reached her parents' house, it felt as if she had stepped into another world. Their village was a long way from the city and the eye of the storm; Tanwen thought at times you might almost even be able to forget there was a war being waged, and that Poland was in the grip of the German armies. Her mother was quiet and unquestioning of everything. Her father came and went, vaguely referring to 'business'. Tanwen's mother said, proudly, that he still received a great many letters, and also telephone calls, and that people often came to the house, wanting to see him about business matters. No, she did not know what any of those business matters were, of course she did not.

The months before Helena's birth – the Library, Yan, the birth itself – began to feel distant, like something in a dream, although news of the war reached them, of course. Warsaw was at the mercy of the Third Reich by now, and most people understood that the city was seen by the Nazis as one of the main goals to complete subjugation of Poland. They viewed it as a core of defiance and potential rebellion, and they were doing everything they could to crush this core before it could spread.

Letters came from Irina at erratic intervals. Tanwen supposed that not all the letters sent actually reached her, because you could no longer trust the postal services. Irina did not put an address at the head of any of the letters, which would be because of the censor. Everything she wrote sounded perfectly innocent and ordinary. She sent good wishes, and said that she, and people Tanwen had known and been close to, were safe and well, and Tanwen had no need to worry. Tanwen knew Irina was talking about Helena, and she was reassured.

*   *   *

Her parents invited neighbours to the house one evening, so that Tanwen could play to them. Tanwen made a show of reluctance, but of course she allowed herself to be coaxed into agreeing. Mother found a white frock with ruffles which had been left in the back of a wardrobe when Tanwen went away to the Academy, and father said delightedly that she must certainly wear that for the evening, she would look a picture.

The frock was frightful. It made her look about fifteen, but the neighbours all smiled indulgently, and said things like, My word, Georg, isn't your little girl clever. Tanwen hated them for not knowing what she had been through, but she smiled, and looked modestly at her feet, and played a Mozart sonata. Father beamed with pride and sat well forward in his chair, as if he could not bear to miss a single note. Seeing this, and later, watching him hand round drinks to the neighbours, and look on approvingly as Tanwen's mother brought in platters of food, Tanwen was very much inclined to think Irina's words had been due to some stupid misunderstanding.

But the day after that evening, the safe-feeling dreamlike world splintered and the nightmare came clawing in.

She had been putting the stupid, frilled frock away, folding it into a small bundle, and stowing it at the bottom of an old suitcase in the guest room where it was not likely to be found and brought to her again for her to wear.

Tucked inside the suitcase was a large envelope, which was probably of no interest whatsoever, and need not be opened. However, it might contain newspaper cuttings about Tanwen, so it was worth taking a look. When she won the Żelazowa Award, Father had gone along to several newspaper offices – local ones here and also a couple of the larger city ones – to tell them about it, saying he believed this was called a human interest story. The result had been a couple of articles – the fact that the award had been given by an anonymous benefactor had spiced it up, of course, and Father had said this would all help her to get into one of the prestigious concert halls. In a way he had been proved right, because the Chopin Library, although small, had been very prestigious indeed.

There was a cutting in the envelope – a magazine report of

the award ceremony for the Żelazowa, and a description of how Tanwen had played the Mozart rondo. She had read it at the time, of course, but it was always nice to read these things again.

But also in the envelope were letters and what looked like notes of a meeting. The top letter was handwritten, and simply headed *Warsaw.* The date was shortly after the Żelazowa Award.

My dear Georg,
Your most generous donation to the Trust's coffers was cleared today, and I can assure you it will be put to good use.

As for the appointment of your young lady, you can now take it as official. I know I can trust you to get from her details of the workings of the Library itself without her realizing she is being manipulated. As you say, she's very young, and only just out of the Academy, so I expect she's still very naïve. To be blunt, this is what we need in those we use as puppets. Have no misgivings about using her, my good friend – think of the eventual glory we shall have in victory.

I am still undecided if you are right about a Resistance strand being woven in the Library, but the attached letter came into my possession recently – better not to ask how! – and could add weight to your suspicions. Please keep it somewhere safe and secret; as well as helping in your investigations, it may also be useful as evidence at some future time.

Since our last meeting, I have heard a whisper that if you are indeed proved right and this rebellion is rooted out, a certain personage might consider giving you a certain honour. I must say no more, but you will know to whom and to what I refer! That said, we must proceed slowly and with extreme caution.

May I advise you to keep your private life separate? The woman with the lodging house may indeed possess all the arts of Salome and Messalina combined, and putting your girl into her house could pay dividends. It could, however, also rebound and jeopardize this entire operation.

Cordially yours.

The signature was not really legible, although by the time Tanwen got to the foot of the page, she was not sure she could have read it if it had been printed in foot-high letters.

Her mind felt as if it was being wrenched into jagged pieces. A puppet, the writer had said, and it was quite dreadfully clear that it was Tanwen he was referring to. Her own father had used her as a puppet – he had deliberately got her into the Chopin Library and then proceeded to get information out of her about its workings and its layout.

Beneath the letter were notes of a meeting held at the Library itself. The members of the Chopin Library Trust had been present, together with Yan and Bruno Sicora.

Yan had objected to the proposal to appoint Tanwen – reading that brought an unexpected pain – but Bruno had supported it. The anonymous donation was referred to, and despite Yan's objections, the Trust had confirmed Tanwen's appointment.

But beneath this was another missive.

Dear friend,

Your suspicions regarding G were initially surprising, but when I thought about it, they answered several questions that had been in my mind.

As you say, we certainly need to know more, and seduction might well bring forth some unguarded confidence from him. If you do feel you can play Mata Hari for a night or two, heaven forbid that I should try to deter you, but you'd better let me know, because we'll need to get T out of the house for the evening. That won't be difficult – I can arrange for a late practice session, which she'll jump at. She's conceived a passion for the maestro – but which of his female musicians don't do that? I expect she'll try to seduce him, but whether or not she'll succeed, I have no idea. He's a deep one, as you know.

Incidentally, I've heard one or two slightly dubious rumours about G's bedroom tastes, so if you do get him into bed, I hope you can cope!

And if he really is a . . . I had better not use the word, but if you are right and G is what you suspect, then we both know what must be done. Such people can't be allowed to live.

Your always irreverent, but unfailingly patriotic Bruno.

As she put down the letter, it was as if white, hurting lights were piercing Tanwen's eyes. She had been used by her father – everything fitted – dates, names, everything. He believed the Library was the base for a spy network against the Nazis, and he was gathering information about it. And he had engineered her post with the Library, even giving them a donation in return for the appointment. Had he engineered the Żelazowa Award, as well? Had he even been the anonymous donor?

Through the sick disbelief, Tanwen was aware of a thread of puzzlement as to how her father had come by Bruno's letter. But how often might her father have been in Irina's house? The memory suddenly came to her of how, when Tanwen had offered to tidy the rooms, Irina said she had more important things to be thinking about. From there it was sickeningly easy for Tanwen to visualize her father furtively searching cupboards and drawers while Irina was not around, looking for scraps of information that might one day be of use. And he had found something; he had found this damning letter, and he had kept it to one day use against Bruno.

Bruno had written that such a traitor could not be allowed to live. He had not used the word traitor, but his meaning had been obvious. Irina had said that if Georg Malek were ever to enter her house again, she would kill him. Had they both really meant that? It certainly sounded like it. When might they do it, though? It might be some way in the future – it had sounded as if their suspicions were still very slight and unformed. They would want to be sure of their facts. Tanwen would want to be sure, as well.

But she thought she would want to be there when they executed her father.

TWENTY-THREE

Thaisa had stood completely still, staring at Helena and the photograph she was holding for what felt like a very long time. It was only when there were voices behind her that the frozen immobility snapped, and she turned to see Phin and the professor and the others coming in.

Nina said, 'We didn't know you were in here. Helena said something about going across to the cloakroom – to freshen up after all the drama.'

'And then we heard the music,' said Phin.

The music.

Thaisa felt as if her legs had turned to cotton threads, but she managed to reach one of the chairs, and sat down, gratefully, clasping her trembling hands together tightly.

To her astonishment, she heard herself say, 'Nina, Lucek, please will you ask Helena who she believes is the person in that photo?'

Lucek spoke to Helena, and for a moment Thaisa thought Helena was not going to answer, but then she looked down at the photograph again. She said, '*Moja matka.*'

Thaisa heard Lucek gasp and she saw Nina start slightly. Then Lucek said, 'She's saying it's a photograph of her mother. Only it can't be – can it?'

'No, of course not.' Thaisa took a deep breath. 'It's a photograph of me,' she said. 'It was taken when I was about seventeen – by my music teacher. She was trying to fathom the workings of a new camera, and we were laughing.' For a moment she was back in that sunlit picture, herself and Alan enjoying the afternoon. She saw, with a pang, how very different she had looked in the photograph – her hair dark, not the pepper-and-salt grey it was now, her eyes bright and happy because of being with Alan and looking forward to the music festival they were going to enter.

She forced herself to say, 'You wouldn't recognize it as me, of course. It was a long time ago, and my hair was dark in those days. But—'

'I can see the resemblance,' said Professor Liripine, unexpectedly. 'The cheekbones and the eyes.'

Thaisa had no idea how to respond to this, so she said, 'I had it framed for my father to have in here, because . . . oh, because I thought I'd like him to have it in the room where he spent most of his time.' She looked at the photo again. 'But he said—'

'Yes?'

'He said in the photograph I looked exactly as my mother looked when she was around that age. When he first met her.'

There was a silence. They're all working it out, thought Thaisa, and heard Lucek translating for Helena. She saw Helena smile and nod, as if this had not surprised her.

There was only one conclusion that could be reached, of course, and everyone would have reached it. The same mother, thought Thaisa. Making us half-sisters. Different father? Yes, it must have been. But she was aware of unexpected warmth at what had just happened. She was able to look at Helena and think that this was someone who belonged to her – it was even someone who might understand about the fears and the strangeness of her own life. She and Helena could talk properly later – there would be a great many things to find out. Nina and Lucek would help with the language. That, too, brought a good feeling. But for the moment . . .

She said, 'Professor – the music. You called it the "Dark Cadence".'

'We think that's what it is. Did you recognize it?'

'I once heard my father play it,' said Thaisa. 'It was just before he died. Many years ago. But I never forgot it. It seemed to me that it was almost being torn from him. My mother was almost distraught at hearing it – she begged him to stop. She said something about being there with him when they had heard it played. "I heard it being played," she said. "And it was a bad way for them to die".'

'Thaisa, you don't have to tell us anything that might be – well, private,' said Phin. 'And we wouldn't try to find out anything you didn't want to talk about.'

Thaisa was grateful. She said, 'You wouldn't think I'd remember a piece of music after so long – and you certainly wouldn't think I'd know the music so well after hearing it just that once. But I do.'

'It isn't music you'd ever forget,' said Lucek. 'Helena must have been very small when she heard it, but she never forgot it, either. It was part of her nightmares.'

'You said it was known as the "Traitor's Music",' said Thaisa, looking back at the professor.

'That's its legend. We've more or less established that it was heard the night the Chopin Library burned.'

'Which means that if we're trusting the legend at all, a traitor died in that fire,' said Phin. 'That he – or even she – was executed. But not in the usual way of being shot or hanged—'

'Burned to death,' said Thaisa, and the memory came again. She said, 'It would have been a bad way to die.'

'Yes.' Phin hesitated, and when he spoke again, Thaisa had the impression that he was choosing his words carefully. He said, 'Is it possible that either of your parents could have been in Warsaw when the Library burned? That they heard the music that night?'

'I don't know. I don't who they were,' said Thaisa. 'Not in the way most people know about their parents. They never spoke about their early lives, although I know they were both Polish, and I'm fairly sure they were both from Warsaw.' She could hardly believe she was saying this – that she was actually step-ping into the dark, forbidden waters at last. *Always be on guard . . . Keep people away . . .* But I can't. Not any longer. And there's Helena— And this is Helena's mother, as well as mine.

Helena's memories might fill in the jagged gaps in Thaisa's knowledge of the past. They might help to bring the truth into the light – it might turn out to be a terrible truth, but finally knowing it might free Thaisa of all the years of uncertainty and the ingrained compulsion to keep the world at bay and the past sealed up. It might also mean that Helena would be freed from the nightmares.

With the feeling that now she really was stepping into those dark waters, she said, 'I don't know what my father might have done as a young man – I don't know what part he might have played in the war, because . . .' She broke off. This was going to be the hardest thing yet, but she would do it. 'He had a Nazi Death's Head ring,' she said. 'I found it one day by accident. What was called a *Totenkopf.*'

Arabella said, softly, 'Heinrich Himmler's infamous award. A silver ring with a skull's head and runic symbols engraved in it. Given for special services to the Third Reich.'

'But only given to high-ranking Nazi officers,' said Thaisa. 'Which begs the question as to why my father had it.'

Helena reached for Lucek's hand, and said something to him. He nodded, then said, 'Helena would like to explain more of what she remembers since hearing the music and seeing the photograph,' said Lucek, after a moment. 'She thinks it might add to what's already known – that it might help Thaisa.' He said, a bit awkwardly, 'She thinks she knew from the first that there was a link with Thaisa.'

'We both knew,' said Thaisa, at once. 'As soon as we saw each other—'

Lucek smiled at her. He said, 'And so if Nina will translate as she speaks—'

'Of course I will. Helena . . .'

Helena appeared to have followed a good deal of this without anyone having to translate for her. She curved her hands around the photograph, and although she was looking down at it, Thaisa had the feeling that she was looking beyond it, as if into some long-ago world.

Then she began to speak.

For Phin, listening to Nina translating Helena's words was a curious experience. Even though it was Nina's voice they listened to, he was intensely aware that they were hearing the memories and emotions of the no-longer-young lady with high cheekbones and dark eyes. This was the voice of that long-ago child, whose terror in a ravaged city had marred her life.

But it was not the ghosts of devastated buildings and ruined streets that were crowding into the quiet room; it was the ghosts of the people that the child had seen and known, recounted with a curious blend of the child's perceptions and the older woman's understanding. And central to all the ghosts was the figure of

the child's mother – a mother who had been the focus of the
child's life. A lady who had looked exactly like the smiling
dark-haired girl in the photograph.

'I mustn't ever call her Mamma, because nobody had to know
who I was. But she was so beautiful and so clever that I used
to follow her when she went out, just so I could look at her.

'Sometimes she went to a big old house – a white stone
house in a square. It was the most beautiful house in the world.
There were boards across the windows, because of the secrets.
The men with clawed boots mustn't find out about them—'

A pause. The professor looked across at Phin and framed the
word, *Nazis*, and Phin nodded.

'You mustn't ever let them see you, those men. I knew that
– people in the dining room said it. It was always Irina who
took me there. I liked it. There was a man with fat cheeks
who cooked for people.'

Irina, thought Phin, reaching for his notebook to write down
the name. And a man with fat cheeks who cooked – Anatol?
Is this all coming together?

'People drank wine there, and laughed and talked. There were
two men who played music – one of them read stories to
me about magic worlds and kings and princesses. I sat on his
knee and he showed me how to pick out the music on the piano.'

'The firebird piano,' said Professor Liripine, very softly.

'Sometimes, when people went to the white house, I followed
them. It was like being part of an adventure – like the children
in the stories. Nobody knew I was there – I was good at not
letting people see me—'

Eerily, there was the impression of a child's innocent glee at
fooling the grown-ups.

'But one day when I went to the house it stopped being an
adventure. One day the nightmare came.'

She broke off and wrapped her arms around her as if for
warmth. Phin said, 'Nina, ask her if she's all right to go on.'

'If she is remembering, she will want to talk,' said Lucek,
eagerly. 'It is – um . . . What is that word you used, doctor?
Healing. Letting the demons shrivel up in the light.'

Phin thought Nina relayed the gist of this to Helena, who
nodded and looked at them gratefully.

'My mamma and the man had to do something important in the house that day. I followed them – I thought it was still the adventure, but it wasn't. The terror had got into the house. And then I couldn't get out – somebody had locked the door, and there were boards over the windows . . .' A pause, as if she might be struggling to reach the memories.

'Somebody was in the house with me – saying I would be safe. But there was something very bad in the house . . . We went down steps to a dark room, and there was something cold down there in the dark . . .'

'Nina – ask her what happened.'

But Helena shook her head at the question. 'She can't reach the memory,' said Nina. 'All she can remember is a coldness and a dark old room, and then someone carrying her through that house – and telling her she would be all right.'

Phin said, 'She's looking back at the memory now, isn't she? She's stepped out of it and she's looking back at it. Sorry, I didn't mean to interrupt. Go on.'

'There was smoke and the sound of a fire crackling . . . And then there was just fear, and I was frightened, because I thought the fire was going to burn us up . . .

'Then suddenly the fire had gone away and I wasn't frightened any more. I was outside the house, only I couldn't remember how I got there. But the fire had stopped, and people had come to help – I remember sitting on the ground for a long time watching them. They were trying to clear the rubble, and a woman saw me and carried me to her house. She said something about me being an orphan of the war and I would be looked after.' Helena made a brief gesture with one hand. 'I think that was the first time I had heard that word, orphan.' She reached for Lucek's hand, and said something, and before Nina could translate, Lucek smiled and said something to her in Polish. Then, for the benefit of the others, he said, 'It was my great-grandmother who found her.'

'But the music had been there . . . I had heard it – it was being played through the fire. It was quite close to me. I never forgot it. And then today Professor Liripine played it and I knew it was the same.' She stopped speaking, but Nina kept hold of her hand.

Phin said softly, 'The "Dark Cadence".'

'Yes,' said the professor.

'The links are being forged, aren't they?' said Phin. 'Anatol heard the "Cadence" that night, as well.'

'And Anatol has got to be the man with fat cheeks who served food in the dining room,' put in Arabella.

'The dining room where someone played the firebird piano.' This was Dr Purslove.

'And Thaisa's parents knew – and feared – the "Cadence",' said Professor Liripine. 'But who was it who tried to save Helena from the fire?'

'And who played the "Cadence" while the Library burned?' said Dr Purslove. 'Was it the same person? Because whoever it was, was inside the place – Anatol was clear about that.'

'And my parents talked about it being a bad way to die,' said Thaisa.

Phin frowned, then said, 'Nina – how much of the scrapbook is left to translate?'

TWENTY-FOUR

Warsaw, mid-1940s

To Yan, one of the most dreadful things, in all the dreadful things that were happening, was the way in which they were all becoming used to the ravaged streets of Warsaw. It was no longer so shocking to find that a once-imposing building had been reduced to rubble overnight, or that some lovely old square had vanished.

Normal life had certainly vanished. The Luftwaffe were bombing the city relentlessly now, and people who did venture out did so warily and in secrecy. Most people knew that there were defiant meetings of small groups behind locked doors and shuttered windows, but hardly anyone knew about the meetings below the Chopin Library. Its windows were boarded up and the rooms empty.

'But one day it could be rebuilt,' Yan said to Bruno. 'If we could send these cruel brutes back, Warsaw could be reclaimed.'

'It'd be a massive task, maestro.'

'I wouldn't care how massive. I'd lay bricks and dig trenches with my own hands. I'd do anything to get back even a part of what's been lost in this city.'

Yan or Bruno went into the Library once a week, doing so openly during daylight.

'To the soldiers' eyes,' said Bruno, 'we're merely checking that the place is secure and no one's living there – no one they'd want to haul off to one of the camps, I mean. If we're seen and questioned, I think that will be credible. Thank God most of the Street of Music is still intact.'

'The word is that the German armies are in retreat on the Eastern Front,' said Yan. 'This *can't* go on much longer.'

But there was a rumour that Himmler had given an order that Warsaw's inhabitants were all to be killed, and that the city was to be what he called 'levelled', as an example to the rest of Europe.

'He won't do it,' said Bruno, but Yan heard, for the first time, a note of uncertainty in Bruno's voice.

Yan and Bruno – often with Irina and Anatol and the former printer – worked and plotted in the deep old scullery below the Library. Alicja was often with them, as well.

'I, too, can fight,' she said, and for the first time there was anger in her voice.

Several times they managed transmissions to and from the main Resistance – always very brief transmissions to minimize the risk of the Germans picking them up, but exchanging information about meetings and about the approach of the Red Army. The Russian soldiers were encountering appalling hardships, but they were coming doggedly and determinedly forwards. People in Anatol's wept with emotion and hope at hearing this, telling one another they would eventually be liberated – if they could only cling to their city a little longer, they would be saved.

It was good to be able to still gather in Anatol's café. It was necessary to keep a wary listen for the approach of the patrols, of course, but there was strength and comfort to be derived from the company. The few children who were still in the city were brought with the adults. It was appalling that such small children had to be part of the bleakness and to sense the fear, but most people thought it would be too dangerous to try to take them elsewhere now. It was difficult and risky enough to get a couple of adults through the blockades – how could you expose children to such terror and uncertainty?

The children had never really known any other way of life, though, and they liked being in the grown-up world of Anatol's. They loved listening to Yan playing, as well. One of them, a dark-haired, dark-eyed little creature, came to sit on his knee when he stopped, and laughed with delight when he showed her how to pick out tunes. She was usually brought by Irina – Yan had no idea if Irina was the child's mother, and these days it was better not to ask who was related to whom. Once, Irina had said something about having originally intended to send the child to Anatol's cousins in the Kampinos Forest.

'But since the mass executions there, it's much too dangerous,' she said. 'You knew about that?'

'Yes.' Yan had been sickened by the stories that had filtered back. The victims had been people whom the Gestapo said were fomenting rebellion – people they called Polish elite – political, cultural, and social elite, they said. There had been doctors, writers, politicians, artists, lawyers. The Gestapo had ordered the cutting down of trees in the beautiful, ancient valley in order to dig ditches, and the bodies had been flung into mass graves.

Certainly that was no place to send a child, and when Irina said she could keep the child safe ('I know the tricks for dodging the oppressors'), Yan thought she was probably right.

One day he looked at a couple of the books brought from Ipatiev House, and took them to Anatol's, where he read the stories to the children, translating them from Russian to Polish as he read. His dark-eyed girl sat on the floor, listening, utterly enrapt.

Irina said, 'She will remember this, Yan. Hopefully not the terror and the secrecy, but the music and the stories. You're giving her a good memory to take from all this horror.'

Yan was absurdly pleased by Irina's words. Several times he thought if there was ever a chance of getting any of the children out of Warsaw to safety, he would make sure that this little one was with them.

It had not occurred to Yan that Tanwen would reappear in Warsaw after so long, so he was totally unprepared to see her walk with apparent unconcern into Anatol's early one evening.

After the initial shock, his first reaction was that she had changed – that something had happened to alter her in some deep, intrinsic way. His second reaction was very different – it was fear. Because although this was the woman with whom he had shared that astonishing passion, it was also the woman to whom, afterwards, he had confessed to committing murder. But surely it was ridiculous to feel so apprehensive? How many years was it since that night – since he had believed for that short time that his Romanov girl had come back? Tanwen would not have waited this long to bring some sort of challenge or to wreak revenge on him.

He was relieved to find that he was able to greet her with reasonable normality, asking how she was, and listening to her talking of how she had been with her parents. It had been a splendid time, she said; it was a very lively part of the country, and there had been all kinds of entertainments and musical evenings which she had been part of. But more recently, of course, she had wanted to be at the centre – she had wanted to come back to Warsaw to help, she said, adopting an air of solemnity. Irina still had her old rooms free, so she was staying there again, although it all felt a bit strange, and as if she had stepped back in time.

Yan, listening, murmuring suitable rejoinders, suddenly saw the younger Tanwen who wanted to impress, and who was probably embroidering the truth. She still had the same habit of tilting her head, but he thought her eyes were wary and watchful. She wore her hair differently, but the autumn glints were still visible.

Turning back to the children, he could not help thinking that there was more to it than feeling needed in the city. Tanwen was here for some purpose of her own. A lover? But he thought it was unlikely that Tanwen – that anyone – would come to this ravaged city purely to be with a lover. What, then, had brought her here?

He stayed late at the restaurant, helping Irina and the printer with the leaflets they were preparing which would call the members of their small group together in a week's time.

'We can meet here at Anatol's,' said Irina. 'We haven't used his cellar for a while, and I don't think it's being watched very particularly. I'm sketching the firebird piano in each one – everyone will know that means to come here.'

The printer bewailed the fact that he could no longer use his printing press. 'But if the oppressors see this leaflet,' he said, 'they will think it's a draft for a concert programme cover.'

'Even though they'll know we couldn't possibly stage a concert in these circumstances?' said Yan.

'I'm not putting a date on it. And I'll smudge it a bit. They'll think it's an old draft.'

Yan did not say that he was beginning to wonder how much longer this could go on. It was all good and fine to tell people that the Red Army were making their dogged way from the east, but how long would it take them? And would they be able to drive back Hitler's armies anyway? It had been all very well to tell Bruno that one day they would reclaim their city, rebuild what had been destroyed, but would that ever really be possible?

As they were preparing to leave, Irina suddenly said to him, 'Yan, I didn't know Tanwen was coming back to Warsaw.'

'Why did she?'

'I don't know, but whatever her reasons, I think we should be careful not to let her know what we're doing. Only the people we're absolutely certain we can trust can know.'

'You don't trust Tanwen?' said Yan.

He thought Irina's eyes slid away, but then she said, 'Not entirely. But then I don't trust anyone any more.'

It was after midnight when Yan walked back to his rooms. He had the book of Russian fairytales with him – the children had listened to two stories that night. Tanwen had listened, as well, quietly sitting in a corner, watching everything. Irina doesn't trust you, thought Yan, remembering. I don't think I do, either. But is that simply because of that night we had together? Or is it because Irina's suspicious? Whatever it is, there's *something* . . .

Putting the book away, he looked at the folded piece of silk that lay at the very bottom of the box. Inside was the miniature of his sunset-haired girl, but also inside the silk was the music that Vadim – his father – had given to him. Yan had promised Vadim that he would destroy it, but he had known he could never do so, and he never had. But now – with danger everywhere – with Tanwen back in Warsaw . . .?

He took out the score and with it came the remembered feeling of someone writing this down a long time ago – doing so in fearful secrecy because no one must know what this was . . .

No one must know . . . But tonight, someone had reappeared in his life who did know. *I murdered Katya*, he had said to Tanwen that night. Could any connection ever be seen between the 'Cadence' music and Katerinburg? Between Katya's death and Yan himself?

He reached into the cupboard for some blank music scores. With the feeling that he was repeating an action that had happened several times over the centuries, he made sure his door was locked, then by the light of a single candle he began, very painstakingly, to copy the music on to the blank score. He made two copies – he would not trust one copy not to be lost or damaged or destroyed. One could stay here with the miniature, and the other could be kept in the safe in his office at the Chopin Library. And then the music Vadim had given him could be burned. He looked at it for a moment, then lit a fire in the small grate in his room in preparation. He sat down at his desk with the 'Cadence' and the blank score.

The copying did not take very long. It was not a very long piece of music. I've disguised you, he thought, at length, sitting back. You're no longer the '*Temnaya Kadentsiya*' – the 'Traitor's Music'. But what name can I give you that won't alert suspicion? He frowned, and then his brow cleared, because of course there was only one piece of music he could use in this deception.

Carefully and clearly, at the top of each score, he wrote *The 'Demon's aria'. Anton Rubinstein.* Beneath this, he wrote '*Ne plach' ditya moya*'.

Now the 'Dark Cadence' could hide behind the sad, beautiful lament that his lost Romanov girl had sung on the way to her own death.

He picked up the original, and with the feeling that he was completing a ritual he deliberately consigned it to the fire.

TWENTY-FIVE

Warsaw, mid-1940s

Tanwen felt strange to be in Warsaw again. She could not entirely believe she had even managed to get here at all, but somehow she had done it.

After finding the documents in the old suitcase, she had watched her father closely. For a long time there had not been even the tiniest wisp of a fact that might weave into actual proof, and even if she had found any wisps, Tanwen admitted to herself that she was not sure what she would do with them.

And then one day, her father announced, casually, that he had to go to Warsaw.

'A nuisance, and a difficult journey,' he said. 'But I still have a seat on several boards, and there's a meeting – sadly to dissolve most of the boards. Documents will have to be signed, and resolutions passed.' He gave her the indulgent smile that she had known since childhood, and that she now believed to be as false as stairs of sand. 'Not into the city itself,' he said. 'I'm not going into the turbulent heart of the war.' He patted her hand, and Tanwen had to force herself not to snatch her own hand away, because every time he touched her, grotesque images flooded her mind. Images of her father with Irina – the two of them grunting and heaving in a bed in the house she had lived in herself . . . 'There are dubious rumours about G's bedroom tastes,' Bruno had written to Irina. 'I hope you can cope.'

Her father left the following day, and Tanwen at once put her own plan into action. She said to her mother that she had had a letter from one of her old Academy friends – there was a concert in the friend's little town, and they would like Tanwen to be part of it. To help with the organization and also to perform, of course. She could stay with the friend for a week or two.

No, it was not a dangerous journey, it would all be perfectly easy and safe. Her mother was completely unsuspicious; Tanwen was not surprised that her father had deceived her so easily and for so long.

And now, at last, she was in Irina's house again, and her rooms at the top of the house were available. 'Empty for many months,' Irina had said. 'No one wants to live in Warsaw now.'

Tanwen did not allow time for Irina to ask why she herself wanted to live in Warsaw again. She looked at Irina from the corners of her eyes as if bashful, and embarked on the lies she had worked out. There was a man, she said, here in Warsaw. But there was a wife in the picture, so it all had to be utterly secret. But she had come to be with him – you snatched at whatever fragments of happiness you could in these times, didn't you? She hoped Irina would understand.

Irina seemed to understand, and Tanwen was relieved, although she had thought it all sounded perfectly plausible. Irina gave Tanwen a key to the front door, warned her about the patrols, and that was all. This was all very good, and everything was going as Tanwen had planned.

What she had not expected was that Helena would still be in the house.

Helena.

Tanwen could not believe that anyone could look at the small lively Helena and not see that she was an exact print of Yan. It was all there – the dark eyes, the slanting cheekbones, the impression of light and life and intelligence. And music, she thought, and saw, as she had seen after Helena was born, the instant, instinctive response to music of any kind.

She had been determined not to show any emotion when she and Yan met again, but several days later, accompanying Irina and Helena to the small restaurant near the Street of Music, she felt something constrict around her heart when Helena ran straight to him. Watching her clamber delightedly on to Yan's knee, and pick out notes on an old piano with him, she wanted to shout to him to recognize Helena for who and what she was. Later, Helena sat with a small group of children who had remained in the city, and listened when Yan read to them from a book of old fairy stories. Tanwen, still watching covertly, thought he had some sort of magic with children – it was as if he knew and understood how their minds and their imaginations worked. This was surprising, because it was not a quality she would have thought he would possess.

She was careful not to let anyone become aware of these thoughts, of course, although Bruno looked at her questioningly a few times, and even Alicja emerged from one of her gloomy moods to study Tanwen thoughtfully. But that was all.

She had a very simple plan. Those letters had suggested that Georg – it was increasingly difficult to think of him as 'Father' – was suspicious of the Chopin Library. If he was here to unmask some kind of Resistance group based inside it, then that was where he would go. He might do so openly, walking nonchalantly across the square in broad daylight, but it was more likely that he would go stealthily, by night. He would reason that it would be night when plotters would gather. So Tanwen had only to slip out of the house each evening – letting Irina assume she was off to see her mythical lover – and conceal herself in one of the dark corners of the square. And wait.

It was curious to find that rather than this nightly vigil being tedious, which Tanwen had expected, it was exciting. There was a feeling of purpose and importance each time she stole through the unlit streets, wrapped in a concealing cloak (it was black, which was not really her colour, but it was all she had been able to find). And later, when the war was over – as one day it would be – she might even be hailed as a heroine. She would be the woman who had patriotically given evidence against her own father. 'I did it for my country,' she would say.

It was not, however, until the third week of her stay in Warsaw that Georg finally appeared. It was a dismal night, with a thin misty rain falling, and, as a nearby church clock chimed nine o'clock, Tanwen heard footsteps come along one of the narrow streets that led into the square. Her heart bumped. It was not unknown for a solitary person to be abroad out here at such an hour, but it was unusual, because people tended to be indoors by this hour. She pressed back into the shadows.

Into the square came the well-known figure, wearing the

familiar long dark overcoat, the collar turned up so that it hid most of the face. Tanwen felt a spiral of triumph. She had been right. He was going into the Library to catch the Resistance group, and Tanwen herself was going in to catch him. She was not sure what she was actually going to do with him, but if the Resistance group was in there, they would know.

He paused, glanced about him, then crossed the square and went around the side of the building. How would he get in? Then Tanwen heard the faint sound of glass breaking. She gave it a couple of moments, then went towards the Library.

She saw the broken window at once. It was near the back of the Library, and it was narrow, but her father had been able to climb through, and Tanwen could do so, as well. Once inside, the remembered scents of the Library closed around her, and she stood very still, listening. Soft footsteps were going towards the back of the house, and then came the sound of a door being opened. The kitchens below ground? It must be. No secret group would carry out their work up here, in these public rooms with their tall windows through which anyone could peer.

She went across the floor, and down the flight of stone steps that led to the scullery. She had never been down here before, but she knew the way, because on the night of the concert these doors had been propped wide, so that the famous tradition of lighting the Iced Polonaise could be followed. Her footsteps echoed in the emptiness, and Tanwen tried to move more stealthily. The steps went quite a long way down, and they were steep, so that it was necessary to put a hand out to the wall once or twice. But she reached the bottom, and there was the scullery. It was unexpectedly large, and it was shadowy and dim. But there was no one here, and Tanwen felt suddenly unsure. There did not seem to be anyone down here, and everywhere was in darkness—

Everywhere was not in darkness. On the other side of the room, a section of timber had been moved out, and propped against the wall, and a dull, smeary light spilled out from the opening. She went towards it, her heart bumping with nerves, but also with a stir of excitement. The opening was easily wide enough to step through, and beyond it she could see stone steps, going down, and tarnished old wall sconces, cobwebs dripping from them. She hesitated, and then heard a murmur of voices from below.

Taking a deep breath, she went cautiously down the wide stairs. The light from below was obviously from candles or maybe oil lamps, because it was flickering wildly, causing shadows to form on the stair wall. It was absurd to think that the shadows watched her, and that at any moment one of them would reach out and snatch her up.

She heard her father's voice say, 'We've never been introduced. But I know you're Bruno Sicora, and you'll certainly know who I am.'

'Georg Malek,' said Bruno. 'I know you.'

'I've been watching you and this house for a while. You're sending messages to the Resistance movement from here. I think my friends and contacts in the Third Reich will be very interested indeed to hear about that.'

'Malek, this isn't what it looks like,' Bruno said, and Georg laughed.

'It's exactly what it looks like. Now, you'll stay here – and if you try to jump me, I'll use this revolver. Be sure of that.'

'I don't doubt it.'

'I'm going back upstairs – I'll have you covered all the time, of course – and I'll replace that panel of timber, and put a barricade across it. Then I'll bring in one of the patrols. How will you – and your sly colleagues – like being marched out to face a firing squad?'

Bruno said, 'I don't think it'll come to that, Malek.'

'No?'

'No,' he said, and there was the sound of a chair being pushed back. With that sound, Tanwen went down the remaining stairs and hurled herself at her father's figure, knocking him to the ground.

The gun went off, deafeningly loud in the underground room, but the bullet went wide, burying itself in the stone wall. Bruno had bounded forward, and grabbed Georg's arms, twisting them behind his back.

'Something to tie them,' he said. 'Quickly. And what on earth are you doing here?'

Tanwen snatched off the belt of her frock, and Bruno bound

her father's wrists tightly behind his back. 'I was watching him,' she said. 'I found out ages ago what he is. I wanted to catch him.'

'You nearly gave me a heart attack erupting down the stairs like that,' said Bruno. 'How did you get in?'

'He—' Tanwen pointed, 'he had broken a window and climbed through. I followed him. The window by the little side door.'

'The boarding was always a bit chancy on that side window,' said Bruno. He tightened the belt around Malek's wrists. 'That should hold all right,' he said. 'And I can use the belt from my trousers for his ankles. That'll be good enough for the moment.'

A stream of curses was coming from Georg as Bruno bound his feet. Tanwen flinched at the vicious spite and hatred in his tone, but Bruno said, 'Curse all you like. You're the one who'll be facing death. A spy against your own people – against Poland – my God, you'll suffer for that.'

Tanwen said, 'Do we leave him here and . . .' She stopped, because finally she was forced to face the practicalities of who they should go to about this. The Nazis ruled here – they ruled all across Poland – and they would certainly inflict their own punishment on the Polish spy – Bruno – who had unmasked one of their men. And on Tanwen herself, as well.

When at last they both straightened up and looked at one another, she saw these thoughts mirrored in Bruno's expression.

He said, 'I think this is one we'll have to deal with ourselves, Tanwen. How far can I trust you? Because he's your father, so—'

'You can trust me to the ultimate,' said Tanwen. 'Whatever we do, I'll never speak of it, not for the rest of my life, or yours.'

'That could be an easy promise to keep, because our lives might not be very long,' said Bruno. 'If we don't handle this right, we could still end up facing that firing squad and it could be very soon.' He looked down at the man lying bound on the floor. 'An honest-to-goodness German spy, I might have almost accepted,' he said. 'Because, damn it all, I'm spying. But this—'

'This is spying against his own people,' said Tanwen.

'Yes. And that,' said Bruno in a soft voice that whispered eerily around the room, 'is why I think he had better die.'

The silence closed down, and they looked at one another. 'Now?' whispered Tanwen at last. 'Here?'

'Yes.'

'How?'

Bruno said, 'The means are to hand.' He reached down to pick up the revolver, but Tanwen put out her hand to stop him.

'No – wait. What about . . . afterwards? Where do we put him? Because he can't be found, can he? Not in here, anyway – it would point back to you. To the people you're working with.' It might point back to Yan, said her mind. Helena's father. Even to Helena herself.

'We can't carry him through the streets,' said Bruno, frowning. 'We'd be seen by the patrols. We probably wouldn't even get him across the square. Only I can't think . . .' He broke off, looking about him, then he said, 'D'you remember Anatol talking about an old ice room? And how Yan said there would be bound to be one in a house of this size?'

'Yes. But where would it be?' Tanwen felt as if she had stepped into a nightmare, and this no longer felt real. She did not look at the figure on the ground, because she did not dare to look at it. She was overwhelmingly grateful for Bruno's presence – somehow he was no longer the flippant person he had been when she first came to Warsaw; he was sharp and purposeful.

As he reached for one of the oil lamps, Tanwen saw for the first time that there was what must be a wireless transmitter on the table, and a notepad. Bruno saw the look.

'Yes, there really is a Resistance network in this place,' he said. 'Very small, but we're doing what we can. Tonight I was sending messages to tell others in the group about a meeting at Anatol's at the end of this week.' He looked across at the figure lying bound in the corner, and said, 'You see, Malek, you were right.'

'I knew it.'

'Would there be a door going into an ice room,' said Tanwen, as Bruno moved the lamp across the walls, then lowered it to the floor.

'If there is, I should think it's more likely to be off this room – maybe below this floor,' said Bruno, kneeling down, and running his hands slowly across the stone floor. 'In fact . . . Ah, what's this?'

Tanwen had seen it at the same time. A section of the stone floor in a corner – a large square of the stones that was slightly out of true with the rest.

'A trapdoor?' she said.

'It could be. Take the lamp and hold it up. And,' said Bruno, looking back over his shoulder, 'keep an eye on that one, as well.'

'He's still tied up,' she said, casting a quick look over her shoulder.

As she said this, there was a hard scraping sound as Bruno prised up the square of stone. It came up unwillingly and it showered dust and debris as it did so. Cold, dry breath came out at them, and Tanwen flinched.

'It's not an ice room,' said Bruno, peering down. 'It's more of an ice pit. My God, it's cold down there. Tilt the lamp, will you?'

The lamplight showed up a cellar-like structure – Tanwen thought it was about nine or ten feet across. There were several deep shelves, and a rickety-looking ladder that extended from beneath the slab.

'And there seems to be an extra layer of stone on the underside of the lid,' said Bruno, still investigating. 'That would seal the place up quite effectively – in fact it has done. There are still slivers of ice on some of the shelves.' He straightened up. 'As graves go, Georg,' he said, 'you could do a lot worse.'

'You're going to put me in there?' For the first time Tanwen heard a note of fear.

'We can't risk letting you live,' said Bruno. 'You'll go running to your masters in Berlin and you'll blow our cover, and we can't let that happen.'

'You won't get away with it.'

'I think we will.'

'*She* won't let you execute me.' It came out with a kind of vicious satisfaction.

'Tanwen?' said Bruno, turning to her. 'Will you let me shoot this creature?'

This creature. This man who had always been in her life. Who had encouraged her, helped her, been proud of her when she achieved something. Yes, but who had been prepared to sell out his own country and his own people to the oppressors – to those greedy, soulless men who were burning Jews wholesale and dragging innocent victims to dreadful concentration camps, and who were destroying cities and cultures. And who had manoeuvred his own daughter into this very building in order to inveigle its secrets from her.

Tanwen said, 'Yes. Yes, I will let you shoot him.' She looked very directly at the man she could no longer think of as her father. He returned her look levelly, and something disquieting stirred within her mind. He's frightened, she thought – but there's something else. Something that's calculating and cunning. But what? Because he can't possibly escape.

She turned back to Bruno. 'Do it,' she said, but as Bruno picked up the revolver that had skittered across the floor, she said, suddenly, 'But not through the head.' *Not splintering the face and the eyes that once had watched her with love and pride . . .*

'No,' said Bruno, as if understanding. 'Not the brain, but the black evil heart of the traitor.'

The shot, when it came, was deafening in the enclosed space, and there was a crackle of flame and the sharp scent of smoke. Tanwen saw Georg's body arch and then fall back, prone, the head dropping to one side. Before she could speak, Bruno said, 'Over and done. I'll push him into the ice pit.' As Tanwen started forward, he said, 'No, I can manage it,' and grasped Georg's ankles, dragging him across the couple of feet to the yawning ice pit. Once there, he tipped him over the edge.

As the body tumbled down, Bruno reached for the stone slab and forced it back down into place. As it clanged home the sound echoed dully, and the movement caused the oil lamps to flicker. Echoes whispered slyly in the corners and the shadows reared up, and then subsided.

Bruno reached for Tanwen's hand. 'And now,' he said, 'we must go back into the world and pretend none of this happened.'

TWENTY-SIX

Warsaw, mid-1940s

But, of course, it was impossible to pretend it had not happened.

Two days later, Bruno sought Tanwen out in Anatol's restaurant, and said, 'I'll have to go back into the Library.'

Tanwen had known, deep down, that they would have to do this, but she said, 'Why?'

'To get rid of the transmitter and anything else that might point back to our group,' he said. 'I can't be sure that he – Malek – hadn't told his people about his suspicions. He said something about, "I always knew". Remember?'

'Yes.'

'And I need to board up the window he broke,' said Bruno. 'We'd made the place as impregnable as we could so that none of the homeless could use it. But I can't leave that window smashed open. I think I can board it up – there are some sections of timber from the false wall that was created to seal off the old stairway and the original scullery. We levered some of them off when we set up the wireless and we put what was left over in Yan's office, I think. I can use those.'

'Is it safe to go back, though?'

'It'll have to be. We daren't risk anyone getting in and finding anything,' said Bruno. 'I've been waiting until Yan and the others are occupied with other things, or I'd have gone back before this.'

'Aren't you going to tell them what's happened?'

'No. I'm just going to say I've had to move the wireless because I can't get a signal any longer, and we need to close down this location. I don't know where I'll move it to, yet, but one thing at a time.'

As he turned to go, Tanwen said, 'Wait. You can't do it on your own. I'll come, too.'

'Better not.'

'No, I'll come.' It was impossible to explain that there had been that moment when, alongside the fear, something very curious had looked out of Georg Malek's eyes. Something that had said, *This isn't the end . . . I'm going to get the better of you . . .* It was absurd to think he could somehow have cheated them – Bruno had shot him, Tanwen had seen him do it, and she had seen Georg recoil and then lie dead on the ground. But there had been that sly look . . . Into her mind came the thought – *I must be absolutely sure . . .*

But she only said, 'It'll be a bit eerie going down there on your own. And I can at least hold the oil lamp and help you carry everything out.'

'I suppose it'll look less suspicious if there are two of us. All right. The transmitter takes apart – we can put the sections in a couple of shopping bags. Not that anyone goes shopping any longer – not that there are many shops left – but it'll be a fair enough cover.'

'All right. When do we do it?'

'This afternoon.'

'In broad daylight?'

'It'll be less noticeable than by night when we'd need lights to see what we're doing.'

It was another unexpected aspect to Bruno that, once inside the Library, he dealt with the broken window efficiently. He had brought nails and a hammer and the planks were in the office where he had said. Tanwen watched as he nailed a thick section of wood across the smashed window, fastening sections on the outside and then on the inside. The hammering echoed in the empty old mansion, and she found herself looking nervously about her, because she could not get rid of the feeling that something had come after them tonight, and that something was huddled in the shadows, watching them.

'All done,' said Bruno, at last, stepping back to survey his work. 'I'll go down for the transmitter. You stay here.'

But again was that thought: *I need to make sure . . .* Tanwen said, 'If I come with you I can help carry things, and—'

'What's wrong?' said Bruno, as Tanwen broke off, and turned

her head in the direction of the door leading down to the sculleries.

'Listen.'

'What? Tanwen, *what?*'

Tanwen said, 'You stopped hammering in those nails at least five minutes ago.'

'Yes.'

'The tapping is still going on.'

They moved at once, Tanwen reaching for Bruno's hand, grateful when it closed warmly around her own.

Together they crossed the hall and went down the steps to the scullery. The tapping seemed to pause, as if listening, and then came again, louder this time. Bruno began tearing away the panel that concealed the old stairway, and Tanwen reached for one of the oil lamps. Her hands were shaking so badly that it took several attempts to get it alight, but the dull glow eventually flared up.

'It'll be something from outside we're hearing, that's all,' said Bruno. 'Or a trapped animal . . . He can't still be alive. I shot him. Straight through the heart. You saw me do it.' He turned a haggard face to her. 'You saw him die,' he said with a kind of angry desperation.

'Yes.' But I saw that sly look, as well, thought Tanwen. The look that said, *This isn't the end . . .*

As the panel came away, and the oil lamp fell on the dark stairway, the tapping came at them like the frantic beating of a laboured heart. And something else. Something that cried out in a hoarse, terrible voice. '*Help me . . .*'

As they went down the stairs, Tanwen holding the lamp as high as possible, the shadows came with them, quivering because she was shaking so badly that the light also shook. Or was it just that? She looked back over her shoulder, but the curve of the stair hid the upper part of it. There was nothing there, of course. It was what was below them that they must focus on.

Here was the old underground cellar that Bruno and others had been using as a secret Resistance room. And in the far corner . . .

Tanwen heard one of them cry out, although she had no idea

which of them it had been. The stone trapdoor lid they had
lowered over the ice pit had been partly pushed up – perhaps
a quarter of the way. A dreadful livid face, its eyes black pits,
its skin crusted with dirt and with tiny glistening particles of
ice, was partly thrust through the tiny gap, staring straight at
them. For a wild moment she thought it could not possibly be
her father, because this was someone whose skin had dried and
withered so that it resembled old, grey stone . . .

'*Help me . . .*'

The words came again, and they both went forward at once.
Bruno grasped the edges of the stone lid, and Tanwen managed
to say, 'Please . . . oh, please, get him out.' It was one thing to
send a bullet cleanly and quickly into the heart of a traitor, but
it was the height of cruelty for someone to have been trapped
down here in the freezing darkness for two days.

Bruno was almost sobbing with the effort of trying to push
the stone lid up. He sat back on his heels, and dragged the back
of his hand across his forehead. 'I can't do it – Jesus God, I
can't shift it – it must have jammed or something snapped when
we lowered it. Malek – for God's sake, man, can't you push
from beneath in some way?'

'I can't. I've been trying for the last two days . . . As soon
as I managed to tear my hands free of the binding.' Then, in a
slightly stronger voice, he said, 'Are you wondering how I
missed the bullet? An old SS trick. You fling your whole body
back seconds before the trigger's pressed. If luck's with you,
the bullet goes over your head.'

'I'll remember that one,' said Bruno. 'And we'll get you out
somehow.' Tanwen set down the lamp, and added her strength
to his efforts, but she thought they all knew it was impossible.
And could they even dare to do it? Warsaw was in the iron grip
of the Nazis, and there was no one to whom they could deliver
a spy. There was no longer that kind of justice in this city or
in this country. And if her father were free he would certainly
tell his masters about the small Resistance group. The thought
flickered on her mind that until two days ago she had had no
idea that the group even existed.

Then the trapped man said, in a harsh, desperate voice, 'Sicora
– you aren't going to manage it. And I'm nearly done for – I'm

half dead already. The cold . . . oh, Christ, you have no idea . . . End it for me. The gun's still on the ground there.'

'I can't.' It came out in an anguished cry.

'Please . . . You can't imagine what it's been like all this time – the cold and the darkness. The grave can't be worse. Tanwen . . .' The dulled eyes flickered round to her. 'Remember I truly loved you. Will you remember that? I was always so proud of you.' Incredibly part of his hand struggled out of the darkness, clawing at the edges of the stones. He had said something about managing to get his hands free of the belt they had tied around his wrists.

As Tanwen knelt down and touched his hand, she saw the silver ring he was wearing. A signet ring? She had never seen him wear such a thing, before. And then the ring caught the candlelight, and she saw that it was not a signet ring at all; it was a thick heavy ring with a grinning skull and tiny engraved symbols.

It did not need Bruno's quick indrawn breath to tell Tanwen what it was. A Nazi Death's Head ring. *Totenkopf.* So they had given him that, she thought, sickened. Services rendered to the Third Reich.

She saw him register that she had seen it, and he said, 'Awarded last week – a small ceremony on the borders. That was why I had to leave home for a time. I promised – my masters – that I would investigate the rumours about this place.'

Somehow Tanwen kept hold of the hand, and tried not to think it felt like touching a cold, ancient stone. She sensed Bruno levelling the revolver, and leaned closer. In a whisper, she managed to say, 'Goodbye, Father,' and there was a brief sense of gratitude that in these last moments she could think of him in that way again. My father. Evil and traitorous, but still my father.

She had thought she was braced for the sound of the shot, but when it came it tore into her senses and she cried out. And this time there could be no mistake. This time the side of Georg Malek's head was shattered – even in the dim light Tanwen could see it.

The dim room tilted and blurred, and little scutterings and patterings seemed to echo around the underground room, as if even the shadows could not bear to look on this any longer. But she saw Bruno throw the gun into the ice pit, and she saw him straighten up.

'Nothing more we can do,' he said, brusquely, and, grabbing her arm, pulled her back up the stairs and into the upper scullery. As they reached the main hall, Tanwen stopped. 'The panel across the old stairway – we didn't replace it.'

'We don't need to,' said Bruno. 'After tonight it won't matter.'

'Why?'

'Because we'll have to destroy everything,' he said. 'You saw how we had to leave him— oh, Tanwen, don't shudder like that, we can solve this. I can solve it. But can't you see that now we really daren't risk anything being found. And it's got to be dealt with quickly, because we can't chance anyone coming in here to look for him.'

'You said – destroy everything . . .?'

Bruno hesitated, and a curious expression came into his eyes. A hardness – as if this was no longer the flippant, insouciant companion of those earlier months, or even the rather more serious young man of the last couple of weeks. He said, 'I'm going to come back later tonight – after Yan's gone to Anatol's. I'm going to lock this place up and then I'm going to burn it to the ground.'

Yan had not been able to relax at Anatol's tonight. He missed Bruno, who could always be relied on to enliven any gathering, but Bruno had said something about going to the Library that evening. The transmitter signal had been weak, he said, and he wanted to see if he could find out what was wrong.

It was ten o'clock when Yan said vaguely to Alicja that he would go along to the Street of Music, and see if Bruno was still there. 'If so, I might be able to help him.'

Alicja, who had been rather languidly helping Anatol to clear tables, said something about not working too late, and Yan went out. The streets were unlit, of course, and it was necessary to go cautiously at this hour, but this was the edge of the city, and it was not as heavily patrolled as other parts. As he entered the square, a small figure darted out of the shadows and ran towards the Library. A child? Yes, for sure. He crossed the square quickly, and went around to the small side door near the back, which they always used. He did not have his keys with him, but if Bruno was still in there, it was likely that he would have left it unlocked, because he nearly always did. Yan and Irina were always telling him it was dangerous.

The door was unlocked, and Yan went in. He would find Bruno, and he would find out about the child, as well. It was not safe for any child to be abroad at this hour. Once in the main hall, he thought that there was a curious feel to the place tonight. Was it simply because it was so dark? But he thought it was more than that. There were odd sounds – seeming to come not from inside, but from outside. It was almost as if the shadows were tiptoeing around the dark old building, quick and furtive, whispering to one another to take care not to be seen. This was an absurd idea, but the impression was so strong that he went over to the tall windows that flanked the main entrance. It was impossible to see through the thick boarding, though, so Yan went across to the Ivory Salon. It was then that he became aware of a smell of smoke. A fire somewhere? He looked around, and as he did so there was a movement from the top of the gilt stairway, and the small dark-eyed girl who came to Anatol's with Irina – the child who listened with such delight to Yan playing the firebird piano and to the old Russian fairy stories – was coming down the stairs.

He saw wariness in her eyes, so he smiled down at her.

'Hello. What are you doing in here?'

'It's a secret. I like to watch—' She stopped, as if aware of saying something she must not, and Yan, intrigued, but not wanting to alarm her, said,

'We know each other quite well, don't we? The music, the piano – and the fairy tales. But I don't know your name.'

'Helena.' She said it carefully, as if she had been taught that telling her name correctly was important.

'That's a very nice name. I'm Yan.'

'I know.'

There was not only the smell of smoke now, there was also the crackle of flames. Yan was increasingly aware of the need to get out of the Library, but he did not want to frighten Helena, and it was likely that Bruno was in the old scullery, so he said, 'Who is it you like to watch? If it's a secret I promise not to tell anyone.'

She hunched a shoulder, and looked about her as if to make sure no one was listening. Then she said, in a whisper, 'She's my mamma, only I mustn't call her that, 'cos I'm not s'posed to know.'

'Your mamma?' Yan stared down at her, and then understanding exploded in his mind. Tanwen! he thought. Dear God, yes, of course! The bone structure – the colouring. And the cheekbones. Why didn't I see it for myself? That one night we had together . . . Oh, Tanwen, why didn't you tell me? Why did you run away – because that's what you did. But you left Helena here. I'm not sure if I can ever forgive you for that.

But even through these tumbling thoughts, even with the knowledge of a fire somewhere, he was aware of a sudden fierce love and pride, because this was exactly how he would have wanted a daughter to look. This was how Katya must have looked at this age.

He said, 'Is your – is your mamma in here?'

'She was with the other man, and I thought they were coming into this house, 'cos they usually do. The door was unlocked, so I could get in. But I've looked everywhere and they aren't here.'

'Was the other man Bruno? The one who plays the firebird piano?'

'Yes.'

'Well, we can go out together now, and I expect we'll find them,' said Yan. He took Helena's hand, and led her towards the side door.

It was always dark here – the door was thick old oak, and even in broad daylight no sliver of light came in. But tonight the darkness felt different. There had been those tiptoeing shadows . . . And there was a fire . . . Once the door was open they would be outside and safe, though.

But when he grasped the door handle, panic clutched at him, because the handle would not move. Yan tried a second and then a third time, pushing and pulling as hard as he could, twisting it back and forth, but without success.

The door was locked, and Yan and his daughter were trapped.

TWENTY-SEVEN

Warsaw, mid-1940s

Whoever had locked the door must have done so in the last ten minutes. The tiptoeing shadows? But there was no time to speculate; he had to find a way to get himself and Helena out.

Leaving Helena on the gilt staircase, he ran through the empty rooms, trying not to succumb to panic. There would be a door unlocked or a window he could break, and they would get out. Even if they had to jump from one of the upper floors it would not matter, because it was better to break both your legs than burn alive. They were not going to burn alive, though, Yan was not going to let it happen. If he could not find a way out, he would find the fire and douse it. He tried to think if the water supply would still be on, but had no idea.

At worst, he could shout through a window for help. The Nazis were burning buildings wholesale and people had become resigned to it, but the Street of Music had not, so far, been touched, so this was one fire that might attract attention. There might already be people out there.

There were no unlocked doors, and the windows in every room were boarded over on the outside. But in one of the upper rooms there was a small narrow space in the boarding, where the two boards did not quite meet. The window was deeply inset, but by pressing against the glass Yan managed to see almost all the way down to the ground. And there the fire was. It was not inside the Library at all; it was outside it. It looked as if rags and bits of wood had been heaped against the main doors, and then set alight. Had those soft-footed shadows he had heard earlier done this? Helena had said she had followed Bruno and Tanwen earlier, and Bruno had certainly intended to come out here tonight. But that had been to look at the wireless. There was no reason why either of those two would set fire to the Chopin Library.

The blaze was directly beneath the elaborate stone canopy over the main doors, and flames were already licking around the stonework, bathing it in livid colour. How long would it be before those flames blazed higher, and the old mansion's fabric began to burn in earnest?

He ran down to the main hall and snatched up a chair, slamming it against one of the narrow windows on the side of the massive double doors. The glass smashed at once, but the chair was no match for the thick heavy planking, and the legs splintered. Yan cursed and threw the chair down, seizing instead a heavy gilt statue from the Ivory Salon. But it was no better; the stone simply broke into pieces and the windows remained stubbornly boarded over.

He beat down fear and looked about him. Was there anywhere he had not checked? What about the lower part of the Library? The sculleries? Something stirred in a corner of his mind, because the main scullery would not offer any escape route, but there was the older one – the one they had found recently, sealed off behind the false wall. The one that had stone floors, and that, if Anatol could be believed, contained an old ice room.

Yan's mind looped back over the years – to the stone slab set deep into the wall, where Katya and the Romanov servant had hidden. Surely, if anything was impervious to fire, an ice room would be. And Anatol had described the Library's ice room – how the famous Frozen Polonaise was kept there and brought up to the sound of violinists playing . . .

He picked Helena up, and carried her down the stone steps to the main scullery.

'It's all perfectly all right,' he said, as she clutched him in fear. 'But we might have to stay down here, just for a while. I'll be with you, though, and it won't be for long.' Please God it really won't be for long, he thought.

It was very dark in the scullery, but there were always candles and matches left to hand. Yan, aware of the irony of lighting a flame in this situation, found a candle and lit it. With that long-ago memory of Ipatiev House, he thrust several more candles and the matches into his pocket.

The last person here – presumably Bruno – had not replaced the panel concealing the original stairs, and the stairway opening yawned blackly. Helena shivered and tried to pull away.

Yan said, 'It's all right. There's nothing to be frightened of.'

The candle flame caused shadows to dance grotesquely on the stair wall as they went down, but here were the original kitchens, and there was the stone shelf with the transmitter. For a moment, Yan wondered if he could transmit a message for help, but the wireless had always been Bruno's province, and he had no idea how to operate it. All he could do was find the ice room, and get the two of them inside it. It ought not to be difficult to locate – it would be set into one of the alcoves, most likely.

And then he held the candle up, and its light fell on something that sent the blood thudding through Yan's body and brought waves of horror and panic rushing down like swooping nightmares.

In the far corner of the old scullery, a section of the stone floor had been partly levered up – like the lid of a trapdoor. Even from here, even in the uncertain light, he could see the faint breath of iciness coming from below. Not an ice room, an ice pit, thought Yan.

But the past was swooping down, smothering him with memories, and for several nightmare moments he was in Ipatiev House again, seeing Katya and the other girl huddled together in that frozen death grip. Because protruding from the partly open stone lid was the head of a man – a terrible head; a nightmare thing of shattered bone and brain and eye on one side, but with the other side grey and frozen, just as those two had been. *Withered and shrunken and dried out, as if something had sucked all the moisture . . . .*

Somehow, Yan managed to say, very calmly, 'Helena – there's nothing for you to be scared of, but will you take this candle very carefully, and go up those stairs and wait for me at the very top. Can you do that? Hold on, I'll light a second one for myself.'

Helena had backed into a corner, a small clenched hand pressing against her mouth, her eyes on the dreadful thing thrusting up out of the stone opening. This is going to haunt her for the rest of her life, thought Yan, appalled. As she ran up the stairs, he forced himself to walk across the stone floor, seeing that one of the man's hands was grasping the edges of the stone, as if he had tried desperately to claw his way to freedom. He had got one arm and part of a shoulder out. But then the lid jammed, and that was as far as you could get, thought Yan. But someone shot you through the head – that's very clear. But why? Who are you? It was then that he saw the silver ring on the man's hand. He had never seen one before, but he knew at once what it was. A Nazi Death's Head ring. Then this man must have been a high-ranking SS or Nazi officer.

Forcing down his revulsion, Yan set the candle down so that its light fell across the terrible head, and reached down to the pocket flap of the man's jacket. It was only just visible and only just reachable, but there might be something in it that would identify him . . . The confused thought that if this was a Nazi – or a Nazi spy – they needed to know who it was.

And there it was. An identity card – the kind that gave the administrative region. There was the green cover, reserved for Poles, and at the foot was a signature and a name. Georg Malek.

Malek. Tanwen's brother? No, too old. Her father? Yan glanced at the date of birth. Yes, it fitted. The region given was Tanwen's home and the card looked genuine. But this man was wearing a Death's Head ring.

Bruno and Tanwen, thought Yan. Did they kill him because he was a Nazi? A spy? It looks like it. And now they're burning this building to destroy the evidence – that's the explanation for the fire. But there was no time to speculate further. He tried again to raise the stone lid, but he already knew it would not move, and he had already acknowledged that the ice pit could not be used to shield them from the fire.

He ran back upstairs. The smoke was denser now, and the crackling of the flames was louder. Helena was crouching on the stairs. She looked up at him, and Yan's heart turned over. He said, 'It was some poor man that someone hurt. You don't need to worry about it, though.'

He scooped her up again – she was struggling, and Yan understood she wanted to run away and hide. But he held onto her, still trying to reassure her, and carried her up to the room where there had been the small gap in the window boards. It was the narrowest of narrow spaces between the two sections of wood, but it might just be possible for Helena, small and light, to squeeze through. Then what? Could she climb out onto the jutting canopy, and then to that lower window sill, and drop down to the ground? It was the longest shot in the world, but it was the only shot Yan could think of.

'D'you see that little opening, Helena?' he said. 'I think you could squeeze through there and get outside.'

There was only a frightened sob in reply, so, with memories of his own childhood Yan said, 'It's a bit of an adventure, really. Escaping and being brave.'

She shook her head.

'Let's try anyway,' said Yan. 'You go first, and I'll follow.' He knew he could not possibly get through the narrow gap himself, but it was important that Helena thought he would be with her. 'You've only got to get onto that square slab just under this window, d'you see it? It's what's called a canopy. It's not very far from the ground,' he said, as she did not speak. 'And once you're on it, you can slither onto that window sill at the side – you see where I mean? And then you can jump onto the ground.'

'And you'll come too?'

He was relieved to hear her respond at last. 'Yes, I will, but it might take a bit longer, because I'll have to break off a bit of that boarding.' He knelt in front of her, taking her hands. 'So when you get down there, don't wait for me. Run as fast as you can and tell somebody – a grown-up – your mamma or Bruno or Irina. Say I'm here in the Library, and they must come. Can you do that?' There was a small worried nod, but her eyes were huge with terror and Yan had no idea if she was fully understanding him. But he could see no other way and this might give her a good chance to get free. Beyond that he did not dare think.

He lifted her onto the sill, still talking as she squeezed through the narrow gap with his help, repeating that she would be safe, that everything would be all right. As she dropped onto the canopy, Yan tried not to think that the fire might suddenly surge up and engulf Helena. But she crawled to the edge and then reached the window sill below it. It was going to be all right. She was slithering to the ground now – it was not very far, but it was far enough for such a small girl. As she reached the ground, smoke billowed up, obscuring his view of her. There was a moment when he thought he saw her, a small shadowy figure through the murk, and then she was gone. Had she managed to run clear?

He went back downstairs and tried again to break through another of the windows, shouting for help as he did so. But he had no idea if anyone was out there or, even if they were, whether he could be heard through the crackling of the flames.

Even if Helena had not reached help, surely Irina and Tanwen would have missed her, and be looking for her. But would it occur to them to come here? Wouldn't Tanwen be giving this place a very wide berth indeed? Because down there in the old scullery . . .

Tanwen's own father. He must have been working for the Nazis, thought Yan, sickened. Working against his own people. And in this building because of the Resistance group – to find out about them – to report back to Berlin. Had Bruno and Tanwen killed him to stop him doing that? Had it been, in effect, a traitor's execution?

But Yan's mind was working on strange levels now – at one level he knew the fear was affecting him, and he knew fear did odd things to a man's mind. But it suddenly seemed over-whelmingly important that Tanwen – Helena's mother – was not suspected of killing Georg Malek. And that Helena did not have to grow up in that shadow or with that knowledge. Was there one last thing he could do for Helena – and for Tanwen? If he did not escape, was there some way in which he could leave clues so that people would know that if Malek's body were to be found, his death had been the justified, justifi-able death of a traitor?

He seized a big portfolio which he sometimes used for music scores. It had a number of thick card pages slotted inside it – he could scribble an account of the truth on one of them. Glancing towards the door leading out to the hall, he saw that the fire had not yet got through the old walls, and he thought he had

a little time left. There might be time to include proof to back
up his account.

Working with frantic haste, he ransacked the drawers of his
desk, finding some Nazi orders that had been sent earlier in the
year. There was a notice about buildings scheduled to be demolished, but the Library was not listed, which might tell some
discerning eye that it had been some other force that had caused
the place to be destroyed tonight.

In his pocket was the fake programme summoning people to
Anatol's restaurant. Irina had drawn that tiny, detailed sketch
of Father Gregory's firebird piano. At the top of the programme
Yan wrote in the name of the 'Dark Cadence', as if it was the
music that would be played at the concert that would not and
could not take place. '*Temnaya Kadentsiya*'. A concert adver-
tising the execution of a traitor. He added a date of October
1944. Anyone finding that would certainly know the programme
to be false – no concert could possibly have taken place at such
a time. He pushed everything into the portfolio – there was
even some glue in the desk, which would make sure the things
stayed in place.

What else? He eyes fell on the music of the 'Cadence' itself
– the music he had disguised as the 'Demon's aria'. For a
moment the shadowy Katerinburg house closed around him,
and his copper-haired Romanov girl was coming down the
stairs towards him, her hands outstretched . . .

He put the music in as well. If anyone with any knowledge
were to play it, they would know it was not the real aria. They
might even know it for the 'Traitor's Music', and understand
something of what had happened tonight.

Almost as an afterthought, he grabbed a handful of letters
and memoranda from his desk drawer. They referred to the
appointment of Tanwen Malek, and he had always thought they
had hinted at a degree of manipulation. Had Tanwen's father
been part of that manipulation? Yan thought he could well
have been. He had kept the documents separate from the main
files for that precise reason – you never knew what you might
want or need to make use of. He would make use of them now
– they should go into the scrapbook with the rest.

The fire was roaring up now, and there was a crash of

something overhead near the front of the building. It's starting
to disintegrate, thought Yan. I don't believe I'm entirely sane
any longer – I don't believe anyone in this situation would be
sane – I could even believe that if I escape this I won't do so
with my mind entirely intact . . .

But he seized the pencil anyway, and began to write.

'I think I have only moments left, but before death overtakes
me I must set down what happened in the Chopin Library
tonight . . .'

It took barely five minutes to write what he wanted to say,
but in those minutes he was aware of the heat as the fire tore
through the old fabric. There were more crashes – the gilt
stairway? – and splinterings as windows were blown. Yan's
hands were shaking badly by this time, mostly from sheer terror,
but also from the frantic compulsion that was driving him to
get this done – to finish before the fire took over. A particularly
loud crash shook the floor of the room, and the pot of glue
teetered slightly, spilling a few drops onto the corner of
the portfolio. Yan cursed, and tore the edges of the page away
where it had touched them.

But it's all done, he thought. I can't do anything more – I've
said what needs saying, and there's no more time. He looked
about him. There was a small safe in his office, used for the
modest amount of cash kept for small day-to-day expenses, and
for any papers or documents. Fire proof? Probably reasonably
so. He dragged the door open and pushed the portfolio inside,
slamming the door. Then he stood very still. There was one
more thing to do before the flames came roaring into the room.
His violin lay in a corner. He was still clinging to the hope that
he would be rescued, but for now . . .

As the flames tore through the great hall and into the Ivory
Salon – the famous hall where once the renowned musicians
and composers of the world had performed, where kings and
princes and doomed tsars had gathered – Yan began to play the
'Dark Cadence'.

Bruno said, and Irina said – even Anatol said – that lying on a
bed and sobbing out reproaches would not do Tanwen any good.
It would not bring back Yan or Helena.

From out of the welter of grief and guilt and sheer scalding horror, Tanwen said, 'But I was the one who killed them. I started the fire.'

'We both started it,' said Bruno, who was slumped in a chair in the corner of Tanwen's bedroom, and who seemed to have aged twenty years in a single night. 'We're both guilty. We locked the door, trapping them. But we didn't know – how could we know – they were both in there. Oh, God, my dearest friend – that gifted man—'

'And a child, barely started on her life,' said Irina, softly.

'We don't know for certain about Helena,' said Bruno. 'We know about Yan, because he told Alicja he was going to the Library. But by the time we knew that, it was too late. But we don't know that Helena—'

'We do. Anatol saw her crossing the square that night, remember?' said Tanwen.

'I was worried,' said Anatol. 'It was so late. I went along to Irina's house to tell her. Irina had thought she was in bed.'

Tanwen, still sobbing, said, 'And if she didn't die in the fire, where is she now? She died, I know she did.' It no longer seemed to matter about letting them know that Helena was her daughter. Tanwen did not care if the entire world knew it.

Alicja, arriving later, sat by Tanwen's bed and held her hand, and said tragedy of all kinds came into people's lives. If only she had stopped Yan from going to the Library that night, she said. Or if she had accompanied him . . . She, too, had her guilt, said Alicja.

It was two days later that Anatol returned, and his chubby face was serious. 'You'll both have to leave Warsaw,' he said to Tanwen, and to Bruno who was constantly in Tanwen's rooms now, and who seemed unable to be by himself any longer. 'They've begun clearing the ruins. Who knows what they might find?'

Burned bodies – a little girl whose life had scarcely started. A gifted, charismatic musician, who had never known he had a daughter . . .

And, thought Tanwen, the body of a man who should have worked for his country against the oppressors, but who worked for the oppressors instead. But wouldn't even the bones have been burned to ash after such a fierce fire? She began to cry all over again.

Anatol was saying that they could not be sure that the fire would not be traced back to Bruno or Tanwen. 'But I went out to the ruins myself early this morning.' He gave a brief shrug. 'I thought perhaps there might be things – clues – that I could cover up.'

'Thank you,' said Bruno. 'You wouldn't find anything, though. It would all be reduced to cinders.'

'I found one thing,' said Anatol. 'And I brought it away before anyone – the oppressors – could find it. I didn't know if it would set people thinking – asking questions.'

'What?'

Anatol produced something small in a screw of newspaper. 'This is a black memory of a black-hearted man,' he said. 'But he was your father, Tanwen, and perhaps there were good times you can one day remember.'

'The Death's Head ring,' said Tanwen, staring down at the silver object inside the paper. 'He was wearing it when we— when he died.'

'It was lying in the rubble,' said Anatol. 'No one saw me pick it up. But there were people around, so I didn't dare look for anything else.'

'I will keep it,' said Tanwen, with decision. 'As a reminder – although I don't know what it's a reminder of. But there might be a day—'

'Papers are being created for you,' said Anatol. 'Yurik is working on them now.' Yurik was the former printer, part of the group, and a person who could be trusted. 'He thinks you should try to get to England – the English are our good friends.'

Tanwen did not care where she went. She did not care when Bruno and Anatol said they were going to Yan's rooms to clear away his things.

'Come with us,' said Anatol. 'There could be something you would like to have, as a memory of him. I have a key – we'll go together.'

'I don't want anything,' said Tanwen, but in the end she agreed. She managed to get up and wash her face and brush her hair. She looked perfectly dreadful. Like Bruno, she looked as if she had aged twenty years. It did not matter. It would never matter again how she looked.

The sight – the atmosphere – of Yan's rooms came at her like a blow.

'But you never came here, did you?' said Bruno.

'No. But seeing all his things . . .' The music, the books, the sight of a jacket carelessly lying across a chair . . . The bed with a patchwork cover where he had slept . . . Tanwen sat down on the bed, and held the pillow against her and did not know how she would bear the weary years ahead. If they had not both died in such a way – if it had not been her fault . . .

Anatol was looking at a box of what looked like children's books, pushed half under a bureau. 'Yan brought these to the restaurant sometimes, to read to the children,' he said.

Children . . . A small dark-eyed girl who had loved to curl up at Yan's feet, and listen to him reading . . . The grief welled up all over again, then Anatol said, 'These should not be destroyed. I'm going to my cousins in the Kampinos Forest soon, but Yurik is staying here. We can leave the books with him.'

'And if there's ever news of Helena,' said Tanwen, eagerly, 'if it turns out that she did get out – wandered off somewhere—'

'For instance, if there's ever a report in a newspaper,' put in Bruno, 'anything about a girl whose name and age might fit—'

'You would like it investigated, and if it should be Helena, you would like her to have the books,' said Anatol, speaking very kindly. 'Yurik would find a way of doing that.'

Tanwen saw he was just saying this to comfort her – that he did not think Helena ever would be found, but she said, 'It would tell her that once she had a family who cared about her.'

'Of course. And the truth need not come out. Yurik could simply say he thinks the books belonged to people who might have known her family. That would be acceptable?'

'Yes,' said Tanwen, gratefully. 'Thank you.'

'Yurik is making your papers in the name of Wyngham,' said Anatol. 'From our own word, *wygnanie*. Exiles. But making it more English, you see. Can you think yet where in England you will go?'

Tanwen said, 'My mother's family was from a part of England
– oh, generations ago – where it borders onto Wales. A small
place called Causwain.' She pronounced it carefully. 'She talked
about it sometimes. The name Tanwen is from Wales.'

Bruno was looking through the stacked music. 'I'd like to
take some of these with us,' he said. 'They won't take up much
room, and it would be a memory.'

Tanwen did not bother to ask how there was suddenly an
'us', but whatever was ahead would probably be a bit easier to
cope with if Bruno was there. The knowledge of what they had
done might even bring them closer together.

'There's a good deal of Mozart,' he was saying, as he looked
along the shelf. 'And Debussy and Chopin, and . . . What on
earth is this?'

'What?'

'It's handwritten,' said Bruno, sitting on the edge of the bed
next to her, and showing her the single sheet of music. 'I think
it's in Yan's hand – I mean the heading is in his hand. It's
the aria from Rubinstein's *Demon.*'

Tanwen stared at the music, and her mind went back to the
night in the Library when Yan had played this, and she had started
to sing it, walking down that marvellous stairway. It had reached
him in some curious way she had never understood and there
had been that explosive passion . . . Suddenly this music was
part of him – something to be treasured, valued . . .

'Let me play it,' she said, grasping Bruno's hand. 'Please.
There's one of his violins here – in that corner.'

'All right. Can you manage if I hold the score up for you?'

'Yes.' If I play this, it'll be as if I'm touching that night when
Helena was conceived, thought Tanwen. It'll be a final hand-
clasp with Yan.

But as the first notes drifted into the room, she knew at once
there was something wrong. This was not the 'Demon's aria'
– the achingly sad farewell of the ill-starred demon to his lost
bride. She faltered, then went on, but she had barely reached
the final bars when Anatol said, 'Dear God – do you know what
you're playing, Tanwen?'

'I know it isn't the 'Demon's aria',' said Tanwen, lowering the
violin, puzzlement briefly taking over from her other emotions.

'It is not,' said Anatol, his face the colour of raw dough. 'It's music known as the "Dark Cadence". It's regarded as music only ever played at the execution of a traitor.'

'I've never heard that story,' said Bruno, turning to stare at him.

'Not very many people have. But the story exists. And so does the music. And,' said Anatol, slowly, 'on the night the Chopin Library burned I heard someone playing it.'

'You recognized it?'

'Oh, yes. I had heard it before,' said Anatol, his voice suddenly filled with sadness.

'Was it someone in the square who was playing it while the Library burned?' said Bruno.

'I don't know. People ran out there, you remember. But there was so much confusion.'

'But does it mean that someone knew what happened?' said Bruno. 'Or saw something?'

'It might. I think,' said Anatol, looking at them, 'that it's now even more vital for you to leave Warsaw, and as soon as possible. If you want the music, you must take it,' he said. 'But really, you should destroy it.'

Bruno nodded, and then looked at Tanwen. 'You understand that none of this must ever be talked of,' he said. 'For the rest of our lives – and perhaps our lives will be lived out together – we can never dare let anyone know that we killed a traitor – a German spy.'

'And that he was my father. And,' said Tanwen, not looking away from him, 'that in trying to destroy the evidence of it, we burned two people alive.'

*　　*　　*

Phin thought that of all the strange things that had come to light during the search for the 'Dark Cadence', the assembly in the White Hart's coffee room after dinner was the strangest.

Nina had driven out to collect Thaisa, who came hesitantly into the dining room, and sat quietly at the table, not saying very much, but rather earnestly following the conversation. At Phin's side, Arabella said softly, 'To us, a meal in a pub is ordinary, but Thaisa's never known such things, poor soul. But she's dressed very carefully for it, I think. A very nice jacket and a silk scarf. Good for her.'

The White Hart had expressed itself delighted to place the coffee room at their disposal again. No, it was no trouble at all; this was a quiet season for them anyway. Please to let them know if any drinks were needed. In the meantime, they would bring coffee.

Thaisa and Helena sat together. Phin said quietly to the professor, 'You can see the likeness between them, can't you? It's in the eyes and the cheekbones.'

'They must both have been very striking when they were younger,' said the professor, thoughtfully. 'What a damned waste of a life it's been for Thaisa. Or has it? She's not all that old yet. There might be all kinds of things she could still do.'

Phin glanced at him, and he made a dismissive gesture. 'When the moment's right I'm going to ask Thaisa what her parents' names were,' said Phin. 'But I think we already know who her mother was.' He reached for the book about *Vanished Temples of Music*, which he had brought down with him, and turned to the chapter on lost music accolades. Tanwen Malek's winsome smile looked out.

The professor stared at it, then said, 'It might be the same girl as that photograph in the music room.'

'Yes. Their mother was undoubtedly Tanwen,' said Phin.

'Did they have the same father, d'you think? The man who played the "Cadence" on his piano as he was dying? Or someone entirely different?'

'I don't know.'

Nina and Lucek had placed the scrapbook on the table in front of them. Nina said, 'If it's all right with everyone, I'm going to try translating an unexpected final section. It's on the very last page and it was stuck to the previous page – almost as if they'd been glued together. Arabella helped me to lever them apart.'

'Nail file,' said Arabella. 'We had to be *very* cautious – we were terrified we were going to tear the pages and lose anything that might be in-between them. But we managed it in the end.'

'I don't think either of us thought there would be anything to find,' said Nina. 'But we were determined not to miss anything. And there was something, and it's here. I saved it to read until we were all together.'

'Handwriting,' said Phin, leaning forward to see.

'It's very faded,' said Arabella, 'and the page itself is torn quite badly at the edges, but Nina thinks she can decipher it.'

'I'll translate aloud as I go,' said Nina. 'And Helena's going to be reading it with me, so we'll all hear what it is at the same time.'

There was a moment before Nina began to read when Phin felt the ghosts creep closer, and he glanced at Thaisa and saw fear in her eyes. As if sensing his regard, she looked up and Phin gave her what he hoped was a reassuring smile.

Then Nina began to read.

I think I have only moments left, but before death overtakes me I must set down what happened in the Chopin Library tonight.

The Library was burned deliberately, by two people who wanted to conceal that they had executed a traitor. The building is burning all around me, as I write this.

I am putting in documents, in case it's thought these are the ravings of a man awaiting a terrible death of his own – that my mind has been turned. Perhaps it has.

Mostly, though, I write this for my daughter. Helena – I believe your mother, Tanwen Malek, helped to execute Georg Malek, who was her father. He was Polish, but a traitor to Poland – to his own people. Almost certainly a Nazi spy. In any country and in any culture that would be regarded as a justifiable act of execution. No blame should ever be attached either to Tanwen or to Bruno Sicora who I think was part of that execution. Bruno has been a good friend and a loyal fighter against the oppressors. He is also a gifted musician. I believe that when all this is over, he will look after Tanwen.

Malek's body is in the old ice pit of this Library. He wears the infamous Nazi Death's Head ring – a badge of his evil against his own people. Proof of what he is and was. In executing him, Tanwen – Bruno also – performed a brave act.

Helena – if you ever read this, believe that even in those few weeks when I knew you – when you sat with me while I played the firebird piano for you and read to you the Russian fairy tales from my own childhood in the Romanov household – you became immensely dear to me. I am grateful that I knew you, even for that short time. Tonight I have tried to save you. I pray that you escaped the fire, and that one day, somehow, somewhere, you might read this.

Your father, Yan Orzek.

Tears were pouring down Arabella's face, and Nina's voice had faltered towards the end of the narrative.

Thaisa was staring at the scrawled writing as if she was afraid that if she looked away it might vanish. Helena was white and stunned. But she's all right, thought Phin. Dear God, what a legacy he left her. If only she had found it years ago – no, I won't think that, I'll just be glad she has it now. She'll be glad. And so will Thaisa. It's broken open the secrets – the secrets her parents must have lived with all their lives, and tried to protect her from. He hoped the two of them would be able to talk about everything in more detail later.

He said, very gently, 'Helena saw something – either the execution itself, or the murdered man afterwards. That was the start of the nightmare. And then being trapped – the fire—'

'No wonder she pushed it away for most of her life,' said Arabella, softly. 'Nina, Lucek – say all that to her, will you? Say we understand.'

As Nina spoke to Helena, Thaisa put out her hand, and Helena grasped it gratefully. It was a shared nightmare, thought Phin. It reached out to Thaisa, as well.

Nina said, carefully, 'Helena is saying she did see it – she's remembering it. A man's head thrusting up out of a stone cellar – as if trapped.'

Helena said, '*Nie żyje. Zimno.*'

She shivered, and Lucek said, 'She's saying – Dead. And cold.'

'Because they'd put him in the old ice pit below the Library,' said Phin. 'Yan says that's where his body was. And Helena saw it.'

'Remember that he was a spy and that he was killed – no, executed – by two brave people,' said the professor. 'Tanwen and Bruno. Thaisa, that man – Bruno – he was your father?'

'Yes. Bruno.'

'"A gifted musician – a loyal fighter against the oppressors",' said the professor, very gently.

'Yes. I'm glad Yan said that about him. I'm glad I'll have that memory – of both of them.' Thaisa's eyes were bright with unshed tears.

'And someone took that ring from Malek at the last,' said Dr Purslove. 'Before or after his execution, I wonder? Or even after the fire – yes, I can see that being done – not as a keepsake, exactly. Perhaps to remove any evidence.'

'And my mother kept it,' said Thaisa. 'Or it was given to her.'

Lucek said, 'What about the Russian books? How would they have got to Helena?'

'I don't think we'll ever know that. Maybe someone found them, and when it was realized Helena was still alive, sent them to her.'

'Thinking she'd remember them?' said Lucek. 'The sad thing is that she didn't.'

It was Arabella who said, 'And Yan Orzek?'

They looked at one another. 'He died in the fire,' said Professor Liripine, at last. 'That must be the "bad death" Thaisa's mother talked about.'

Phin said, 'A bad death. But a remarkable legacy.'

EPILOGUE

'We're going to Warsaw at the start of the month,' said Phin to Thaisa. 'Arabella and myself, that is. We're meeting Nina and Lucek and Helena, and we'll be staying in Warsaw for about a week. I do wish you'd come with us, Thaisa. It's said to be a beautiful city, and you could see all the places your . . . your mother would have known.'

'I'd like to come,' said Thaisa, slowly. 'It would be a big thing for me after the years of . . . Well, of not travelling, or doing anything much at all. And I'd like to think that in the future I will. Helena has said there's an open invitation to stay with her – with Lucek's family. But the thing is, that I've had this letter.' She passed it to Phin.

Dear Thaisa,

I hope all's well with you after our astonishing time in Causwain. It was a remarkable and emotional few days, wasn't it? Theo Purslove is already writing it all up, although I daresay I shall have to edit a good deal of what he writes, because he's very much given to exaggeration and embroidering the facts.

You'll perhaps recall we had a brief conversation about the music of William Boyce, after I noticed how many of his works you had on CD. There's a weekend of Boyce's music here in Durham next month – performances of most of the symphonies and some discussion sessions. I've been asked to read a paper on him – only a short thing, but hopefully interesting.

It occurred to me that if you're free, you might like to come up to Durham and be part of it all. I could book you into the Golden Hind, which is a pleasant and comfortable small hotel, and I think you would enjoy the music and the various (quite modest) events. It's likely that Theodore will be wending his way north for it too, so there'll be one other familiar face.

I look forward to hearing soon.

Very kindest regards,

Ernest Liripine.

'The dates clash with your trip,' said Thaisa. 'And since the professor was kind enough to invite me—'

'You think you should go to Durham,' said Phin, managing not to smile.

'Well, I do think I should. Don't you?'

'Yes,' said Phin, very firmly. 'Yes, I definitely think you should.'

'The Street of Music,' said Arabella, with deep pleasure.

'Near enough to it, anyway,' said Lucek, who could hardly get over the delight of having Phin and Arabella in Warsaw, and actually taking them to his and Nina's coffee house. Nina would be there ahead of them with Helena, so as to secure a nice table for them. She was really good at that kind of thing.

'This is lovely,' said Arabella, as they went inside. 'Oh, and there's Nina and Helena – oh, it's so good to see you all again.'

Phin liked the little coffee place, and he liked the obvious closeness between Lucek and Nina. The staff were friendly; they were charmed to hear these were two English friends visiting their city. There were suggestions from a waitress who spoke very good English as to what might be good to eat and drink.

'And we have a very delicious iced pudding which you could have after your lunch,' said the waitress. 'A very old recipe – the man who once owned this restaurant, years and years ago, had it from his father.'

Phin and Arabella stared at one another, then, with one voice, said, 'Iced Polonaise.'

'It is a simplified version of the original, but still very good, and I can order it for you.'

'Yes, please. And,' said Phin, 'could you tell me – the man who owned this restaurant: what was his name?'

The waitress beamed. 'He was Anatol,' she said. 'Much loved

by everyone. When the war ended, he left Warsaw to live with
family – the Kampinos Forest, I think. But he had kept the
restaurant open through the war years – this is known and
we like to tell our customers the stories. There were plottings
– the Resistance, you understand – and very hard times indeed,
which are not to be forgotten. But almost always a good supper
could be had at Anatol's. Also, music.'

'Music?'

'There was – today we would say live music. A piano given
to the restaurant during the war years – given by an elderly
man who had been Anatol's good friend. People played on it
for customers. There are stories of one brilliant pianist—'

'A brilliant pianist?' said Phin.

'Yes, and there is still the piano he always played. When the
restaurant took over the next-door premises the piano was
moved in there. That is the part we open up in the evenings,
when we have large groups coming in – there is more room
for larger tables. But I think it was always felt that the piano
was a part of the restaurant's history, so it was kept, and it is
regularly tuned.'

'Could we see it? The piano?' Phin hardly dared ask.

'Of course. Wait – I will put on some lights.'

'The firebird piano,' said Arabella, softly, as they stood
in the inner room. She looked at Helena. 'This is almost too
much to bear.'

Phin said to the waitress, 'Would you let my friend play it,
just very briefly? We think it once belonged to . . . to someone
from her childhood.'

'It would mean so much to her – to all of us,' put in Lucek.

'But of course. We shall like that very much.'

As they walked across to the piano, Arabella said, 'Phin –
d'you see that?'

'Something's been set into the front,' said Phin. 'On the
right-hand side of the stand.'

'It's a tiny painting,' said Nina, looking closely. 'A miniature.
Very beautiful.'

The helpful waitress said, 'No one ever knew who she was,
that lady in the painting. But the man who played the piano
always brought it with him, and put it on the keyboard when

he played. Perhaps a lost lover. When he died the miniature was left here, so it was decided to embed – is that the word? – it into the piano. A small memory of our pianist.'

Phin said, as casually as he could, 'I suppose the years when this man played here – that would be before the war?'

'No, no, it was afterwards,' she said. 'When people were starting to return to Warsaw.'

'And the man came here then?'

'Yes. He was scarred – his face—' She made a brief gesture, indicating her own cheeks. 'No one knew how it had happened, and there had been so many atrocities in those years. But it added to the romance of him. Stories were told – probably none of them true – about how he had escaped from the Nazis – or how he had been a person of importance who had been caught up in a plot and been damaged as a result. That he had wandered in many places by himself, before somehow finding his way here. But I do not think anyone ever knew the truth.'

'And his identity was never discovered,' said Phin, thoughtfully.

'No. No one ever recognized him or claimed him.'

'So much of Warsaw was lost during those years,' said Lucek. 'So much history – so many identities and families were torn apart.'

'And a great many people were driven out of Warsaw,' put in Nina.

'It was a time of great confusion,' agreed the waitress. 'People vanished, and when that happened . . .' A philosophic shrug. 'It was not expected to see them again. But wherever he had come from, that mystery man, and whatever had been done to him, after a time he found a place for himself and a life. He worked for the rebuilding of this city – organizing concerts and music events, and getting the donations. A lot of the rebuilding was done by volunteers.'

Nina said, 'I think there were organizations – state funded, but also many voluntary set-ups. And people came from all parts of the country to rebuild the city after the war.'

The waitress was clearly interested. She said, 'At Anatol's, we have always liked to keep our mystery man's piano as our own private memorial.'

Phin pounced on the last words. 'Your own "private" memorial?'

'There is an official memorial to him in a small garden near here. I can tell you directions.'

As the five of them walked through the streets to the small garden the waitress had described, Phin's heart was pounding with nervous anticipation. It won't be even remotely connected, he thought. And yet . . . Could he have escaped the fire that night? And returned later on, but with his memory gone, never knowing who he was? Unrecognizable, and unrecognized?

Then Lucek said, 'I've been here before.' He turned eagerly to Helena, who was already nodding and looking at the square with the small garden just beyond it. 'We used to bring our lunch,' said Lucek.

The memorial was a small stone plinth, the area around it meticulously cultivated. There was wording on the plinth itself – it was weathered, but it looked legible.

'Lucek?' said Nina. 'This is for you to translate.'

Lucek stared at the lettering, then began to translate.

A small remembrance of a man whose own memory was erased by the devastation of this city in World War II, and whose real name was never known – but who worked selflessly with various organizations to help raise funds for the city's rebuilding.

Whoever he was, and whatever he had once been, he was a man of charm and warmth and generosity, and was a gifted musician.

He was known, simply, as 'The Maestro'.

He will never be forgotten.